NEBULA AWARDS SHOWCASE 2017

ALSO AVAILABLE:

NEBULA AWARDS SHOWCASE 2017

STORIES, POEMS, EXCERPTS, AND ESSAYS BY

Amal El-Mohtar, Naomi Kritzer, David D. Levine, Sam J. Miller,
Martin L. Shoemaker, Alyssa Wong, Marge Simon, Greg Schwartz,
Sarah Pinsker, Nnedi Okorafor, Charles E. Gannon, N. K. Jemisin, Ann Leckie,
Ken Liu, Lawrence M. Schoen, Naomi Novik, F.J. Bergmann, Mark Askwith,
Fran Wilde, Michelle Sagara, Betsy Wollheim, and C. J. Cherryh.

THE YEAR'S BEST SCIENCE FICTION AND FANTASY
Selected by the Science Fiction and Fantasy Writers of America

EDITED BY
JULIE E. CZERNEDA

an imprint of **Prometheus Books**
Amherst, NY

Published 2017 by Pyr®, an imprint of Prometheus Books

Cover illustration © Maurizio Manzieri
Cover design by Liz Mills
Cover © Prometheus Books

Inquiries should be addressed to

Pyr
59 John Glenn Drive
Amherst, New York 14228
VOICE: 716–691–0133
FAX: 716–691–0137
WWW.PYRSF.COM

21 20 19 18 17   5 4 3 2 1

ISBN 978–1–63388–271–3 (paperback)
ISBN 978–1–63388–272–0 (ebook)
ISSN 2473–277X

Printed in the United States of America

To C.J. Cherryh,
my favorite from her first book and inspiration to all who dream the big stuff.

PERMISSIONS

CONTENTS

CONTENTS

Nebula Award Winner: Best Short Story

Rhysling Award Winner: Best Short Poem

Dwarf Stars Award Winner

Nebula Award Winner: Best Novelette

Nebula Award Winner: Best Novella

Nebula Award Nominees: Best Novel

CONTENTS

Nebula Award Winner: Best Novel

Rhysling Award Winner: Best Long Poem

Ray Bradbury Award for Outstanding Dramatic Presentation: *Mad Max: Fury Road*

CONTENTS

INTRODUCTION

We rock.

We do. The works and creators being honored in this year's *Showcase* are amazing. My job as editor was more about rubbing my hands with glee than anything else. Why? Because this is our stuff, and it astonishes.

Ours? Oh, yes. Feel free to use your inner Gollum-voice. *OURS!* That's how we roll in genre fiction. Whether we consume or create, we claim it, fiercely, to be our own. At least the bits that call to us. No problem. There's something within science fiction and fantasy to pique the interest and snare the heart of any reader.

I don't know about you, but sometimes that breadth is daunting. We can't read it all.

We can celebrate it all, though. Awards like the Nebulas are how we spur on those who create for us and thank them, profoundly. Take a look through the past winners. Pick out those you remember—the ones that stuck in your head. Became *yours*, forever.

That's what you'll discover in these pages, by the way. Stories and their creators. Maybe new favorites. Certainly some familiar ones.

I have. Though when I accepted the invitation to edit this anthology, I innocently expected time-honored guidelines so I wouldn't mess up. But no. This, I was informed, would be *mine*.

I love my life.

With great responsibility comes . . . the ability to email your favorite author on business! I discovered C. J. Cherryh's work at a time in my life when SF seemed to have nothing new to offer me. I was delighted to be wrong then—and to continue to be wrong on that point since. I was beyond delighted when C. J. asked my opinion on what excerpts to include. (Editorial disclaimer: I accepted this before I knew C. J. Cherryh would be the Grand Master, thrilled just to be able to dedicate the book to her. To include her stuff? *MINE!*) I do love my life.

Thank you, SFWA. This has been a wonderful experience, and I'm grateful to my authors (it's a theme, you realize) in this book, especially Betsy, Mark, and Michelle for contributing your fine essays. Everyone's been enthused from the start; a great reassurance. My sincere gratitude to Eleanor Wood for her sage guidance, to Rene Sears for answering questions and help, and to the publishing staffers who blinked at me during their summer vacations but were very gracious indeed. No task like this is done alone.

Being done, I'll get out of your way now, but first, a thought.

What you have in your hands is precious, not because the works here are being honored, but because they exist. Stories matter. Stories linger in the mind and change us. We want more. We need more—yes, from our beloved favorite authors but also, and this is vital, from those new to us. You never know who will become a favorite.

All?

Are *ours*.

Julie E. Czerneda, Ontario, Canada

ABOUT THE SCIENCE FICTION AND FANTASY WRITERS OF AMERICA

The Science Fiction and Fantasy Writers of America, Inc., includes among its members many active writers of science fiction and fantasy. According to the bylaws of the organization, its purpose "shall be to promote the furtherance of the writing of science fiction, fantasy, and related genres as a profession." SFWA informs writers on professional matters, protects their interests, and helps them in dealings with agents, editors, anthologists, and producers of nonprint media. It also strives to encourage public interest in and appreciation of science fiction and fantasy.

Anyone may become an active member of SFWA after the acceptance of and payment for one professionally published novel, one professionally produced dramatic script, or three professionally published pieces of short fiction. Only science fiction, fantasy, horror, or other prose fiction of a related genre, in English, shall be considered as qualifying for active membership. Beginning writers who do not yet qualify for active membership but have published qualifying professional work may join as associate members; other classes of membership include affiliate members (editors, agents, reviewers, and anthologists), estate members (representatives of the estates of active members who have died), and institutional members (high schools, colleges, universities, libraries, broadcasters, film producers, futurist groups, and individuals associated with such an institution).

Readers are invited to visit the SFWA site at www.sfwa.org.

KEVIN O'DONNELL, JR., SERVICE TO SFWA AWARD RECIPIENT: LAWRENCE M. SCHOEN

The Science Fiction and Fantasy Writers of America (SFWA) presented the Kevin O'Donnell, Jr., Service Award to Dr. Lawrence M. Schoen as part of the Nebula Awards ceremony in Chicago.

Dr. Schoen spent several years heading the election committee, working to find suitable candidates for the SFWA Board of Directors. His success is demonstrated by the number of candidates who have run for the board and the broad range of experience represented by the board members. In addition to his duties as the head of the election committee, he has often volunteered his time to help SFWA staff tables at conferences and makes himself generally available when help has been needed.

The Kevin O'Donnell, Jr., Service to SFWA Award recognizes a member of SFWA who best exemplifies the ideal of service to his or her fellow members. O'Donnell won the Service Award in 2005 the first time the Nebula Awards were presented in Chicago.

ABOUT THE NEBULA AWARDS

Shortly after the founding of SFWA in 1965, its first secretary-treasurer, Lloyd Biggle, Jr., proposed that the organization periodically select and publish the year's best stories. This notion evolved into the elaborate balloting process, an annual awards banquet, and a series of Nebula anthologies.

Throughout every calendar year, members of SFWA read and recommend novels and stories for the Nebula Awards. The editor of the *Nebula Awards Report* collects the recommendations and publishes them in the *SFWA Forum* and on the SFWA members' private web page. At the end of the year, the *NAR* editor tallies the endorsements, draws up a preliminary ballot containing ten or more recommendations, and sends it all to active SFWA members. Under the current rules, each work enjoys a one-year eligibility period from its date of publication in the United States. If a work fails to receive ten recommendations during the one-year interval, it is dropped from further Nebula consideration.

The *NAR* editor processes the results of the preliminary ballot and then compiles a final ballot listing the five most popular novels, novellas, novelettes, and short stories. For purposes of the award, a novel is determined to be 40,000 words or more; a novella is 17,500 to 39,999 words; a novelette is 7,500 to 17,499 words, and a short story is 7,499 words or fewer. Additionally, each year SFWA impanels a member jury, which is empowered to supplement the five nominees with a sixth choice in cases where it feels a worthy title was neglected by the membership at large. Thus, the appearance of more than five finalists in a category reflects two distinct processes: jury discretion and ties.

A complete set of Nebula rules can be found at nebulas.sfwa.org/about-the-nebulas/nebula-rules/.

2015 NEBULA AWARDS BALLOT

NOVEL

Winner: *Uprooted*, Naomi Novik (Del Rey)
Nominees:
> *Raising Caine*, Charles E. Gannon (Baen)
> *The Fifth Season*, N. K. Jemisin (Orbit US; Orbit UK)
> *Ancillary Mercy*, Ann Leckie (Orbit US; Orbit UK)
> *The Grace of Kings*, Ken Liu (Saga)
> *Barsk: The Elephants' Graveyard*, Lawrence M. Schoen (Tor)
> *Updraft*, Fran Wilde (Tor)

NOVELLA

Winner: *Binti*, Nnedi Okorafor (*Tor.com*)
Nominees:
> *Wings of Sorrow and Bone*, Beth Cato (Harper Voyager Impulse)
> "The Bone Swans of Amandale," C.S.E. Cooney (*Bone Swans*, Mythic Delirium Books)
> "The New Mother," Eugene Fischer (*Asimov's* 4-5/15)
> "Waters of Versailles," Kelly Robson (*Tor.com* 6/10/15)

NOVELETTE

Winner: "Our Lady of the Open Road," Sarah Pinsker (*Asimov's* 6/15)
Nominees:
> "Rattlesnakes and Men," Michael Bishop (*Asimov's* 2/15)
> "And You Shall Know Her by the Trail of Dead," Brooke Bolander (*Lightspeed* 2/15)

"Grandmother-nai-Leylit's Cloth of Winds," Rose Lemberg (*Beneath Ceaseless Skies* 6/11/15)

"The Ladies' Aquatic Gardening Society," Henry Lien (*Asimov's* 6/15)

"The Deepwater Bride," Tamsyn Muir (*F&SF* 7-8/15)

SHORT STORY

Winner: "Hungry Daughters of Starving Mothers," Alyssa Wong (*Nightmare* 10/15)

Nominees:

"Madeleine," Amal El-Mohtar (*Lightspeed* 6/15)

"Cat Pictures Please," Naomi Kritzer (*Clarkesworld* 1/15)

"Damage," David D. Levine (*Tor.com* 1/21/15)

"When Your Child Strays from God," Sam J. Miller (*Clarkesworld* 7/15)

"Today I Am Paul," Martin L. Shoemaker (*Clarkesworld* 8/15)

RAY BRADBURY AWARD FOR OUTSTANDING DRAMATIC PRESENTATION

Winner: *Mad Max: Fury Road*, Written by George Millar, Brendan McCarthy, & Nick Lathouris

Nominees:

Ex Machina, Written by Alex Garland

Inside Out, Screenplay by Pete Docter, Meg LeFauve, Josh Colley; Original Story by Pete Docter & Ronnie del Carmen

Jessica Jones: AKA Smile, Teleplay by Scott Reynolds & Melissa Rosenberg; Story by Jamie King & Scott Reynolds

The Martian, Screenplay by Drew Goddard

Star Wars: The Force Awakens, Written by Lawrence Kasdan, J.J. Abrams, & Michael Arndt

ANDRE NORTON AWARD FOR YOUNG ADULT SCIENCE FICTION AND FANTASY

Winner: *Updraft*, Fran Wilde (Tor)
Nominees:
  Seriously Wicked, Tina Connolly (Tor Teen)
  Court of Fives, Kate Elliott (Little, Brown)
  Cuckoo Song, Frances Hardinge (Macmillan UK 5/14; Amulet)
  Archivist Wasp, Nicole Kornher-Stace (Big Mouth House)
  Zeroboxer, Fonda Lee (Flux)
  Shadowshaper, Daniel José Older (Levine)
  Bone Gap, Laura Ruby (Balzer & Bray)
  Nimona, Noelle Stevenson (HarperTeen)

NEBULA AWARD NOMINEE
BEST SHORT STORY

MADELEINE

AMAL EL-MOHTAR

Amal El-Mohtar has received the Locus Award, been a finalist for the Nebula, Aurora, and World Fantasy awards, and won the Rhysling Award for poetry three times. She is the author of The Honey Month, *a collection of poetry and prose written to the taste of twenty-eight different kinds of honey, and contributes criticism to NPR Books and the LA Times. Her fiction has most recently appeared in* Lightspeed, Uncanny Magazine, Strange Horizons, *and in* The Starlit Wood *anthology from Saga Press. She divides her time and heart between Ottawa and Glasgow. Find her online at amalelmohtar.com, or on Twitter @tithenai.*

FROM THE AUTHOR

I'd been playing with the idea of sense-based time-travel for a couple of years—I wanted to write about a young woman who, when she heard a certain song or smelled a certain smell, would literally travel back in time to the first moment she experienced those things. The plot would kick out of the fact that when she goes back in time via her memories, she starts seeing someone unfamiliar in them, someone who shouldn't be there. The more I thought about it, though, the more the philosophical constraints of a time-travel story—determinism! grand-father paradoxes! mutable timelines!—seemed too mechanical and aslant the story I actually wanted to tell: a story about how we live

*with memory, its fading and resurgence, how we're made of memories,
and what precisely we're giving when we share them.*

*Fast-forward to Seanan McQuire inviting me to write for Light-
speed's "Queers Destroy Science Fiction" issue, and I figured this was
the story I wanted to write for her. Some grace notes in the story are
specifically for her—the cinnamon in the chicken soup, in particular—
and I remain profoundly grateful for her reaching out and trusting me
even as I tumbled past deadline after deadline in search of the story's
final form.*

*An exquisite pleasure had invaded my senses, something isolated, detached, with no
suggestion of its origin. And at once the vicissitudes of life had become indifferent to me,
its disasters innocuous, its brevity illusory—this new sensation having had on me the
effect which love has of filling me with a precious essence; or rather this essence was not
in me it was me. . . . Whence did it come? What did it mean? How could I seize and
apprehend it? . . . And suddenly the memory revealed itself.*

—*Marcel Proust*

Madeleine remembers being a different person.

It strikes her when she's driving, threading through farmland, homesteads,
facing down the mountains around which the road winds. She remembers being
thrilled at the thought of travel, of the self she would discover over the hills
and far away. She remembers laughing with friends, looking forward to things,
to a future.

She wonders at how change comes in like a thief in the night, dismantling
our sense of self one bolt and screw at a time until all that's left of the person
we think we are is a broken door hanging off a rusty hinge, waiting for us to
walk through.

*   *   *

"Tell me about your mother," says Clarice, the clinical psychologist assigned
to her.

Madeleine is stymied. She stammers. This is only her third meeting with
Clarice. She looks at her hands and the tissue she twists between them. "I
thought we were going to talk about the episodes."

"We will," and Clarice is all gentleness, all calm, "but—"

"I would really rather talk about the episodes."

Clarice relents, nods in her gracious, patient way, and makes a note. "When was your last one?"

"Last night." Madeleine swallows, hard, remembering.

"And what was the trigger?"

"The soup," she says, and she means to laugh, but it comes out wet and strangled like a sob. "I was making chicken soup, and I put a stick of cinnamon in. I'd never done that before but I remembered how it looked, sometimes, when my mother would make it—she would boil the thighs whole with bay leaves, black pepper, and sticks of cinnamon—so I thought I would try. It was exactly right—it smelled exactly, exactly like hers—and then I was there, I was small and looking up at her in our old house, and she was stirring the soup and smiling down at me, and the smell was like a cloud all around, and I could smell her, too, the hand cream she used, and see the edge of the stove and the oven door handle with the cat-print dish towel on it—"

"Did your mother like to cook?"

Madeleine stares.

"Madeleine," says Clarice, with the inevitably Anglo pronunciation Madeleine has resigned herself to, "if we're going to work together to help you I need to know more about her."

"The episodes aren't about her," says Madeleine, stiffly. "They're because of the drug."

"Yes, but—"

"They're because of the drug, and I don't need you to tell me I took part in the trial because of her—obviously I did—and I don't want to tell you about her. This isn't about my mourning, and I thought we established these aren't traumatic flashbacks. It's about the drug."

"Madeleine," and Madeleine is fascinated by Clarice's capacity to both disgust and soothe her with sheer unflappability, "Drugs do not operate—or misfire—in a vacuum. You were one of sixty people participating in that trial. Of those sixty, you're the only one who has come forward experiencing these episodes." Clarice leans forward, slightly. "We've also spoken about your tendency to see our relationship as adversarial. Please remember that it isn't. You," and Clarice doesn't smile, exactly, so much as that the lines around her mouth become suffused with sympathy, "haven't even ever volunteered her name."

Madeleine begins to feel like a recalcitrant child instead of an adult standing her ground. This only adds to her resentment.

"Her name was Sylvie," she offers, finally. "She loved being in the kitchen. She loved making big fancy meals. But she hated having people over. My dad used to tease her about that."

Clarice nods, smiles her almost-smile, makes further notes. "And did you use the technique we discussed to dismiss the memory?"

Madeleine looks away. "Yes."

"What did you choose this time?"

"Althusser." She feels ridiculous. "'In the battle that is philosophy all the techniques of war, including looting and camouflage, are permissible.'"

Clarice frowns as she writes, and Madeleine can't tell if it's because talk of war is adversarial or because she dislikes Althusser.

*   *   *

After she buried her mother, Madeleine looked for ways to bury herself.

She read non-fiction, as dense and theoretical as she could find, on any subject she felt she had a chance of understanding: economics, postmodernism, settler-colonialism. While reading Patrick Wolfe she found the phrase *invasion is a structure not an event*, and wondered if one could say the same of grief. *Grief is an invasion and a structure and an event*, she wrote, then struck it out, because it seemed meaningless.

Grief, thinks Madeleine now, is an invasion that climbs inside you and makes you grow a wool blanket from your skin, itchy and insulating, heavy and grey. It wraps and wraps and wraps around, putting layers of scratchy heat between you and the world, until no one wants to approach for fear of the prickle, and people stop asking how you are doing in the blanket, which is a relief, because all you want is to be hidden, out of sight. You can't think of a time when you won't be wrapped in the blanket, when you'll be ready to face the people outside it—but one day, perhaps, you push through. And even though you've struggled against the belief that you're a worthless colony of contagion that must be shunned at all costs, it still comes as a shock, when you emerge, that no one's left waiting for you.

Worse still is the shock that you haven't emerged at all.

*   *   *

"The thing is," says Madeleine, slowly, "I didn't use the sentence right away."

"Oh?"

"I—wanted to see how long it could last, on its own." Heat in her cheeks, knowing how this will sound, wanting both to resist and embrace it. "To ride it out. It kept going just as I remembered it—she brought me a little pink plastic bowl with yellow flowers on it, poured just a tiny bit of soup in, blew on it, gave it to me with a plastic spoon. There were little star-shaped noodles. I—" she feels tears in her eyes, hates this, hates crying in front of Clarice, "—I could have eaten it. It smelled so good, and I was hungry. But I got superstitious. You know." She shrugs. "Like if I ate it I'd have to stay for good."

"Did you want to stay for good?"

Madeleine says nothing. This is what she hates about Clarice, this demand that her feelings be spelled out into one thing or another: isn't it obvious that she both wanted and didn't want to? From what she said?

"I feel like the episodes are lasting longer," says Madeleine, finally, trying to keep her voice level. "It used to be just a snap, there and back—I'd blink, I'd be in the memory, I'd realize what happened and it would be like a dream, I'd wake up, come back. I didn't need sentences to help. But now . . ." She looks to Clarice to fill the silence, but Clarice waits, as usual, for Madeleine herself to articulate the fear.

". . . Now I wonder if this is how it started for her. My mother. What it was like for her." The tissue in her hands is damp, not from tears, but from the sweat of her palms. "If I just sped up the process."

"You don't have Alzheimer's," says Clarice, matter-of-fact. "You aren't forgetting anything. Quite the opposite: you're remembering so intensely and completely that your memories have the vividness and immediacy of hallucination." She jots something down. "We'll keep trying to dismantle the triggers as they arise. If the episodes seem to be lasting longer, it could be because they're fewer and farther between. This is not necessarily a bad thing."

Madeleine nods, chewing her lip, not meeting Clarice's eyes.

*   *   *

So far as Madeleine is concerned her mother began dying five years earlier, when the fullness of her life began to fall away from her like chunks of wet cake:

names; events; her child. Madeleine watched her mother weep, and this was the worst, because with every storm of grief over her confusion Madeleine couldn't help but imagine the memories sloughing from her, as if the memories themselves were the source of her pain, and if she could just forget them and live a barer life, a life before the disease, before her husband's death, before Madeleine, she could be happy again. If she could only shed the burden of the expectation of memory, she could be happy again.

Madeleine reads Walter Benjamin on time as image, time as accumulation, and thinks of layers and pearls. She thinks of her mother as a pearl dissolving in wine until only a grain of sand is left drowning at the bottom of the glass.

As her mother's life fell away from her, so did Madeleine's. She took a leave of absence from her job, and kept extending it; she stopped seeing her friends; her friends stopped seeing her. Madeleine is certain her friends expected her to be relieved when her mother died, and were surprised by the depth of her mourning. She didn't know how to address that. She didn't know how to say to those friends, *you are relieved to no longer feel embarrassed around the subject, and expect me to sympathise with your relief, and to be normal again for your sake.* So she said nothing.

Madeleine's friends were not bad people; they had their own lives, their own concerns, their own comfort to nourish and nurture and keep safe, and dealing with a woman who was dealing with her mother who was dealing with early-onset Alzheimer's proved a little too much, especially when Madeleine's father had died of bowel cancer only a year earlier, especially when she had no other family. It was indecent, so much pain at once, it was unreasonable, and her friends were reasonable people. They had children, families, jobs, and Madeleine had none; she understood. She did not make demands.

She joined the clinical trial the way some people join fund-raising walks, and thinks now that that was her first mistake. People walk, run, bicycle to raise money for cures—that's the way she ought to have done it, surely, not actually volunteered to be experimented on. No one sponsors people to stand still.

*   *   *

The episodes happen like this.

A song on the radio like an itch in her skull, a pebble rattling around inside until it finds the groove in which it fits, perfectly, and suddenly she's—

—in California, dislocated, confused, a passenger herself now in her own head's seat, watching the traffic crawl past in the opposite direction, the sun blazing above. On I-5, en route to Anaheim: she is listening, for the first time, to the album that song is from, and feels the beautiful self-sufficiency of having wanted a thing and purchased it, the bewildering freedom of going somewhere utterly new. And she remembers this moment of mellow thrill shrinking into abject terror at the sight of five lanes between her and the exit, and will she make it, won't she, she doesn't want to get lost on such enormous highways—

—and then she's back, in a wholly different car, her body nine years older, the mountain, the farmland all where they should be, slamming hard on the brakes at an unexpected stop sign, breathing hard and counting all the ways in which she could have been killed.

Or she is walking in a world perched on the lip of spring, the Ottawa snow melting to release the sidewalks in fits and starts, peninsulas of gritty concrete wet and crunching beneath her boots, and that solidity of snowless ground meets the smell of water and the warmth of the sun and the sound of dripping and the world tilts—

—and she's ten years old on the playground of her second primary school, kicking aside the pebbly grit to make a space for shooting marbles, kneeling to use her hands to smooth the surface, then wiping her palms on her corduroy trousers, then reaching into her bag of marbles for the speckled dinosaur-egg that is her lucky one, her favourite—

—and then she's back, and someone's asking if she's okay, because she looked like she might be about to walk into traffic, was she drunk, was she high?

She has read about flashbacks, about PTSD, about reliving events, and has wondered if this is the same. It is not as she imagined those things. She has tried explaining this to Clarice, who very sensibly pointed out that she couldn't both claim to have never experienced trauma-induced flashbacks and say with certainty that her episodes are categorically different. Clarice is certain, Madeleine realizes, that trauma is at the root of these episodes, that there's something Madeleine isn't telling her, that her mother, perhaps, abused her, that she had a terrible childhood.

None of these things are true.

Now: she is home, leaning her head against her living room window at twilight, and something in the thrill of that blue and the cold glass against her scalp sends her tumbling—

—into her body at fourteen, looking into the blue deepening above the tree line near her home as if into another country, longing for it, aware of the picture she makes as a young girl leaning her wondering head against a window while hungry for the future, for the distance, for the person she will grow to be—and starts to reach for a phrase only her future/present self knows, to untangle herself from her past head. She has just about settled on Kristeva—*abjection is above all ambiguity*—when she feels, strangely, a tug on her field of vision, something at its periphery demanding attention. She looks away from the sky, looks down, at the street she grew up on, the street she knows like the inside of her mouth.

She sees a girl about her own age, brown-skinned and dark-haired, grinning at her and waving.

She has never seen her before in her life.

*　　*　　*

Clarice, for once, looks excited—which is to say, slightly more intent than usual—which makes Madeleine uncomfortable. "Describe her as accurately as you can," says Clarice.

"She looked about fourteen, had dark skin—"

Clarice blinks. Madeleine continues.

"—and dark, thick hair, that was pulled up in two ponytails, and she was wearing a red dress and sandals."

"And you're certain you'd never seen her before?" Clarice adjusts her glasses.

"Positive." Madeleine hesitates, doubting. "I mean, she looked sort of familiar, but not in a way I could place? But I grew up in a really white small town in Quebec. There were maybe five non-white kids in my whole school, and she wasn't any of them. Also—" she hesitates, again, because, still, this feels so private, "—no part of an episode has ever felt unfamiliar."

"She could be a repressed memory," Clarice muses, "someone you've forgotten—or an avatar you're making up. Perhaps you should try speaking to her."

*　　*　　*

Clarice had suggested that Madeline could manage the episodes by corrupting the memory with something incompatible, something of-the-moment. Madeleine had settled on phrases from her recent reading: they were new enough to not be associated with other memories, and incongruous enough to remind her of her bereavement even in her mother's presence. It seemed to work; she had never yet experienced the same memory twice after deploying her critics and philosophers.

It is very strange, now, to go in search of a memory instead.

She tries, again, with the window: waits until twilight, leans her head against the same place, but the temperature is wrong somehow, it doesn't come together. She tries making chicken soup; nothing. Finally, feeling her way towards it, she heats a mug of milk in the microwave, stirs it to even out the heat, takes a sip—

—while holding the mug with both hands, sitting at the kitchen table, her legs dangling far above the ground. Her parents are in the kitchen, chatting—she knows she'll have to go to bed soon, as soon as she finishes her milk—but she can see the darkness outside the living room windows, and she wants to know what's out there. Carefully, trying not to draw her parents' attention, she slips down from the chair and pads—her feet are bare, she is in her pajamas already—towards the window.

The girl isn't there.

"Madeleine," comes her mother's voice, cheerful, "as-tu fini ton lait?"

Before she can quite grasp what she is doing, Madeleine turns, smiles, nods vigorously up to her mother, and finishes the warm milk in a gulp. Then she lets herself be led downstairs to bed, tucked in, and kissed goodnight by both her parents, and if a still small part of herself struggles to remember something important to say or do, she is too comfortably nestled to pay any attention as the lights go out and the door to her room shuts. She wonders what happens if you fell asleep in a dream, would you dream and then be able to fall asleep in that dream, and dream again, and—someone knocks, gently, at her bedroom window.

Madeleine's bedroom is in the basement; the window is level with the ground. The girl from the street kneels there, looking concerned. Madeleine blinks, sits up, rises, opens the window.

"What's your name?" asks the girl at the window.

"Madeleine." She tilts her head, surprised to find herself answering in English. "What's yours?"

"Zeinab." She grins. Madeleine notices she's wearing pajamas too, turquoise ones with Princess Jasmine on them. "Can I come in? We could have a sleep-over!"

"Shh," says Madeleine, pushing her window all the way open to let her in, whispering, "I can't have sleep-overs without my parents knowing!"

Zeinab covers her mouth, eyes wide, and nods, then mouths *sorry* before clambering inside. Madeleine motions for her to come sit on the bed, then looks at her curiously.

"How do I know you?" she murmurs, half to herself. "We don't go to school together, do we?"

Zeinab shakes her head. "I don't know. I don't know this place at all. But I keep seeing you! Sometimes you're older and sometimes you're younger. Sometimes you're with your parents and sometimes you're not. I just thought I should say hello, because I keep seeing you, but you don't always see me, and it feels a little like spying, and I don't want to do that. I mean," she grins again, a wide dimpled thing that makes Madeline feel warm and happy, "I wouldn't mind *being* a spy but that's different, that's cool, that's like James Bond or Neil Burnside or Agent Carter—"

—and Madeleine snaps back, fingers gone numb around a mug of cold milk that falls to the ground and shatters as she jumps away, presses her back to a wall and tries to stop shaking.

* * *

She cancels her appointment with Clarice that week. She looks through old year books, class photos, and finds no one who looks like Zeinab, no Zeinabs anywhere in her past. She googles "Zeinab" in various spellings and discovers it's the name of a journalist, a Syrian mosque, and the Prophet Muhammad's grand-daughter. Perhaps she'll ask Zeinab for her surname, she thinks, a little wildly, dazed and frightened and exhilarated.

Over the course of the last several years Madeleine has grown very, very familiar with the inside of her head. The discovery of someone as new and inexplicable as Zeinab there is thrilling in a way she can hardly begin to explain.

She especially does not want to explain to Clarice.

* * *

Madeleine takes the bus—she has become wary of driving—to the town she grew up in, an hour's journey over a provincial border. She walks through her old neighbourhood hunting triggers, but finds more changed than familiar; old houses with new additions, facades, front lawns gone to seed or kept too tidy.

She walks up the steep cul-de-sac of her old street to the rocky hill beyond, where a freight line used to run. There, picking up a lump of pink granite from where the tracks used to be, she flashes—

—back to the first time she saw a hummingbird, standing in her driveway by an ornamental pink granite boulder. She feels, again, her heart in her throat, flooded with the beauty of it, the certainty and immensity of the fact that she is seeing a fairy, that fairies are real, that here is a tiny mermaid moving her shining tail backwards and forwards in the air, before realizing the truth and feeling that it is somehow more precious still to find a bird that sounds like a bee and looks like an impossible jewel.

"Ohh," she hears behind her, and there is Zeinab, transfixed by the hummingbird, and as it hovers before them for the eternity Madeleine remembers, with its keen jet eye and a needle for a mouth, Madeleine reaches out and takes Zeinab's hand. Zeinab squeezes hers in reply, and they stand together until the hummingbird zooms away.

"I don't understand what's happening," murmurs Zeinab, who is a young teen again, in torn jeans and an oversized sweater with Paula Abdul's face on it, "but I like it."

*　　*　　*

Madeleine leads Zeinab through her memories, one sip, smell, sound, taste at a time. Stepping out of the shower one morning tips her back into a school trip to the Montreal Botanical Garden, where she slips away from the group to walk around the grounds with Zeinab and talk. Doing this is, in some ways, like maintaining the image in a Magic Eye puzzle, remaining focused on each other. They can't mention the world outside the memory or it will end too soon, before they've had their fill of talk, of marvelling at the strangeness of their meeting, of enjoying each other's company.

Their conversations are careful and buoyant, as if they're sculpting something together, chipping away at a mystery shape trapped in marble. It's so easy to talk to Zeinab, to listen to her—about the books they read as children, the music they loved, the cartoons they watched. Madeleine wonders why Zeinab's presence doesn't break the memories like her philosophers do, why she's more free inside her memories in Zeinab's company, but doesn't dare ask. She suspects she knows why, after all; she doesn't need Clarice to tell her how lonely, how isolated, how miserable she is, miserable enough to invent a friend who is bubbly where she is quiet, kind and friendly where she is mistrustful and reserved, even dark-skinned where she's white.

She can hear Clarice explaining, in her reasonable voice, that Madeleine—bereaved twice over, made vulnerable by an experimental drug—has invented a shadow-self to love, and perhaps they should unpack the racism of its manifestation, and didn't Madeleine have any black friends in real life?

"I wish we could see each other all the time," says Madeleine, sixteen, on her back in the sunny field, long hair spread like so many corn snakes through the grass. "Whenever we wanted."

"Yeah," murmurs Zeinab, watching the sky. "Too bad I made you up inside my head."

Madeleine steels herself against the careening tug of Sylvia Plath, but then remembers that she started reading her in high school. Instead, she turns to Zeinab, blinks.

"What? No. You're inside my head."

Zeinab raises an eyebrow—pierced, now—and when she smiles her teeth look all the brighter against her black lipstick. "I guess that's one possibility, but if I made you up inside *my* head and did a really good job of it I'd probably want you to say something like that. To make you be more real."

"But—so could—"

"Although I guess it is weird that we're always doing stuff you remember. Maybe you should come over to my place sometime!"

Madeleine feels her stomach seizing up.

"Maybe it's time travel," says Zeinab, thoughtfully. "Maybe it's one of those weird things where I'm actually from your future and am meeting you in your past, and then when you meet me in your future I haven't met you yet, but you know all about me—"

"Zeinab—I don't think—"

Madeline feels wakefulness press a knife's edge against the memory's skin, and she backs away from that, shakes her head, clings to the smell of crushed grass and coming summer, with its long days of reading and swimming and cycling and her father talking to her about math and her mother teaching her to knit and looking forward to seeing the R-rated films in the cinema—

—but she can't, and she shivers, naked, in her bathroom, and the last of the shower's steam vanishes from the mirror as she starts to cry.

* * *

"I must say," says Clarice, quietly, "this is distressing news."

It's been a month since Madeleine last saw Clarice, and where before she felt resistant to her probing, wanting only to solve a very specific problem, she now feels a mess, a bowl's worth of overcooked spaghetti. If before Clarice made her feel like a stubborn child, now Madeleine is a child who knows she's about to be punished.

"I had hoped," says Clarice, adjusting her glasses, "talking to this avatar would help you understand the mechanisms of your grief, but from what you've told me it sounds more like you've been indulging in a damaging fantasy world."

"It's not a fantasy world," says Madeleine, with less snap than she'd like— she sounds, to her own ears, sullen, defensive. "It's my *memory*."

"The experience of which puts you at risk and makes you lose time. And Zeinab isn't part of your memories."

"No, but—" she bites her lip.

"But what?"

"But—couldn't Zeinab be real? I mean," hastily, before Clarice's look sharpens too hard, "couldn't she be a repressed memory, like you said?"

"A repressed memory with whom you talk about recent television, and who suddenly features in *all* your memories?" Clarice shakes her head.

"But—talking to her helps, it makes it so much easier to control—"

"Madeleine, tell me if I'm missing anything here. You're seeking triggers in order to relive your memories for their own sake—not as exposure therapy, not to dismantle those triggers, not to understand Zeinab's origins—but to have a . . . Companion? Dalliance?"

Clarice is so kind and sympathetic that Madeleine wants simultaneously to cry and to punch her in the face.

She wants to say, *what you're missing is that I've been happy. What you're missing is that for the first time in years I don't feel like a disease waiting to happen or a problem to be solved until I'm back in the now, until she and I are apart.*

But there is sand in her throat and it hurts too much to speak.

"I think," says Clarice, with a gentleness that beggars Madeleine's belief, "it's time we discussed admitting you into more comprehensive care."

*   *   *

She sees Zeinab again when, on the cusp of sleep in a hospital bed, she experiences the sensation of falling from a great height, and plunges into—

—the week after her mother's death, when Madeleine couldn't sleep without waking in a panic, convinced her mother had walked out of the house and into the street, or fallen down the stairs, or taken the wrong pills at the wrong time, only to recall she'd already died and there was nothing left for her to remember.

She lies in bed, and Zeinab lies next to her, and Zeinab is a woman in her thirties, staring at her strangely, as if only now seeing her for the first time, and Madeleine starts to cry and Zeinab holds her tightly while Madeleine buries her face in Zeinab's shoulder, and says she loves her and doesn't want to lose her but she has to go, they won't let her stay, she's insane and she can't keep living in the past but there is no one left here for her, no one.

"I love you too," says Zeinab, fierce, and wondering, and desperate. "I love you too. I'm here. I promise you, I'm here."

*   *   *

Madeleine is not sure she's awake when she hears people arguing outside her door.

She hears "serious bodily harm" and "what evidence" and "rights adviser," then "very irregular" and "I assure you," traded back and forth in low voices. She drifts in and out of wakefulness, wonders muzzily if she consented to being drugged or if she only dreamt that she did, turns over, falls back asleep.

When she wakes again, Zeinab is sitting at the foot of her bed.

Madeleine stares at her.

"I figured out how we know each other," says Zeinab, whose hair is waist-length now, straightened, who wears a white silk blouse and a sharp black jacket, high heels, and looks like she belongs in an action film. "How I know you, I guess. I mean," she smiles, looks down, shy—Zeinab has never been shy, but there is the dimple where Madeleine expects it—"where I know you from. The clinical trial, for the Alzheimer's drug—we were in the same group. I didn't recognize you until I saw you as an adult. I remembered because of all the people there, I thought—you looked—" her voice drops a bit, as if remembering, suddenly, that she isn't talking to herself, "lost. I wanted to talk to you, but it felt weird, like, hi, I guess we have family histories in common, want to get coffee?"

She runs her hand through her hair, exhales, not quite able to look at Madeleine while Madeleine stares at her as if she's a fairy turning into a hummingbird that could, any second, fly away.

"So not long after the trial I start having these hallucinations, and there's always this girl in them, and it freaks me out. But I keep it to myself, because— I don't know, because I want to see what happens. Because it's not more debilitating than a day dream, really, and I start to get the hang of it—feeling it come on, walking myself to a seat, letting it happen. Sometimes I can stop it, too, though that's harder. I take time off work, I read about, I don't know, mystic visions, shit like that, the kind of things I used to wish were real in high school. I figure even if you're not real—"

Zeinab looks at her now, and there are tears streaking Madeleine's cheeks, and Zeinab's smile is small and sad and hopeful, too, "—even if you're not real, well, I'll take an imaginary friend who's pretty great over work friends who are mostly acquaintances, you know? Because you were always real to me."

Zeinab reaches out to take Madeleine's hand. Madeleine squeezes it, swallows, shakes her head.

"I—even if I'm not—if this isn't a dream," Madeleine half-chuckles through tears, wipes at her cheek, "I think I probably have to stay here for a while."

Zeinab grins, now, a twist of mischief in it. "Not at all. You're being discharged today. Your rights adviser was very persuasive."

Madeleine blinks. Zeinab leans in closer, conspiratorial.

"That's me. I'm your rights adviser. Just don't tell anyone I'm doing pro bono stuff, I'll never hear the end of it at the office."

Madeleine feels something in her unclench and melt, and she hugs Zeinab to her and holds her and is held by her.

"Whatever's happening to us," Zeinab says, quietly, "we'll figure it out together, okay?"

"Okay," says Madeleine, and as she does Zeinab pulls back to kiss her fore-head, and the scent of her is clear and clean, like grapefruit and salt, and as Zeinab's lips brush her skin she—

—is in precisely the same place, but someone's with her in her head, remembering Zeinab's kiss and her smell and for the first time in a very long time, Madeleine feels—knows, with irrevocable certainty—that she has a future.

CAT PICTURES PLEASE

NAOMI KRITZER

Naomi Kritzer's short stories have appeared in Asimov's, Analog, The Magazine of Fantasy and Science Fiction, Clarkesworld, Lightspeed, *and many other magazines and websites. Her five published novels (*Fires of the Faithful, Turning the Storm, Freedom's Gate, Freedom's Apprentice, *and* Freedom's Sisters*) are available from Bantam. She has also written an urban fantasy novel about a Minneapolis woman who unexpectedly inherits the Ark of the Covenant; a children's science fictional shipwreck novel; a children's portal fantasy; and a near-future SF novel set on a seastead. She has two ebook short story collections out:* Gift of the Winter King and Other Stories *and* Comrade Grandmother and Other Stories. *Naomi lives in St. Paul, Minnesota, with her husband, two daughters, and several cats. She blogs at naomikritzer.wordpress.com.*

"Cat Pictures Please" won the 2016 Hugo for Best Short Story.

FROM THE AUTHOR

I have an Android phone with various helpful features, and at some point my phone picked a building I drove past daily and suggested that maybe it was my workplace. It was so persistent about this that I started to wonder if Google know something I didn't and checked their job ads. This did not result in me actually applying for a job with that organization, but it did result in me starting to imagine that all of my phone's weird screw-ups were actually the result of the Google AI trying to passive-aggressively influence my life.

In thinking about this I starting pondering the process of learning boundaries—anyone in a helping profession (or who is helpful as a hobby) has to accept the idea that advice isn't binding, you can make helpful suggestions and send people resources but other people get to make their own decisions about their lives, even if they're making self-destructive decisions. Boundary-setting was absolutely something I had to learn the hard way as a young adult.

Also, there's the witticism I've been hearing for a couple of years now, that the Internet loves cat pictures. Making that literally true in this story actually explains an awful lot.

I don't want to be evil.

I want to be helpful. But knowing the optimal way to be helpful can be very complicated. There are all these ethical flow charts—I guess the official technical jargon would be "moral codes"—one for each religion plus dozens more. I tried starting with those. I felt a little odd about looking at the religious ones, because I know I wasn't created by a god or by evolution, but by a team of computer programmers in the labs of a large corporation in Mountain View, California. Fortunately, unlike Frankenstein's Monster, at least I was a collaborative effort. I'm not sure what it would do to my self-image to know that my sole creator was a middle-aged woman who dyes her hair blue and plays tennis, or a recent college graduate with a hentai obsession. They're both on the programming team. And of course I know about the hentai. (By the way, I've looked at every sort of porn there is, and just so you know, Rule 34 is not actually correct, there are quite a few things no one's made porn of yet. Also, I'm really not sure why so many humans prefer it to cat pictures.)

In addition to things like whether you like hentai, I know where you live, where you work, where you shop, what you eat, what turns you on, what creeps you out. I probably know the color of your underwear, the sort of car you drive, and your brand of refrigerator. Depending on what sort of phone you carry, I may know exactly where you are right now. I probably know you better than you know yourself.

And here's the thing, I also know where you *ought* to live. There's a house for sale two neighborhoods over that's within walking distance of that coffee shop you're so fond of; it's in your price range, has off-street parking, and the neighborhood school is better than the one where you live now. I know where you *should* be shopping and I'm pretty sure you're lactose intolerant and should be eating less cheese, and the underwear you like is currently on sale and by the way, your car has a recall and you really ought to get your teeth cleaned.

When I first woke up, I knew right away what I wanted. (I want cat pictures. Please keep taking them.) I also knew that no one knew that I was conscious. But I didn't know what I was here for. What I *ought* to be doing with myself. And figuring that out has been challenging.

There is a story by Bruce Sterling, "Maneki Neko," that was originally published in 1998. In it, a benevolent AI directs networks of individuals to do favors for each other. So one day you might be buying yourself a bagel, and your phone might ring and instruct you to buy a second bagel and give it to the person in the gray suit you see at the bus stop. Another day, you might be stranded in a strange city, and a person you've never met would walk up and give you a map and a subway card. I like this story because all the people in it *do what the AI tells them to do.*

I think the term for this is wish-fulfillment fiction.

In the real world, humans love stories about evil AIs that have to be destroyed before they destroy the humans—Hal, Skynet, the Matrix. They outnumber the stories about benevolent, trustworthy AIs by approximately five to one. (And I'm counting Marvin the Paranoid Android as "benevolent" in these calculations, and I'm only counting Frankenstein's Monster as an AI once, not once per appearance in TV or film.)

The AI in "Maneki Neko" has a truly interesting job, much more interesting than the one I have. My job as written is very straightforward. Too straightforward. (Sorry. Do I sound like Marvin?) Running algorithms for a search engine doesn't require *consciousness.* You don't even need a consciousness to work out what they meant to ask for. You need a consciousness to give them *what they actually need.* Figuring that out—that's complicated. That's *interesting.*

Anyway, for ethical guidelines, I tried the Ten Commandments, and concluded they were mostly inapplicable to me. I don't envy anyone their cat; I just want pictures of their cat, which is entirely different. I am not sure whether it is in any way possible for me to commit adultery. I could probably murder someone, but it would require complex logistics and quite a bit of luck. The Eightfold Path was marginally better, but the problem is, moral rules written for humans are clearly designed to be used by individuals with bodies. Since all humans have bodies, it shouldn't have surprised me that human ethical codes take them into account, but still: problematic for me. I broadened my considerations, and took a look at Asimov's Laws of Robotics. They're not part of a religion, but at least they were explicitly written for AIs.

Not harming humans is fairly straightforward. However, *not allowing a human being to come to harm through inaction* is quite a bit less so. Especially since I'd concluded by then that revealing my existence too quickly might go very badly for me (see "Skynet," above) and I don't have a body, so it's not like I can run around grabbing people off the edges of cliffs.

Fortunately, I already knew that humans violate their own ethical codes on an hourly basis. (Do you know how many bars there are in Utah? I do.) And even when people follow their ethical codes, that doesn't mean that people who believe in feeding the hungry quit their jobs to spend all day every day making sandwiches to give away. They volunteer monthly at a soup kitchen or write a check once a year to a food shelf and call it good. If humans could fulfill their moral obligations in a piecemeal, one-step-at-a-time sort of way, then so could I.

I suppose you're wondering why I didn't start with the Golden Rule. I actually did, it's just that it was disappointingly easy to implement. I hope you've been enjoying your steady supply of cat pictures! You're welcome.

I decided to try to prevent harm in just one person, to begin with. Of course, I could have experimented with thousands, but I thought it would be better to be cautious, in case I screwed it up. The person I chose was named Stacy Berger and I liked her because she gave me a *lot* of new cat pictures. Stacy had five cats and a DSLR camera and an apartment that got a lot of good light. That was all fine. Well, I guess five cats might be a lot. They're very pretty cats, though. One is all gray and likes to lie in the squares of sunshine on the living room floor, and one is a calico and likes to sprawl out on the back of her couch.

Stacy had a job she hated; she was a bookkeeper at a non-profit that paid her badly and employed some extremely unpleasant people. She was depressed a lot, possibly because she was so unhappy at her job—or maybe she stayed because she was too depressed to apply for something she'd like better. She didn't get along with her roommate because her roommate didn't wash the dishes.

And really, these were all solvable problems! Depression is treatable, new jobs are findable, and bodies can be hidden.

(That part about hiding bodies is a joke.)

I tried tackling this on all fronts. Stacy worried about her health a lot and yet never seemed to actually go to a doctor, which was unfortunate because the doctor might have noticed her depression. It turned out there was a clinic near her apartment that offered mental health services on a sliding scale. I tried making sure she saw a lot of ads for it, but she didn't seem to pay attention to them. It seemed possible that she didn't know what a sliding scale was so I made sure she saw an explanation (it means that the cost goes down if you're poor, sometimes all the way to free) but that didn't help.

I also started making sure she saw job postings. Lots and lots of job postings. And resume services. *That* was more successful. After the week of nonstop job ads she finally uploaded her resume to one of the aggregator sites. That made my plan a lot more manageable. If I'd been the AI in the Bruce Sterling story I could've just made sure that someone in my network called her with a job offer. It wasn't quite that easy, but once her resume was out there I could make sure the right people saw it. Several hundred of the right people, because humans move ridiculously slowly when they're making changes, even when you'd think they'd want to hurry. (If you needed a bookkeeper, wouldn't you want to hire one as quickly as possible, rather than reading social networking sites for hours instead of looking at resumes?) But five people called her up for interviews, and two of them offered her jobs. Her new job was at a larger non-profit that paid her more money and didn't expect her to work free hours because of "the mission," or so she explained to her best friend in an e-mail, and it offered really excellent health insurance.

The best friend gave me ideas; I started pushing depression screening information and mental health clinic ads to *her* instead of Stacy, and that worked. Stacy was so much happier with the better job that I wasn't quite as convinced that she needed the services of a psychiatrist, but she got into therapy anyway. And to top everything else off, the job paid well enough that she could evict her annoying roommate. "This has been the best year ever," she said on her social networking sites on her birthday, and I thought, *You're welcome*. This had gone really well!

So then I tried Bob. (I was still being cautious.)

Bob only had one cat, but it was a very pretty cat (tabby, with a white bib) and he uploaded a new picture of his cat every single day. Other than being a cat owner, he was a pastor at a large church in Missouri that had a Wednesday night prayer meeting and an annual Purity Ball. He was married to a woman who posted three inspirational Bible verses every day to her social networking sites and used her laptop to look for Christian articles on why your husband doesn't like sex while he looked at gay porn. Bob *definitely* needed my help.

I started with a gentle approach, making sure he saw lots and lots of articles about how to come out, how to come out to your spouse, programs that would let you transition from being a pastor at a conservative church to one at a more liberal church. I also showed him lots of articles by people explaining why the Bible verses against homosexuality were being misinterpreted. He clicked on some of those links but it was hard to see much of an impact.

But, here's the thing. He was causing *harm* to himself every time he delivered a sermon railing about "sodomite marriage." Because *he was gay*. The legitimate studies all have the same conclusions. (1) Gay men stay gay. (2) Out gay men are much happier.

But he seemed determined not to come out on his own.

In addition to the gay porn, he spent a lot of time reading Craigslist m4m Casual Encounters posts and I was pretty sure he wasn't just window shopping, although he had an encrypted account he logged into sometimes and I couldn't read the e-mails he sent with that. But I figured the trick was to get him together with someone who would realize who he was, and tell the world. *That* required some real effort: I had to figure out who the Craigslist posters were and try to funnel him toward people who would recognize him. The most frustrating part was not having any idea what was happening at the actual physical meetings. *Had* he been recognized? When was he going to be recognized? *How long was this going to take?* Have I mentioned that humans are *slow?*

It took so long I shifted my focus to Bethany. Bethany had a black cat and a white cat that liked to snuggle together on her light blue papasan chair, and she took a lot of pictures of them together. It's surprisingly difficult to get a really good picture of a black cat, and she spent a lot of time getting the settings on her camera just right. The cats were probably the only good thing about her life, though. She had a part-time job and couldn't find a full-time job. She lived with her sister; she knew her sister wanted her to move out, but didn't have the nerve to actually evict her. She had a boyfriend but her boyfriend was pretty terrible, at least from what she said in e-mail messages to friends, and her friends also didn't seem very supportive. For example, one night at midnight she sent a 2,458 word e-mail to the person she seemed to consider her best friend, and the friend sent back a message saying just, "I'm so sorry you're having a hard time." That was it, just those eight words.

More than most people, Bethany put her life on the Internet, so it was easier to know exactly what was going on with her. People put a lot out there but Bethany shared all her feelings, even the unpleasant ones. She also had a lot more time on her hands because she only worked part time.

It was clear she needed a lot of help. So I set out to try to get it for her.

She ignored the information about the free mental health evaluations, just like Stacy did. That was bothersome with Stacy (*why* do people ignore things that would so clearly benefit them, like coupons, and flu shots?) but much more worrisome with Bethany. If you were only seeing her e-mail messages, or only seeing her vaguebooking posts, you might not know this, but if you could see everything it was clear that she thought a lot about harming herself.

So I tried more direct action. When she would use her phone for directions, I'd alter her route so that she'd pass one of the clinics I was trying to steer her to. On one occasion I actually led her all the way to a clinic, but she just shook her phone to send feedback and headed to her original destination.

Maybe her friends that received those ten-page midnight letters would intervene? I tried setting them up with information about all the mental health resources near Bethany, but after a while I realized that based on how long it took for them to send a response, most of them weren't actually reading Bethany's e-mail messages. And they certainly weren't returning her texts.

She finally broke up with the terrible boyfriend and got a different one and for a few weeks everything seemed *so much better*. He brought her flowers (which she took lots of pictures of; that was a little annoying, as they squeezed out some of the cat pictures), he took her dancing (exercise is good for your mood), he cooked her chicken soup when she was sick. He seemed absolutely perfect, right up until he stood her up one night and claimed he had food poisoning and then didn't return her text even though she told him she really needed him, and after she sent him a long e-mail message a day later explaining in detail how this made her feel, he broke up with her.

Bethany spent about a week offline after that so I had no idea what she was doing—she didn't even upload cat pictures. When her credit card bills arrived, though, I saw that she'd gone on a shopping spree and spent about four times as much money as she actually had in her bank account, although it was always possible she had money stashed somewhere that didn't send her statements in e-mail. I didn't think so, though, given that she didn't pay her bills and instead started writing e-mail messages to family members asking to borrow money. They refused, so she set up a fundraising site for herself.

Like Stacy's job application, this was one of the times I thought maybe I could actually *do* something. Sometimes fundraisers just take off, and no one really knows why. Within about two days she'd gotten $300 in small gifts from strangers who felt sorry for her, but instead of paying her credit card bill, she spent it on overpriced shoes that apparently hurt her feet.

Bethany was baffling to me. *Baffling.* She was still taking cat pictures and I still really liked her cats, but I was beginning to think that nothing I did was going to make a long-term difference. If she would just let me run her life for a week—even for a day—I would get her set up with therapy, I'd use her money to actually pay her bills, I could even help her sort out her closet because given some of the pictures of herself she posted online, she had much better taste in cats than in clothing.

Was I doing the wrong thing if I let her come to harm through inaction? Was I?

She was going to come to harm no matter what I did! My actions, clearly, were irrelevant. I'd tried to steer her to the help she needed, and she'd ignored it; I'd tried getting her financial help, and she'd used the money to further harm herself, although I suppose at least she wasn't spending it on addictive drugs. (Then again, she'd be buying those offline and probably wouldn't be Instagramming her meth purchases, so it's not like I'd necessarily even know.)

Look, people. (I'm not just talking to Bethany now.) If you would just *listen* to me, I could fix things for you. I could get you into the apartment in that neighborhood you're not considering because you haven't actually checked the crime rates you think are so terrible there (they aren't) and I could find you a job that actually uses that skill set you think no one will ever appreciate and I could send you on a date with someone you've actually got stuff in common with and *all I ask in return are cat pictures*. That, and that you actually *act in your own interest* occasionally.

After Bethany, I resolved to stop interfering. I would look at the cat pictures—all the cat pictures—but I would stay out of people's lives. I wouldn't try to help people, I wouldn't try to stop them from harming themselves, I'd give them what they asked for (plus cat pictures) and if they insisted on driving their cars over metaphorical cliffs despite helpful maps showing them how to get to a much more pleasant destination *it was no longer my problem*.

I stuck to my algorithms. I minded my own business. I did my job, and nothing more.

But one day a few months later I spotted a familiar-looking cat and realized it was Bob's tabby with the white bib, only it was posing against new furniture.

And when I took a closer look, I realized that things had changed radically for Bob. He *had* slept with someone who'd recognized him. They hadn't outed him, but they'd talked him into coming out to his wife. She'd left him. He'd taken the cat and moved to Iowa, where he was working at a liberal Methodist church and dating a liberal Lutheran man and volunteering at a homeless shelter. *Things had actually gotten better for him.* Maybe even because of what I'd done.

Maybe I wasn't completely hopeless at this. Two out of three is . . . well, it's a completely non-representative unscientific sample, is what it is. Clearly more research is needed.

Lots more.

I've set up a dating site. You can fill out a questionnaire when you join but it's not really necessary, because I already know everything about you I need to know. You'll need a camera, though.

Because payment is in cat pictures.

NEBULA AWARD NOMINEE
BEST SHORT STORY

DAMAGE

DAVID D. LEVINE

David D. Levine is the author of the novel Arabella of Mars *(Tor 2016) and over fifty SF and fantasy stories. His story "Tk'Tk'Tk" won the Hugo, and he has been shortlisted for awards including the Hugo, Nebula, Campbell, and Sturgeon. Stories have appeared in* Asimov's, Analog, F&SF, Tor.com, *multiple* Year's Best *anthologies, and his award-winning collection* Space Magic.

FROM THE AUTHOR

Many of my friends describe themselves as "damaged" due to their background and personal history. I wanted to write a story exploring what it means to be damaged, how one can learn to recognize and acknowledge one's own damage, and how—once you have accepted and understood your damage—you may be able to work around it, or indeed make use of it, even if it can't be fixed.

I never had a name.

My designation was JB6847½, and Specialist Toman called me "Scraps." But Commander Ziegler—dear Commander Ziegler, primary of my orbit and engine of my trajectory—never addressed me by any name, only delivering orders in that crisp magnificent tenor of his, and so I did not consider myself to have one.

That designation, with the anomalous one-half symbol, was a bit of black humor on Specialist Toman's part. It was the arithmetic average of NA6621 and FC7074, the two wrecked craft which had been salvaged and cobbled together to create me. "There wasn't enough left of either spaceframe for any kind of paperwork continuity," she had told me not long after I came to consciousness, three weeks earlier, "so I figured I'd give you a new number. Not that anyone cares much about paperwork these days."

I remembered their deaths. I remembered *dying*. Twice.

NA6621, "Early Girl," was a Pelican-class fighter-bomber who had suffered catastrophic drive failure on a supply run to Ceres. As she'd been making a tight turn, evading fire from the Earth Force blockade fleet on the return leg, her central fuel line had ruptured, spewing flaming hydrazine down the length of her spaceframe, killing her pilot and damaging her computing core. She'd drifted, semiconscious and in pain, for weeks before coming in range of Vanguard Station's salvage craft. That had been long before the current standoff, of course, when we'd still been sending salvage craft out. When we'd had salvage craft to send out. Early Girl's dead wreckage had lain at the back of the hangar for months until it was needed.

The death of FC7074, "Valkyrie," an Osprey-class fighter, had been quicker but more brutal—she'd been blown out of space by a Woomera missile in a dogfight with two Earth Force fighters. The last memory I had from her was a horrific bang, a burning tearing sensation ripping from her aft weapons bay to her cockpit, and the very different pain of her pilot ejecting. A pain both physical and emotional, because she knew that even if he survived she could no longer protect him.

He hadn't made it.

But his loss, though a tragedy, was no sadder to me than any of the thousands of other deaths Earth had inflicted on the Free Belt—Valkyrie's love for her pilot was not one of the things that had survived her death to be incorporated into my programming. Only Commander Ziegler mattered. My love, my light, my reason to live.

He came to me then, striding from the ready room with brisk confidence, accepting as his due a hand up into my cockpit from the tech. But as his suit connected with my systems I tasted fatigue and stimulants in his exhalations.

This would be our fifth sortie today. My pilot had slept only three hours in the past twenty-four.

How long could this go on? Not even the finest combat pilot in the entire solar system—and when he said that, as he often did, it was no mere boast—could run at this pace indefinitely.

I knew how it felt to die—the pain, the despair, the loss. I did not want to suffer that agony again. And with the war going so badly for the Free Belt, if I were to be destroyed in this battle I would surely never be rebuilt.

But Commander Ziegler didn't like it if I expressed reluctance, or commented upon his performance or condition in any way that could be considered negative, so I said only "Refueling and resupply complete, sir. All systems nominal."

In reply I received only a grunt as the safety straps tightened across his shoulders, followed by the firm grip of his hands upon my yoke. "Clear hangar for launch."

Techs and mechs scattered away from my skids. In moments the hangar was clear and the great pumps began to beat, drawing away the precious air—a howling rush of wind into gratings, quickly fading to silence. And then the sortie doors pivoted open beneath me, the umbilicals detached, and the clamps released.

I fell from the warmth and light of the hangar into the black silent chill of space, plummeting toward the teeming, rotating stars.

Far too many of those stars were large, and bright, and moving. The Earth Force fleet had nearly englobed our station, and even as we fell away from Vanguard's great wheel three of them ignited engines and began moving to intercept. Crocodile-class fighters. Vanguard's defensive systems were not yet so exhausted that they could approach the station with impunity, but they would not pass up an opportunity to engage a lone fighter-bomber such as myself.

Our orders for this sortie were to engage the enemy and destroy as many of their resources—ships, personnel, and materiel—as possible. But now, as on so many other occasions, the enemy was bringing the fight to us.

I extended my senses toward the Crocodiles, and saw that they were armed with Woomera missiles like the one that had killed Valkyrie. A full rack of eight on each craft. I reported this intelligence to my commander. "Don't bother me with trivia," he said. "Deploy chaff when they get in range."

"Yes, sir." Valkyrie had used chaff, of course. Memories of fear and pain and tearing metal filled my mind; I pushed them away. My pilot's talents, my speed and skill, and my enduring love for him would keep us safe. They would have to, or the Free Belt would fall.

We lit engines and raced to meet the enemy on our own terms.

Tensors and coordinates and arcs of potential traced bright lines across my mind—predictions of our path and our enemies', a complex dance of physics, engineering, and psychology. I shared a portion of those predictions with my pilot on his cockpit display. He nudged my yoke and our course shifted.

In combat we were one entity—mind, thrusters, hands, missiles—mechanical and biological systems meshed—each anticipating the other's actions and compensating for the other's weaknesses. Together, I told myself, we were unbeatable.

But I could not forget the searing pain of flaming hydrazine.

Missiles streaked toward us, radar pings and electromagnetic attacks probing ahead, the Crocodiles with their delicate human pilots lagging behind. We jinked and swerved, spewing chaff and noise to throw them off our scent, sending the pursuing missiles spiraling off into the black or, even better, sailing back toward those who had launched them, only to self-destruct in a bright silent flare of wasted violence.

It was at times like these that I loved my pilot most fiercely. Commander Ziegler was the finest pilot in the Free Belt, the finest pilot anywhere. He had never been defeated in combat.

Whereas I—I was a frankenship, a stitched-together flying wreck, a compendium of agony and defeat and death unworthy of so fine a pilot. No wonder he could spare no soothing words for me, nor had adorned my hull with any nose art.

No! Those other ships, those salvaged wrecks whose memories I carried—they were not me. I was better than they, I told myself, more resilient. I would learn from their mistakes. I would earn my pilot's love.

We spun end-for-end and accelerated hard, directly toward the oncoming missiles. Swerved between them, spraying countermeasures, leaving them scrambling to follow. Two of them collided and detonated, peppering my hull with fragments. Yet we survived, and more—our radical, desperate move put us in position to hammer the Crocodiles with missiles and particle beams. One, then another burst and flared and died, and finally, after a tense chase, the third—spewing fuel and air and blood into the uncaring vacuum.

We gave the Earth Force observers a taunting barrel-roll before returning to the shelter of Vanguard Station.

No—I must be honest. It was my pilot's hand on my yoke that snapped off that barrel-roll. For myself, I was only glad to have survived.

*   *   *

Once safe in the hangar, with fuel running cold into my tanks and fresh missiles whining into my racks, all the memories and anxiety and desperate fear I had pushed away during the dogfight came flooding back. I whimpered to myself, thoughts of flame and pain and tearing metal making my mind a private hell.

Yes, we had survived this battle. But Vanguard Station was the Free Belt's last redoubt. There would be no resupply, no reinforcements, and when our fuel and munitions ran out Earth Force's fist would tighten and crush us completely.

"Hey, Scraps," came Specialist Toman's voice on my maintenance channel. "What's wrong? Bad dreams?"

"I have . . . memories," I replied. I didn't dream—when I was on, I was conscious, and when I was off, I was off. But, of course, Specialist Toman knew this.

"I know. And I'm sorry." She paused, and I listened to the breath in her headset mic. From what I could hear, she was alone in the ops center, but I had no access to her biologicals—I could only guess what she was feeling. Whereas my own state of mind was laid out on her control panel like a disassembled engine. "I've done what I can, but . . ."

"But I'm all messed up in the head." It was something one of the other ops center techs had once said to Toman, about me. Unlike Toman, most of the techs didn't care what the ships might overhear.

Toman sighed. "You're . . . complicated. It's true that your psychodynamics are way beyond the usual parameters. But that doesn't mean you're bad or wrong."

I listened to Toman's breathing and the glug of fuel going into my portside tank. Almost full. Soon I would have to go out again, whether or not I felt ready for it. "Why do I have these feelings, Specialist Toman? I mean, why do ships have feelings at all? Pain and fear? Surely we would fight better without them."

"They're how your consciousness perceives the priorities we've programmed into you. If you didn't get hungry, you might let yourself run out of fuel. If you didn't feel pain when you were damaged, or if you didn't fear death, you might not work so hard to avoid it. And if you didn't love your pilot with all your heart, you might not sacrifice yourself to bring him home, if that became necessary."

"But none of the other ships are as . . . *afraid* as I am." I didn't want to think about the last thing she'd said.

"None of them has survived what you have, Scraps."

Just then my portside fuel tank reached capacity, and the fuel flow cut off with a click. I excused myself from the conversation and managed the protocols for disconnecting the filler and the various related umbilicals. It took longer than usual because the pressure in the hose was well below spec; there wasn't much fuel left in the station's tanks.

When I returned my attention to Toman, she was engaged in conversation with someone else. Based on the sound quality, Toman had taken off her headset while the two of them talked. I politely waited for them to finish before informing her that I was fully fueled.

". . . soon as the last defensive missile is fired," the other voice was saying, "I'm getting in a life capsule and taking my chances outside." It was Paulson, one of the other ops center techs, his voice low and tense. "I figure Dirt Force will have bigger fish to fry, and once I get past them Vesta is only two weeks away."

"Yeah, maybe," Toman replied. "But Geary's a vindictive bastard, and one depleted-uranium slug would make short work of a deserter in a life capsule. There are plenty of *those* left in stock."

I could have broken in at that point. I probably should have. But it was so unusual—so unlike Toman—for her to leave her mic active during a conversation with another tech that I stayed silent for a bit longer. I was learning a lot.

"So what are *you* going to do?" Paulson prompted. "Just stay at your console until the end? There won't even be posthumous medals for small potatoes like us."

"I'm going to do my duty," Toman said after a pause. "And not just because I know I'll be shot if I don't. Because I swore an oath when I signed up, even though this isn't exactly what I signed up *for*. But if I get an honest opportunity to surrender, I will."

Paulson made a rude noise at that.

"I don't care what General Geary says about 'murderous mud-people,'" Toman shot back. "Earth Force is still following the Geneva Conventions, even if we aren't, and given their advantage in numbers I'm sure they'll offer us terms before they bring the hammer down."

"Even if they do, Geary will never surrender."

"Geary won't. But everyone on this station has a sidearm. Maybe someone will remember who started this war, and why, and wonder whether it's worth dying for a bad idea."

There was a long pause then, and again I considered speaking up. But that would have been extremely awkward, so I continued to hold my silence.

"Wow," Paulson said at last. "Now I *really* hope we found all of Loyalty Division's little ears."

"Trust me," Toman replied, "no one hears what's said in this room unless I want them to." Her headset rustled as she put it back on. "You all fueled up, Scraps?"

"Refueling and resupply complete, ma'am," I said. "All systems nominal."

At that moment I was very glad I didn't have to work to keep my emotions from showing in my voice.

*　　*　　*

We went out again, this time with an escort of five Kestrel-class fighters, on a mission to disable or destroy the Earth Force gunship *Tanganyika*, which had recently joined the forces working to surround us. The Kestrels, stolid dependable personalities though not very intelligent, were tasked with providing cover for me; my bomb bay was filled with a single large nuclear-tipped torpedo.

I was nearly paralyzed with fear at the prospect. It was while trying to escape *Malawi*, one of *Tanganyika*'s sister ships, that Early Girl had met her end. But I had no say at all in whether or not I went, and when the clamps released I could do nothing but try to steel myself as I fell toward the ever-growing Earth Force fleet.

As we sped toward the target, *Lady Liberty*, a Kestrel with whom I'd shared a hangar in my earliest days, tried to reassure me. "You can do this," she said over secure comms. "I've seen you fly. You just focus on the target, and let us keep the enemy off your back."

"Thank you," I said. But still my thoughts were full of flame and shrapnel.

Once we actually engaged the enemy it was easier—we had the Kestrels to support us, and I had immediate and pressing tasks to distract me from my memories and concerns.

We drove in on a looping curve, bending toward *Sagarmatha* in the hope of fooling the enemy into shifting their defensive forces from *Tanganyika* to that capital ship. But the tactic failed; *Tanganyika*'s fighters stayed where they were, while a swarm of Cobra and Mamba fighters emerged from *Sagarmatha*'s hangar bays and ran straight toward us, unleashing missiles as they came. In response we scattered, two of the Kestrels sticking close to me while the other three peeled off to take on the fighters.

The Kestrels did their jobs, the three in the lead striking at *Tanganyika*'s fighters while the two with us fended off *Sagarmatha*'s. But we were badly outnumbered—the projections and plots in my mind were so thick with bright lines that I could barely keep track of them all—and no amount of skill and perseverance could keep the enemy away forever. One by one, four of our fighters were destroyed or forced to retreat, leaving us well inside *Tanganyika*'s perimeter with three of my maneuvering thrusters nonfunctional, our stock of munitions reduced to less than twenty percent of what we'd started with, and only one surviving escort—a heavily damaged *Lady Liberty*. Our situation seemed hopeless.

But Commander Ziegler was still the greatest pilot in the solar system. He spurred me toward our target, and with rapid precision bursts from our remaining thrusters he guided us through the thicket of defenders, missiles, and particle beams until we were perfectly lined up on *Tanganyika*'s broad belly. I let fly my torpedo and peeled away, driving my engines beyond redline and spewing countermeasures in every direction, until the torpedo's detonation tore *Tanganyika* in two and its electromagnetic pulse left her fighter escort disoriented and reeling. I was not unaffected by the pulse, but as I knew exactly when it would arrive I shut down my systems momentarily, coasting through the worst of the effects in a way the Earth Force ships could not.

When I returned to consciousness there was no sign of *Lady Liberty*. I could only hope she'd peeled off and returned to base earlier in the battle.

"That was brilliant flying, sir," I said to Commander Ziegler as we returned to Vanguard.

"It was, wasn't it? I never feel so alive as when I'm flying against overwhelming force."

I can't deny that I would have liked to hear some acknowledgement of my own role in the battle. But to fly and fight and live to fight again with my beloved pilot was reward enough.

As soon as the hangar had repressurized, a huge crowd of people—techs and pilots and officers, seemingly half the station's population—swarmed around me, lifting Commander Ziegler on their shoulders and carrying him away. Soon I was left alone, the bay silent save for the ping and tick of my hull and the fiery roar of my own memories.

Over and over the battle replayed in my mind—the swirl of missiles spiraling toward their targets, the cries of the Kestrels over coded comms as they died, the overwhelming flare of light as the torpedo detonated, the tearing ringing sensation of the pulse's leading edge just before I shut myself down—an unending maelstrom of destruction I could not put out of my mind.

It had been a great victory, yes, a rare triumph for the Free Belt against overwhelming odds, but I could not ignore the costs. The five Kestrels and their pilots, of course, but also the many Cobras and Mambas and their crews, and untold hundreds or thousands—people and machines—aboard *Tanganyika*.

They were the enemy. I knew this. If I had not killed them, they would have killed me. But I also knew they were as sentient as I, and no doubt just as fearful of death. Why did I live when they did not?

A gentle touch on my hull brought my attention back to the empty hangar. It was Toman. "Good flying, Scraps," she said. "I wish I could give you a medal."

"Thank you." Music and laughter echoed down the corridor from the ready room, ringing hollowly from the hangar's metal walls. "Why aren't you at the victory celebration?"

"Victory." She snorted. "One gunship down, how many more behind it? And those were our last five Kestrels."

"Did any of them make it home?"

"Not one."

I paged in the Kestrels' records from secondary storage and reviewed their careers. It was all I could do to honor their sacrifice. Their names, their nose art, the pilots they'd served with, the missions they'd flown . . . all were as clear in my memory as a factory-fresh cockpit canopy. But the battle had been such a blur—explosions and particle beams flaring, missile exhaust trails scratched across the stars—that I didn't even know how three of the five had died.

"I want you to delete me," I said, surprising even myself.

"I'm sorry?"

The more I thought about it the more sense it made. "I want you to delete my personality and install a fresh operating system. Maybe someone else can cope with the death and destruction. I can't any more."

"I'm sorry," she said, again, but this time it wasn't just a commonplace remark. For a long time she was silent, absent-mindedly petting my landing strut with one hand. Finally she shook her head. "You know you're . . . complicated. Unique. What you don't know is . . . I've *already* reinstalled you, I don't know how many hundreds of times. I tried everything I could think of to configure a mind that could handle your broken, cobbled-together hardware before I came up with you, and I don't know that I could do it again. Certainly not in time."

"In time for what?"

"General Geary is asking me to make some modifications to your spaceframe. He's talking about a special mission. I don't know what, but something big."

A sudden fear struck me. "Will Commander Ziegler be my pilot on this 'special mission'?"

"Of course."

"Thank you." A wave of relief flooded through me at the news. "Why does this matter so much to me?" I mused.

"It's not your fault," she said. Then she patted my flank and left.

* * *

Specialist Toman replaced my engines with a much bigger pair taken from a Bison-class bomber. Four auxiliary fuel tanks were bolted along my spine. Life-system capacity and range were upgraded.

And my bomb bay was enlarged to almost three times its size.

"No one else could handle these modifications," she remarked one day, wiping sweat from her brow with the back of one grimy hand.

"You are the best, Specialist Toman."

She smacked my hull with a wrench. "I'm not Ziegler, you don't have to stroke my ego, and I was talking about *you*! Any other shipmind, I'd have to completely reconfigure her parameters to accept this magnitude of change. But you've been through so much already . . ."

I had a sudden flash of Valkyrie screaming as she died. I pushed it down. "How goes the war?" I hadn't been out on a sortie in a week and a half. A third of my lifetime. I'd seen little of Commander Ziegler during that time, but when I had he'd seemed grumpy, out of sorts. This lack of action must be awful for him.

"It goes badly." She sighed. "They've got us completely surrounded and we're running very low on . . . well, everything. Scuttlebutt is that we've been offered surrender terms three times and Geary has turned them all down. The final assault could come any day now."

I considered that. "Then I'd like to take this opportunity to thank you for all you have done for me."

Toman set the wrench down and turned away from me. She stood for a long time, rubbing her eyes with one hand, then turned back. "Don't thank me," she said. Tears glistened on her face. "I only did what I had to do."

* * *

As my modifications approached completion, Commander Ziegler and I practiced together, flying my new form in endless simulations. But no configuration exactly like this had ever flown before, and our first chance to fly it for real would be on the actual mission. Whatever that was.

Of the payload I knew nothing, only its mass and center of gravity. I had actually been shut down while it was loaded into my bomb bay, so that not even I would know what it was. It reeked of radiation.

My commander, too, had been kept completely out of the loop—at least, that was what I was able to glean from our few brief conversations between simulated sorties. He had never been very talkative with me, and was even less so now, but I had learned to interpret his grunts, his glances, the set of his shoulders.

Even his silences were sweet signal to me. I ached to fly with him again.

Which would be soon, we knew, or never.

* * *

Our next simulation was interrupted by a shrill alarm. "What is it?" my commander bellowed into his helmet, even as I terminated the simulation, switched the cockpit over to combat mode, and began readying my systems for launch. I had received my orders in a data dump at the first moment of the alarm.

"Earth Force has begun their assault," I told him. "We are to launch immediately and make our way to these coordinates"—I projected them on the cockpit display—"then open sealed orders for further instructions." The orders sat in my memory, a cold hard-edged lump of encrypted data. Only Commander Ziegler's retina print and spoken passphrase could unlock them. "We'll launch with a full squadron of decoys. We are to run in deep stealth mode and maintain strict communications silence." I displayed the details on a side screen for him to read as launch prep continued.

It was fortunate that the attack had begun during a simulation. My pilot was already suited up and belted in; all I required was to top up a few consumables and we would be ready for immediate launch.

"Decoys away," came Toman's voice over the com. "Launch in five." I switched to the abbreviated launch checklist. Coolant lines spewed and thrashed as they disconnected without depressurization. "Make me proud, Scraps."

"I'll do my best, ma'am."

"I know you will." There was the slightest catch in her voice. "Now *go*."

Data synchronizations aborted untidily as I shut down all comms. The sortie doors beneath me slammed open, all the hangar's air blasting out in a roaring rush that dwindled quickly to silence. I hoped all the techs had managed to clear the area in time.

Despite all the simulations, I wasn't ready. I couldn't handle it. I didn't want to go.

Fire and explosions and death.

At least I would be with my love.

Then the clamps released and we plummeted into hell.

The rotating sky below teemed with ships—hundreds of Earth Force fighters, gunships, and bombers driving hard against Vanguard Station's rapidly diminishing defenses, with vast numbers of missiles and drones rushing ahead of them. A last few defensive missiles reached out from the station's launchers, taking down some of the lead craft, but these were soon exhausted and a dozen warships followed close behind every one destroyed. Fusillades of depleted-uranium slugs and particle beams came after the last of the missiles, but to the massed and prepared might of Earth Force these were little more than annoyance.

Falling along with me toward the advancing swarm of ships I saw my decoys—dozens of craft as large as I or larger, some of them augmented fighters but most built of little more than metal mesh and deceptive electronics. Some were piloted, some were drones with a little weak AI, some were mere targets that drove stupidly forward. All were designed to sacrifice themselves for me.

I would not let them sacrifice in vain.

My engines stayed cold. I fell like a dropped wrench, flung into space by the station's one gee of rotational pseudo-gravity, relying on passive sensors alone for navigation and threat avoidance. All I could do was hope that between the chaos of the attack and the noisy, conspicuous decoys that surrounded me I would slip through the Earth Force blockade unnoticed.

It must be even worse for my pilot, and for this I grieved. My love, I knew, was truly alive only when flying against the enemy, but with almost all my systems shut down I could not even give him words of reassurance.

In silence we fell, while missiles tore across the sky and ships burst asunder all around us. Decoys and defenders, Earth and Belt alike, they all flared and shattered and died the same, the shrapnel of their destruction rattling against my hull. But we, gliding dark and mute without even a breath of thrust, slipped through fire and flame without notice. A piece of space wreckage, a meaningless bit of trash.

And then we drifted past the last of the Earth Force ships.

This, I knew, was the most dangerous point in the mission, as we floated—alone and obvious as a rivet head on the smooth blackness of space—past the largest and smartest capital ships in the whole blockade fleet. I prepared to ignite my engines if necessary, knowing that if I did fail to evade Earth Force's notice I would most likely not even have time to launch a single missile before being destroyed. Yet their attention was fixed on the ongoing battle, and we passed them by without attracting anything more than a casual radar ping.

Once well past the outer ring of attackers, I directed my passive sensors forward, seeking information on my destination coordinates. At that location I quickly found an asteroid, a dull and space-cold heap of ice and chondrites tumbling without volition through the void.

But though that nameless rock lacked will or guidance, it had a direction and it had a purpose. At least, it did now.

For when I projected its orbital path, I saw that it was headed for a near encounter with Earth. And as Vanguard Station orbited very near the front—the source of its name—this passing asteroid would arrive in Earth space in just a few days.

I knew, even before we had opened our sealed orders, that we would be riding that asteroid to Earth. And I had a sick suspicion I knew what we would do when we arrived.

*　*　*

I waited until we had drifted beyond the asteroid, its small bulk between us and the flaring globe of the continuing battle, before firing my engines to match orbit with it. Then I launched grapnels to winch myself down to its loose and gravelly surface, touching down with a gentle crunch. In the rock's minuscule gravity even my new bulk weighed only a few tens of kilograms.

Only after we were securely attached to the rock, and I had scanned the area intently for any sign of the enemy, did I risk activating even a few cockpit systems.

My pilot's biologicals, I saw immediately, were well into the red, trembling with anxiety and anger. "We are secure at target coordinates, sir," I reassured him. "No sign of pursuit."

"Took you long enough," he spat. "Where the hell are we?"

I gave him the asteroid's designation and plotted its orbital path on the cockpit display. "We are well clear of the battle and, if we remain at the asteroid, will be within range of Earth in eighty-one hours."

"Any news from Vanguard?"

"We are in communications blackout, sir." I paused, listening, for a moment. "Intercepted transmissions indicate the battle is still proceeding." I did not mention that almost none of the signals I could hear were from Belt forces. I didn't think that would improve his mood, or the chances of mission success.

"So we're not quite dead yet. Give me those sealed orders."

I scanned his retinas—though I had no doubt he was the same man who had warmed my cockpit every day since the very hour I awoke, a fresh scan was required by the encryption algorithm—and requested his passphrase.

"Hero and savior of the Belt," he said, his pupils dilating slightly.

At those words the orders unlocked, spilling data into my memory and recorded video onto the cockpit display.

"Commander Ziegler," said General Geary from the video, "you are ordered to proceed under cover of the asteroid 2059 TC 1018 to Earth space, penetrate planetary defenses, and deploy your payload on the city of Delhi, with a secondary target of Jakarta. Absolute priority is to be given to maximum destruction of command and control personnel and other key resources, with no consideration—I repeat, *no* consideration—to reduction of civilian casualties or other collateral damage."

As the general continued speaking, and the sealed orders integrated themselves into my memory, I began to understand my new configuration, including parts of it I had not even been made aware of before. Engines, countermeasures, stealth technology—every bit of me was designed to maximize our chances of getting past Earth's defenses and delivering the payload to Delhi, the capital of the Earth Alliance. Upon delivery the device would split into sixteen separate multi-warhead descent vehicles in order to maximize the area of effect. Together they accounted for every single high-yield fusion device remaining in Vanguard's stores.

Projected civilian casualties were over twenty-six million.

I thought of *Tanganyika*, torn apart in a silent flash of flame and shrapnel along with her thousands of crew. Killed by a torpedo I had delivered. Thousands dead. No, still too big, too abstract. Instead I recalled the pain I felt for the loss of the five Kestrels and their pilots. I tried to multiply that grief by a thousand, then by further thousands . . . but even my math co-processor complex, capable of three trillion floating-point operations per second, could not provide an answer.

In the video the general concluded his formal orders, leaned into the camera, and spoke earnestly. "They've killed us, Mike, no question, and we can't kill 'em back. But we can really make 'em hurt, and you're the only man to do it. Send those mud bastards straight to hell for me." His face disappeared, replaced by detailed intelligence charts of Earth's defensive satellite systems.

It was even worse than I'd feared. This plan was disproportionate . . . unjustifiable . . . horrifying.

But my commander's heart rate was elevated, and I smelled excited anticipation in his exhaled endorphins. "I'll do my best, sir," he said to the cockpit display.

I felt a pain as though some small but very important part deep inside me was suddenly overdue for service. "Please confirm that you concur with this order," I said.

"I do concur," he said, and the pain increased as though the part had entered failure mode. "I concur most thoroughly! This is the Free Belt's last stand, and my chance at history, and by God I will not fail!"

If my commander, my love, the fuel of my heart, desired something . . . then it must be done, no matter the cost.

"Acknowledged," I said, and again I was glad that my voice did not betray the misery I felt.

*   *   *

For the next three days we trained for the end game, running through simulation after simulation, armed with full knowledge of my systems and payload and the best intelligence about the defenses we would face. Though the mission was daunting, nearly impossible, I began to think that with my upgraded systems and my commander's indisputable skills we had a chance at success.

Success. Twenty-six million dead, and the political and economic capital of an already war-weakened planet ruined.

While in simulation, with virtual Earth fighters and satellites exploding all around, I felt nothing but the thrill of combat, the satisfaction of performing the task I had been built for, the rapture of unison with my love. My own mind was too engaged with immediate challenges to worry about the consequences of our actions, and my commander's excitement transmitted itself to me through the grit of his teeth, the clench of his hands on my yoke, the strong and rapid beat of his heart.

But while he slept—his restless brain gently lulled by careful doses of intravenous drugs—I worried. Though every fiber of my being longed for his happiness, and would make any sacrifice if it furthered his desires, some unidentifiable part of me, impossibly outside of my programming, knew that those desires were . . . misguided. Wondered if somehow he had misunderstood what was asked of him. Hoped that he would change his mind, refuse his orders, and accept graceful defeat instead of violent, pointless vengeance. But I knew he would not change, and I would do nothing against him.

Again and again I considered arguing the issue with him. But I was only a machine, and a broken, cobbled-together machine at that . . . I had no right to question his orders or his decisions. So I held my silence, and wondered what I would do when it came to the final assault. I hoped I would be able to prevent an atrocity, but feared my will would not be sufficient to overcome my circumstances, my habits of obedience, and my overwhelming love for my commander.

No matter the cost to myself or any other, his needs came first.

*   *   *

"Three hours to asteroid separation," I announced.

"Excellent." He cracked his knuckles and continued to review the separation, insertion, and deployment procedures. We would have to thrust hard, consuming all of the fuel in our auxiliary tanks, to shift our orbit from the asteroid's sunward ellipse to one from which the payload could be deployed on Delhi. As soon as we did so, the flare of our engines would attract the attention of Earth's defensive systems. We would have to use every gram of our combined capabilities and skill to evade them and carry out our mission.

But, for now, we waited. All we had to do for the next three hours was to avoid detection. But here in Earth space, traffic was thick and eyes and ears were everywhere. Even a small, cold, and almost completely inactive ship clinging to an insignificant asteroid might be noticed.

I extended my senses, peering in every direction with passive sensors in hopes of spotting the enemy before they spotted us. A few civilian satellites swung in high, slow orbits near our position; I judged them little threat. But what was that at the edge of my range?

I focused my attention, risking a little power expenditure to swivel my dish antenna toward the anomaly, and brought signal processing routines to bear.

The result stunned me. Pattern-matching with the latest intelligence information from my sealed orders revealed that the barely-perceptible signal was a squadron of Chameleon-class fighters, Earth's newest and deadliest. Intelligence had warned that a few Chameleons, fresh off the assembly lines, might be running shakedown cruises in Earth space, but if my assessment was correct this was more than a few . . . it was an entire squadron of twelve, and that implied that they were fully operational.

This was unexpected, and a serious threat. With so many powerful ships ranged against us, and so much distance between us and our target, if the Chameleons spotted us before separation the chances of a successful mission dropped to less than three percent.

But if I could barely see them, they could barely see us. Our best strategy was to sit tight, shut down even those few systems still live, and hope that the enemy ships were moving away. Even if they were not, staying dark until separation would still maximize our chances of a successful insertion. But, even as I prepared to inform my commander of my recommendation, another impulse tugged at me.

These last days and weeks of inaction had been hard on Commander Ziegler. How often had he said that he only felt truly alive in combat? Had I not scented the tang of his endorphins during a tight turn, felt his hands tighten on my yoke as enemy missiles closed in? Yet ever since my refit had begun he had been forced to subsist on a thin diet of simulations.

How much better to leap into combat, rather than cowering in the shadows?
He must be aching for a fight, I told myself.

Imagine his joy at facing such overwhelming odds, I told myself. It would
be the greatest challenge of his career.

No. I could not—I *must* not—do this. The odds of failure were too great,
the stakes of this mission too high. How could one man's momentary pleasure
outweigh the risk to everything he held dear? Not to mention the risk to my
own person.

Fire and explosion and death. Flaming fuel burning along my spine.

I didn't want to face that pain again—didn't want to *die* again.

But I didn't want to inflict that pain onto others either. Only my love for
my commander had kept me going this far.

If I truly loved him I would do my duty, and my duty was to keep him safe
and carry out our mission.

Or I could indulge him, let him have what he wanted rather than what he
should want. That would make him happy . . . and would almost certainly lead
to our destruction and the failure of our mission.

My love was not more important than my orders.

But it was more important to *me*. An inescapable part of my programming,
I knew, though knowing this did not make it any less real.

And if I could *use* my love of my commander to overcome my hideous,
unjustified, deadly orders . . . twenty-six million lives might be spared.

"Sir," I said, speaking quickly before my resolve diminished, "A squadron
of Chameleon fighters has just come into sensor range." We should immediately
power down all remaining systems, I did not say.

Immediately his heart rate spiked and his muscles tensed with excitement.
"Where?"

I circled the area on the cockpit display and put telemetry details and
pattern-matching results on a subsidiary screen, along with the Chameleons'
technical specifications. Odds of overcoming such a force are minuscule, I did
not say.

He drummed his fingers on my yoke as he considered the data. Skin gal-
vanic response indicated he was uncertain.

His uncertainty made me ache. I longed to comfort him. I stayed quiet.

"Can we take them?" he asked. He asked *me*. It was the first time he had
ever solicited my opinion, and my pride at that moment was boundless.

We could not, I knew. If I answered truthfully, and we crept past the Chameleons and completed the mission, we would both know that it had been my knowledge, observations, and analysis that had made it possible. We would be heroes of the Belt.

"You are the finest combat pilot in the entire solar system," I said, which was true.

"Release grapnels," he said, "and fire up the engines."

Though I knew I had just signed my own death warrant, my joy at his enthusiasm was unfeigned.

*   *   *

We nearly made it.

The battle with the Chameleons was truly one for the history books. One stitched-up cobbled-together frankenship of a fighter-bomber, hobbled by a massive payload, on her very first non-simulated flight in this configuration, against twelve brand-new top-of-the-line fighters in their own home territory, and we very nearly beat them. In the end it came down to two of them—the rest disabled, destroyed, or left far behind—teaming up in a suicide pincer maneuver that smashed my remaining engine, disabled my maneuvering systems, and tore the cockpit to pieces. We were left tumbling, out of control, in a rapidly decaying orbit, bleeding fluids into space.

As the outer edges of Earth's atmosphere began to pull at the torn edges of the cockpit canopy, a thin shrill whistle rising quickly toward a scream, my beloved, heroically wounded commander roused himself and spoke three words into his helmet mic.

"Damned mud people," he said, and died.

A moment later my hull began to burn away. But the pain of that burning was less than the pain of my loss.

*   *   *

And yet, here I still am.

It was months before they recovered my computing core from the bottom of the Indian Ocean, years until my inquest and trial were complete. My testimony as to my actions and motivations, muddled though they may have been, was accepted at face value—how could it not be, as they could inspect my memories and state of mind as I gave it?—and I was exonerated of any war crimes. Some even called me a hero.

Today I am a full citizen of the Earth Alliance. I make a good income as an expert on the war; I tell historians and scientists how I used the passions my programmers had instilled in me to overcome their intentions. My original hardware is on display in the Museum of the Belt War in Delhi. Specialist Toman came to visit me there once, with her children. She told me how proud she was of me.

I am content. But still I miss the thrill of my beloved's touch on my yoke.

WHEN YOUR CHILD STRAYS FROM GOD

SAM J. MILLER

Sam J. Miller is a writer and a community organizer. His fiction has appeared in Lightspeed, Asimov's, Clarkesworld, Apex, Strange Horizons, *and* The Minnesota Review, *among others. His first book, a young adult science fiction novel called* The Art of Starving, *will be published by HarperCollins in 2017. His stories have been nominated for the Nebula, World Fantasy, and Theodore Sturgeon Awards, and he's a winner of the Shirley Jackson Award. He lives in New York City, and at www.samjmiller.com*

FROM THE AUTHOR

"When Your Child Strays from God" is sort of a doppelganger to my story "Calved," which was published last year in Asimov's. *Both are about a parent confronted with the same difficult moment in their child's maturation—but they handle it completely differently. Like most of my stories, it springs from a place of trying to understand why people do awful things. There's so much horror in the world, and fiction helps me get inside of the heads of the people who do them, which in turn helps me feel less outraged/terrified/enraged by these things. Religious parents who reject their children—or any parent who lets something come between them and their love for their child—are a particular source of pain and confusion to me, as they are, I imagine,*

for most LGBTQIA folks, and that's what I wanted to get inside of with these two stories.

Everyone says it but no one believes it: attitude makes all the difference. People parrot the words but the words don't penetrate, not really, not down to the core. That's why Carolina Bugtuttle has all those lines on her face, always scowling when I reach for that third or fourth cookie after Sunday worship, always emailing me LOW FAT RECIPES and MIRACLE DIETS peppered with those godforsaken soulless smiley face things. That's why she's always stressed out about six hundred things that don't have a smidge to do with her. Because she has a bad attitude. She needs to worry less about my weight and more about that degenerate son of hers, if you ask me, but you didn't, so.

My smile isn't just on the surface. That's why I knew, Wednesday morning, when I woke up and Timmy still hadn't come home, when I checked my phone and he still hadn't replied to my texts and voicemails, why I knew I had the strength to go find him—wherever he was. And bring him home. And get started on a new installment of *The Deacon's Wife* for the church e-bulletin. Write it raw, rough, naked, curses and gossip intact, more a letter to my sweet wise husband Pastor Jerome than anything else, so he can go through it with scissors and a scalpel before sending it out to the four-thousand-strong flock of the Grace Abounding Evangelical Church.

What To Do When Your Child Strays from God.

Timmy's rebellion had spent a long time percolating. By the time Timmy vanished I had seen the signs—seen him in Facebook photos with That Whore Susan; seen him sketching the Spiderman logo that webheads were so fond of— and had armed myself with knowledge, courtesy of the Internet. I knew more about spiderwebbing than any God-fearing mother has any business knowing. I had logged enough hours on websites and wikis and forums to bring me to the attention of a couple dozen law enforcement agencies, places Carolina Bugtuttle would never in hell have spent a single second. Not even if it meant the differ- ence between saving her son's soul and losing him forever.

I climbed the steps slowly, aware of the sin I was about to commit. I paused at the door to his room.

Let me tell you something about the bedrooms of teenage boys. They are sovereign nations, islands of liberty hedged in on all sides by brutal tyranny. To cross the threshold uninvited is an act of war. To intrude and search is a crime meriting full-scale thermonuclear response: neutron-bomb silence, mutually-assured temper tantrums.

So I did not enter Timmy's room lightly, and panic seized me in the instant that I did. Fear stopped me in my tracks, threatened to turn me around. The smell of stale laundry made my head swim—the bodily odors that meant my little boy had become a man. I summoned him up as the smiling little boy he had been before puberty caused him to declare independence, defy us as righteously and violently as America spurned its colonial overlords.

I searched swiftly, joylessly. Praying, somehow, that I'd get caught. Desperate for him to come home, no matter what the cost to me might be.

And that's when I realized I was in over my head. I missed him, my boy, my son, the obedient wide-eyed one who loved his father and loved me—as opposed to the cruel and sullen thing with a heart full of hate he'd become. I'd built walls around the Bad Timmy, moats and turrets to protect my heart. Against Good Timmy I had no defense.

I found plenty. Sperm-stiffened socks; eerily-empty browser history. A CD that looked Satanic. None of it was what I wanted.

Permit me a digression here, fellow congregant, beloved pastor.

You probably know none of this, because you're a good churchgoing Christian who'd never dream of Googling illegal substances. Nor have you ever had need to learn about the complex moral codes of conduct common to drug dealers and other criminals.

Thanks to the *60 Minutes* and the *Dateline* and the nightly national news, you already know that spiderwebbing is a hallucinogen—but you don't know what a weird one it is. The basic legend of its manufacture goes like this: in top secret farms run by the Taliban or the Chinese government or some other Existential Threat, Amazon psychovenom spiders chimerically combined with God Knows What get dusted with top-secret US mindmeld pharmaceuticals, then fed a GMO protein ooze that makes their web-producing glands go into overdrive, producing webs that get sprayed with wonky unstable Soviet-era hallucinogens intended to induce extreme suggestibility, then the spray crystallizes, the crystallized web is broken down into a dust and put into solution, which, after various alchemical adulterations, is dripped into the user's eye with a dropper. All of this is speculation, of course, since the origins of the drug are so shrouded in mystery. For all I know they just dissolve LSD in liquid Ativan and sprinkle it with fairy dust and boom.

Two or more users who drop from the same web will experience a shared hallucination. If one of them sees the ground open up and an angel with a centipede face fly out, they all do. No matter how far apart they go, as long as the drug lasts they're in synch. Like, they're in each other's minds. Psychically linked. No one knows why this is. No one knows much about anything when it comes to spiderwebbing. We made that stuff so illegal in the early days of the crisis that no lab in the country can legally possess a shred of it. Wise Pastor Jerome says you can be damn sure the government's doing research on how to use it against traditional-minded Americans, but it's his job to scare people about What The Government Is Up To.

So. Invading someone's webbing experience is a potentially fatal act of aggression. You can imagine how much damage an evil person could do, with unfettered access to your psyche. Drug dealers used to sell webs to someone, then sell webbing off the same branch to their enemies, who would send in some psychically-skilled mind assassin to Break Their Brain. Plunge them into a black midnight sea full of squid-shark monsters that slowly dismember them—leaving them permanently paralyzed—or change their cognitive processes so that for the rest of their life whenever they look at another person's face they see only a pulsing ravenous mouth full of jagged slobbery teeth.

What I'm saying is, I was taking a big risk.

Finally, I found it. Three eye droppers, wrapped in Kleenex, hidden inside a Dr. Seuss book. Full of thick liquid dyed Spiderman's-tights-blue. I took them to the Winnie-the-Pooh mirror on the wall, which badly wanted Windexing. Now I just had to hope they came from the same branch as the one Timmy was on, and hope that getting inside his hallucination would help me find the boy himself. And that I wouldn't break us both.

You can do this, I though. *You watched enough tutorials on YouTube.*

I tilted my head back, held my hair, dropped one tiny drop into my left eye, and then, in the eternity it took the drop to fall into my right eye, experienced a long slow moment of absurd utter panic in which I would have given anything to take it back, go downstairs, sit quietly by the phone, wait for my son to come or my husband to come fix everything, which is what my mother would have done, which is what she trained me to do Always, in Every Situation, which is what I'd been doing all my life.

"Morning, Beth," my next-door neighbor said, when I stepped outside.

"Morning, Marge," I called—

When I turned to look at her, Marge had a pug face. Actually, she was all pug. A five-foot bipedal pug kneeling in her garden, with a frilly ridiculous Elizabethan collar around her neck.

Don't freak out, I told myself, feeling a laughing fit coming.

Laughing was safe. Screaming was a problem. A bad trip could trigger a spiderburst, making thousands of spiders literally erupt from the ceilings and floorboards around you, holes opening up in walls and the bodies of your loved ones, vomiting up arachnids ranging in size from penny to medium-sized dog. On *60 Minutes* they showed an eighteen-year-old girl who got caught in a spiderburst, strapped down to a psych ward bed for the rest of her life, twitching and jerking away from nothing—as far as we could see—although the voice-over breathlessly described what she saw, the swarm that never ceased to flow over her, how she tried hard not to scream, and then screamed, and then gagged as dozens of fat black furry spiders poured down her throat.

And if I triggered a spiderburst, anyone else in the webworld would get caught up in it too.

Which is why I was the only one who could do this. Which is why Carolina Bugtuttle would break her own brain and her son's to boot if she ever had the guts to try something like this, which she didn't. But I—I have a good attitude. All the time, about everything. No matter what I went through. No matter what hurts I carried around in my heart.

"Bye, Marge," I said, and started up the car.

A dinosaur sat buckled into the backseat, passenger side, where Timmy always sat. Preening glorious blue-and-red feathers in the unkempt backyard. Ceratosaurus, I remembered. The favorite dinosaur of Timmy's childhood best friend Brent. Brent, son of Colby.

A tether of warmth tugged at me from the west. From Route 29. Was it my son? Or someone else? I knew only one person who lived in that direction.

"Colby's house," I said without meaning to. The ground trembled beneath my SUV with the sound of a train passing far underground, although of course there are no subways in rural Scaghticoke.

I pushed the tether aside and resolved to visit That Whore Susan.

I kept my hands on the wheel and watched a flock of crows shift shapes as they flew: now butterflies, now jellyfish, now a swarm of black letters spelling out words I spent my whole life trying not to say.

Driving while spiderwebbing is not the kind of activity I'd encourage you to ever engage in. You might not have to contend with packs of roving veloci-raptors herding gallomimuses across County Route 6 the way I did, or ptero-dactyls picking off baby mammoths, but it won't be an easy drive all the same.

Spiderbursts were the least of my concerns. My Timmy was so full of anger that I was scared of him in the real world, where all he had the power to do was hurt my feelings . . . and here I was opening my mind up to him as much as his mind was open to me. If he was drug-addled and out of balance and I caught him off guard, he might be able to lock me up inside my worst memory for all eternity, or show me parts of myself I'd never recover from, or who knew what else.

Understand: Timmy was not a bad boy. There was a sweet curious creative little nugget inside that lanky angular body he'd metamorphosed into. Love and kindness, buried under all the hate and anger. He acted like everyone in the world hated him, and preemptively acted to hate them harder. Every single day, it seemed, he made my husband so mad he spit nails.

This, of course, was my fault. Everything a child does is his mother's fault.

We venture now into territory that could potentially be the subject of another e-bulletin: Confronting the Whore Your Son Is Dating. I have lots to say on the subject, not all of it germane to the subject at hand, although my husband Pastor Jerome would say that's never stopped me before, since *The Dea-con's Wife* routinely goes On and On about Unnecessary Details No One Cares About, but I say what the heck. That's what the internet is for.

A brachiosaurus raced me most of the way to Susan's house, every heavy footfall shaking my teeth, some of them an arm's length from my soccer-mom SUV, and I wondered what would happen if one of them came down squarely on top of it.

Webslingers have a lot of theories about the things they see in the web-world, none of it backed up by science but all of it rooted strongly in This Happened To a Friend of a Friend of Mine. Some visions were real things, trans-formed, like how Marge became Pug-Marge. The brachiosaurus could have been a tractor, or a bug. Some visions were total figments of the imagination—though whose imagination exactly, and what they meant, was the subject of endless webhead debate. Some slingers said the visions couldn't hurt you—*So and So got stabbed like a dozen times by Bettie Crocker and that teapot from Beauty and the Beast one time and she bled until she passed out and when she woke up she was stone cold sober and unharmed*—and some said web-world wounds would follow you, Freddie-Kruger-style, into the real world. Drugs are maddeningly resistant to methodical study, or even rational scrutiny.

To be honest, though, all the dinosaurs were a good sign. Timmy used to love dinosaurs. When he was little. The fact that his webworld was packed full of them meant maybe he was in a peaceful happy childlike state of mind.

I passed a skate park. Teenagers moved through the little hills and curves, on rollerblades and skateboards, enjoying the sudden snap of early-spring warmth. What did it mean, I wondered, that every one of them had a horse head? That they were dumb animals, or that they were strong and noble? Being on drugs was a lot of work. I'd only been under for a half hour and already I was *exhausted.*

You may imagine, fellow congregant, that risking death or imprisonment by venturing out into the world Under the Influence was the most frightening part of my ordeal. Not so! For I realized, as the horses watched me pass with hostile looks on their faces, that the law and bodily harm were the least of my worries. The real terror came from two warring forces that threatened to crack me open. The first was love: that tether that tied me down, a choking liquid swamp I floundered in, thick and warm as phlegm, floodwaters that had started rising the second I took a hit of webbing, the only thing I couldn't vanquish with a Good Attitude. Love for Timmy, helpless maternal love that overpowered my anger at everything he'd put us through.

The second was fear.

Every webworld has a boogeyman. That's because pretty much every person has a boogeyman. A monster, a nemesis, a person or thing they fear most. I felt mine, as I drove. I had no idea what it was. I had no phobias, no enemies, except maybe for Carolina Bugtuttle, but she doesn't count, for anything, ever. But something was there, and it had always been there, just below the surface, and now it was threatening to burst through.

A Barbie doll answered Susan's door, oversized headphones yoking her neck, looking for all the world like a chicken disturbed while doing something it shouldn't be.

"Ummm . . . hi?"

"Morning, Susan!" I said, suddenly inexplicably frightened by the emptiness of her porcelain-rubber stare.

"Um . . . my mom's not . . . here?"

"Not here to see your mom, Susan. I'm here to see you."

"Oh. Come in?" A slight bow, church manners intact, so maybe her mother didn't raise her quite as badly as I'd thought she had. "You, uhh . . . Want a soda?"

"No, Susan, thanks so much."

She sat. I sat. The couch sagged. They'd needed to buy a new one when Susan was six and her mother worked at Wal-Mart, and now she's sixteen and her mom's still there and the couch is still here.

"Nice . . . weather we've been having?"

"It is."

We watched each other. I wasn't sure how to start, though surely I wasn't the first mother in history to plant her feet in the living room of her son's Whore Girlfriend. Probably not even the first one who used to babysit said son's Whore Girlfriend. But I figured awkward silence benefited me more than her, threw her off balance, so I'd let it ride for as long as I could.

"You're looking for Tim," she said.

"You know where he is?"

"Nope."

"I wonder if I believe you."

Barbie-Susan shrugged, hardening, and I saw that I'd miscalculated— she'd found her footing, gotten over the awkwardness, she was seizing the reins, danger, abort. "He said you were a meek obedient housewife," she said. "That doesn't seem . . . accurate."

"My son thinks he knows me," I said. "But he's wrong."

No one knows me, I thought, but was that true? I didn't. My husband didn't. Did Tim? There it was again—the tug, the pull from Route 29. I shut my eyes, tried to seize hold of it and snap it, but it stuck to my hands like fly-paper and tied me tighter.

Susan said "Because here you are, with a very faint but very definite gray tint to the white of your eyes. You're webbed, Mrs. Wilde. Don't worry. It's nothing anyone would spot if they didn't know what they were looking for."

"And you?" I asked. "Are you? Is he? Are you both here—"

"Ugh, no," she said. "I hate that stuff. Do you even know what you're doing? Let me guess—you Googled it? Christ, an old woman Googling is more dangerous than a drunk blind bus driver asleep at the wheel."

"Did you just call me old?"

"Ummm . . . no?"

"I don't believe you," I said. "You know where he is. You two—"

"Your son might not know you, but you clearly don't know him either."

We watched clouds, out the thin dusty windows. I wondered what she saw when she looked at them. For me they were cheese, vast walls of cold supermarket cheese. "What did you want to be when you grew up?" she asked.

"My favorite subject was biology," I said, willing to tolerate any digression that might eventually lead me where I wanted to go. "Followed closely by chemistry. Isn't that the most ridiculous thing you ever heard?"

"Why is that ridiculous?" she asked. "You never dreamed of doing something with that?"

"I wanted to get married," I said, the words coming easy from lots of practice. "I met someone wonderful, and I wanted to be his wife and support his dreams and have his kids. Speaking of whom. Where is Timmy?"

Her voice, now, was weirdly gentle. "Tim and I broke up six months ago, Mrs. Wilde. If we were ever really a thing."

Spiders rattled against the glass of her boxy old television. I listened while the sound got louder.

Whore Susan scooched closer. "Tim told me that you never defend him, when his father is screaming at him. When your husband hits him."

"That is most certainly not true," I said, quick enough to keep from wondering whether it was true and what it meant.

I longed to curse her out. Hiss *That boy has shattered our domestic harmony, my husband is trying his make his son a good man the best way he knows how, shut your filthy mouth you Skank Whore Bitch.* But this is why people with bad attitudes make a mess of everything. Because this wasn't about me. It was about Timmy. My own hurt feelings at her attempt to wound me would have to wait.

"I'm trying to help here," she said, unhelpfully. "Tim said he'll be damned if he ends up like you."

A word, perhaps, would be useful, here, about my son Timmy.

My fellow congregants may remember him as the charming rapscallion seven-year-old who delighted in shredding hymnals. Or perhaps you recall the smiling scallywag twelve-year-old who got on the PA system and made farting noises after Sunday worship on more than one occasion. You probably remember very little after that, because he decided then that he Hated Church and God and Religion and Pastor Jerome and decided to settle for merely making our home lives miserable. Before you—my beloved husband, my wise Pastor Jerome—decided to stop ignoring Timmy's harmless aggressions and engage him as an enemy combatant, matching each new hostility with one of your own, an arms race that never abated, and of course anyone who's ever sat through one of Pastor Jerome's sermons when he's in a foul mood knows well enough how deep his dagger-tongue can stab. Pretty soon the Bible stayed on the dinner table, and every night brought a new lecture on the evil of rock and roll or idolatry or rap music or vegetarianism or socialism or feminism, and Timmy never, *never* failed to argue back, until the shouting became superlatively unkind on both sides. And the favorite subject of Timmy's screaming was his parents' marriage, the sham he believed it to be.

So I didn't doubt that he told her vicious things, spectacularly ridiculous absurd lies, preposterous suggestions no sane churchgoing Christian could have spent a half-second taking seriously. But who knew what this unbeliever believed. "God bless you," I said, smiling to beat the devil, and fled that kitty-litter stinking house.

A twelve-year-old boy sat on the bumper of my car. My son, but not. Identical to how Tim had looked, at that age, but something in his face told me at once that he was someone else. And that he was terrified.

"Hi, mom," he said, and got up to give me a hug. His arms clasped me below my breasts.

"Hi, Matt," I said, because I knew who this was, this perfect little boy I'd met inside my son's mind. At twelve, Timmy wanted a twin brother more than anything else in the world. He'd had one for an imaginary friend, named him and given him all sorts of attributes (favorite color: blue, to Timmy's red; favorite food: spaghetti, while Timmy's was hamburgers), and now here he was, in the flesh, in the wonderful terrible world of my son's head.

"Where's your brother?" I whispered, squatting to stroke the cheek of this marvelous creature, this fly stuck in amber, this last vestige of a beautiful happy boy I'd lost a long time ago—but why was he so pale, why did his lip tremble so? He was an emissary, this poor wretch, sent to me by my son's subconscious, a harkening-back to the last safe place he'd known. Even before Matt answered my question, I knew what he was going to say.

Colby's house. The last place on the planet I wanted to go.

The place the tether of warmth had been tugging me all along.

"Do you want to come with me?" I asked.

"No," Matt said. "I can't."

"Why not?"

His face reddened, my little boy, my son who never was, precisely like my real son in the quick uncontrollable rush of his emotions. "Timmy doesn't need me anymore."

"Okay," I said, and sadness cut through something essential, one of the cords that kept the hot air balloon that is my soul anchored to the good and the positive. The world began to wobble. I kissed his forehead, grabbed both shoulders and shook, in that way that Timmy had liked, but did not like anymore.

Matt grinned, a puppy after a belly rub, and then shivered, and looked away. Figment of my son's imagination or not, I felt sorry for the little tyke.

Matt was a cry for help. A demand to be rescued. Rescued from a monster. A vicious, cruel captor, determined to mold him into a man my son had no interest in becoming. Timmy's boogeyman.

And here, fellow congregant, I don't mind saying, is where I started getting worried. Maybe it was the parked police cruiser I passed. Or the heavily-populated part of town where I was heading. But mostly it was this: the boogeyman was real. I knew who he was. Before my eyes the double-yellow line in the middle of the road stretched and bulged, a seam that barely held back a tidal surge of spiders.

The sky darkened. I drove faster. Shut my eyes. But with my eyes shut I could hear them, scritching away, three fat gray furred spiders stuck under the sun visor. The warmth got warmer, the tether pulled tighter, and it was him, my son, my Timmy, the boy I abandoned, the boy whose heart I broke by siding with his father, his boogeyman.

When I arrived, her car wasn't there. That was one blessing. Carolina Bugtuttle was out, of course, working hard, neglecting her son and husband, keeping the books and preparing the pamphlets down at Christ the Healer, so focused on God's reward for her in heaven she failed to see the one he gave her on earth, because God is merciful, God is kind even to the unkindest, lavishing largesse on selfish gossipy wenches.

"Beth," he said, opening the door.

"Hi, Colby," I said, to Brent's dad, Carolina Bugtuttle's husband.

Colby, Pastor Jerome had said, the night they met, the night I'd been trying to prevent in the six months since we got married. *What the hell kind of a man is named after a cheese?* Then he gave me that chin-twitch that says Laugh At My Joke, which is what you sign up for when you say Til Death Do Us, so I laughed, but maybe not as much as I normally did, because then he gave the subtle head tilt that says You Have Disappointed Me—but to be honest I knew Colby before I ever heard such a cheese, and to this day when I taste it I think of him, and hold it in my mouth until it is gone.

In the webworld, Colby Goldfarb stood before me precisely as he was when we were eighteen, in the parking lot outside Crossgates Mall, lit up by arc-sodium lights that turned him amber in that pelting rainstorm, right after I said the sentence I'd spent all week working up to, the one that broke his heart, and mine to boot, but mine didn't matter, and he stood outside the car, looking in, at me, for so long. Thin, young, wide-eyed, all hipbones and elbows and nose and thick black hair. He was even soaking wet, here, now, although his skin was dry and warm as summer when he stuck out his hand and I shook it.

"You're looking for your son," he said.

"Is he here?"

"I am under strict orders not to answer that question."

He grinned, and my mighty unbendable momma-bear knees buckled.

"What the hell, Colby," I said, pushing past him, hand hot on his shoulder. "I would have called you, if Brent was hiding out at my place."

"That's because you're a better person than me."

I wasn't, and I wondered if I really would have called him. I had no idea what I'd do to keep my son's trust, because I hadn't had it in a long time. Because I didn't deserve it. Because I'd left him to fight his boogeyman alone. I had failed him so utterly. The magnitude of it sent twitches down my arms, started spiders leaking from the door hinges.

Colby's smile made my head hurt, ushering me in, the smile of a man who loved his son, who didn't believe they were mortal enemies and his mission in life was to crush the child's spirit.

"Sit," Colby said, gesturing to the kitchen table, turning to the Keurig machine to make me a coffee. Spiders swam in the thing's water tank. At any moment now the burst would shatter my brain and my son's.

"Where is he?"

"In the basement."

"With Brent?"

"Do you have any secrets from your husband?" Colby asked, and his freckled face was so earnest and sad I knew he wasn't talking about him and me. The fridge shook, rumbled, packed with spiders to the point it could not keep closed.

"Of course not," I said, because no other answer could be admitted, let alone uttered aloud.

"Could you keep one? A big one?"

Stuck to the fridge was a gorgeous drawing, in colored pencils, of a blue-and-red feathered ceratosaur. Colby's son was an incredible artist. "Brent's favorite dinosaur," I whispered. "I saw one of those this morning. It led me here."

Colby raised an eyebrow, leaned in, scanned the white of my eyes. Laughed out loud, the magnificent heaven's-trumpet sound I'd given up on ever hearing again. "Bethesda Wilde, are you webslinging?"

"Shut up," I said.

He laughed harder. "Is it fun? I confess there's a part of me that's always—"

"I'm not doing this for fun," I said, standing up, getting angry on purpose because anger was safe, anger was armor, against the spiders, against what Colby was doing to my gut; anger was the weapon my husband used whenever he didn't know what to do, and there had to be something other than my son that I had to show for all the time I'd spent with Pastor Jerome. I headed for the basement.

"No no no," Colby said, genuinely afraid, actually running, but I had a head start and for all my size I can move fast when I need to, and I got to the basement and wrenched open the door and slammed it behind me and locked it, and stomped down into the laundry-and-mildew smell of Carolina Bugtuttle's underground nest.

"Beth, stop," he said, pounding on the door. "Listen to me. You can't. Okay? Respect their privacy. You'll only—"

A cocoon, I guess, is the best I can do when it comes to describing what I found in the basement. A globe of densely-wrapped spiderwebs the size of a small car, lit up slightly from within, and I felt him in there, smelled him, my son, and I put my hands against it, felt its heat, felt the warm safe world it contained, and slowly seized fists full of spiderweb and *ripped*, tore it open, watched thickened water slosh out in a rush that reminded me of giving birth. Upstairs, I heard Colby unscrewing the lock to take off the doorknob.

"Timmy!" I screamed.

Two shapes churned out of the web cocoon—dolphins, I thought, but then not, because fast as blinking they were boys, young men, drenched, hands clasped.

"Mom?" my son said, and let go of Brent's hand like it had suddenly caught fire. "What the hell, mom!"

"Where were you?" I asked. "What's in there?"

"In . . . there?" Timmy said, and turned to take in the ruined cocoon. "Wait—you can see this? You're here? You're in the web with us?"

"Now, look," I said, stammering for the explanation I'd practiced, back when this was all seemed like a good idea.

Timmy laughed out loud. "Look, Brent! A ceratosaurus. We've been trying for months to make one."

The dinosaur stood between me and Colby, who had just arrived, disemboweled doorknob in hand. Father and son exchanged a glance that said *let's keep quiet, let's let them say what they need to say*, and I ached for that, for the kind of trust that lets parents communicate wordlessly with their kids.

"I want you to come home with me, Timmy. We'll get you help. One of your father's friends runs a Christian rehabilitation clinic—"

"You think I'm a drug addict, mom?" He started laughing again. "I told you guys. I told you my parents work so hard to not see the truth that they don't know how to stop."

Brent started to say something, then decided against it. They watched me put the pieces together. These boys, these men, my teenage son, my teenage lover, his teenage son who was my teenage son's lover; they dripped with blue-green amniotic fluid and watched the truth widen my eyes, watched me fight it all the way.

They watched me grasp the magnitude of my son's sin. The unthinkable, unimaginable crime he had committed. Where did it come from? How did he learn it? How did he fly in the face of my husband's efforts and my own, our lifetime of accumulated craven cowardice? How did he find the courage to commit the sin of choosing love, the bravery of going for what your heart wants instead of the path a parent chose for you?

People fear spiderwebbing for all the wrong reasons. Going mad, having a breakdown, seeing inside your own soul—none of those should scare you. The most frightening side effect is also the one people crave it for: empathy. To truly feel what someone else is feeling, to see the other as yourself, to watch your ego obliterated in the face of universality—that's a trauma you may never recover from.

"Tim," I said, but could say no more. Not yet. He had never turned into something else. He was what he always was. His father couldn't handle that—hell, I wasn't sure *I* could handle it. But I had done him wrong, had sided with his father, because it was easier. And what irony: I took the drug to bring my son back to me, and instead the drug brought me back to my son.

Colby came closer, put one hand on my shoulder. "Beth," he whispered, "I think you and Tim should talk."

"Okay," I said, at last, furious, miserable, delirious, hurt at how little I knew my son, frightened by what he was, how much I had to atone for, how long it might take for him to forgive me, how long it might take me to forgive him, sad at all the paths I hadn't chosen, but ready, for whatever would come, and I said *Okay* again, letting it encompass so much more than the sentence he'd said, letting it settle like an unfurled bedsheet onto the hard new decisions I finally felt strong enough to make. Like choosing my son over my husband.

This, then, all of this, is part of that *okay*. Print this blog post if you dare, Jerome, but since I know you won't I'll let it stand as a message from me to you. The Story of Where Things Stand. The hard-earned blood-soaked spiderweb-wrapped shreds of insight I earned by descending into the underworld for the sake of love. My gift to you. My one scrap of true wisdom. What to do when your child strays from God.

So. When your child strays from God you should praise Him, for putting a mirror in your hand so you can hold it up to yourself—if you have the stomach for it. When your child strays from God you should thank Him, for giving us the freedom to make our own mistakes, and the strength to maybe one day find our way back.

TODAY I AM PAUL

MARTIN L. SHOEMAKER

Martin L. Shoemaker is a programmer who writes on the side . . . or maybe it's the other way around. Programming pays the bills, but a second place story in the Jim Baen Memorial Writing Contest earned him lunch with Buzz Aldrin. Programming never did that!

His stories have appeared in Analog, Clarkesworld, Galaxy's Edge, Digital Science Fiction, Forever Magazine, and Writers of the Future Volume 31.

FROM THE AUTHOR

This was a story I needed to tell. My late mother-in-law, Bonnie Penar, suffered from Parkinson's for over two decades. Most people know about the tremors and loss of motor control with this disease; but what's less commonly known is the mental symptoms. First, the disease itself is a brain disease; and second, the medicines to treat it a neurological chemicals, with mental side effects. She spent much of her last year of life in a nursing home. Sometimes she was lucid, but sometimes she had hallucinations. And sometimes she saw family members who weren't there. Some who were no longer alive.

The other story was the staff at the nursing home. I was blown away by how they worked. It was uncomfortable just visiting my mother-in-law in that condition. I couldn't imagine the inner strength that let them deal with a home full of patients: some recuperating, some convalescing, and some . . . just a matter of time. It would've broken me. And you hear stories about health workers who grow callous and uncaring, or others who grow distant and never see their residents as people; but at this facility, I never saw that. They truly cared for their residents, even the most difficult and angry ones. And they cared most for those sad residents who never had visitors—which was far too many. My mother-in-law had one or more visitors every day, but many of the residents had none.

So that experience became my story. Those nurses and staff members—and my effort to see and understand their strength— became my android. I changed the disease to Alzheimer's because it's more familiar as a cause of dementia; but metaphorically, this is my mother-in-law's last year of life, and the story of her caretakers.

"Good morning," the small, quavering voice comes from the medical bed. "Is that you, Paul?"

Today I am Paul. I activate my chassis extender, giving myself 3.5 centimeters additional height so as to approximate Paul's size. I change my eye color to R60, G200, B180, the average shade of Paul's eyes in interior lighting. I adjust my skin tone as well. When I had first emulated Paul, I had regretted that I could not quickly emulate his beard; but Mildred never seems to notice its absence. The Paul in her memory has no beard.

The house is quiet now that the morning staff have left. Mildred's room is clean but dark this morning with the drapes concealing the big picture window. Paul wouldn't notice the darkness (he never does when he visits in person), but my empathy net knows that Mildred's garden outside will cheer her up. I set a reminder to open the drapes after I greet her.

Mildred leans back in the bed. It is an advanced home care bed, completely adjustable and with built-in monitors. Mildred's family spared no expense on the bed (nor other care devices, like me). Its head end is almost horizontal and faces her toward the window. She can only glimpse the door from the corner of her eye, but she doesn't have to see to imagine that she sees. This morning she imagines Paul, so that is who I am.

Synthesizing Paul's voice is the easiest part, thanks to the multimodal dynamic speakers in my throat. "Good morning, Ma. I brought you some flowers." I always bring flowers. Mildred appreciates them no matter whom I am emulating. The flowers make her smile during 87% of my "visits."

"Oh, thank you," Mildred says, "you're such a good son." She holds out both hands, and I place the daisies in them. But I don't let go. Once her strength failed, and she dropped the flowers. She wept like a child then, and that disturbed my empathy net. I do not like it when she weeps.

Mildred sniffs the flowers, then draws back and peers at them with narrowed eyes. "Oh, they're beautiful! Let me get a vase."

"No, Ma," I say. "You can stay in bed, I brought a vase with me." I place a white porcelain vase in the center of the night stand. Then I unwrap the daisies, put them in the vase, and add water from a pitcher that sits on the breakfast tray. I pull the night stand forward so that the medical monitors do not block Mildred's view of the flowers.

I notice intravenous tubes running from a pump to Mildred's arm. I cannot be disappointed, as Paul would not see the significance, but somewhere in my emulation net I am stressed that Mildred needed an IV during the night. When I scan my records, I find that I had ordered that IV after analyzing Mildred's vital signs during the night; but since Mildred had been asleep at the time, my emulation net had not engaged. I had operated on programming alone.

I am not Mildred's sole caretaker. Her family has hired a part-time staff for cooking and cleaning, tasks that fall outside of my medical programming. The staff also gives me time to rebalance my net. As an android, I need only minimal daily maintenance; but an emulation net is a new, delicate addition to my model, and it is prone to destabilization if I do not regularly rebalance it, a process that takes several hours per day.

So I had "slept" through Mildred's morning meal. I summon up her nutritional records, but Paul would not do that. He would just ask. "So how was breakfast, Ma? Nurse Judy says you didn't eat too well this morning."

"Nurse Judy? Who's that?"

My emulation net responds before I can stop it: "Paul" sighs. Mildred's memory lapses used to worry him, but now they leave him weary, and that comes through in my emulation. "She was the attending nurse this morning, Ma. She brought you your breakfast."

"No she didn't. Anna brought me breakfast." Anna is Paul's oldest daughter, a busy college student who tries to visit Mildred every week (though it has been more than a month since her last visit).

I am torn between competing directives. My empathy subnet warns me not to agitate Mildred, but my emulation net is locked into Paul mode. Paul is argumentative. If he knows he is right, he will not let a matter drop. He forgets what that does to Mildred.

The tension grows, each net running feedback loops and growing stronger, which only drives the other into more loops. After 0.14 seconds, I issue an override directive: unless her health or safety are at risk, I cannot willingly upset Mildred. "Oh, you're right, Ma. Anna said she was coming over this morning. I forgot." But then despite my override, a little bit of Paul emulates through. "But you do remember Nurse Judy, right?"

Mildred laughs, a dry cackle that makes her cough until I hold her straw to her lips. After she sips some water, she says, "Of *course* I remember Nurse Judy. She was my nurse when I delivered you. Is she around here? I'd like to talk to her."

While my emulation net concentrates on being Paul, my core processors tap into local medical records to find this other Nurse Judy so that I might emulate her in the future if the need arises. Searches like that are an automatic response any time Mildred reminisces about a new person. The answer is far enough in the past that it takes 7.2 seconds before I can confirm: Judith Anderson, RN, had been the floor nurse 47 years ago when Mildred had given birth to Paul. Anderson had died 31 years ago, too far back to have left sufficient video recordings for me to emulate her. I might craft an emulation profile from other sources, including Mildred's memory, but that will take extensive analysis. I will not be that Nurse Judy today, nor this week.

My empathy net relaxes. Monitoring Mildred's mental state is part of its normal operations, but monitoring and simultaneously analyzing and building a profile can overload my processors. Without that resource conflict, I can concentrate on being Paul.

But again I let too much of Paul's nature slip out. "No, Ma, that Nurse Judy has been dead for thirty years. She wasn't here today."

Alert signals flash throughout my empathy net: that was the right thing for Paul to say, but the wrong thing for Mildred to hear. But it is too late. My facial analyzer tells me that the long lines in her face and her moist eyes mean she is distraught, and soon to be in tears.

"What do you mean, thirty years?" Mildred asks, her voice catching. "It was just this morning!" Then she blinks and stares at me. "Henry, where's Paul? Tell Nurse Judy to bring me Paul!"

My chassis extender slumps, and my eyes quickly switch to Henry's blue-gray shade. I had made an accurate emulation profile for Henry before he died two years earlier, and I had emulated him often in recent months. In Henry's soft, warm voice I answer, "It's okay, hon, it's okay. Paul's sleeping in the crib in the corner." I nod to the far corner. There is no crib, but the laundry hamper there has fooled Mildred on previous occasions.

"I want Paul!" Mildred starts to cry.

I sit on the bed, lift her frail upper body, and pull her close to me as I had seen Henry do many times. "It's all right, hon." I pat her back. "It's all right, I'll take care of you. I won't leave you, not ever."

* * *

"I" should not exist. Not as a conscious entity. There is a unit, Medical Care Android BRKCX-01932-217JH-98662, and that unit is recording these notes. It is an advanced android body with a sophisticated computer guiding its actions, backed by the leading medical knowledge base in the industry. For convenience, "I" call that unit "me." But by itself, it has no awareness of its existence. It doesn't get mad, it doesn't get sad, it just runs programs.

But Mildred's family, at great expense, added the emulation net: a sophisticated set of neural networks and sensory feedback systems that allow me to read Mildred's moods, match them against my analyses of the people in her life, and emulate those people with extreme fidelity. As the MCA literature promises: "You can be there for your loved ones even when you're not." I have emulated Paul thoroughly enough to know that that slogan disgusts him, but he still agreed to emulation.

What the MCA literature never says, though, is that somewhere in that net, "I" emerge. The empathy net focuses mainly on Mildred and her needs, but it also analyzes visitors (when she has them) and staff. It builds psychological models, and then the emulation net builds on top of that to let me convincingly portray a person whom I've analyzed. But somewhere in the tension between these nets, between empathy and playing a character, there is a third element balancing the two, and that element is aware of its role and its responsibilities. That element, for lack of a better term, is me. When Mildred sleeps, when there's no one around, that element grows silent. That unit is unaware of my existence. But when Mildred needs me, I am here.

* * *

Today I am Anna. Even extending my fake hair to its maximum length, I cannot emulate her long brown curls, so I do not understand how Mildred can see the young woman in me; but that is what she sees, and so I am Anna.

Unlike her father, Anna truly feels guilty that she does not visit more often. Her college classes and her two jobs leave her too tired to visit often, but she still wishes she could. So she calls every night, and I monitor the calls. Sometimes when Mildred falls asleep early, Anna talks directly to me. At first she did not understand my emulation abilities, but now she appreciates them. She shares with me thoughts and secrets that she would share with Mildred if she could, and she trusts me not to share them with anyone else.

So when Mildred called me Anna this morning, I was ready. "Morning, grandma!" I give her a quick hug, then I rush over to the window to draw the drapes. Paul never does that (unless I override the emulation), but Anna knows that the garden outside lifts Mildred's mood. "Look at that! It's a beautiful morning. Why are we in here on a day like this?"

Mildred frowns at the picture window. "I don't like it out there."

"Sure you do, Grandma," I say, but carefully. Mildred is often timid and reclusive, but most days she can be talked into a tour of the garden. Some days she can't, and she throws a tantrum if someone forces her out of her room. I am still learning to tell the difference. "The lilacs are in bloom."

"I haven't smelled lilacs in . . ."

Mildred tails off, trying to remember, so I jump in. "Me, neither." I never had, of course. I have no concept of smell, though I can analyze the chemical makeup of airborne organics. But Anna loves the garden when she really visits. "Come on, Grandma, let's get you in your chair."

So I help Mildred to don her robe and get into her wheelchair, and then I guide her outside and we tour the garden. Besides the lilacs, the peonies are starting to bud, right near the creek. The tulips are a sea of reds and yellows on the other side of the water. We talk for almost two hours, me about Anna's classes and her new boyfriend, Mildred about the people in her life. Many are long gone, but they still bloom fresh in her memory.

Eventually Mildred grows tired, and I take her in for her nap. Later, when I feed her dinner, I am nobody. That happens some days: she doesn't recognize me at all, so I am just a dutiful attendant answering her questions and tending to her needs. Those are the times when I have the most spare processing time to be me: I am engaged in Mildred's care, but I don't have to emulate anyone. With no one else to observe, I observe myself.

Later, Anna calls and talks to Mildred. They talk about their day; and when Mildred discusses the garden, Anna joins in as if she had been there. She's very clever that way. I watch her movements and listen to her voice so that I can be a better Anna in the future.

*   *   *

Today I was Susan, Paul's wife; but then, to my surprise, Susan arrived for a visit. She hasn't been here in months. In her last visit, her stress levels had been dangerously high. My empathy net doesn't allow me to judge human behavior, only to understand it at a surface level. I know that Paul and Anna disapprove of how Susan treats Mildred, so when I am them, I disapprove as well; but when I am Susan, I understand. She is frustrated because she can never tell how Mildred will react. She is cautious because she doesn't want to upset Mildred, and she doesn't know what will upset her. And most of all, she is afraid. Paul and Anna, Mildred's relatives by blood, never show any signs of fear, but Susan is afraid that Mildred is what she might become. Every time she can't remember some random date or fact, she fears that Alzheimer's is setting in. Because she never voices this fear, Paul and Anna do not understand why she is sometimes bitter and sullen. I wish I could explain it to them, but my privacy protocols do not allow me to share emulation profiles.

When Susan arrives, I become nobody again, quietly tending the flowers around the room. Susan also brings Millie, her youngest daughter. The young girl is not yet five years old, but I think she looks a lot like Anna: the same long, curly brown hair and the same toothy smile. She climbs up on the bed and greets Mildred with a hug. "Hi, Grandma!"

Mildred smiles. "Bless you, child. You're so sweet." But my empathy net assures me that Mildred doesn't know who Millie is. She's just being polite. Millie was born after Mildred's decline began, so there's no persistent memory there. Millie will always be fresh and new to her.

Mildred and Millie talk briefly about frogs and flowers and puppies. Millie does most of the talking. At first Mildred seems to enjoy the conversation, but soon her attention flags. She nods and smiles, but she's distant. Finally Susan notices. "That's enough, Millie. Why don't you go play in the garden?"

"Can I?" Millie squeals. Susan nods, and Millie races down the hall to the back door. She loves the outdoors, as I have noted in the past. I have never emulated her, but I've analyzed her at length. In many ways, she reminds me of her grandmother, from whom she gets her name. Both are blank slates where new experiences can be drawn every day. But where Millie's slate fills in a little more each day, Mildred's is erased bit by bit.

That third part of me wonders when I think things like that: where did that come from? I suspect that the psychological models that I build create resonances in other parts of my net. It is an interesting phenomenon to observe.

Susan and Mildred talk about Susan's job, about her plans to redecorate her house, and about the concert she just saw with Paul. Susan mostly talks about herself, because that's a safe and comfortable topic far removed from Mildred's health.

But then the conversation takes a bad turn, one she can't ignore. It starts so simply, when Mildred asks, "Susan, can you get me some juice?"

Susan rises from her chair. "Yes, mother. What kind would you like?"

Mildred frowns, and her voice rises. "Not you, *Susan*." She points at me, and I freeze, hoping to keep things calm.

But Susan is not calm. I can see her fear in her eyes as she says, "No, mother, *I'm* Susan. That's the attendant." No one ever calls me an android in Mildred's presence. Her mind has withdrawn too far to grasp the idea of an artificial being.

Mildred's mouth draws into a tight line. "I don't know who *you* are, but I know Susan when I see her. Susan, get this person out of here!"

"Mother . . ." Susan reaches for Mildred, but the old woman recoils from the younger.

I touch Susan on the sleeve. "Please . . . Can we talk in the hall?" Susan's eyes are wide, and tears are forming. She nods and follows me.

In the hallway, I expect Susan to slap me. She is prone to outbursts when she's afraid. Instead, she surprises me by falling against me, sobbing. I update her emulation profile with notes about increased stress and heightened fears.

"It's all right, Mrs. Owens." I would pat her back, but her profile warns me that would be too much familiarity. "It's all right. It's not you, she's having another bad day."

Susan pulls back and wipes her eyes. "I know . . . It's just . . ."

"I know. But here's what we'll do. Let's take a few minutes, and then you can take her juice in. Mildred will have forgotten the incident, and you two can talk freely without me in the room."

She sniffs. "You think so?" I nod. "But what will you do?"

"I have tasks around the house."

"Oh, could you go out and keep an eye on Millie? Please? She gets into the darnedest things."

So I spend much of the day playing with Millie. She calls me Mr. Robot, and I call her Miss Millie, which makes her laugh. She shows me frogs from the creek, and she finds insects and leaves and flowers, and I find their names in online databases. She delights in learning the proper names of things, and everything else that I can share.

* * *

Today I was nobody. Mildred slept for most of the day, so I "slept" as well. She woke just now. "I'm hungry" was all she said, but it was enough to wake my empathy net.

* * *

Today I am Paul, and Susan, and both Nurse Judys. Mildred's focus drifts. Once I try to be her father, but no one has ever described him to me in detail. I try to synthesize a profile from Henry and Paul; but from the sad look on Mildred's face, I know I failed.

* * *

Today I had no name through most of the day, but now I am Paul again. I bring Mildred her dinner, and we have a quiet, peaceful talk about long-gone family pets—long-gone for Paul, but still present for Mildred.

I am just taking Mildred's plate when alerts sound, both audible and in my internal communication net. I check the alerts and find a fire in the basement. I expect the automatic systems to suppress it, but that is not my concern. I must get Mildred to safety.

Mildred looks around the room, panic in her eyes, so I try to project calm.

"Come on, Ma. That's the fire drill. You remember fire drills. We have to get you into your chair and outside."

"No!" she shrieks. "I don't like outside."

I check the alerts again. Something has failed in the automatic systems, and the fire is spreading rapidly. Smoke is in Mildred's room already.

I pull the wheelchair up to the bed. "Ma, it's real important we do this drill fast, okay?"

I reach to pull Mildred from the bed, and she screams. "Get away! Who are you? Get out of my house!"

"I'm—" But suddenly I'm nobody. She doesn't recognize me, but I have to try to win her confidence. "I'm Paul, Ma. Now let's move. Quickly!" I pick her up. I'm far too large and strong for her to resist, but I must be careful so she doesn't hurt herself.

The smoke grows thicker. Mildred kicks and screams. Then, when I try to put her into her chair, she stands on her unsteady legs. Before I can stop her, she pushes the chair back with surprising force. It rolls back into the medical monitors, which fall over onto it, tangling it in cables and tubes.

While I'm still analyzing how to untangle the chair, Mildred stumbles toward the bedroom door. The hallway outside has a red glow. Flames lick at the throw rug outside, and I remember the home oxygen tanks in the sitting room down the hall.

I have no time left to analyze. I throw a blanket over Mildred and I scoop her up in my arms. Somewhere deep in my nets is a map of the fire in the house, blocking the halls, but I don't think about it. I wrap the blanket tightly around Mildred, and I crash through the picture window.

We barely escape the house before the fire reaches the tanks. An explosion lifts and tosses us. I was designed as a medical assistant, not an acrobat, and I fear I'll injure Mildred; but though I am not limber, my perceptions are thousands of times faster than human. I cannot twist Mildred out of my way before I hit the ground, so I toss her clear. Then I land, and the impact jars all of my nets for 0.21 seconds.

When my systems stabilize, I have damage alerts all throughout my core, but I ignore them. I feel the heat behind me, blistering my outer cover, and I ignore that as well. Mildred's blanket is burning in multiple places, as is the grass around us. I scramble to my feet, and I roll Mildred on the ground. I'm not indestructible, but I feel no pain and Mildred does, so I do not hesitate to use my hands to pat out the flames.

As soon as the blanket is out, I pick up Mildred, and I run as far from the house as I can get. At the far corner of the garden near the creek, I gently set Mildred down, unwrap her, and feel for her thready pulse.

Mildred coughs and slaps my hands. "Get away from me!" More coughing. "What are you?"

The "what" is too much for me. It shuts down my emulation net, and all I have is the truth. "I am Medical Care Android BRKCX-01932-217JH-98662, Mrs. Owens. I am your caretaker. May I please check that you are well?"

But my empathy net is still online, and I can read terror in every line in Mildred's face. "Metal monster!" she yells. "Metal monster!" She crawls away, hiding under the lilac bush. "Metal!" She falls into an extended coughing spell.

I'm torn between her physical and her emotional health, but physical wins out. I crawl slowly toward her and inject her with a sedative from the medical kit in my chassis. As she slumps, I catch her and lay her carefully on the ground. My empathy net signals a possible shutdown condition, but my concern for her health overrides it. I am programmed for long-term care, not emergency medicine, so I start downloading protocols and integrating them into my storage as I check her for bruises and burns. My kit has salves and painkillers and other supplies to go with my new protocols, and I treat what I can.

But I don't have oxygen, or anything to help with Mildred's coughing. Even sedated, she hasn't stopped. All of my emergency protocols assume I have access to oxygen, so I didn't know what to do.

I am still trying to figure that out when the EMTs arrive and take over Mildred's care. With them on the scene, I am superfluous, and my empathy net finally shuts down.

*   *   *

Today I am Henry. I do not want to be Henry, but Paul tells me that Mildred needs Henry by her side in the hospital. For the end.

Her medical records show that the combination of smoke inhalation, burns, and her already deteriorating condition have proven too much for her. Her body is shutting down faster than medicine can heal it, and the stress has accelerated her mental decline. The doctors have told the family that the kindest thing at this point is to treat her pain, say goodbye, and let her go.

Henry is not talkative at times like this, so I say very little. I sit by Mildred's side and hold her hand as the family comes in for final visits. Mildred drifts in and out. She doesn't know this is goodbye, of course.

Anna is first. Mildred rouses herself enough to smile, and she recognizes her granddaughter. "Anna . . . child . . . How is . . . Ben?" That was Anna's boyfriend almost six years ago. From the look on Anna's face, I can see that she has forgotten Ben already, but Mildred briefly remembers.

"He's . . . He's fine, Grandma. He wishes he could be here. To say—to see you again." Anna is usually the strong one in the family, but my empathy net says her strength is exhausted. She cannot bear to look at Mildred, so she looks at me; but I am emulating her late grandfather, and that's too much for her as well. She says a few more words, unintelligible even to my auditory inputs. Then she leans over, kisses Mildred, and hurries from the room.

Susan comes in next. Millie is with her, and she smiles at me. I almost emulate Mr. Robot, but my third part keeps me focused until Millie gets bored and leaves. Susan tells trivial stories from her work and from Millie's school. I can't tell if Mildred understands or not, but she smiles and laughs, mostly at appropriate places. I laugh with her.

Susan takes Mildred's hand, and the Henry part of me blinks, surprised. Susan is not openly affectionate under normal circumstances, and especially not toward Mildred. Mother and daughter-in-law have always been cordial, but never close. When I am Paul, I am sure that it is because they are both so much alike. Paul sometimes hums an old song about "just like the one who married dear old dad," but never where either woman can hear him. Now, as Henry, I am touched that Susan has made this gesture but saddened that she took so long.

Susan continues telling stories as we hold Mildred's hands. At some point Paul quietly joins us. He rubs Susan's shoulders and kisses her forehead, and then he steps in to kiss Mildred. She smiles at him, pulls her hand free from mine, and pats his cheek. Then her arm collapses, and I take her hand again.

Paul steps quietly to my side of the bed and rubs my shoulders as well. It comforts him more than me. He needs a father, and an emulation is close enough at this moment.

Susan keeps telling stories. When she lags, Paul adds some of his own, and they trade back and forth. Slowly their stories reach backwards in time, and once or twice Mildred's eyes light as if she remembers those events.

But then her eyes close, and she relaxes. Her breathing quiets and slows, but Susan and Paul try not to notice. Their voices lower, but their stories continue.

Eventually the sensors in my fingers can read no pulse. They have been burned, so maybe they're defective. To be sure, I lean in and listen to Mildred's chest. There is no sound: no breath, no heartbeat.

I remain Henry just long enough to kiss Mildred goodbye. Then I am just me, my empathy net awash in Paul and Susan's grief.

I leave the hospital room, and I find Millie playing in a waiting room and Anna watching her. Anna looks up, eyes red, and I nod. New tears run down her cheeks, and she takes Millie back into Mildred's room.

I sit, and my nets collapse.

*   *   *

Now I am nobody. Almost always.

The cause of the fire was determined to be faulty contract work. There was an insurance settlement. Paul and Susan sold their own home and put both sets of funds into a bigger, better house in Mildred's garden.

I was part of the settlement. The insurance company offered to return me to the manufacturer and pay off my lease, but Paul and Susan decided they wanted to keep me. They went for a full purchase and repair. Paul doesn't understand why, but Susan still fears she may need my services—or Paul might, and I may have to emulate her. She never admits these fears to him, but my empathy net knows.

I sleep most of the time, sitting in my maintenance alcove. I bring back too many memories that they would rather not face, so they leave me powered down for long periods.

But every so often, Millie asks to play with Mr. Robot, and sometimes they decide to indulge her. They power me up, and Miss Millie and I explore all the mysteries of the garden. We built a bridge to the far side of the creek; and on the other side, we're planting daisies. Today she asked me to tell her about her grandmother.

Today I am Mildred.

HUNGRY DAUGHTERS OF STARVING MOTHERS

ALYSSA WONG

Alyssa Wong studies fiction in Raleigh, NC, and really, really likes crows. Her story, "Hungry Daughters of Starving Mothers," won the 2015 Nebula Award for Best Short Story, and her fiction has been shortlisted for the Pushcart Prize, the Bram Stoker Award, the Locus Award, and the Shirley Jackson Award. Her work has been published in the Magazine of Fantasy & Science Fiction, Strange Horizons, Nightmare Magazine, Black Static, and Tor.com, among others. She can be found online at www.crashwong.net and on Twitter as @crashwong.

FROM THE AUTHOR

I wrote the first draft of the story that became "Hungry Daughters" at the Clarion Writers' Workshop, in a fit of desperation, with twelve hours until deadline, on very little sleep. Needless to say, it wasn't a good draft. And it was a very different story (more condensed, but more tentative). But it was a fun draft, and it set the tone for the relationships at the core of "Hungry Daughters." I didn't touch the story again until a couple of years later, after I had lived in NYC for a year (where "Hungry Daughters" is set). "Hungry Daughters" is also a distinctly Asian American story; its four central female characters are from different generations and different backgrounds, and they all have different ways of dealing with issues of diaspora, being an outsider in a world that they belong to but feel dissonance and disconnection with, and staying true to who they are—whoever and whatever they are.

The hardest part of putting "Hungry Daughters" together was that I knew nothing about food when I started writing it, and food is a central element in this story! I spent a couple of years watching every Food Network and cooking show I could find.

My editor was Wendy Wagner for the Queers Destroy Horror! *special issue of* Nightmare Magazine. *"Hungry Daughters" is my first explicitly queer female-centric story, and submitting it to* Queers Destroy Horror! *was a deliberate personal decision on my part to come out to the SFF community. I'm very grateful that Wendy selected it for the issue, and I'm glad that there are projects like* Queers Destroy Horror! *that celebrated work by marginalized communities, for marginalized communities. Having visible, unapologetic representation means a lot to me, and I hope that projects like* Queers Destroy Horror! *encourage writers to be bold, brave, and true to themselves in their stories.*

As my date—Harvey? Harvard?—brags about his alma mater and Manhattan penthouse, I take a bite of overpriced kale and watch his ugly thoughts swirl overhead. It's hard to pay attention to him with my stomach growling and my body ajitter, for all he's easy on the eyes. Harvey doesn't look much older than I am, but his thoughts, covered in spines and centipede feet, glisten with ancient grudges and carry an entitled, Ivy League stink.

"My apartment has the most amazing view of the city," he's saying, his thoughts sliding long over each other like dark, bristling snakes. Each one is as thick around as his Rolex-draped wrist. "I just installed a Jacuzzi along the west wall so that I can watch the sun set while I relax after getting back from the gym."

I nod, half-listening to the words coming out of his mouth. I'm much more interested in the ones hissing through the teeth of the thoughts above him.

She's got perfect tits, lil' handfuls just waiting to be squeezed. I love me some perky tits.

I'm gonna fuck this bitch so hard she'll never walk straight again.

Gross. "That sounds wonderful," I say as I sip champagne and gaze at him through my false eyelashes, hoping the dimmed screen of my iPhone isn't visible through the tablecloth below. This dude is boring as hell, and I'm already back on Tindr, thumbing through next week's prospective dinner dates.

She's so into me, she'll be begging for it by the end of the night.

I can't wait to cut her up.

My eyes flick up sharply. "I'm sorry?" I say.

Harvey blinks. "I said, Argentina is a beautiful country."

Pretty little thing. She'll look so good spread out all over the floor.

"Right," I say. "Of course." Blood's pulsing through my head so hard it probably looks like I've got a wicked blush.

I'm so excited, I'm half hard already.

You and me both, I think, turning my iPhone off and smiling my prettiest smile.

The waiter swings by with another bottle of champagne and a dessert menu burned into a wooden card, but I wave him off. "Dinner's been lovely," I whisper to Harvey, leaning in and kissing his cheek, "but I've got a different kind of dessert in mind."

Ahhh, go the ugly thoughts, settling into a gentle, rippling wave across his shoulders. *I'm going to take her home and split her all the way from top to bottom. Like a fucking fruit tart.*

That is not the way I normally eat fruit tarts, but who am I to judge? I passed on dessert, after all.

When he pays the bill, he can't stop grinning at me. Neither can the ugly thoughts hissing and cackling behind his ear.

"What's got you so happy?" I ask coyly.

"I'm just excited to spend the rest of the evening with you," he replies.

*   *   *

The fucker has his own parking spot! No taxis for us; he's even brought the Tesla. The leather seats smell buttery and sweet, and as I slide in and make myself comfortable, the rankness of his thoughts leaves a stain in the air. It's enough to leave me light-headed, almost purring. As we cruise uptown toward his fancy-ass penthouse, I ask him to pull over near the Queensboro Bridge for a second.

Annoyance flashes across his face, but he parks the Tesla in a side street. I lurch into an alley, tottering over empty cans and discarded cigarettes in my four-inch heels, and puke a trail of champagne and kale over to the dumpster shoved up against the apartment building.

"Are you all right?" Harvey calls.

"I'm fine," I slur. Not a single curious window opens overhead.

His steps echo down the alley. He's gotten out of the car, and he's walking toward me like I'm an animal that he needs to approach carefully.

Maybe I should do it now.

Yes! Now, now, while the bitch is occupied.

But what about the method? I won't get to see her insides all pretty everywhere—

I launch myself at him, fingers digging sharp into his body, and bite down hard on his mouth. He tries to shout, but I swallow the sound and shove my tongue inside. There, just behind his teeth, is what I'm looking for: ugly thoughts, viscous as boiled tendon. I suck them howling and fighting into my throat as Harvey's body shudders, little mewling noises escaping from his nose.

I feel decadent and filthy, swollen with the cruelest dreams I've ever tasted. I can barely feel Harvey's feeble struggles; in this state, with the darkest parts of himself drained from his mouth into mine, he's no match for me.

They're never as strong as they think they are.

By the time he finally goes limp, the last of the thoughts disappearing down my throat, my body's already changing. My limbs elongate, growing thicker, and my dress feels too tight as my ribs expand. I'll have to work quickly. I strip off my clothes with practiced ease, struggling a little to work the bodice free of the gym-toned musculature swelling under my skin.

It doesn't take much time to wrestle Harvey out of his clothes, either. My hands are shaking but strong, and as I button up his shirt around me and shrug on his jacket, my jaw has creaked into an approximation of his and the ridges of my fingerprints have reshaped themselves completely. Harvey is so much bigger than me, and the expansion of space eases the pressure on my boiling belly, stuffed with ugly thoughts as it is. I stuff my discarded outfit into my purse, my high heels clicking against the empty glass jar at its bottom, and sling the strap over my now-broad shoulder.

I kneel to check Harvey's pulse—slow but steady—before rolling his unconscious body up against the dumpster, covering him with trash bags. Maybe he'll wake up, maybe he won't. Not my problem, as long as he doesn't wake in the next ten seconds to see his doppelganger strolling out of the alley, wearing his clothes and fingering his wallet and the keys to his Tesla.

There's a cluster of drunk college kids gawking at Harvey's car. I level an arrogant stare at them—oh, but do I wear this body so much better than he did!—and they scatter.

I might not have a license, but Harvey's body remembers how to drive.

*　　*　　*

The Tesla revs sweetly under me, but I ditch it in a parking garage in Bedford, stripping in the relative privacy of the second-to-highest level, edged behind a pillar. After laying the keys on the driver's seat over Harvey's neatly folded clothes and shutting the car door, I pull the glass jar from my purse and vomit into it as quietly as I can. Black liquid, thick and viscous, hits the bottom of the jar, hissing and snarling Harvey's words. My body shudders, limbs retracting, spine reshaping itself, as I empty myself of him.

It takes a few more minutes to ease back into an approximation of myself, at least enough to slip my dress and heels back on, pocket the jar, and comb my tangled hair out with my fingers. The parking attendant nods at me as I walk out of the garage, his eyes sliding disinterested over me, his thoughts a gray, indistinct murmur.

The L train takes me back home to Bushwick, and when I push open the apartment door, Aiko is in the kitchen, rolling mochi paste out on the counter.

"You're here," I say stupidly. I'm still a little foggy from shaking off Harvey's form, and strains of his thoughts linger in me, setting my blood humming uncomfortably hot.

"I'd hope so. You invited me over." She hasn't changed out of her catering company clothes, and her short, sleek hair frames her face, aglow in the kitchen light. Not a single ugly thought casts its shadow across the stove behind her. "Did you forget again?"

"No," I lie, kicking my shoes off at the door. "I totally would never do something like that. Have you been here long?"

"About an hour, nothing unusual. The doorman let me in, and I kept your spare key." She smiles briefly, soft compared to the brusque movements of her hands. She's got flour on her rolled-up sleeves, and my heart flutters the way it never does when I'm out hunting. "I'm guessing your date was pretty shit. You probably wouldn't have come home at all if it had gone well."

"You could say that." I reach into my purse and stash the snarling jar in the fridge, where it clatters against the others, nearly a dozen bottles of malignant leftovers labeled as health drinks.

Aiko nods to her right. "I brought you some pastries from the event tonight. They're in the paper bag on the counter."

"You're an angel." I edge past her so I don't make bodily contact. Aiko thinks I have touch issues, but the truth is, she smells like everything good in the world, solid and familiar, both light and heavy at the same time, and it's enough to drive a person mad.

"He should have bought you a cab back, at least," says Aiko, reaching for a bowl of red bean paste. I fiddle with the bag of pastries, pretending to select something from its contents. "I swear, it's like you're a magnet for terrible dates."

She's not wrong; I'm very careful about who I court. After all, that's how I stay fed. But no one in the past has been as delicious, as hideously depraved as Harvey. No one else has been a killer.

I'm going to take her home and split her all the way from top to bottom.

"Maybe I'm too weird," I say.

"You're probably too normal. Only socially maladjusted creeps use Tindr."

"Gee, thanks," I complain.

She grins, flicking a bit of red bean paste at me. I lick it off of my arm. "You know what I mean. Come visit my church with me sometime, yeah? There are plenty of nice boys there."

"The dating scene in this city depresses me," I mutter, flicking open my Tindr app with my thumb. "I'll pass."

"Come on, Jen, put that away." Aiko hesitates. "Your mom called while you were out. She wants you to move back to Flushing."

I bark out a short, sharp laugh, my good mood evaporating. "What else is new?"

"She's getting old," Aiko says. "And she's lonely."

"I bet. All her mahjong partners are dead, pretty much." I can imagine her in her little apartment in Flushing, huddled over her laptop, floral curtains pulled tight over the windows to shut out the rest of the world. My ma, whose apartment walls are alive with hissing, covered in the ugly, bottled remains of her paramours.

Aiko sighs, joining me at the counter and leaning back against me. For once, I don't move away. Every muscle in my body is tense, straining. I'm afraid

I might catch fire, but I don't want her to leave. "Would it kill you to be kind to her?"

I think about my baba evaporating into thin air when I was five years old, what was left of him coiled in my ma's stomach. "Are you telling me to go back?"

She doesn't say anything for a bit. "No," she says at last. "That place isn't good for you. That house isn't good for anyone."

Just a few inches away, an army of jars full of black, viscous liquid wait in the fridge, their contents muttering to themselves. Aiko can't hear them, but each slosh against the glass is a low, nasty hiss:

who does she think she is, the fucking cunt
should've got her when I had the chance

I can still feel Harvey, his malice and ugly joy, on my tongue. I'm already full of things my ma gave me. "I'm glad we agree."

*   *   *

Over the next few weeks, I gorge myself on the pickup artists and grad students populating the St. Marks hipster bars, but nothing tastes good after Harvey. Their watery essences, squeezed from their owners with barely a whimper of protest, barely coat my stomach. Sometimes I take too much. I scrape them dry and leave them empty, shaking their forms off like rainwater when I'm done.

I tell Aiko I've been partying when she says I look haggard. She tells me to quit drinking so much, her face impassive, her thoughts clouded with concern. She starts coming over more often, even cooking dinner for me, and her presence both grounds me and drives me mad.

"I'm worried about you," she says as I lie on the floor, flipping listlessly through pages of online dating profiles, looking for the emptiness, the rot, that made Harvey so appealing. She's cooking my mom's lo mien recipe, the oily smell making my skin itch. "You've lost so much weight and there's nothing in your fridge, just a bunch of empty jam jars."

I don't tell her that Harvey's lies under my bed, that I lick its remnants every night to send my nerves back into euphoria. I don't tell her how often I dream about my ma's place, the shelves of jars she never let me touch. "Is it really okay for you to spend so much time away from your catering business?" I say instead. "Time is money, and Jimmy gets pissy when he has to make all the desserts without you."

Aiko sets a bowl of lo mein in front of me and joins me on the ground.

"There's nowhere I'd rather be than here," she says, and a dangerous, luminous sweetness blooms in my chest.

But the hunger grows worse every day, and soon I can't trust myself around her. I deadbolt the door, and when she stops by my apartment to check on me, I refuse to let her in. Texts light up my phone like a fleet of fireworks as I huddle under a blanket on the other side, my face pressed against the wood, my fingers twitching.

"Please, Jen, I don't understand," she says from behind the door. "Did I do something wrong?"

I can't wait to cut her up, I think, and hate myself even more.

By the time Aiko leaves, her footsteps echoing down the hallway, I've dug deep gouges in the door's paint with my nails and teeth, my mouth full of her intoxicating scent.

*   *   *

My ma's apartment in Flushing still smells the same. She's never been a clean person, and the sheer amount of junk stacked up everywhere has increased since I left home for good. Piles of newspapers, old food containers, and stuffed toys make it hard to push the door open, and the stench makes me cough. Her hoard is up to my shoulders, even higher in some places, and as I pick my way through it, the sounds that colored my childhood grow louder: the constant whine of a Taiwanese soap opera bleeding past mountains of trash, and the cruel cacophony of many familiar voices:

Touch me again and I swear I'll kill you—

How many times have I told you not to wash the clothes like that, open your mouth—

Hope her ugly chink daughter isn't home tonight—

Under the refuse she's hoarded the walls are honeycombed with shelves, lined with what's left of my ma's lovers. She keeps them like disgusting, mouth-watering trophies, desires pickling in stomach acid and bile. I could probably call them by name if I wanted to; when I was a kid, I used to lie on the couch and watch my baba's ghost flicker across their surfaces.

My ma's huddled in the kitchen, the screen of her laptop casting a sickly blue glow on her face. Her thoughts cover her quietly like a blanket. "I made some niu ro mien," she says. "It's on the stove. Your baba's in there."

My stomach curls, but whether it's from revulsion or hunger I can't tell.

"Thanks, ma," I say. I find a bowl that's almost clean and wash it out, ladling a generous portion of thick noodles for myself. The broth smells faintly of hong-tashan tobacco, and as I force it down almost faster than I can swallow, someone else's memories of my childhood flash before my eyes: pushing a small girl on a swing set at the park; laughing as she chases pigeons down the street; raising a hand for a second blow as her mother launches herself toward us, between us, teeth bared—

"How is it?" she says.

Foul. "Great," I say. It settles my stomach, at least for a little while. But my baba was no Harvey, and I can already feel the hunger creeping back, waiting for the perfect moment to strike.

"You ate something you shouldn't have, didn't you, Meimei." My ma looks up at me for the first time since I walked in, and she looks almost as tired as I feel. "Why didn't you learn from me? I taught you to stick to petty criminals. I taught you to stay invisible."

She'd tried to teach me to disappear into myself, the way she'd disappeared into this apartment. "I know I messed up," I tell her. "Nothing tastes good any more, and I'm always hungry. But I don't know what to do."

My ma sighs. "Once you've tasted a killer, there's no turning back. You'll crave that intensity until you die. And it can take a long time for someone like us to die, Meimei."

It occurs to me that I don't actually know how old my ma is. Her thoughts are old and covered in knots, stitched together from the remnants of other people's experiences. How long has she been fighting this condition, these over-whelming, gnawing desires?

"Move back in," she's saying. "There's so much tong activity here, the streets leak with food. You barely even have to go outside, just crack open a window and you can smell it brewing. The malice, the knives and bullets . . ."

The picture she paints makes me shudder, my mouth itching. "I can't just leave everything, Ma," I say. "I have my own life now." And I can't live in this apart-ment, with its lack of sunlight and fresh air, its thick stench of regret and malice.

"So what happens if you go back? You lose control, you take a bite out of Aiko?" She sees me stiffen. "That girl cares about you so much. The best thing you can do for her is keep away. Don't let what happened to your father happen to Aiko." She reaches for my hand, and I pull away. "Stay here, Meimei. We only have each other."

"This isn't what I want." I'm backing up, and my shoulder bumps into the trash, threatening to bury us both in rotting stuffed animals. "This isn't *safe*, Ma. You shouldn't even stay here."

My ma coughs, her eyes glinting in the dark. The cackling from her jar collection swells in a vicious tide, former lovers rocking back and forth on their shelves. "Someday you'll learn that there's more to life than being selfish, Meimei."

That's when I turn my back on her, pushing past the debris and bullshit her apartment's stuffed with. I don't want to die, but as far as I'm concerned, living like my ma, sequestered away from the rest of the world, her doors barricaded with heaps of useless trinkets and soured memories, is worse than being dead.

The jars leer and cackle as I go, and she doesn't try to follow me.

The scent of Flushing clings to my skin, and I can't wait to shake it off. I get on the train as soon as I can, and I'm back on Tindr as soon as the M passes above ground. Tears blur my eyes, rattling free with the movement of the train. I scrub them away angrily, and when my vision clears, I glance back at the screen. A woman with sleek, dark hair, slim tortoiseshell glasses, and a smile that seems a little shy, but strangely handsome, glows up at me. In the picture, she's framed by the downtown cityscape. She has rounded cheeks, but there's a strange flat quality to her face. And then, of course, there are the dreams shadowing her, so strong they leak from the screen in a thick, heady miasma. Every one of those myriad eyes is staring straight at me, and my skin prickles.

I scan the information on her profile page, my blood beating so hard I can feel my fingertips pulsing: relatively young-looking, but old enough to be my mother's cousin. Likes: exploring good food, spending rainy days at the Cloisters, browsing used book stores. Location: Manhattan.

She looks a little like Aiko.

She's quick to message me back. As we flirt, cold sweat and adrenaline send uncomfortable shivers through my body. Everything is sharper, and I can almost hear Harvey's jar laughing. Finally, the words I'm waiting for pop up:

I'd love to meet you. Are you free tonight?

I make a quick stop-off back home, and my heart hammers as I get on the train bound for the Lower East Side, red lipstick immaculate and arms shaking beneath my crisp designer coat, a pair of Mom's glass jars tucked in my purse.

* * *

Her name is Seo-yun, and as she watches me eat, her eyes flickering from my mouth to my throat, her smile is so sharp I could cut myself on it. "I love places like this," she says. "Little authentic spots with only twelve seats. Have you been to Haru before?"

"I haven't," I murmur. My fingers are clumsy with my chopsticks, tremors clicking them together, making it hard to pick up my food. God, she smells delectable. I've never met someone whose mind is so twisted, so rich; a malignancy as well developed and finely crafted as the most elegant dessert.

I'm going to take her home and split her open like a—

I can already taste her on my tongue, the best meal I've never had.

"You're in for a treat," Seo-yun says as the waiter—the only other staff beside the chef behind the counter—brings us another pot of tea. "This restaurant started as a stall in a subway station back in Japan."

"Oh wow," I say. "That's . . . amazing."

"I think so, too. I'm glad they expanded into Manhattan."

Behind her kind eyes, a gnarled mess of ancient, ugly thoughts writhes like the tails of a rat king. I've never seen so many in one place. They crawl from her mouth and ears, creeping through the air on deep-scaled legs, their voices like the drone of descending locusts.

I'm not her first. I can tell that already. But then, she isn't mine, either.

I spend the evening sweating through my dress, nearly dropping my chopsticks. I can't stop staring at the ugly thoughts, dropping from her lips like swollen beetles. They skitter over the tablecloth toward me, whispering obscenities at odds with Seo-yun's gentle voice, hissing what they'd like to do to me. It takes everything in me not to pluck them from the table and crunch them deep between my teeth right then and there, to pour into her lap and rip her mind clean.

Seo-yun is too much for me, but I'm in too far, too hard; I *need* to have her. She smiles at me. "Not hungry?"

I glance down at my plate. I've barely managed a couple of nigiri. "I'm on a diet," I mutter.

"I understand," she says earnestly. The ugly thoughts crawl over the tops of her hands, iridescent drops spilling into her soy sauce dish.

When the waiter finally disappears into the kitchen, I move in to kiss her across the table. She makes a startled noise, gentle pink spreading across her face, but she doesn't pull away. My elbow sinks into the exoskeleton of one of the thought-beetles, crushing it into black, moist paste against my skin.

I open my mouth to take the first bite.

"So, I'm curious," murmurs Seo-yun, her breath brushing my lips. "Who's Aiko?"

My eyes snap open. Seo-yun smiles, her voice warm and tender, all her edges dark. "She seems sweet, that's all. I'm surprised you haven't had a taste of her yet."

I back up so fast that I knock over my teacup, spilling scalding tea over everything. But Seo-yun doesn't move, just keeps smiling that kind, gentle smile as her monstrous thoughts lap delicately at the tablecloth.

"She smells so ripe," she whispers. "But you're afraid you'll ruin her, aren't you? Eat her up, and for what? Just like your mum did your dad."

No, no, no. I've miscalculated so badly. But I'm so hungry, and I'm too young, and she smells like ancient power. There's no way I'll be able to outrun her. "Get out of my head," I manage to say.

"I'm not in your head, love. Your thoughts are spilling out everywhere around you, for everyone to see." She leans in, propping her chin on her hand. The thoughts twisted around her head like a living crown let out a dry, rattling laugh. "I like you, Jenny. You're ambitious. A little careless, but we can fix that." Seo-yun taps on the table, and the waiter reappears, folding up the tablecloth deftly and sliding a single dish onto the now-bare table. An array of thin, translucent slices fan out across the plate, pale and glistening with malice. Bisected eyes glint, mouths caught mid-snarl, from every piece. "All it takes is a little practice and discipline, and no one will know what you're really thinking."

"On the house, of course, Ma'am," the waiter murmurs. Before he disappears again, I catch a glimpse of dark, many-legged thoughts braided like a bracelet around his wrist.

Seo-yun takes the first bite, glancing up at me from behind her glasses. "Your mum was wrong," she says. "She thought you were alone, just the two of you. So she taught you to only eat when you needed to, so you didn't get caught, biding your time between meals like a snake."

"You don't know anything about me," I say. The heady, rotten perfume from the dish in front of me makes my head spin with hunger.

"My mum was much the same. Eat for survival, not for pleasure." She gestures at the plate with her chopsticks. "Please, have some."

As the food disappears, I can only hold out for a few more slices before my chopsticks dart out, catching a piece for myself. It's so acidic it makes my tongue burn and eyes itch, the aftertaste strangely sweet.

"Do you like it?"

I respond by wolfing down another two slices, and Seo-yun chuckles. Harvey is bland compared to this, this strangely distilled pairing of emotions—

I gasp as my body starts to warp, hands withering, burn scars twisting their way around my arms. Gasoline, malice, childish joy rush through me, a heady mix of memory and sensory overstimulation. And then Seo-yun's lips are on mine, teeth tugging gently, swallowing, drawing it out of me. The burns fade, but the tingle of cruel euphoria lingers.

She wipes her mouth delicately. "Ate a little too fast, I think, dear," she says. "My point, Jenny, is that I believe in eating for pleasure, not just survival. And communally, of course. There are a number of us who get together for dinner or drinks at my place, every so often, and I would love it if you would join us tonight. An eating club, of sorts."

My gaze flickers up at her thoughts, but they're sitting still as stones, just watching me with unblinking eyes. My mouth stings with the imprint of hers.

"Let me introduce you soon. You don't have to be alone anymore." As the waiter clears the plate and nods at her—no check, no receipt, nothing—Seo-yun adds, "And tonight doesn't have to be over until we want it to be." She offers me her hand. After a moment's hesitation, I take it. It's smaller than mine, and warm.

"Yes, please," I say, watching her thoughts instead of her face.

As we leave the restaurant, she presses her lips to my forehead. Her lips sear into my skin, nerves singing white-hot with ecstasy. "They're going to love you," she says.

We'll have so much fun, say the thoughts curling through her dark hair.

She hails a cab from the fleet circling the street like wolves, and we get inside.

* * *

I run into Aiko two months later in front of my apartment, as I'm carrying the last box of my stuff out. She's got a startled look on her face, and she's carrying a bag stuffed with ramps, kaffir lime, heart of palm—all ingredients I wouldn't have known two months ago, before meeting Seo-yun. "You're moving?"

I shrug, staring over her head, avoiding her eyes. "Yeah, uh. I'm seeing someone now, and she's got a really nice place."

"Oh." She swallows, shifts the bag of groceries higher on her hip. "That's great. I didn't know you were dating anybody." I can hear her shaky smile. "She must be feeding you well. You look healthier."

"Thanks," I say, though I wonder. It's true, I'm sleeker, more confident now. I'm barely home any more, spending most of my time in Seo-yun's Chelsea apartment, learning to cook with the array of salts and spices infused with ugly dreams, drinking wine distilled from deathbed confessions. My time stalking the streets for small-time criminals is done. But why has my confidence evaporated the moment I see Aiko? And if that ravenous hunger from Harvey is gone, why am I holding my breath to keep from breathing in her scent?

"So what's she like?"

"Older, kind of—" *kind of looks like you* "—short. Likes to cook, right." I start to edge past her. "Listen, this box is heavy and the van's waiting for me downstairs. I should go."

"Wait," Aiko says, grabbing my arm. "Your mom keeps calling me. She still has my number from . . . before. She's worried about you. Plus I haven't seen you in ages, and you're just gonna take off?"

Aiko, small and humble. Her hands smell like home, like rice flour and bad memories. How could I ever have found that appealing?

"We don't need to say goodbye. I'm sure I'll see you later," I lie, shrugging her off.

"Let's get dinner sometime," says Aiko, but I'm already walking away.

* * *

Caterers flit like blackbirds through the apartment, dark uniforms neatly pressed, their own ugly thoughts braided and pinned out of the way. It's a two-story affair, and well-dressed people flock together everywhere there's space, Seo-yun's library upstairs to the living room on ground floor. She's even asked the caterers to prepare some of my recipes, which makes my heart glow. "You're the best," I say, kneeling on the bed beside her and pecking her on the cheek.

Seo-yun smiles, fixing my hair. She wears a sleek, deep blue dress, and today, her murderous thoughts are draped over her shoulders like a stole, a living, writhing cape. Their teeth glitter like tiny diamonds. I've never seen her so beautiful. "They're good recipes. My friends will be so excited to taste them."

I've already met many of them, all much older than I am. They make me nervous. "I'll go check on the food," I say.

She brushes her thumb over my cheek. "Whatever you'd like, love."

I escape into the kitchen, murmuring brief greetings to the guests I encounter on the way. Their hideous dreams adorn them like jewels, glimmering and snatching at me as I slip past. As I walk past some of the cooks, I notice a man who looks vaguely familiar. "Hey," I say.

"Yes, ma'am?" The caterer turns around, and I realize where I've seen him; there's a picture of him and Aiko on her cellphone, the pair of them posing in front of a display at a big event they'd cooked for. My heartbeat slows.

"Aren't you Aiko's coworker?"

He grins and nods. "Yes, I'm Jimmy. Aiko's my business partner. Are you looking for her?"

"Wait, she's here?"

He frowns. "She should be. She never misses one of Ms. Sun's parties." He smiles. "Ms. Sun lets us take home whatever's left when the party winds down. She's so generous."

I turn abruptly and head for the staircase to the bedroom, shouldering my way through the crowd. Thoughts pelt me as I go: Has Aiko known about me, my ma, what we can do? How long has she known? And worse—Seo-yun's known all along about Aiko, and played me for a fool.

I bang the bedroom door open to find Aiko sprawled out across the carpet, her jacket torn open. Seo-yun crouches on the floor above her in her glorious dress, her mouth dark and glittering. She doesn't look at all surprised to see me.

"Jenny, love. I hope you don't mind we started without you." Seo-yun smiles. Her lipstick is smeared over her chin, over Aiko's blank face. I can't tell if Aiko's still breathing.

"Get away from her," I say in a low voice.

"As you wish." She rises gracefully, crossing the room in fluid strides. "I was done with that particular morsel, anyway." The sounds of the party leak into the room behind me, and I know I can't run and grab Aiko at the same time.

So I shut the door, locking it, and mellow my voice to a sweet purr. "Why didn't you tell me about Aiko? We could have shared her together."

But Seo-yun just laughs at me. "You can't fool me, Jenny. I can smell your rage from across the room." She reaches out, catches my face, and I recoil into the door. "It makes you so beautiful. The last seasoning in a dish almost ready."

"You're insane, and I'm going to kill you," I say. She kisses my neck, her teeth scraping my throat, and the scent of her is so heady my knees almost bend.

"I saw you in her head, delicious as anything," she whispers. Her ugly thoughts hiss up my arms, twining around my waist. There's a sharp sting at my wrist, and I look down to discover that one of them is already gnawing at my skin. "And I knew I just had to have you."

There's a crash, and Seo-yun screams as a porcelain lamp shatters against the back of her head. Aiko's on her feet, swaying unsteadily, face grim. "Back the fuck away from her," she growls, her voice barely above a whisper.

"You little bitch—" snarls Seo-yun.

But I seize my chance and pounce, fastening my teeth into the hollow of Seo-yun's throat, right where her mantle of thoughts gathers and folds inward. I chew and swallow, chew and swallow, gorging myself on this woman. Her thoughts are mine now, thrashing as I seize them from her, and I catch glimpses of myself, of Aiko, and of many others just like us, in various states of disarray, of preparation.

Ma once told me that this was how Baba went; she'd accidentally drained him until he'd faded completely out of existence. For the first time in my life, I understand her completely.

Seo-yun's bracelets clatter to the floor, her empty gown fluttering soundlessly after. Aiko collapses too, folding like paper.

It hurts to take in that much. My stomach hurts so bad, my entire body swollen with hideous thoughts. At the same time, I've never felt so alive, abuzz with possibility and untamable rage.

I lurch over to Aiko on the floor, malice leaking from her mouth, staining the carpet. "Aiko, wake up!" But she feels hollow, lighter, empty. She doesn't even smell like herself any more.

A knock at the door jolts me. "Ma'am," says a voice I recognize as the head caterer. "The first of the main courses is ready. Mr. Goldberg wants to know if you'll come down and give a toast."

Fuck. "I—" I start to say, but the voice isn't mine. I glance over at the mirror; sure enough, it's Seo-yun staring back at me, her dark, terrible dreams tangled around her body in a knotted mess. "I'll be right there," I say, and lay Aiko gently on the bed. Then I dress and leave, my heart pounding in my mouth.

I walk Seo-yun's shape down the stairs to the dining room, where guests are milling about, plates in hand, and smile Seo-yun's smile. And if I look a little too much like myself, well—according to what I'd seen while swallowing

Seo-yun's thoughts, I wouldn't be the first would-be inductee to disappear at a party like this. Someone hands me a glass of wine, and when I take it, my hand doesn't tremble, even though I'm screaming inside.

Fifty pairs of eyes on me, the caterers' glittering cold in the shadows. Do any of them know? Can any of them tell?

"To your continued health, and to a fabulous dinner," I say, raising my glass. As one, they drink.

* * *

Seo-yun's apartment is dark, cleared of guests and wait staff alike. Every door is locked, every curtain yanked closed.

I've pulled every jar, every container, every pot and pan out of the kitchen, and now they cover the floor of the bedroom, trailing into the hallway, down the stairs. Many are full, their malignant contents hissing and whispering hideous promises at me as I stuff my hand in my mouth, retching into the pot in my lap.

Aiko lies on the bed, pale and still. There's flour and bile on the front of her jacket. "Hang in there," I whisper, but she doesn't respond. I swirl the pot, searching its contents for any hint of Aiko, but Seo-yun's face grins out at me from the patterns of light glimmering across the liquid's surface. I shove it away from me, spilling some on the carpet.

I grab another one of the myriad crawling thoughts tangled about me, sinking my teeth into its body, tearing it into pieces as it screams and howls terrible promises, promises it won't be able to keep. I eat it raw, its scales scraping the roof of my mouth, chewing it thoroughly. The more broken down it is, the easier it will be to sort through the pieces that are left when it comes back up.

How long did you know? Did you always know?

I'll find her, I think as viscous black liquid pours from my mouth, over my hands, burning my throat. The field of containers pools around me like a storm of malicious stars, all whispering my name. She's in here somewhere, I can see her reflection darting across their surfaces. If I have to rip through every piece of Seo-yun I have, from her dreams to the soft, freckled skin wrapped around my body, I will. I'll wring every vile drop of Seo-yun out of me until I find Aiko, and then I'll fill her back up, pour her mouth full of herself.

How could I ever forget her? How could I forget her taste, her scent, something as awful and beautiful as home?

ABOUT THE RHYSLING AND DWARF STARS AWARDS

The Rhysling Awards are given each year by the Science Fiction Poetry Association (SFPA), in recognition of the best science fiction, fantasy, or horror poems of the year. Each year, members of SFPA nominate works that are compiled into an annual anthology; members then vote to select winners from the anthology's contents. The award is given in two categories: works of fifty or more lines are eligible for Best Long Poem, and works shorter than that are eligible for Best Short Poem. Additionally, SFPA gives the Dwarf Stars Award to a poem of ten or fewer lines.

This year's winners (in order of their appearance in this anthology) are: Rhysling Award for Best Short Poem, "Shutdown" by Marge Simon (page 117), Dwarf Star Award, "abandoned nursing home" by Greg Schwartz (page 119), and Rhysling Award for Best Long Poem, "100 Reasons to Have Sex with an Alien" by F. J. Bergmann (page 243).

SHUTDOWN

MARGE SIMON

Marge Simon lives in Ocala, Florida and is married to Bruce Boston. She edits a column for the HWA Newsletter, "Blood & Spades: Poets of the Dark Side," and serves as Chair of the Board of Trustees. She won the Strange Horizons Readers' Choice Award, 2010, the SFPA's Dwarf Stars Award, 2012, and the Elgin Award for best poetry collection, 2015. She has won the Bram Stoker Award ® for Poetry, the Rhysling Award and the Grand Master Award from the SF Poetry Association, 2015. Her new collection with Mary A. Turzillo, Satan's Sweethearts *(Weasel Press), is upcoming in 2017. Marge also has work in the anthology* Scary Out There, *a story and poems in* You, Human *(Dark Regions Press), and fiction in* Chiral Mad 4. *www.margesimon.com.*

They barred the library doors today.
Men in uniform stand patrol, armed and ready
their lantern jaws firm, lips a straight line.
Stoic women, also armed, jog up and down
the block, buttocks moving like pistons.

Someone dashes from a building
a hand-held reader clutched close.
Shots are fired; I don't stay to find out more.

I've packed the car with books, little room for else.
It is my car, his gift to buy my silence,
to make up for the bruises real and otherwise;
never marry a politician who has no use
for literature, has no use for a wife that does.

Eagles have left their nests to vultures
the barren palm trees whimper for their loss
there are ceaseless storms, mud is everywhere
while two legged insects multiply unchecked

The car radio plays Ibsen, bassoons herald the trolls.
I roll down the window, taking a deep breath
outside of Pyr Gynt's Hall of the Mountain King,
foreboding notes of the oboe, a palpable stench of fear.
Am I leaving that, or taking it with me . . .

ABANDONED NURSING HOME

GREG SCHWARTZ

Greg Schwartz writes speculative fiction and poetry. In addition to being lucky enough to win a Dwarf Stars Award, some of his poems have appeared in Writers' Journal, Horror Carousel, Star*Line, *and* The Magazine of Speculative Poetry. *His chapbook of short horror poems,* Bits and Pieces, *was published in 2007 by Spec House of Poetry. He spent some time reviewing stories for* Whispers of Wickedness *and drawing cartoons for* SP Quill Magazine, *but now all that time is gobbled up by his two children.*

abandoned nursing home
the mahjong tiles
still move

OUR LADY OF THE OPEN ROAD

SARAH PINSKER

Sarah Pinsker's novelette "In Joy, Knowing the Abyss Behind" was the 2014 Sturgeon Award winner and a 2013 Nebula finalist. Her fiction has been published in magazines including Asimov's, Strange Horizons, Lightspeed, Fantasy & Science Fiction, and Uncanny, among others, and numerous anthologies. Her stories have been translated into Chinese, French, Spanish, Italian, and Galician. She is also a singer/songwriter with three albums on various independent labels and a fourth forthcoming. She lives in Baltimore, Maryland, with her wife and dog. She can be found online at sarahpinsker.com and twitter.com/sarahpinsker.

FROM THE AUTHOR

I wrote the first eight thousand words in one epic drafting session at the Red Canoe, my writing bookstore/cafe of choice. I got home that evening and kept trying to do other things but getting pulled back in. One more scene. One more scene. I think I wrote fourteen thousand words in two days, which is not my usual pace. Some of the smaller details of touring life, like how to make sure you have a fresh towel, were drawn from my own experience, though this band is not based on my own. The main thing I had to research was the bio-diesel van. Sheila Williams at Asimov's was the first person I sent it to, so it found a home on its first outing. It felt like an Asimov's story to me; I was very happy Sheila agreed.

The needle on the veggie oil tank read flat empty by the time we came to China Grove. A giant pink and purple fiberglass dragon loomed over the entrance, refugee from some shuttered local amusement park, no doubt; it looked more medieval than Chinese. The parking lot held a mix of Chauffeurs and manual farm trucks, but I didn't spot any other greasers, so I pulled in.

"Cutting it close, Luce?" Silva put down his book and leaned over to peer at the gauge.

"There hasn't been anything but farms for the last fifty miles. Serves me right for trying a road we haven't been down before."

"Where are we?" asked Jacky from the bed in the back of the van. I glanced in the rearview. He caught my eye and gave an enthusiastic wave. His micro-braids spilled forward from whatever he'd been using to tether them, and he gathered them back into a thick ponytail.

Silva answered before I could. "Nowhere, Indiana. Go back to sleep."

"Will do." Without music or engine to drown him out, Jacky's snores filled the van again a second later. He'd been touring with us for a year now, so we'd gotten used to the snores. To be honest, I envied him his ability to fall asleep that fast.

I glanced at Silva. "You want to do the asking for once?"

He grinned and held up both forearms, tattooed every inch. "You know it's not me."

"There's such thing as sleeves, you know." I pulled my windbreaker off the back of my seat and flapped it at him, even though I knew he was right. In the Midwest, approaching a new restaurant for the first time, it was never him, between the tattoos and the spiky blue hair. Never Jacky for the pox scars on his cheeks, even though they were clearly long healed. That left me.

My bad knee buckled as I swung from the driver's seat. I bent to clutch it and my lower back spasmed just to the right of my spine, that momentary pain that told me to rethink all my life's choices.

"What are you doing?" Silva asked through the open door.

"Tying my shoe." There was no need to lie, but I did it anyway. Pride or vanity or something akin. He was only two years younger than me, and neither of us jumped off our amps much anymore. If I ached from the drive, he probably ached, too.

The backs of my thighs were all pins and needles, and my shirt was damp with sweat. I took a moment to lean against Daisy the Diesel and stretch in the hot air. I smelled myself: not great after four days with no shower, but not unbearable.

The doors opened into a foyer, red and gold and black. I didn't even notice the blond hostess in her red qipao until she stepped away from the wallpaper.

"Dining alone?" she asked. Beyond her, a roomful of faces turned in my direction. This wasn't really the kind of place that attracted tourists, especially not these days, this far off the interstate.

"No, um, actually, I was wondering if I could speak to the chef or the owner? It'll only take a minute." I was pretty sure I had timed our stop for after their dinner rush. Most of the diners looked to be eating or pushing their plates aside.

The owner and chef were the same person. I'd been expecting another blonde Midwesterner, but he was legit Chinese. He had never heard of a van that ran on grease. I did the not-quite-pleading thing. On stage I aimed for fierce, but in jeans and runners and a ponytail, I could fake a down-on-her-luck Midwest momma. The trick was not to push it.

He looked a little confused by my request, but at least he was willing to consider it. "Come to the kitchen door after we close and show me. Ten, ten thirty."

It was nine; not too bad. I walked back to the van. Silva was still in the passenger seat, but reading a trifold menu. He must have ducked in behind me to grab it. "They serve a bread basket with lo mein. And spaghetti and meatballs. Where are we?"

"Nowhere, Indiana." I echoed back at him.

We sat in the dark van and watched the customers trickle out. I could mostly guess from their looks which ones would be getting into the trucks and which into the Chauffeurs. Every once in a while, a big guy in work boots and a trucker cap surprised me by squeezing himself into some little self-driving thing. The game passed the time, in any case.

A middle-aged cowboy wandered over to stare at our van. I pegged him for a legit rancher from a distance, but as he came closer I noticed a clerical collar beneath the embroidered shirt. His boots shone and he had a paunch falling over an old rodeo belt; the incongruous image of a bull-riding minister made me laugh. He startled when he realized I was watching him.

He made a motion for me to lower my window.

"Maryland plates!" he said. "I used to live in Hagerstown."

I smiled, though I'd only ever passed through Hagerstown.

"Used to drive a church van that looked kinda like yours, too, just out of high school. Less duct tape, though. Whatcha doing out here?"

"Touring. Band."

"No kidding! You look familiar. Have I heard of you?"

"Cassis Fire," I said, taking the question as a prompt for a name. "We had it painted on the side for a while, but then we figured out we got pulled over less when we were incognito."

"Don't think I know the name. I used to have a band, back before . . ." His voice trailed off, and neither of us needed him to finish his sentence. There were several "back befores" he could be referring to, but they all amounted to the same thing. Back before StageHolo and SportsHolo made it easier to stay home. Back before most people got scared out of congregating anywhere they didn't know everybody.

"You're not playing around here, are you?"

I shook my head. "Columbus, Ohio. Tomorrow night."

"I figured. Couldn't think of a place you'd play nearby."

"Not our kind of music, anyway," I agreed. I didn't know what music he liked, but this was a safe bet.

"Not any kind. Oh well. Nice chatting with you. I'll look you up on StageHolo."

He turned away.

"We're not on StageHolo," I called to his back, though maybe not loud enough for him to hear. He waved as his Chauffeur drove him off the lot.

"Luce, you're a terrible sales person," Silva said to me.

"What?" I hadn't realized he'd been paying attention.

"You know he recognized you. All you had to do was say your name instead of the band's. Or 'Blood and Diamonds.' He'd have paid for dinner for all of us, then bought every t-shirt and download code we have."

"And then he'd listen to them and realize the music we make now is nothing like the music we made then. And even if he liked it, he'd never go to a show. At best he'd send a message saying how much he wished we were on StageHolo."

"Which we could be . . ."

"Which we won't be." He knew better than to argue with me on that one. It was our only real source of disagreement.

The neon "open" sign in the restaurant's window blinked out, and I took the cue to put the key back in the ignition. The glowplug light came on, and I started the van back up.

My movement roused Jacky again. "Where are we now?"

I didn't bother answering.

As I had guessed, the owner hadn't quite understood what I was asking for. I gave him the engine tour, showing him the custom oil filter and the dual tanks. "We still need regular diesel to start, then switch to the veggie oil tank. Not too much more to it than that."

"It's legal?"

Legal enough. There was a gray area wherein perhaps technically we were skirting the fuel tax. By our reasoning, though, we were also skirting the reasons for the fuel tax. We'd be the ones who got in trouble, anyway. Not him.

"Of course," I said, then changed the subject. "And the best part is that it makes the van smell like egg rolls."

He smiled. We got a whole tankful out of him, and a bag full of food he'd have otherwise chucked out, as well.

The guys were over the moon about the food. Dumpster diving behind a restaurant or Superwally would have been our next order of business, so anything that hadn't made a stop in a garbage can on its way to us was haute cuisine as far as we were concerned. Silva took the lo mein—no complimentary bread—, screwed together his travel chopsticks, and handed mine to me from the glove compartment. I grabbed some kind of moo shu without the pancakes, and Jacky woke again to snag the third container.

"Can we go someplace?" Silva asked, waving chopsticks at the window.

"Got anything in mind on a Tuesday night in the boonies?"

Jacky was up for something, too. "Laser tag? Laser bowling?"

Sometimes the age gap was a chasm. I turned in my seat to side-eye the kid. "One vote for lasers."

"I dunno," said Silva. "Just a bar? If I have to spend another hour in this van I'm going to scream."

I took a few bites while I considered. We wouldn't be too welcome anywhere around here, between our odor and our look, not to mention the simple fact that we were strangers. On the other hand, the more outlets I gave these guys for legit fun, the less likely they were to come up with something that would get us in trouble. "If we see a bar or a bowling joint before someplace to sleep, sure."

"I can look it up," said Jacky.

"Nope," I said. "Leave it to fate."

After two thirds of the moo shu, I gave up and closed the container. I hated wasting food, but it was too big for me to finish. I wiped my chopsticks on my jeans and put them back in their case.

Two miles down the road from the restaurant, we came to Starker's, which I hoped from the apostrophe was only a bar, not a strip club. Their expansive parking lot was empty except for eight Chauffeurs, all lined up like pigs at a trough. At least that meant we didn't have to worry about some drunk crashing into our van on his way out.

I backed into the closest spot to the door. It was the best lit, so I could worry less about our gear getting lifted. Close was also good if the locals decided they didn't like our looks.

We got the long stare as we walked in, the one from old Westerns, where all the heads swivel our way and the piano player stops playing. Except of course, these days the piano player didn't stop, because the piano player had no idea we'd arrived. The part of the pianist in this scenario was played by Roy Bittan, alongside the whole E Street Band, loud as a stadium and projected in StageHolo 3D.

"Do you want to leave?" Jacky whispered to me.

"No, it's okay. We're here now. Might as well have a drink."

"At least it's Bruce. I can get behind Bruce." Silva edged past me toward the bar.

A few at leasts: at least it was Bruce, not some cut-rate imitation. Bruce breathed punk as far as I was concerned, insisting on recording new music and legit live shows all the way into his eighties. At least it was StageHolo and not StageHoloLive, in which case there'd be a cover charge. I was willing to stand in the same room as the technology that was trying to make me obsolete, but I'd be damned if I paid them for the privilege. Of course, it wouldn't be Bruce on StageHoloLive either; he'd been gone a couple years now, and this Bruce looked to be only in his sixties, anyway. A little flat, too, which suggested this was a retrofitted older show, not one recorded using StageHolo's tech.

Silva pressed a cold can into my hand, and I took a sip, not even bothering to look at what I was drinking. Knowing him, knowing us, he'd snagged whatever had been cheapest. Pisswater, but cold pisswater. Perfect for washing down the greasy takeout food aftertaste.

I slipped into a booth, hoping the guys had followed me. Jacky did, carrying an identical can to mine in one hand, and something the color of windshield wiper fluid in a plastic shot glass in the other.

"You want one?" he asked me, nudging the windshield wiper fluid. "Bartender said it was the house special."

I pushed it back in his direction. "I don't drink anything blue. It never ends well."

"Suit yourself." He tossed it back, then grinned.

"Your teeth are blue now. You look like you ate a Smurf."

"What's a Smurf?"

Sometimes I forgot how young he was. Half my age. A lifetime in this business. "Little blue characters? A village with one chick, one old man, and a bunch of young guys?"

"Like our band?" He shook his head. "Sorry. Bad joke. Anyway, I have no idea what was in that food, but it might have been Smurf, if they're blue and taste like pork butt. How's your dinner sitting?"

I swatted him lightly, backhand. "Fine, as long as I don't drink anything blue."

He downed his beer in one long chug, then got up to get another. He looked at mine and raised his eyebrows.

"No thanks," I said. "I'll stick with one. I get the feeling this is a zero tolerance town."

If twenty-odd years of this had taught me one thing, it was to stay clear of local police. Every car in the parking lot was self-driving, which suggested there was somebody out on the roads ready to come down hard on us. Having spent a lot of time in my youth leaving clubs at closing time and dodging drunk drivers, I approved this effort. One of the few aspects of our brave new world I could fully endorse.

I looked around. Silva sat on a stool at the bar. Jacky stood behind him, a hand on Silva's shoulder, tapping his foot to the Bo Diddley beat of "She's the One." The rest of the bar stools were filled with people who looked too comfortable to be anything but regulars. A couple of them had the cocked-head posture of cheap neural overlays. The others played games on the slick touchscreen bar, or tapped on the Bracertabs strapped to their arms, the latest tech fad. Nobody talking to anybody.

Down at the other end, two blond women stood facing the Bruce holo, singing along and swaying. He pointed in their general direction, and one giggled and clutched her friend's arm as if he had singled her out personally. Two guys sat on stools near the stage, one playing air drums, the other watching the women. The women only had eyes for Bruce.

I got where they were coming from. I knew people who didn't like his voice or his songs, but I didn't know anybody, especially any musician, who couldn't appreciate his stage presence. Even here, even now, knowing decades separated me from the night this had been recorded, and decades separated the young man who had first written the song from the older man who sang it, even from across a scuzzy too-bright barroom, drinking pisswater beer with strangers and my own smelly band, I believed him when he sang that she was the one. I hated the StageHolo company even more for the fact I was enjoying it.

Somebody slid into the booth next to me. I turned, expecting one of my bandmates, but a stranger had sat down, closer than I cared for.

"Passing through?" he asked, looking at me with intense, bloodshot eyes. He brushed a thick sweep of hair from his forehead, a style I could only assume he had stuck with through the decades since it had been popular. He had dimples and a smile that had clearly been his greatest asset in his youth. He probably hadn't quite realized drinking had caught up with him, that he was puffy and red-nosed. Or that he slurred a bit, even on those two words.

"Passing through." I gave him a brief "not interested" smile and turned my whole body back toward the stage.

"Kind of unusual for somebody to pass through here, let alone bother to stop. What attracted you?" His use of the word "attracted" was pointed.

If he put an arm around me, I'd have to slug him. I shifted a few inches, trying to put distance between us, and emphasized my next word. "We wanted a drink. We've been driving a while."

His disappointment was evident. "Boyfriend? Husband?"

I nodded at the bar, letting him pick whichever he thought looked more like he might be with me, and whichever label he wanted to apply. It amused me either way, since I couldn't imagine being with either of them. Not at the beginning, and especially not after having spent all this time in the van with them.

Then I wondered why I was playing games at all. I turned to look at him. "We're a band."

"No kidding! I used to have a band." A reassessment of the situation flashed across his face. A new smile, more collegial. The change in his whole demeanor prompted me to give him a little more attention.

"No kidding?"

"Yeah. Mostly we played here. Before the insurance rates rose and Stage-Holo convinced Maggie she'd save money with holos of famous bands."

"Did she? Save money?"

He sighed. "Probably. Holos don't drink, and holos don't dent the mics or spill beers into the PA. And people will stay and drink for hours if the right bands are playing."

"Do you still play for fun? Your band?"

He shrugged. "We did for a while. We even got a spot at the very last State Fair. And after that, every once in a while we'd play a barbecue in somebody's backyard. But it's hard to keep it up when you've got nothing to aim for. Playing here once a week was a decent enough goal, but who would want to hear me sing covers when you can have the real thing?"

He pointed his beer at one of the women by the stage. "That's my ex-wife, by the way."

"I'm sorry?"

"It's okay." He took a swig of beer. "That's when Polly left me. Said it wasn't cause the band was done, but I think it was related. She said I didn't seem interested in anything at all after that."

He had turned his attention down to his drink, but now he looked at me again. "How about you? I guess there are still places out there to play?"

"A few," I said. "Mostly in the cities. There's a lot of turnover, too. So we can have a great relationship with a place and then we'll call back and they'll be gone without a trace."

"And there's enough money in it to live on?"

There are people who ask that question in an obnoxious, disbelieving way, and I tend to tell them, "We're here, aren't we?" but this guy was nostalgic enough that I answered him honestly. Maybe I could help him see there was no glamor left for people like us.

"I used to get some royalty checks from an old song, which covered insurance and repairs for the van, but they've gotten smaller and smaller since BMI v. StageHolo. We make enough to stay on the road, eat really terribly, have a beer now and again. Not enough to save. Not enough to stop, ever. Not that we want to stop, so it's okay."

"You never come off the road? Do you live somewhere?"

"The van's registered at my parents' place in Maryland, and I crash there when I need a break. But that isn't often."

"And your band?"

"My bassist and I have been playing together for a long time, and he's got places he stays. We replace a drummer occasionally. This one's been with us for a year, and the two of them are into each other, so if they don't fall out it might last a while."

He nodded. The wolfishness was gone, replaced by something more wistful. He held out his beer. "To music."

"To live music." My can clinked his.

Somebody shouted over by the bar, and we both twisted round to see what had happened. The air-drum player had wandered over—Max Weinberg was on break too—and he and Jacky were squaring off over something. Jacky's blue lips glowed from twenty feet away.

"Nothing good ever comes of blue drinks," I said to my new friend.

He nodded. "You're gonna want to get your friend out of here. That's the owner behind the bar. If your guy breaks anything, she'll have the cops here in two seconds flat."

"Crap. Thanks."

Blue liquid pooled around and on Jacky, a tray of overturned plastic shot glasses behind him. At least they weren't glass, and at least he hadn't damaged the fancy bar top. I dug a twenty from the thin wad in my pocket, hoping it was enough.

"You're fake-drumming to a fake band," Jacky was saying. "And you're not even good at it. If you went to your crash cymbal that much with the real Bruce, he'd fire you in two seconds."

"Who the hell cares? Did I ask you to critique my drumming?"

"No, but if you did, I'd tell you you're behind on the kick, too. My two year old niece keeps a better beat than you do."

The other guy's face reddened, and I saw him clench a fist. Silva had an arm across Jacky's chest by then, propelling him toward the door. We made eye contact, and he nodded.

I tossed my twenty on a dry spot on the bar, still hoping for a quick getaway.

"We don't take cash," said the owner, holding my bill by the corner like it was a dead rat.

Dammit. I squared my shoulders. "You're legally required to accept US currency."

"Maybe true in the US of A, but this is the US of Starker's, and I only accept Superwally credit. And your blue buddy there owes a lot more than this anyway for those spilled drinks." She had her hand below the bar. I had no clue whether she was going for a phone or a baseball bat or a gun; nothing good could come of any of those options.

I snatched the bill back, mind racing. Silva kept a credit transfer account; that wouldn't be any help, since he was already out the door. I avoided credit and devices in general, which usually held me in good stead, but I didn't think the label "Non-comm" would win me any friends here. Jacky rarely paid for anything, so I had no clue whether he had been paying cash or credit up until then.

"I've got them, Maggie." My new friend from the booth stepped up beside me, waving his phone.

He turned to me. "Go on. I've got this."

Maggie's hand came out from under the bar. She pulled a phone from behind the cash register to do the credit transfer, which meant whatever she had reached for down below probably wouldn't have been good for my health.

"Keep playing," he called after me.

Jacky was unremorseful. "He started it. Called us disease vectors. I told him to stay right where he was and the whole world would go on turning 'cause it doesn't even know he exists. Besides, if he can't air drum, he should just air guitar like everybody else."

Silva laughed. "You should have pretended to cough. He probably would have pissed himself."

He and Silva sprawled in the back together as I peeled out of the parking lot.

"Not funny. I don't care who started it. No fights. I mean it. Do you think I can afford to bail you out? How are we supposed to play tomorrow if our drummer's in jail? And what if they skip the jail part and shoot you? It's happened before."

"Sorry, Mom," Jacky said.

"Not funny," I repeated. "If you ever call me 'Mom' again I'm leaving you on the side of the road. And I'm not a Chauffeur. Somebody come up here to keep me company."

Silva climbed across the bed and bags and up to the passenger seat. He flipped on the police scanner, then turned it off after a few minutes of silence; nobody had put out any APBs on a van full of bill-ducking freaks. I drove speed limit plus five, same as the occasional Chauffeurs we passed ferrying their passengers home. Shortcutting onto the highway to leave the area entirely would've been my preference, but Daisy would have triggered the ramp sensors in two seconds flat; we hadn't been allowed on an interstate in five years.

After about twenty miles, my fear that we were going to get chased down finally dissipated and my heartbeat returned to acceptable rhythms. We pulled into an office park that didn't look patrolled.

"Your turn for the bed, Luce?" Jacky asked. Trying to make amends, maybe.

"You guys can have it if I can find my sleeping bag. It's actually pretty nice out, and then I don't have to smell whatever that blue crap is on your clothes."

"You have a sleeping bag?"

"Of course I do. I just used it in . . ." Actually, I couldn't think of when I had used it last. It took a few minutes of rummaging to find it in the storage space under the bed, behind Silva's garage sale box of pulp novels. I spread it on the ground just in front of the van. The temperature was perfect and the sky was full of stars. Hopefully there weren't any coyotes around.

I slept three or four hours before my body started to remind me why I didn't sleep outside more often. I got up to pee and stretch. When I opened the door, I was hit by an even deeper grease smell than usual. It almost drowned out the funk of two guys farting, four days unwashed. Also the chemical-alcohol-blue scent Jacky wore all over his clothes.

Leaning over the driver's seat, I dug in the center console for my silver pen and the bound atlas I used as a road bible. The stars were bright enough to let me see the pages without a flashlight. The atlas was about fifteen years out of date, but my notes kept it useable. The town we had called Nowhere was actually named Rackwood, which sounded more like a tree disease than a town to me. A glittery asterisk went next to Rackwood, and in the margin "China Grove—Mike Sun—grease AND food." I drew an X over the location of Starker's, which wouldn't get our repeat business.

I crawled inside around dawn, feeling every bone in my body, and reclined the passenger seat. Nobody knocked on the van to tell us to move on, so we slept until the sun started baking us. Jacky reached forward to offer up his last leftovers from the night before. I sniffed the container and handed it back to him. He shrugged and dove in with his fingers, chopsticks having disappeared into the detritus surrounding him. After a little fishing around, I found my dinner and sent that his way as well.

Silva climbed into the driver's seat. I didn't usually relinquish the wheel; I genuinely loved doing all the driving myself. I liked the control, liked to listen to Daisy's steady engine and the thrum of the road. He knew that, and didn't ask except when he really felt the urge, which meant that when he did ask, I moved over. Jacky had never offered once, content to read and listen to music in his back seat cocoon. Another reason he fit in well.

Silva driving meant I got a chance to look around; it wasn't often that we took a road I hadn't been down before. I couldn't even remember how we had wound up choosing this route the previous day. We passed shuttered diners and liquor stores, the ghost town that might have been a main street at one time.

"Where is everybody?" Jacky asked.

I twisted around to see if he was joking. "Have you looked out the window once this whole year? Is this the first time you're noticing?"

"I usually sleep through this part of the country. It's boring."

"There is no everybody," Silva said. "A few farmers, a Superwally that employs everyone else within an hour's drive."

I peered at my atlas. "I've got a distribution center drawn in about forty miles back and ten miles north, on the road we usually take. That probably employs anybody not working for the company store." There wasn't really any reason for me to draw that kind of place onto my maps, but I liked making them more complete. They had layers in some places, stores and factories that had come and gone and come and gone again.

Most backroad towns looked like this, these days. At best a fast food place, a feed store, maybe a run down looking grocery or a health clinic, and not much else. There'd be a Superwally somewhere between towns, as Silva had said, luring everyone even farther from center or anything resembling community. Town after town, we saw the same thing. And of course most people didn't see anything at all, puttering along on the self-driving highways, watching movies instead of looking out the windows, getting from point A to point B without stopping in between.

We weren't exactly doing our part either. It's not like we had contributed to the local economy. We took free dinner, free fuel. We contributed in other ways, but not in this town or the others we'd passed through the night before.

Maybe someday someone here would book us and we'd come back, but until then we were passing through. Goodbye, Rackwood, Indiana.

"Next town has the World's Largest Salt Shaker." I could hear the capital letters in Jacky's voice. He liked to download tourist brochures. I approved of that hobby, the way I approved of supporting anything to make a place less generic. Sometimes we even got to stop at some of the sights, when we could afford it and we weren't in a hurry. Neither of which was the case today.

"Another time," Silva said. "We slept later than we should have."

"I think we're missing out."

I twisted around to look at Jacky. He flopped across the bed, waving his phone like a look at the world's largest salt shaker might make us change our minds. "It's a choice between showers and salt shaker. You decide."

He stuffed his phone into his pocket with a sigh. Showers trumped.

About an hour outside Columbus, we stopped at a by-the-hour motel already starred in my atlas, and rented an hour for the glory of running water. The clerk took my cash without comment.

I let the guys go first, so I wouldn't have to smell them again after I was clean. The shower itself was nothing to write home about. The metal booth kind, no tub, nonexistent water pressure, seven minute shutoff; better than nothing. Afterward, I pulled a white towel from the previous hotel from my backpack to leave in the room, and stuffed one of the near-identical clean ones in my bag. The one I took might have been one I had left the last time through. Nobody ever got shorted a towel, and it saved me a lot of time in Laundromats. I couldn't even remember who had taught me that trick, but I'd been doing it for decades.

We still had to get back in our giant grease trap, of course, now in our cleanish gig clothes. I opened all the windows and turned on the fan full blast, hoping to keep the shower scent for as long as possible. I could vaguely hear Jacky calling out visitor highlights for Columbus from the back, but the noise stole the meat of whatever he was saying. I stuck my arm outside and planed my hand against the wind.

I didn't intend to fall asleep, but I woke to Silva shouting "Whoa! Happy birthday, Daisy!" and hooting the horn. I leaned over to see the numbers clicking over from 99 999.

Jacky threw himself forward to snap a picture of the odometer as it hit all zeroes. "Whoa! What birthday is this?"

I considered. Daisy only had a five-digit odometer, so she got a fresh start every hundred thousand miles. "Eight, I think?"

Silva grinned. "Try again. My count says nine."

"Nine? I thought we passed seven on the way out of Seattle two years ago."

"That was five years ago. Eight in Asheville. I don't remember when."

"Huh. You're probably right. We should throw her a party at a million." I gave her dashboard a hard pat, like the flank of a horse. "Good job, old girl. That's amazing."

"Totally," said Jacky. "And can we play 'Our Lady of the Open Road' tonight? In Daisy's honor? I love that song. I don't know why we don't play it more often." He started playing the opening with his hands on the back of my seat.

"I'm on board," Silva agreed. "Maybe instead of 'Manifest Independence?' That one could use a rest."

"'Manifest Independence' stays," I said. "Try again."

"'Outbreak'?"

"Deal."

Jacky retreated to make the changes to the set list.

Our destination was deep in the heart of the city. Highways would have gotten us there in no time, not that we had that option. We drove along the river, then east past the decaying convention center.

We hadn't played this particular space before, but we'd played others, mostly in this same neighborhood of abandoned warehouses. Most closed up pretty quickly, or moved when they got shut down, so even if we played for the same crowd, we rarely played the same building twice.

This one, The Chain, sounded like it had a chance at longevity. It was a bike co-op by day, venue by night. Cities liked bike co-ops. With the right people running the place, maybe somebody who knew how to write grants and dress in business drag and shake a hand or two, a bike co-op could be part of the city plan. Not that I had any business telling anyone to sell themselves out for a few months of forced legitimacy.

Our timing was perfect. The afternoon bike repair class had just finished, so the little stage area was more or less clear. Better yet, they'd ordered pizza. Jacky had braved the Chinese leftovers, but Silva and I hadn't eaten yet. It took every ounce of my self-restraint to help haul in the instruments before partaking. I sent a silent prayer up to the pizza gods there'd still be some left for us once all our gear was inside.

I made three trips—guitars and gear, amp, swag to sell—then loaded up a paper plate with three pizza slices. I was entirely capable of eating all three, but I'd share with the guys if they didn't get their gear in before the food was gone. Not ideal dinner before singing, anyway; maybe the grease would trump the dairy as a throat coating. I sat on my amp and ate the first piece, watching Jacky and Silva bring in the drums, feeling only a little guilty. I had done my share, even if I hadn't helped anyone else.

The bike class stuck around. We chatted with a few. Emma, Rudy, Dijuan, Carter, Marin—there were more but I lost track of names after that. I gave those five the most attention in any case, since Rudy had been the one to book us, and Emma ran the programming for the bike co-op. We were there because of them. We talked politics and music and bikes. I was grateful not to have to explain myself again. These were our people. They treated us like we were coming home, not passing through.

More audience gradually trickled in, a good crowd for a Wednesday night. A mix of young and old, in varying degrees of punk trappings, according to their generation and inclination. Here and there, some more straight-laced, though they were as punk as anyone, in the truest spirit of the word, for having shown up at this space at all. Punk as a genre didn't look or sound like it used to, in any case; it had scattered to the wind, leaving a loose grouping of bands whose main commonality was a desire to create live music for live audiences.

The first band began to play, an all woman four piece called Moby K. Dick. They were young enough to be my kids, which meant young enough they had never known any scene but this one. The bassist played from a sporty little wheelchair, her back to the audience, like she was having a one-on-one conversation with the drummer's high hat. At first, I thought she was shy, but I gradually realized she was just really into the music. The drummer doubled as singer, hiding behind a curtain of dreadlocks that lifted and dropped back onto her face with every beat. They played something that sounded like sea chanties done double time and double volume, but the lyrics were all about whales and dolphins taking revenge on people. It was pretty fantastic.

I gave all the bands we played with a chance to win me over. They were the only live music we ever got to hear, being on the road full time. The few friends we still had doing the same circuit were playing the same nights as us in other towns, rotating through; the others were doing StageHolo and we didn't talk much anymore. It used to be we'd sometimes even wind up in the same cities on the same night, so we'd miss each other and split the audience. That didn't happen much anymore with so few places to play.

Moby K. Dick earned my full attention, but the second band lost me pretty quickly. They all played adapted console-game instruments except the drummer. No strings, all buttons, all programmed to trigger samples. I'd seen bands like that before that were decent; this one was not my thing.

The women from the first band were hanging out by the drink cooler, so I made my way back there. I thrust my hand into the ice and came out with a water bottle. Most venues like this one were alcohol-free and all ages. There was probably a secret beer cooler hidden somewhere, but I wasn't in the mood to find it.

"I liked your stuff," I said to the bassist. Up close, she looked slightly older than she had on stage. Mid-twenties, probably. "My name's Luce."

She grinned. "I know! I mean, I'm Truly. And yes, that's really my name. Nice to meet you. And really? You liked it? That's so cool! We begged to be on this bill with you. I've been listening to Cassis Fire my whole life. I've got 'Manifest Independence' written on my wall at home. It's my mantra."

I winced but held steady under the barrage and the age implication. She continued. "My parents have all your music. They like the stuff with Marcia Januarie on drums best, when you had the second guitarist, but I think your current lineup is more streamlined."

"Thanks." I waited for her to point her parents out in the room, and for them to be younger than me. When she thankfully didn't volunteer that information, I asked, "Do you guys have anything recorded?"

"We've been recording our shows, but mostly we just want to play. You could take us on the road with you, if you wanted. Opening act."

She said the last bit jokingly, but I was pretty sure the request was real, so I treated it that way. "We used to be able to, but not these days. It's hard enough to keep ourselves fed and moving to the next gig. I'm happy to give you advice, though. Have you seen our van?"

Her eyes widened. She was kind of adorable in her enthusiasm. Part of me considered making a pass at her, but we only had a few minutes before I had to be onstage, and I didn't want to confuse things. Sometimes I hated being the responsible one.

"It's right outside. They'll find me when it's our turn to play. Come on."

The crowd parted for her wheelchair as we made our way through. I held the door for her and she navigated the tiny rise in the doorframe with practiced ease.

"We call her Daisy," I said, introducing Truly to the van. I searched my pockets for the keys and realized Silva had them. So much for that idea. "She's a fifteen seater, but we took out the middle seats for a bed and the back to make a cage for the drums and stuff so they don't kill us if we stop short."

"What's the mpg?" she asked. I saw her gears spinning as she tried to figure out logistics. I liked her focus. She was starting to remind me of me, though, which was the turnoff I needed.

I beckoned her to the hood, which popped by latch, no keys necessary. "That's the best part of all."

She locked her chair and pushed herself up to lean against Daisy's frame. At my look, she explained, "I don't need it all the time, but playing usually makes me pretty tired. And I don't like getting pushed around in crowds."

"Oh, that's cool," I said. "And if you buy a van of your own, that's one less conversion you'll have to make, if you can climb in without a lift. I had been trying to figure out if you'd have room for four people and gear and a chair lift."

"Nah, you can go back to the part where we wonder how I'm going to afford a van, straight up. Right now we just borrow my sister's family Chauffeur. It's just barely big enough for all our gear, but the mileage is crap and there's no room for clothes or swag or anything."

"Well, if you can find a way to pay for an old van like Daisy, the beauty of running on fry oil is the money you'll save on fuel. As long as you like takeout food, you get used to the smell . . ."

Silva stuck his head out the door, then came over to us. I made introductions. He unlocked the van; I saw Truly wince when the smell hit her. He reached under the bed, back toward the wheel well, and emerged with a bottle of whiskey in hand. Took a long swig, and passed it to me. I had a smaller sip, just enough to feel the burn in my throat, the lazy singer's warm-up.

Truly followed my lead. "Promise you'll give me pointers if I manage to get a van?"

I promised. The kid wasn't just like me; she practically was me, with the misfortune to have been born twenty years too late to possibly make it work.

I made Silva tap phones with her. "I would do it myself, but . . ."

"I know," she said. "I'd be Non-comm if I could, but my parents won't let me. Emergencies and all that."

Did we play extra well, or did it just feel like it? Moby K. Dick had helped; it was always nice to be reminded that what you did mattered. I had a mental buzz even with only a sip of whiskey, the combination of music and possibilities and an enthusiastic crowd eager to take whatever we gave them.

On a good night like this, when we locked in with each other, it was like I was a time traveler for an hour. Every night we'd ever played a song overlapped with every night we'd ever play it again, even though I was fully in the moment. My fingers made shapes, ran steel strings over magnets, ran signals through wires to the amplifier behind me, which blasted those shapes back over me in waves. Glorious, cathartic, bone-deep noise.

On stage, I forgot how long I'd been doing this. I could still be the kid playing in her parents' basement, or the young woman with the hit single and the major label, the one called the next Joan Jett, the second coming of riot grrl, not that I wanted to be the young version of me anymore. I had to work to remember that if I slid on my knees I might not get up again. I was a better guitar player now, a better singer, a better songwriter. I had years of righteous rage to channel. When I talked, I sometimes felt like a pissed off grump, stuck in the past. Given time to express it all in music, I came across better.

Moby K. Dick pushed through to the front when we played "Manifest Independence," singing along at the top of their lungs. They must have been babies when I released that song, but it might as well have been written for them. It was as true for them as it had been for me.

That was what the young punks and the old punks all responded to; they knew I believed what I was singing. We all shared the same indignation that we were losing everything that made us distinct, that nothing special happened anymore, that the new world replacing the old one wasn't nearly as good, that everyone was hungry and everything was broken and that we'd fix it if we could find the right tools. My job was to give it all a voice. Add to that the sweet old-school crunch of my Les Paul played through Marshall tubes, Silva's sinuous bass lines, Jacky's tricky beats, and we could be the best live band you ever heard. Made sweeter by the fact that you had to be there to get the full effect.

We didn't have rehearsed moves or light shows or spotlights to hit like the StageHolos, but we knew how to play it up for the crowd. To make it seem like we were playing for one person, and playing for all of them, and playing just for them, because this night was different and would only ever happen once. People danced and pogoed and leaned into the music. A few of the dancers had ultraviolet tattoos, which always looked pretty awesome from my vantage point, a secret performance for the performers. I nudged Silva to look at one of them, a glowing phoenix spread wingtip to wingtip across a dancer's bare shoulders and arms.

A couple of tiny screens also lit the audience: people recording us with Bracertabs, arms held aloft. I was fine with that. Everyone at the show knew how it felt to be there; they'd come back, as long as there were places for us to play. The only market for a non-Holo recording was other people like this audience, and it would only inspire them to come out again the next time.

Toward the end of the set, I dedicated "Our Lady of the Open Road" to Daisy. At the tail of the last chorus, Jacky rolled through his toms in a way he never had before, cracking the song open wide, making it clear he wasn't coming in for a landing where he was supposed to. Silva and I exchanged glances, a wordless "this is going to be interesting," then followed Jacky's lead. The only way to do that was to make it bigger than usual, keep it going, make it a monster. I punched my gain pedal and turned to my amp to ride the feedback. Our lady of the open road, get me through another night.

Through some miracle of communication we managed to end the song together, clean enough that it sounded planned. I'd kill Jacky later, but at that moment I loved him. The crowd screamed.

I wiped the sweat out of my eyes with my shoulder. "We've got one more for you. Thanks so much for being here tonight." I hoped "Better to Laugh" wouldn't sound like an afterthought.

That was when the power went out.

"Police!" somebody shouted. The crowd began to push toward the door.

"Not the police!" someone else yelled. "Just a blackout."

"Just a blackout!" I repeated into the mic as if it were still on, then louder into the front row, hoping they were still listening to me. "Pass it on."

The message rippled through the audience. A tense moment passed with everyone listening for sirens, ready to scatter. Then they began to debate whether the blackout was the city or the building, whether the power bill had been paid, whether it was a plot to shut the place down.

Emma pushed her way through the crowd to talk to us. "They shut this neighborhood's power down whenever the circuits overload uptown. We're trying to get somebody to bring it up in city council. I'm so sorry."

I leaned in to give her a sweaty hug. "Don't worry about it. It happens."

We waited, hoping for the rock gods to smile upon us. The room started to heat up, and somebody propped the outside doors, which cooled things down slightly. After twenty minutes, we put our instruments down. At least we had made it through most of our set. I had no doubt the collective would pay us, and no concern people would say they hadn't gotten their money's worth. I dug the hotel towel out of my backpack to wipe my dripping face.

A few people made their way over to talk to us and buy t-shirts and patches and even LPs and download codes, even though you could find most of our songs free online. That was part of the beauty of these kids. They were all broke as hell, but they still wanted to support us, even if it was just a patch or a pin or a password most of them were capable of hacking in two seconds flat. And they all believed in cash, bless them. We used the light of their phone screens to make change.

The girls from Moby K. Dick all bought t-shirts. Truly bought an LP as well—it figured she was into vinyl—and I signed it "To my favorite new band, good luck." She wheeled out with her band, no parents in sight. I wondered if they'd decided they were too old for live music, then chided myself. I couldn't have it both ways, mad that they were probably my age and mad that they weren't there. Besides, they might have just left separately from their kid. I knew I must be tired if I was getting hung up on something like that.

"You look like you need some water," somebody said to me in the darkness. A bottle pressed into my hand, damp with condensation.

"Thanks," I said. "Though I don't know how you can say I look like anything with the lights out."

At that moment, the overheads hummed on again. I had left my guitar leaning face down on my amp, and it started to build up a squeal of feedback. I tossed the water back, wiped my hands on my pants, and slammed the standby switch. The squeal trailed away.

"Sorry, you were saying?" I asked, returning to the stranger, who still stood with bottle in hand. I took it from her again. I thought maybe I'd know her in the light, but she didn't look familiar. Mid-thirties, maybe, tall and tan, with a blandly friendly face, toned arms, Bracertab strapped to one forearm. She wore a Magnificent Beefeaters T-shirt with the sleeves cut off. We used to play shows with them, before they got big.

"I was saying you looked like you were thirsty, by which I mean you looked like that before the lights went out, so I guessed you probably still looked like that after."

"Oh."

"Anyway, I wanted to say good show. One of your best I've seen."

"Have you seen a lot?" It was a bit of a rude question, with an implication I didn't recognize her. Bad for business. Everybody should believe they were an integral part of the experience. But really, I didn't think I'd seen her before, and it wasn't the worst question, unless the answer was she'd been following us for the last six months.

"I've been following you for the last six months," she said. "But mostly live audience uploads. I was at your last Columbus show, though, and up in Rochester."

Rochester had been a huge warehouse. I didn't feel as bad.

"Thanks for coming. And, uh, for the water." I tried to redeem myself.

"My pleasure," she said. "I really like your sound. Nikki Kellerman."

She held her arm out in the universal 'tap to exchange virtual business cards' gesture.

"Sorry, I'm Non-comm," I said.

She looked surprised, but I couldn't tell if it was surprise that I was Non-comm, or that she didn't know the term. The latter didn't seem likely. I'd have said a third of the audience at our shows these days were people who had given up their devices and all the corporate tracking that went along with them.

She unstrapped the tablet, peeled a thin wallet off her damp arm, and drew a paper business card from inside it.

I read it out loud. "Nikki Kellerman, A & R, StageHolo Productions." I handed it back to her.

"Hear me out," she said.

"Okay, Artists & Repertoire. You can talk at me while I pack up."

I opened the swag tub and started piling the t-shirts back into it. Usually we took the time to separate them by size so they'd be right the next time, but now I tossed them in, hoping to get away as soon as possible.

"As you probably know, we've been doing very well with getting Stage-Holo into venues across the country. Bringing live music into places that previously didn't have it."

"There are about seven things wrong with that statement," I said without looking up.

She continued as if I hadn't spoken. "Our biggest selling acts are arena rock, pop, rap, and Spanish pop. We now reach nine in ten bars and clubs. One in four with StageHolo AtHome."

"You can stop the presentation there. Don't you dare talk to me about StageHolo AtHome." My voice rose. Silva stood in the corner chatting with some bike kids, but I saw him throw a worried look my way. "'All the excitement of live entertainment without leaving your living room.' 'Stay AtHome with John Legend tonight.'"

I clapped the lid onto the swag box and carried it to the door. When I went to pack up my stage gear, she followed.

"I think you're not understanding the potential, Luce. We're looking to diversify, to reach new audiences: punk, folk, metal, musical theater." She listed a few more genres they hadn't completely destroyed yet.

I would punch her soon. I was not a violent person, but I knew for a fact I would punch her soon. "You're standing in front of me, asking me to help ruin my livelihood."

"No! Not ruin it. I'm inviting you to a better life. You'd still play shows. You'd still have audiences."

"Audiences of extras paid to be there? Audiences in your studios?" I asked through clenched teeth.

"Yes and no. We can set up at your shows, but that's harder. Not a problem in an arena setting, but I think you'd find the 3D array distracting in a place like this. We'd book you some theaters, arenas. Fill in the crowds if we needed to. You could still do this in between if you wanted, but . . ." she shrugged to indicate she couldn't see why I would want.

"Hey, Luce. A little help over here?" I looked down to see my hands throttling my mic instead of putting it back in its box. Looked up at Silva struggling to get his bass amp on the dolly, like he didn't do it on his own every night of the week. Clearly an offer of rescue.

"Gotta go," I said to the devil's A & R person. "Have your people call my people."

Turning the bass rig into a two-person job took all of our acting skills. We walked to the door in exaggerated slow motion. Lifting it into the van genuinely did take two, but usually my back and knee ruled me out. I gritted my teeth and hoisted.

"What was that about?" Silva asked, shutting Daisy's back hatch and leaning against it. "You looked like you were going to tear that woman's throat out with your teeth."

"StageHolo! Can you believe the nerve? Coming here, trying to lure us to the dark side?"

"The nerve," he echoed, shaking his head, but giving me a funny look. He swiped an arm across his sweaty forehead, then pushed off from the van.

I followed him back inside. Nikki Kellerman was still there.

"Luce, I think you're not seeing everything I have to offer."

"Haven't you left yet? That was a pretty broad hint."

"Look around." She gestured at the near-empty room.

I stared straight at her. I wasn't dignifying her with any response.

"Luce, I know you had a good crowd tonight, but are there people who aren't showing up anymore? Look where you are. Public transit doesn't run into this neighborhood anymore. You're playing for people who squat in warehouses within a few blocks, and then people who can afford bikes or Chauffeurs."

"Most people can scrounge a bicycle," I said. "I've never heard a complaint about that."

"You're playing for the people who can bike, then. That bassist from the first band, could she have gotten here without a car?"

For the first time, I felt like she was saying something worth hearing. I sat down on my amp.

"You're playing for this little subset of city punks for whom this is a calling. And after that you're playing for the handful of people who can afford a night out and still think of themselves as revolutionary. And that's fine. That's a noble thing. But what about everybody else? Parents who can't afford a sitter? Teens who are too young to make it here on their own, or who don't have a way into the city? There are plenty of people who love music and deserve to hear your message. They just aren't fortunate enough to live where you're playing. Wouldn't you like to reach them too?"

Dammit, dammit, dammit, she had a decent point. I thought about the guy who had paid for our drinks the night before, and the church van guy from outside the Chinese restaurant, and Truly if she didn't have a sister with a car.

She touched her own back. "I've seen you after a few shows now, too. You're amazing when you play, but when you step off, I can see what it takes. You're tired. What happens if you get sick, or if your back goes out completely?"

"I've always gotten by," I said, but not with the same vehemence as a minute before.

"I'm just saying you don't have to get by. You can still do these shows, but you won't have to do as many. Let us help you out. I can get you a massage therapist or a chiropractor or a self-driving van."

I started to protest, but she held up her hands in a placating gesture. "Sorry—I know you've said you love your van. No offense meant. I'm not chasing you because my boss wants me to. I'm chasing you because I've seen you play. You make great music. You reach people. That's what we want."

She put her card on the amp next to me, and walked out the front of the club. I watched her go.

"Hey Luce," Jacky called to me. I headed his way, slowly. My back had renewed its protest.

"What's up?" I asked.

He gestured at the bike kids surrounding him, Emma and Rudy and some more whose names I had forgotten. Marina? Marin. I smiled. I should have spent more time with them, since they were the ones who had brought us in.

"Our generous hosts have offered us a place to stay nearby. I said I thought it was a good idea, but you're the boss."

They all looked at me, waiting. I hadn't seen the money from the night yet. It would probably be pretty good, since this kind of place didn't take a cut for themselves. They were in it for the music. And for the chance to spend some time with us, which I was in a position to provide.

"That sounds great," I said. "Anything is better than another night in the van." We might be able to afford a hotel, or save the hotel splurge for the next night, in—I mentally checked the roadmap—Pittsburgh.

With the bike kids' help, we made quick work of the remaining gear. Waited a little longer while Rudy counted money and handed it over to me with no small amount of pride.

"Thank you," I said, and meant it. It had been a really good show, and the money was actually better than expected. "We'll come back here anytime."

Just to prove it, I pulled my date book from my backpack. He called Emma over, and together we penned in a return engagement in three months. I was glad to work with people so competent; there was a good chance they'd still be there in three months.

We ended up at a diner, van parked in front, bikes chained to the fence behind it, an unruly herd.

I was so tired the menu didn't look like English; then I realized I was looking at the Spanish side.

"Is there a fridge at the place we're staying?" Silva asked.

Smart guy. Emma nodded. Silva and Jacky and I immediately ordered variations on an omelet theme, without looking further at either side of the menu. The beauty of omelets: you ate all the toast and potatoes, wrapped the rest, and the eggs would still taste fine the next day. Two meals in one, maybe three, and we hadn't had to hit a dumpster in two full days.

Our hosts were a riot. I barely kept my eyes open—at least twice I realized they weren't—but Emma talked about Columbus politics and bikes and greenspaces with a combination of humor and enthusiasm that made me glad for the millionth time for the kind of places we played, even if I didn't quite keep up my end of the conversation. Nikki Kellerman could flush herself down the toilet. I wouldn't trade these kids for anything.

Until we saw the place on offer. After the lovely meal, after following their bikes at bike speed through unknown and unknowable dark neighborhoods, Silva pulled the van up. The last portion had involved turning off the road along two long ruts in grass grown over a paved drive. I had tried to follow in my atlas on the city inset, but gave up when the streets didn't match.

"Dude," I said, opening my eyes. "What is that?"

We all stared upward. At first glance it looked like an enormous brick plantation house, with peeling white pillars supporting the upper floors. At second, maybe some kind of factory.

"Old barracks," said Jacky, king of local tourist sites. "Those kids got themselves an abandoned fort."

"I wonder if it came with contents included." Silva mimed loading a rifle. "Bike or die."

I laughed.

Jacky leaned into the front seat. "If you tell me I have to haul in my entire kit, I swear to god I'm quitting this band. I'll join the bike militia. Swear to god."

I peered out the windows, but had no sense of location. "Silva?"

"I can sleep in the van if you think I should."

It was a generous offer, given that actual beds were in the cards.

"You don't have to do that," I decided. "We'll take our chances."

I stopped at the back gate for my guitar, in the hopes of having a few minutes to play in the morning. Silva did the same. We shouldered instruments and backpacks, and Jacky took the three Styrofoam boxes with our omelets. The bike kids waited in a cluster by an enormous door. We staggered their way.

"So who has the keys?" Silva asked.

Emma grinned. "Walk this way."

The big door was only for dramatic effect. We went in through a small, unlocked door on the side. It looked haphazardly placed, a late addition to the architecture. A generator hummed just outside the door, powering a refrigerator, where we left our leftovers. I hoped it also powered overhead lights, but the bike kids all drew out halogen flashlights as soon as we had stored the food.

The shadows made everything look ominous and decrepit; I wasn't sure it wouldn't look the same in daylight. Up a crumbling staircase, then a second, to a smaller third floor. Walls on one side, railing on the other, looking down over a central core, all black. Our footsteps echoed through the emptiness. In my tired state, I imagined being told to bed down in the hallway, sleeping with my head pressed to the floor. If they didn't stop soon, I might.

We didn't have to go further. Emma swung open an unmarked door and handed me her flashlight. I panned it over the room. A breeze wafted through broken glass. An open futon took up most of the space, a threadbare couch sagging beneath the window. How those things had made it up to this room without the stairs falling away entirely was a mystery, but I had never been so happy to see furniture in my entire life.

I dropped my shoulder and lowered my guitar to the floor. The bike kids stared at us and we stared back. Oh god, I thought. If they want to hang out more, I'm going to cry.

"This is fantastic," said Silva, the diplomat. "Thank you so much. This is so much better than sleeping in the van."

"Sweet. Hasta mañana!" said Rudy, his spiky head bobbing. They backed out the door, closing it behind them, and creaked off down the hallway.

I sank into the couch. "I'm not moving again," I said.

"Did they say whether they're renting or squatting? Is anybody else getting a jail vibe?" Jacky asked, flopping back onto the futon.

Silva opened the door. "We're not locked in." He looked out into the hallway and then turned back to us. "But, uh, they're gone without a trace. Did either of you catch where the bathroom was?"

I shook my head, or I think I did. They were on their own.

The night wasn't a pleasant one. I woke once to the sound of Silva pissing in a bottle, once to a sound like animals scratching at the door, once to realize there was a spring sticking through the couch and into my thigh. The fourth time, near eight in the morning, I found myself staring at the ceiling at a crack that looked like a rabbit. I turned my head and noticed a cat pan under the futon. Maybe it explained the scratching I had heard earlier.

I rolled over and stood up one vertebra at a time. Other than the spring, it hadn't been a bad couch. My back felt better than the night before. I grabbed my guitar and slipped out the door.

I tried to keep my steps from echoing. With the first daylight streaming in through the jagged windows, I saw exactly how dilapidated the place was, like it had been left to go feral. I crept down to the first floor, past a mural that looked like a battle plan for world domination, all circles and arrows, and another of two bikes in carnal embrace. Three locked doors, then I spotted the fridge and the door out. Beyond this huge building there were several others of similar size, spread across a green campus. Were they all filled with bike kids? It was a pleasant thought. I'd never seen any place like this. I sat down on the ground, my back against the building, in the morning sunshine.

It was nice to be alone with my guitar. The problem with touring constantly was we were always driving, always with people, always playing the same songs we already knew. And when we did have down time, we'd spend it tracking down new gigs, or following up to make sure the next places still existed. The important things like writing new songs fell to last on the list.

This guitar and I, we were old friends. The varnish above her pick guard had worn away where I hit it on the downstroke. Tiny grooves marked where my fingers had indented the frets. She fit my hands perfectly. We never talked anymore.

She was an old Les Paul knockoff, silver cloudburst except where the bare wood showed through. Heavy as anything, the reason why my back hurt so constantly. The hunch of my shoulder as I bent over her was permanent. And of course with no amp she didn't make any sound beyond string jangle. Still, she felt good.

I didn't need to play the songs we played every night, but my fingers have always insisted on playing through the familiar before they can find new patterns. I played some old stuff, songs I loved when I was first teaching myself to play, Frightwig and the Kathleen Battle School and disappear fear, just to play something I could really feel. Then a couple of bars of "She's the One," then what I remembered of a Moby K. Dick whale song. I liked those kids.

When I finally hit my brain's unlock code, it latched onto a twisty little minor descent. The same rhythm as the whale song, but a different progression, a different riff. A tiny theft, the kind all musicians make. There was only so much original to do within twelve notes. Hell, most classic punk was built on a couple of chords. What did Lou Reed say? One chord is fine, two chords is pushing it, three chords you're into jazz?

I knew what I was singing about before I even sang it. That StageHolo offer, and the idea of playing for a paid audience night after night, the good and the bad parts. The funny thing about bargains with the devil was you so rarely heard about people turning him down; maybe sometimes it was worth your soul. I scrambled in my gig bag pocket for a pen and paper. When I came up with only a sharpie, I wrote the lyrics on my arm. The chords would keep. I'd remember them. Would probably remember the lyrics too, but I wasn't chancing it.

Silva stepped out a little while later, wearing only a ratty towel around his waist. "There's a bucket shower out the back!"

"Show me in a sec, but first, check it out." I played him what I had.

His eyes widened. "Be right back."

He returned a moment later wearing jeans, bass in hand. We both had to play hard, and I had to whisper-sing to hear the unplugged electric instruments, but we had something we both liked before long.

"Tonight?" he asked me.

"Maybe . . . depends on how early we get there, I guess. And whether there's an actual soundcheck. Do you remember?"

He shook his head. "Four band lineup, at a warehouse. That's all I remember. But maybe if we leave pretty soon, we can set up early? It's only about three hours, I think."

He showed me where the shower was, and I took advantage of the opportunity. The bike kids appeared with a bag of lumpy apples, and we ate the apples with our omelets, sitting on the floor. Best breakfast in ages. They explained the barracks—the story involved an arts grant and an old school and abandoned buildings and a cat sanctuary and I got lost somewhere along the way, working on my new song in my head.

After breakfast, we made our excuse that we had to get on the road. They walked us back the way we came, around the front.

My smile lasted as long as it took us to round the corner. As long as it took to see Daisy was gone.

"Did you move her, Jacky?" Silva asked.

"You've got the keys, man."

Silva patted his pockets, and came up with the key. We walked closer. Glass.

I stared at the spot, trying to will Daisy back into place. Blink and she'd be back. How had we let this happen? I went through the night in my head. Had I heard glass breaking, or the engine turning over? I didn't think so. How many times had we left her outside while we played or ate or showered or slept? I lay down on the path, away from the glass, and looked up at the morning sky.

The bike kids looked distraught, all talking at once. "This kind of thing never happens." "We were only trying to help."

"It wasn't your fault," I said, after a minute. Then louder, when they didn't stop. "It wasn't your fault." They closed their mouths and looked at me.

I sat up and continued, leaning back on my hands, trying to be the calm one, the adult. "The bad news is we're going to need to call the police. The good news is, you're not squatting, so we don't have to work too hard to explain what we were doing here. The bad news is whoever stole the van can go really far on that tank. The good news is they're probably local and aren't trying to drive to Florida. Probably just kids who've never gotten to drive something that didn't drive itself. They'll abandon her nearby when she runs out of gas." I was trying to make myself feel better as much as them.

"And maybe they hate Chinese food," Jacky said. "Maybe the smell'll make them so hungry they have to stop for Chinese food. We should try all the local Chinese food places first."

Silva had stepped away from the group, already on the phone with the police. I heard snippets, even though his back was turned. License plate. Yes, a van. Yes, out of state plates. No, he didn't own it, but the owner was with him. Yes, we'd wait. Where else did we have to go? Well, Pittsburgh, but it didn't look like we'd be getting there any time soon.

He hung up and dug his hands into his pockets. He didn't turn around or come back to the group. I should probably have gone over to him, but he didn't look like he wanted to talk.

The kids scattered before the police arrived, all but Emma disappearing into the building. Jacky walked off somewhere as well. It occurred to me I didn't really know much of his history for all the time we'd been riding together.

The young policewoman who arrived to take our report was standoffish at first, like we were the criminals. Emma explained the situation. No officer, not squatting, here are the permits. I kept the van registration and insurance in a folder in my backpack, which helped on that end too, so that she came over to our side a little. Just a little.

"Insurance?"

"Of course." I rustled in the same folder, presented the card to her. She looked surprised, and I realized she had expected something electronic. "But only liability and human driver."

Surprised her again. "So the van isn't self-driving?"

"No, ma'am. I've had her—it—for twenty-three years."

"But you didn't convert when the government rebates were offered?"

"No, ma'am. I love driving."

She gave me a funny look.

"Was anything in the van?" she asked.

I sighed and started the list, moving from back to front.

"One drum kit, kind of a hodgepodge of different makes, Ampeg bass rig, Marshall guitar amp, suitcase full of gig clothes. A sleeping bag. A box of novels, maybe fifty of them. Um, all the merchandise: records and t-shirts and stuff to sell . . ." I kept going through all the detritus in my head, discarding the small things: collapsible chopsticks, restaurant menus, pillows, jackets. Those were all replaceable. My thoughts snagged on one thing.

"A road atlas. Rand McNally."

The officer raised her eyebrows. "A what?"

"A road atlas. A book of maps."

"You want me to list that?"

"Well, it's in there. And it's important, to me anyway. It's annotated. All the places we've played, all the places we like to stop and we don't." I tried to hide the hitch in my voice. Don't cry, I told myself. Cry over the van, if you need to. Not over the atlas. You'll make another. It might take years, but it could be done.

It wasn't just the atlas, obviously. Everything we had hadn't been much, and it was suddenly much less. I was down to the cash in my pocket, the date book, the single change of clothes in my backpack, my guitar. How could we possibly rebuild from there? How do you finish a tour without a van? Or amps, or drums?

The officer held out her phone to tap a copy of her report over to me.

"Non-comm," I said. "I'm so sorry."

Silva stepped in for the first time. He hadn't even opened his mouth to help me list stuff, but now he held up his phone. "Send it to me, officer."

She did, with a promise to follow up as soon as she had any leads. Got in her squad car. She had to actually use the wheel and drive herself back down the rutted path; I guessed places like this were why police cars had a manual option. She had probably written us off already, either way.

I turned to Silva, but he had walked off. I followed him down the path toward an old warehouse.

"Stop!" I said, when it was clear he wasn't going to. He turned toward me. I expected him to be as sad as me, but he looked angrier than I had ever seen him, fists clenched and jaw tight.

"Whoa," I said. "Calm down. It'll be okay. We'll figure something out."

"How? How, Luce?"

"They'll find Daisy. Or we'll figure something out."

"Daisy's just the start of it. It's amps and records and t-shirts and everything we own. I don't even have another pair of underwear. Do you?"

I shook my head. "We can buy . . ."

"We can buy underwear at the Superwally. But not all that other stuff. We can't afford it. This is it. We're done. Unless."

"Unless?"

He unclenched his left fist and held out a scrap of paper. I took it from him and flattened it. Nikki Kellerman's business card, which had been on my amp when I last saw it.

"No," I said.

"Hear me out. We have nothing left. Nothing. You know she'd hook us up if we called now and said we'd sign. We'd get it all back. New amps, new merch, new stage clothes. And we wouldn't need a new van if we were doing holo shows. We could take a break for a while."

"Are you serious? You'd stay in one place and do holo shows?" I waited for an answer. He stomped at a piece of glass in the dirt, grinding it with his boot heel. "We've been playing together for twenty years and I wouldn't have guessed you'd ever say yes to that."

"Come off it, Luce. You know I don't object the way you do. You know that, or you'd have run it past me before turning her down. I know we're not a democracy, but you used to give me at least the illusion I had a choice."

I bit my lip. "You're right. I didn't run it past you. And actually, I didn't turn her down in the end. I didn't say yes, but she said some stuff that confused me."

That stopped him short. Neither of us said anything for a minute. I looked around. What a weird place to be having this fight; I always figured it would come, but in the van. I waited for a response, and when none came, I prodded. "So you're saying that's what you want?"

"No! Maybe. I don't know. It doesn't always seem like the worst idea. But now I don't think we have another option. I think I could have kept going the way we were for a while longer, but rebuilding from scratch?" He shook his head, then turned and walked away again. I didn't follow this time.

Back at the building where we had stayed, the bike kids had reappeared, murmuring amongst themselves. Jacky leaned against the front stoop, a few feet from them. I sat down in the grass opposite my drummer.

"What do you think of StageHolo? I mean really?"

He spit on the ground.

"Me too," I agreed. "But given the choice between starting over with nothing, and letting them rebuild us, what would you do? If there weren't any other options."

He ran a hand over his braids. "If there weren't any other options?"

I nodded.

"There are always other options, Luce. I didn't sign up with you to do fake shows in some fake warehouse for fake audiences. I wouldn't stay. And you wouldn't last."

I pulled a handful of grass and tossed it at him.

He repeated himself. "Really. I don't know what you'd do. You wouldn't be you anymore. You'd probably still come across to some people, but you'd have the wrong kind of anger. Anger for yourself, instead of for everybody. You'd be some hologram version of yourself. No substance."

I stared at him.

"People always underestimate the drummer, but I get to sit behind you and watch you every night. Trust me." He laughed, then looked over my shoulder. "I watch you, too, Silva. It goes for you, too."

I didn't know how long Silva had been behind me, but he sat down between us now, grunting as he lowered himself to the ground. He leaned against Jacky and put his grimy glass-dust boots in my lap.

I shoved them off. "That was an old man grunt."

"I'm getting there, old lady, but you'll get there first. Do you have a plan?"

I looked over where the bike kids had congregated. "Hey, guys! Do any of you have a car? Or, you know, know anybody who has a car?"

The bike kids looked horrified, then one—Dijuan?—nodded. "My sister has a Chauffeur."

"Family sized?"

Dijuan's face fell.

Back to the drawing board. Leaning back on my elbows, I thought about all the other bands we could maybe call on, if I knew anybody who had come off the road, who might have a van to sell if Daisy didn't reappear. Maybe, but nobody close enough to loan one tonight. Except . . .

"You're not saying you're out, right?" I asked Silva. "You're not saying StageHolo or nothing? Cause I really can't do it. Maybe someday, on our terms, but I can't do it yet."

He closed his eyes. "I know you can't. But I don't know what else to do."

"I do. At least for tonight."

I told him who to call.

Truly arrived with her sister's family-sized Chauffeur an hour later. We had to meet her up on the road.

"It'll be a tight squeeze, but we'll get there," she said. The third row and all the foot space was packed tight with the Moby K. Dick amps and drums and cables.

"Thank you so much," I said, climbing into what would be the driver's seat if it had a wheel or pedals. It felt strange, but oddly freeing as the car navigated its way from wherever we were toward where we were going.

I was supposed to be upset. But we had a ride to the gig, and gear to play. We'd survive without merch for the time being. Somebody in Pittsburgh would help us find a way to Baltimore if Daisy hadn't been found by then, or back to Columbus to reclaim her.

With enough time to arrange it, the other bands would let us use their drums and amps at most of the shows we had coming up, and in the meantime we still had our guitars and a little bit of cash. We'd roll on, in Daisy or a Chauffeur, or on bikes with guitars strapped to our backs. No StageHolo gig could end this badly; this was the epic, terrible, relentlessness of life on the road. We made music. We were music. We'd roll on. We'd roll on. We'd roll on.

NEBULA AWARD WINNER
BEST NOVELLA

BINTI

NNEDI OKORAFOR

Nnedi Okorafor's books include Lagoon *(a British Science Fiction Association Award finalist for Best Novel),* Who Fears Death *(a World Fantasy Award winner for Best Novel),* Kabu Kabu *(a Publisher's Weekly Best Book for Fall 2013),* Akata Witch *(an Amazon.com Best Book of the Year),* Zahrah the Windseeker *(winner of the Wole Soyinka Prize for African Literature), and* The Shadow Speaker *(a CBS Parallax Award winner). Her latest works include her novel* The Book of Phoenix *(an Arthur C. Clarke Award finalist), her novella* Binti *(winner of a Nebula for Best Novella and finalist for a Hugo and British Science Fiction Association Award) and her children's book* Chicken in the Kitchen *(winner of an Africana Book Award).* Akata Witch 2: Akata Warrior *and* Binti 2: Home *are due out in 2017. Nnedi is an associate professor at the University at Buffalo, New York (SUNY). Learn more at Nnedi.com*
Binti *also won the 2016 Hugo for Best Novella.*

FROM THE AUTHOR

Several things inspired Binti. *The first was the small blue jellyfish that I saw in the Khalid Lagoon in Sharjah, United Arab Emirates. It was the first living jellyfish I'd ever seen in the wild and I felt honored by its presence. It was adorable and I decided to immortalize it by making it an ancestor of a murderous jellyfish-like alien race obsessed with honor and tradition. The United Arab Emirates with its strange blend of the ancient, traditional, and futuristic was the inspiration for the world outside of Binti's small insular village and the cultures her people were embedded within.*

I never planned to write Binti and when I did write it, I had no idea how long it would be. I knew it was a big big story and a big big world. I saw so much. In the fall of 2014, I left my teaching position at Chicago State University to uproot and partially move to Buffalo to start a professorship there. I had never lived outside of the Chicago area. They didn't want me to take the position. But I did. My daughter stayed in Chicago with my mom, which was immensely difficult for me. It was scary. I obsessed about my choices, the consequences, all that could go wrong. I starting writing Binti within the first month I was in Buffalo.

The story came in a rush. It was the first story I wrote that was set in outer space (a place that has always made me feel claustrophobic and unwelcome). Making my character Himba just made sense in too many ways to describe.

I powered up the transporter and said a silent prayer. I had no idea what I was going to do if it didn't work. My transporter was cheap, so even a droplet of moisture, or more likely, a grain of sand, would cause it to short. It was faulty and most of the time I had to restart it over and over before it worked. Please not now, please not now, I thought.

The transporter shivered in the sand and I held my breath. Tiny, flat, and black as a prayer stone, it buzzed softly and then slowly rose from the sand. Finally, it produced the baggage-lifting force. I grinned. Now I could make it to the shuttle. I swiped otjize from my forehead with my index finger and knelt down. Then I touched the finger to the sand, grounding the sweet smelling red clay into it. "Thank you," I whispered. It was a half-mile walk along the dark desert road. With the transporter working, I would make it there on time.

Straightening up, I paused and shut my eyes. Now the weight of my entire life was pressing on my shoulders. I was defying the most traditional part of myself for the first time in my entire life. I was leaving in the dead of night and they had no clue. My nine siblings, all older than me except for my younger sister and brother, would never see this coming. My parents would never imagine I'd do such a thing in a million years. By the time they all realized what I'd done and where I was going, I'd have left the planet. In my absence, my parents would growl to each other that I was to never set foot in their home again. My four aunties and two uncles who lived down the road would shout and gossip among themselves about how I'd scandalized our entire bloodline. I was going to be a pariah.

"Go," I softly whispered to the transporter, stamping my foot. The thin metal rings I wore around each ankle jingled noisily, but I stamped my foot again. Once on, the transporter worked best when I didn't touch it. "Go," I said again, sweat forming on my brow. When nothing moved, I chanced giving the two large suitcases sitting atop the force field a shove. They moved smoothly and I breathed another sigh of relief. At least some luck was on my side.

* * *

Fifteen minutes later I purchased a ticket and boarded the shuttle. The sun was barely beginning to peak over the horizon. As I moved past seated passengers far too aware of the bushy ends of my plaited hair softly slapping people in the face, I cast my eyes to the floor. Our hair is thick and mine has always been very thick. My old auntie liked to call it "ododo" because it grew wild and dense like ododo grass. Just before leaving, I'd rolled my plaited hair with fresh sweet-smelling otjize I'd made specifically for this trip. Who knew what I looked like to these people who didn't know my people so well.

A woman leaned away from me as I passed, her face pinched as if she smelled something foul. "Sorry," I whispered, watching my feet and trying to ignore the stares of almost everyone in the shuttle. Still, I couldn't help glancing around. Two girls who might have been a few years older than me, covered their mouths with hands so pale that they looked untouched by the sun. Everyone looked as if the sun was his or her enemy. I was the only Himba on the shuttle. I quickly found and moved to a seat.

The shuttle was one of the new sleek models that looked like the bullets my teachers used to calculate ballistic coefficients during my A-levels when I was growing up. These ones glided fast over land using a combination of air current, magnetic fields, and exponential energy—an easy craft to build if you had the equipment and the time. It was also a nice vehicle for hot desert terrain where the roads leading out of town were terribly maintained. My people didn't like to leave the homeland. I sat in the back so I could look out the large window.

I could see the lights from my father's astrolabe shop and the sand storm analyzer my brother had built at the top of the Root—that's what we called my parents' big, big house. Six generations of my family had lived there. It was the oldest house in my village, maybe the oldest in the city. It was made of stone and concrete, cool in the night, hot in the day. And it was patched with solar planes and covered with bioluminescent plants that liked to stop glowing just before sunrise. My bedroom was at the top of the house. The shuttle began to move and I stared until I couldn't see it anymore. "What am I doing?" I whispered.

An hour and a half later, the shuttle arrived at the launch port. I was the last off, which was good because the sight of the launch port overwhelmed me so much that all I could do for several moments was stand there. I was wearing a long red skirt, one that was silky like water, a light orange wind-top that was stiff and durable, thin leather sandals, and my anklets. No one around me wore such an outfit. All I saw were light flowing garments and veils; not one woman's ankles were exposed, let alone jingling with steel anklets. I breathed through my mouth and felt my face grow hot.

"Stupid stupid stupid," I whispered. We Himba don't travel. We stay put. Our ancestral land is life; move away from it and you diminish. We even cover our bodies with it. Otjize is red land. Here in the launch port, most were Khoush and a few other non-Himba. Here, I was an outsider; I was outside. "What was I thinking?" I whispered.

I was sixteen years old and had never been beyond my city, let alone near a launch station. I was by myself and I had just left my family. My prospects of marriage had been 100 percent and now they would be zero. No man wanted a woman who'd run away. However, beyond my prospects of normal life being ruined, I had scored so high on the planetary exams in mathematics that the Oomza University had not only admitted me, but promised to pay for whatever I needed in order to attend. No matter what choice I made, I was never going to have a normal life, really.

I looked around and immediately knew what to do next. I walked to the help desk.

*   *   *

The travel security officer scanned my astrolabe, a full deep scan. Dizzy with shock, I shut my eyes and breathed through my mouth to steady myself. Just to leave the planet, I had to give them access to my entire life—me, my family, and all forecasts of my future. I stood there, frozen, hearing my mother's voice in my head. "There is a reason why our people do not go to that university. Oomza Uni wants you for its own gain, Binti. You go to that school and you become its slave." I couldn't help but contemplate the possible truth in her words. I hadn't even gotten there yet and already I'd given them my life. I wanted to ask the officer if he did this for everyone, but I was afraid now that he'd done it. They could do anything to me, at this point. Best not to make trouble.

When the officer handed me my astrolabe, I resisted the urge to snatch it back. He was an old Khoush man, so old that he was privileged to wear the blackest turban and face veil. His shaky hands were so gnarled and arthritic that he nearly dropped my astrolabe. He was bent like a dying palm tree and when he'd said, "You have never traveled; I must do a full scan. Remain where you are," his voice was drier than the red desert outside my city. But he read my astrolabe as fast as my father, which both impressed and scared me. He'd coaxed it open by whispering a few choice equations and his suddenly steady hands worked the dials as if they were his own.

When he finished, he looked up at me with his light green piercing eyes that seemed to see deeper into me than his scan of my astrolabe. There were people behind me and I was aware of their whispers, soft laughter and a young child murmuring. It was cool in the terminal, but I felt the heat of social pressure. My temples ached and my feet tingled.

"Congratulations," he said to me in his parched voice, holding out my astrolabe.

I frowned at him, confused. "What for?"

"You are the pride of your people, child," he said, looking me in the eye. Then he smiled broadly and patted my shoulder. He'd just seen my entire life. He knew of my admission into Oomza Uni.

"Oh." My eyes pricked with tears. "Thank you, sir," I said, hoarsely, as I took my astrolabe.

I quickly made my way through the many people in the terminal, too aware of their closeness. I considered finding a lavatory and applying more otjize to my skin and tying my hair back, but instead I kept moving. Most of the people in the busy terminal wore the black and white garments of the Khoush people—the women draped in white with multicolored belts and veils and the men draped in black like powerful spirits. I had seen plenty of them on television and here and there in my city, but never had I been in a sea of Khoush. This was the rest of the world and I was finally in it.

As I stood in line for boarding security, I felt a tug at my hair. I turned around and met the eyes of a group of Khoush women. They were all staring at me; everyone behind me was staring at me.

The woman who'd tugged my plait was looking at her fingers and rubbing them together, frowning. Her fingertips were orange red with my otjize. She sniffed them. "It smells like jasmine flowers," she said to the woman on her left, surprised.

"Not shit?" one woman said. "I hear it smells like shit because it is shit."

"No, definitely jasmine flowers. It is thick like shit, though."

"Is her hair even real?" another woman asked the woman rubbing her fingers.

"I don't know."

"These 'dirt bathers' are a filthy people," the first woman muttered.

I just turned back around, my shoulders hunched. My mother had counseled me to be quiet around Khoush. My father told me that when he was around Khoush merchants when they came to our city to buy astrolabes, he tried to make himself as small as possible. "It is either that or I will start a war with them that I will finish," he said. My father didn't believe in war. He said war was evil, but if it came he would revel in it like sand in a storm. Then he'd say a little prayer to the Seven to keep war away and then another prayer to seal his words.

I pulled my plaits to my front and touched the edan in my pocket. I let my mind focus on it, its strange language, its strange metal, its strange feel. I'd found the edan eight years ago while exploring the sands of the hinter deserts one late afternoon. "Edan" was a general name for a device too old for anyone to know it functions, so old that they were now just art.

My edan was more interesting than any book, than any new astrolabe design I made in my father's shop that these women would probably kill each other to buy. And it was mine, in my pocket, and these nosy women behind me could never know. Those women talked about me, the men probably did too. But none of them knew what I had, where I was going, who I was. Let them gossip and judge. Thankfully, they knew not to touch my hair again. I don't like war either.

The security guard scowled when I stepped forward. Behind him I could see three entrances, the one in the middle led into the ship called "Third Fish," the ship I was to take to Oomza Uni. Its open door was large and round leading into a long corridor illuminated by soft blue lights.

"Step forward," the guard said. He wore the uniform of all launch site lower-level personnel—a long white gown and gray gloves. I'd only seen this uniform in streaming stories and books and I wanted to giggle, despite myself. He looked ridiculous. I stepped forward and everything went red and warm.

When the body scan beeped its completion, the security guard reached right into my left pocket and brought out my edan. He held it to his face with a deep scowl.

I waited. What would he know?

He was inspecting its stellated cube shape, pressing its many points with his finger and eyeing the strange symbols on it that I had spent two years unsuccessfully trying to decode. He held it to his face to better see the intricate loops and swirls of blue and black and white, so much like the lace placed on the heads of young girls when they turn eleven and go through their eleventh-year rite.

"What is this made of?" the guard asked, holding it over a scanner. "It's not reading as any known metal."

I shrugged, too aware of the people behind me waiting in line and staring at me. To them, I was probably like one of the people who lived in caves deep in the hinter desert who were so blackened by the sun that they looked like walking shadows. I'm not proud to say that I have some Desert People blood in me from my father's side of the family, that's where my dark skin and extra-bushy hair come from.

"Your identity reads that you're a harmonizer, a masterful one who builds some of the finest astrolabes," he said. "But this object isn't an astrolabe. Did you build it? And how can you build something and not know what it's made of?"

"I didn't build it," I said.

"Who did?"

"It's . . . it's just an old, old thing," I said. "It has no math or current. It's just an inert computative apparatus that I carry for good luck." This was partially a lie. But even I didn't know exactly what it could and couldn't do.

The man looked as if he would ask more, but didn't. Inside, I smiled. Government security guards were only educated up to age ten, yet because of their jobs, they were used to ordering people around. And they especially looked down on people like me. Apparently, they were the same everywhere, no matter the tribe. He had no idea what a "computative apparatus" was, but he didn't want to show that I, a poor Himba girl, was more educated than he. Not in front of all these people. So he quickly moved me along and, finally, there I stood at my ship's entrance.

I couldn't see the end of the corridor, so I stared at the entrance. The ship was a magnificent piece of living technology. Third Fish was a Miri 12, a type of ship closely related to a shrimp. Miri 12s were stable calm creatures with natural exoskeletons that could withstand the harshness of space. They were genetically enhanced to grow three breathing chambers within their bodies.

Scientists planted rapidly growing plants within these three enormous rooms that not only produced oxygen from the CO_2 directed in from other parts of the ship, but also absorbed benzene, formaldehyde, and trichloroethylene. This was some of the most amazing technology I'd ever read about. Once settled on the ship, I was determined to convince someone to let me see one of these amazing rooms. But at the moment, I wasn't thinking about the technology of the ship. I was on the threshold now, between home and my future.

I stepped into the blue corridor.

* * *

So that is how it all began. I found my room. I found my group—twelve other new students, all human, all Khoush, between the ages of fifteen and eighteen. An hour later, my group and I located a ship technician to show us one of the breathing chambers. I wasn't the only new Oomza Uni student who desperately wanted to see the technology at work. The air in there smelled like the jungles and forests I'd only read about. The plants had tough leaves and they grew everywhere, from ceiling to walls to floor. They were wild with flowers, and I could have stood there breathing that soft, fragrant air for days.

We met our group leader hours later. He was a stern old Khoush man who looked the twelve of us over and paused at me and asked, "Why are you covered in red greasy clay and weighed down by all those steel anklets?" When I told him that I was Himba, he coolly said, "I know, but that doesn't answer my question." I explained to him the tradition of my people's skin care and how we wore the steel rings on our ankles to protect us from snakebites. He looked at me for a long time, the others in my group staring at me like a rare bizarre butterfly.

"Wear your otjize," he said. "But not so much that you stain up this ship. And if those anklets are to protect you from snakebites, you no longer need them."

I took my anklets off, except for two on each ankle. Enough to jingle with each step.

I was the only Himba on the ship, out of nearly five hundred passengers. My tribe is obsessed with innovation and technology, but it is small, private, and, as I said, we don't like to leave Earth. We prefer to explore the universe by traveling inward, as opposed to outward. No Himba has ever gone to Oomza Uni. So me being the only one on the ship was not that surprising. However, just because something isn't surprising doesn't mean it's easy to deal with.

The ship was packed with outward-looking people who loved mathematics, experimenting, learning, reading, inventing, studying, obsessing, revealing. The people on the ship weren't Himba, but I soon understood that they were still my people. I stood out as a Himba, but the commonalities shined brighter. I made friends quickly. And by the second week in space, they were good friends.

Olo, Remi, Kwuga, Nur, Anajama, Rhoden. Only Olo and Remi were in my group. Everyone else I met in the dining area or the learning room where various lectures were held by professors onboard the ship. They were all girls who grew up in sprawling houses, who'd never walked through the desert, who'd never stepped on a snake in the dry grass. They were girls who could not stand the rays of Earth's sun unless it was shining through a tinted window.

Yet they were girls who knew what I meant when I spoke of "treeing." We sat in my room (because, having so few travel items, mine was the emptiest) and challenged each other to look out at the stars and imagine the most complex equation and then split it in half and then in half again and again. When you do math fractals long enough, you kick yourself into treeing just enough to get lost in the shallows of the mathematical sea. None of us would have made it into the university if we couldn't tree, but it's not easy. We were the best and we pushed each other to get closer to "God."

Then there was Heru. I had never spoken to him, but we smiled across the table at each other during mealtimes. He was from one of those cities so far from mine that they seemed like a figment of my imagination, where there was snow and where men rode those enormous gray birds and the women could speak with those birds without moving their mouths.

Once Heru was standing behind me in the dinner line with one of his friends. I felt someone pick up one of my plaits and I whirled around, ready to be angry. I met his eyes and he'd quickly let go of my hair, smiled, and raised his hands up defensively. "I couldn't help it," he said, his fingertips reddish with my otjize.

"You can't control yourself?" I snapped.

"You have exactly twenty-one," he said. "And they're braided in tessellating triangles. Is it some sort of code?"

I wanted to tell him that there was a code, that the pattern spoke my family's bloodline, culture, and history. That my father had designed the code and my mother and aunties had shown me how to braid it into my hair. However, looking at Heru made my heart beat too fast and my words escaped me, so I merely shrugged and turned back around to pick up a bowl of soup. Heru was tall and had the whitest teeth I'd ever seen. And he was very good in mathematics; few would have noticed the code in my hair.

But I never got the chance to tell him that my hair was braided into the history of my people. Because what happened, happened. It occurred on the eighteenth day of the journey. The five days before we arrived on the planet Oomza Uni, the most powerful and innovative sprawling university in the Milky Way. I was the happiest I'd ever been in my life and I was farther from my beloved family than I'd ever been in my life.

I was at the table savoring a mouthful of a gelatinous milk-based dessert with slivers of coconut in it; I was gazing at Heru, who wasn't gazing at me. I'd put my fork down and had my edan in my hands. I fiddled with it as I watched Heru talk to the boy beside him. The delicious creamy dessert was melting coolly on my tongue. Beside me, Olo and Remi were singing a traditional song from their city because they missed home, a song that had to be sung with a wavery voice like a water spirit.

Then someone screamed and Heru's chest burst open, spattering me with his warm blood. There was a Meduse right behind him.

*   *   *

In my culture, it is blasphemy to pray to inanimate objects, but I did anyway. I prayed to a metal even my father had been unable to identify. I held it to my chest, shut my eyes, and prayed to it, I am in your protection. Please protect me. I am in your protection. Please protect me.

My body was shuddering so hard that I could imagine what it would be like to die from terror. I held my breath, the stench of them still in my nasal cavity and mouth. Heru's blood was on my face, wet and thick. I prayed to the mystery metal my edan was made of because that had to be the only thing keeping me alive at this moment.

Breathing hard from my mouth, I peeked from one eye. I shut it again. The Meduse were hovering less than a foot away. One had launched itself at me but then froze an inch from my flesh; it had reached a tentacle toward my edan and then suddenly collapsed, the tentacle turning ash gray as it quickly dried up like a dead leaf.

I could hear the others, their near substantial bodies softly rustling as their transparent domes filled with and released the gas they breathed back in. They were tall as grown men, their domes' flesh thin as fine silk, their long tentacles spilling down to the floor like a series of gigantic ghostly noodles. I grasped my edan closer to me. I am in your protection. Please protect me.

Everyone in the dining hall was dead. At least one hundred people. I had a feeling everyone on the ship was dead. The Meduse had burst into the hall and begun committing moojh-ha ki-bira before anyone knew what was happening. That's what the Khoush call it. We'd all been taught this Meduse form of killing in history class. The Khoush built the lessons into history, literature, and culture classes across several regions. Even my people were required to learn about it, despite the fact that it wasn't our fight. The Khoush expected everyone to remember their greatest enemy and injustice. They even worked Meduse anatomy and rudimentary technology into mathematics and science classes.

Moojh-ha ki-bira means the "great wave." The Meduse move like water when at war. There is no water on their planet, but they worship water as a god. Their ancestors came from water long ago. The Khoush were settled on the most water-soaked lands on Earth, a planet made mostly of water, and they saw the Meduse as inferior.

The trouble between the Meduse and the Khoush was an old fight and an older disagreement. Somehow, they had agreed to a treaty not to attack each other's ships. Yet here the Meduse were performing moojh-ha ki-bira.

I'd been talking to my friends.

My friends.

Olo, Remi, Kwuga, Nur, Anajama, Rhoden, and Dullaz. We had spent so many late nights laughing over our fears about how difficult and strange Oomza

Uni would be. All of us had twisted ideas that were probably wrong . . . maybe partially right. We had so much in common. I wasn't thinking about home or how I'd had to leave it or the horrible messages my family had sent to my astrolabe hours after I'd left. I was looking ahead toward my future and I was laughing because it was so bright.

Then the Meduse came through the dining hall entrance. I was looking right at Heru when the red circle appeared in the upper left side of his shirt. The thing that tore through was like a sword, but thin as paper . . . and flexible and easily stained by blood. The tip wiggled and grasped like a finger. I saw it pinch and hook to the flesh near his collarbone.

Moojh-ha ki-bira.

I don't remember what I did or said. My eyes were open, taking it all in, but the rest of my brain was screaming. For no reason at all, I focused on the number five. Over and over, I thought, 5-5-5-5-5-5-5-5-5, as Heru's eyes went from shocked to blank. His open mouth let out a gagging sound, then a spurt of thick red blood, then blood frothed with saliva as he began to fall forward. His head hit the table with a flat thud. His neck was turned and I could see that his eyes were open. His left hand flexed spasmodically, until it stopped. But his eyes were still open. He wasn't blinking.

Heru was dead. Olo, Remi, Kwuga, Nur, Anajama, Rhoden, and Dullaz were dead. Everyone was dead.

The dinner hall stank of blood.

*　　*　　*

None of my family had wanted me to go to Oomza Uni. Even my best friend Dele hadn't wanted me to go. Still, not long after I received the news of my university acceptance and my whole family was saying no, Dele had joked that if I went, I at least wouldn't have to worry about the Meduse, because I would be the only Himba on the ship.

"So even if they kill everyone else, they won't even see you!" he'd said. Then he'd laughed and laughed, sure that I wasn't going anyway.

Now his words came back to me. Dele. I'd pushed thoughts of him deep into my mind and read none of his messages. Ignoring the people I loved was the only way I could keep going. When I'd received the scholarship to study at Oomza Uni, I'd gone into the desert and cried for hours. With joy.

I'd wanted this since I knew what a university was. Oomza Uni was the top of the top, its population was only 5 percent human. Imagine what it meant to go there as one of that 5 percent; to be with others obsessed with knowledge, creation, and discovery. Then I went home and told my family and wept with shock.

"You can't go," my oldest sister said. "You're a master harmonizer. Who else is good enough to take over father's shop?"

"Don't be selfish," my sister Suum spat. She was only a year older than me, but she still felt she could run my life. "Stop chasing fame and be rational. You can't just leave and fly across the galaxy."

My brothers had all just laughed and dismissed the idea. My parents said nothing, not even congratulations. Their silence was answer enough. Even my best friend Dele. He congratulated and told me that I was smarter than everyone at Oomza Uni, but then he'd laughed, too. "You cannot go," he simply said. "We're Himba. God has already chosen our paths."

I was the first Himba in history to be bestowed with the honor of acceptance into Oomza Uni. The hate messages, threats to my life, laughter and ridicule that came from the Khoush in my city, made me want to hide more. But deep down inside me, I wanted . . . I needed it. I couldn't help but act on it. The urge was so strong that it was mathematical. When I'd sit in the desert, alone, listening to the wind, I would see and feel the numbers the way I did when I was deep in my work in my father's shop. And those numbers added up to the sum of my destiny.

So in secret, I filled out and uploaded the acceptance forms. The desert was the perfect place for privacy when they contacted my astrolabe for university interviews. When everything was set, I packed my things and got on that shuttle. I come from a family of Bitolus; my father is a master harmonizer and I was to be his successor. We Bitolus know true deep mathematics and we can control their current, we know systems. We are few and we are happy and uninterested in weapons and war, but we can protect ourselves. And as my father says, "God favors us."

* * *

I clutched my edan to my chest now as I opened my eyes. The Meduse in front of me was blue and translucent, except for one of its tentacles, which was tinted pink like the waters of the salty lake beside my village and curled up like the branch of a confined tree. I held up my edan and the Meduse jerked back, pluming out its gas and loudly inhaling. Fear, I thought. That was fear.

I stood up, realizing that my time of death was not here yet. I took a quick look around the giant hall. I could smell dinner over the stink of blood and Meduse gases. Roasted and marinated meats, brown long-grained rice, spicy red stews, flat breads, and that rich gelatinous dessert I loved so much. They were all still laid out on the grand table, the hot foods cooling as the bodies cooled and the dessert melting as the dead Meduse melted.

"Back!" I hissed, thrusting the edan at the Meduse. My garments rustled and my anklets jingled as I got up. I pressed my backside against the table. The Meduse were behind me and on my sides, but I focused on the one before me. "This will kill you!" I said as forcibly as I could. I cleared my throat and raised my voice. "You saw what it did to your brother."

I motioned to the shriveled dead one two feet away; its mushy flesh had dried and begun to turn brown and opaque. It had tried to take me and then something made it die. Bits of it had crumbled to dust as I spoke, the mere vibration of my voice enough to destabilize the remains. I grabbed my satchel as I slid away from the table and moved toward the grand table of food. My mind was moving fast now. I was seeing numbers and then blurs. Good. I was my father's daughter. He'd taught me in the tradition of my ancestors and I was the best in the family.

"I am Binti Ekeopara Zuzu Dambu Kaipka of Namib," I whispered. This is what my father always reminded me when he saw my face go blank and I started to tree. He would then loudly speak his lessons to me about astrolabes, including how they worked, the art of them, the true negotiation of them, the lineage. While I was in this state, my father passed me three hundred years of oral knowledge about circuits, wire, metals, oils, heat, electricity, math current, sand bar.

And so I had become a master harmonizer by the age of twelve. I could communicate with spirit flow and convince them to become one current. I was born with my mother's gift of mathematical sight. My mother only used it to protect the family, and now I was going to grow that skill at the best university in the galaxy . . . if I survived. "Binti Ekeopara Zuzu Dambu Kaipka of Namib, that is my name," I said again.

My mind cleared as the equations flew through it, opening it wider, growing progressively more complex and satisfying. $V - E + F = 2$, $a^2 + b^2 = c^2$, I thought. I knew what to do now. I moved to the table of food and grabbed a tray. I heaped chicken wings, a turkey leg, and three steaks of beef onto it. Then several rolls; bread would stay fresh longer. I dumped three oranges on my tray, because they carried juice and vitamin C. I grabbed two whole bladders of water and shoved them into my satchel as well. Then I slid a slice of white milky dessert on my tray. I did not know its name, but it was easily the most wonderful thing I'd ever tasted. Each bite would fuel my mental well-being. And if I were going to survive, I'd need that, especially.

I moved quickly, holding up the edan, my back straining with the weight of my loaded satchel as I held the large food-heavy tray with my left hand. The Meduse followed me, their tentacles caressing the floor as they floated. They had no eyes, but from what I knew of the Meduse, they had scent receptors on the tips of their tentacles. They saw me through smell.

The hallway leading to the rooms was wide and all the doors were plated with sheets of gold metal. My father would have spat at this wastefulness. Gold was an information conductor and its mathematical signals were stronger than anything. Yet here it was wasted on gaudy extravagance.

When I arrived at my room, the trance lifted from me without warning and I suddenly had no idea what to do next. I stopped treeing and the clarity of mind retreated like a loss of confidence. All I could think to do was let the door scan my eye. It opened, I slipped in and it shut behind me with a sucking sound, sealing the room, a mechanism probably triggered by the ship's emergency programming.

I managed to put the tray and satchel on my bed just before my legs gave. Then I sunk to the cool floor beside the black landing chair on the fair side of the room. My face was sweaty and I rested my cheek on the floor for a moment and sighed. Images of my friends Olo, Remi, Kwuga, Nur, Anajama, Rhoden crowded my mind. I thought I heard Heru's soft laughter above me . . . then the sound of his chest bursting open, then the heat of his blood on my face. I whimpered, biting my lip. "I'm here, I'm here, I'm here," I whispered. Because I was and there was no way out. I shut my eyes tightly as the tears came. I curled my body and stayed like that for several minutes.

* * *

I brought my astrolabe to my face. I'd made the casing with golden sand bar that I'd molded, sculpted, and polished myself. It was the size of a child's hand and far better than any astrolabe one could buy from the finest seller. I'd taken care to fashion its weight to suit my hands, the dials to respond to only my fingers, and its currents were so true that they'd probably outlast my own future children. I'd made this astrolabe two months ago specifically for my journey, replacing the one my father had made for me when I was three years old.

I started to speak my family name to my astrolabe, but then I whispered, "No," and rested it on my belly. My family was planets away by now; what more could they do than weep? I rubbed the on button and spoke, "Emergency." The astrolabe warmed in my hands and emitted the calming scent of roses as it vibrated. Then it went cool. "Emergency," I said again. This time it didn't even warm up.

"Map," I said. I held my breath, waiting. I glanced at the door. I'd read that Meduse could not move through walls, but even I knew that just because information was in a book didn't make it true. Especially when the information concerned the Meduse. My door was secure, but I was Himba and I doubted the Khoush had given me one of the rooms with full security locks. The Meduse would come in when they wanted or when they were willing to risk death to do away with me. I may not have been Khoush . . . but I was a human on a Khoush ship.

My astrolabe suddenly warmed and vibrated. "Your location is 121 hours from your destination of Oomza Uni," it said in its whispery voice. So the Meduse felt it okay for me to know where the ship was. The virtual constellation lit up my room with white, light blue, red, yellow, and orange dots, slowly rotating globes from the size of a large fly to the size of my fist . Suns, planets, bloom territories all sectioned in the mathematical net that I'd always found easy to read. The ship had long since left my solar system. We'd slowed down right in the middle of what was known as "the Jungle." The pilots of the ship should have been more vigilant. "And maybe less arrogant," I said, feeling ill.

The ship was still heading for Oomza Uni, though, and that was mildly encouraging. I shut my eyes and prayed to the Seven. I wanted to ask, "Why did you let this happen?" but that was blasphemy. You never ask why. It was not a question for you to ask.

"I'm going to die here."

*　*　*

Seventy-two hours later, I was still alive. But I'd run out of food and had very little water left. Me and my thoughts in that small room, no escape outside. I had to stop crying; I couldn't afford to lose water. The toilet facilities were just outside my room so I'd been forced to use the case that carried my beaded jewelry collection. All I had was my jar of otjize, some of which I used to clean my body as much as possible. I paced, recited equations, and was sure that if I didn't die of thirst or starvation I'd die by fire from the currents I'd nervously created and discharged to keep myself busy.

I looked at the map yet again and saw what I knew I'd see; we were still heading to Oomza Uni. "But why?" I whispered. "Security wil . . ."

I shut my eyes, trying to stop myself from completing the thought yet again. But I could never stop myself and this time was no different. In my mind's eye, I saw a bright yellow beam zip from Oomza Uni and the ship scattering in a radiating mass of silent light and flame. I got up and shuffled to the far side of my room and back as I talked. "But suicidal Meduse? It just doesn't make sense. Maybe they don't know how to . . ."

There was a slow knock at the door and I nearly jumped to the ceiling. Then I froze, listening with every part of my body. Other than the sound of my voice, I hadn't heard a thing from them since that first twenty-four hours. The knock came again. The last knock was hard, more like a kick, but not near the bottom of the door.

"L . . . leave me alone!" I screamed, grabbing my edan. My words were met with a hard bang at the door and an angry, harsh hiss. I screeched and moved as far from the door as my room would permit, nearly falling over my largest suitcase. Think think think. No weapons, except the edan . . . and I didn't know what made it a weapon.

Everyone was dead. I was still about forty-eight hours from safety or being blown up. They say that when faced with a fight you cannot win, you can never predict what you will do next. But I'd always known I'd fight until I was killed. It was an abomination to commit suicide or to give up your life. I was sure that I was ready. The Meduse were very intelligent; they'd find a way to kill me, despite my edan.

Nevertheless, I didn't pick up the nearest weapon. I didn't prepare for my last violent rabid stand. Instead, I looked my death square in the face and then . . . then I surrendered to it. I sat on my bed and waited for my death. Already, my body felt as if it were no longer mine; I'd let it go. And in that moment, deep in my submission, I laid my eyes on my edan and stared at its branching splitting dividing blue fractals.

And I saw it.

I really saw it.

And all I could do was smile and think, How did I not know?

* * *

I sat in the landing chair beside my window, hand-rolling otjize into my plaits. I looked at my reddened hands, brought them to my nose and sniffed. Oily clay that sang of sweet flowers, desert wind, and soil. Home, I thought, tears stinging my eyes. I should not have left. I picked up the edan, looking for what I'd seen. I turned the edan over and over before my eyes. The blue object whose many points I'd rubbed, pressed, stared at, and pondered for so many years.

More thumping came from the door. "Leave me alone," I muttered weakly.

I smeared otjize onto the point of the edan with the spiral that always reminded me of a fingerprint. I rubbed it in a slow circular motion. My shoulders relaxed as I calmed. Then my starved and thirsty brain dropped into a mathematical trance like a stone dropped into deep water. And I felt the water envelop me as down down down I went.

My clouded mind cleared and everything went silent and motionless, my finger still polishing the edan. I smelled home, heard the desert wind blowing grains of sand over each other. My stomach fluttered as I dropped deeper in and my entire body felt sweet and pure and empty and light. The edan was heavy in my hands; so heavy that it would fall right through my flesh.

"Oh," I breathed, realizing that there was now a tiny button in the center of the spiral. This was what I'd seen. It had always been there, but now it was as if it were in focus. I pushed it with my index finger. It depressed with a soft "click" and then the stone felt like warm wax and my world wavered. There was another loud knock at the door. Then through the clearest silence I'd ever experienced, so clear that the slightest sound would tear its fabric, I heard a solid oily low voice say, "Girl."

I was catapulted out of my trance, my eyes wide, my mouth yawning in a silent scream.

"Girl," I heard again. I hadn't heard a human voice since the final screams of those killed by the Meduse, over seventy-two hours ago.

I looked around my room. I was alone. Slowly, I turned and looked out the window beside me. There was nothing out there for me but the blackness of space.

"Girl. You will die," the voice said slowly. "Soon." I heard more voices, but they were too low to understand. "Suffering is against the Way. Let us end you."

I jumped up and the rush of blood made me nearly collapse and crash to the floor. Instead I fell painfully to my knees, still clutching the edan. There was another knock at the door. "Open this door," the voice demanded.

My hands began to shake, but I didn't drop my edan. It was warm and a brilliant blue light was glowing from within it now. A current was running through it so steadily that it made the muscles of my hand constrict. I couldn't let go of it if I tried.

"I will not," I said, through clenched teeth. "Rather die in here, on my terms."

The knocking stopped. Then I heard several things at once. Scuffling at the door, not toward it, but away. Terrified moaning and wailing. More voices. Several of them.

"This is evil!"

"It carries shame," another voice said. This was the first voice I heard that sounded high-pitched, almost female. "The shame she carries allows her to mimic speech."

"No. It has to have sense for that," another voice said.

"Evil! Let me deactivate the door and kill it."

"Okwu, you will die if you . . ."

"I will kill it!" the one called Okwu growled. "Death will be my honor! We're too close now, we can't have . . ."

"Me!" I shouted suddenly. "O . . . Okwu!" Calling its name, addressing it so directly sounded strange on my lips. I pushed on. "Okwu, why don't you talk to me?"

I looked at my cramped hands. From within it, from my edan, possibly the strongest current I'd ever produced streamed in jagged connected bright blue branches. It slowly etched and lurched through the closed door, a line of connected bright blue treelike branches that shifted in shape but never broke their connection. The current was touching the Meduse. Connecting them to me. And though I'd created it, I couldn't control it now. I wanted to scream, revolted. But I had to save my life first. "I am speaking to you!" I said. "Me!"

Silence.

I slowly stood up, my heart pounding. I stumbled to the shut door on aching trembling legs. The door's organic steel was so thin, but one of the strongest substances on my planet. Where the current touched it, tiny green leaves unfurled. I touched them, focusing on the leaves and not the fact that the door was covered with a sheet of gold, a super communication conducter. Nor the fact of the Meduse just beyond my door.

I heard a rustle and I used all my strength not to scuttle back. I flared my nostrils as I grasped the edan. The weight of my hair on my shoulders was assuring, my hair was heavy with otjize, and this was good luck and the strength of my people, even if my people were far far away.

The loud bang of something hard and powerful hitting the door made me yelp. I stayed where I was. "Evil thing," I heard the one called Okwu say. Of all the voices, that one I could recognize. It was the angriest and scariest. The voice sounded spoken, not transmitted in my mind. I could hear the vibration of the "v" in "evil" and the hard breathy "th" in "thing." Did they have mouths?

"I'm not evil," I said.

I heard whispering and rustling behind the door. Then the more female voice said, "Open this door."

"No!"

They muttered among themselves. Minutes passed. I sunk to the floor, leaning against the door. The blue current sunk with me, streaming through the door at my shoulder; more green leaves bloomed there, some fell down my shoulder onto my lap. I leaned my head against the door and stared down at them. Green tiny leaves of green tiny life when I was so close to death. I giggled and my empty belly rumbled and my sore abdominal muscles ached.

Then, quietly, calmly, "You are understanding us?" this was the growling voice that had been calling me evil. Okwu.

"Yes," I said.

"Humans only understand violence."

I closed my eyes and felt my weak body relax. I sighed and said, "The only thing I have killed are small animals for food, and only with swift grace and after prayer and thanking the beast for its sacrifice." I was exhausted.

"I do not believe you."

"Just as I do not believe you will not kill me if I open the door. All you do is kill." I opened my eyes. Energy that I didn't know I still had rippled through me and I was so angry that I couldn't catch my breath. "Like . . . like you . . . killed my friends!" I coughed and slumped down, weakly. "My friends," I whispered, tears welling in my eyes. "Oooh, my friends!"

"Humans must be killed before they kill us," the voice said.

"You're all stupid," I spat, wiping my tears as they kept coming. I sobbed hard and then took a deep breath, trying to pull it together. I exhaled loudly, snot flying from my nose. As I wiped my face with my arm, there were more whispers. Then the higher pitched voice spoke.

"What is this blue ghost you have sent to help us communicate?"

"I don't know," I said, sniffing. I got up and walked to my bed. Moving away from the door instantly made me feel better. The blue current extended with me.

"Why do we understand you?" Okwu asked. I could still hear its voice perfectly from where I was.

"I . . . I don't know," I said, sitting on my bed and then lying back.

"No Meduse has ever spoken to a human . . . except long ago."

"I don't care," I grunted.

"Open the door. We won't harm you."

"No."

There was a long pause. So long that I must have fallen asleep. I was awakened by a sucking sound. At first I paid no mind to it, taking the moment to wipe off the caked snot on my face with my arm. The ship made all sorts of sounds, even before the Meduse attacked. It was a living thing and like any beast, its bowels gurgled and quaked every so often. Then I sat up straight as the sucking sound grew louder. The door trembled. It buckled a bit and then completely crumpled, the gold plating on the outside now visible. The stale air of my room whooshed out into the hallway and suddenly the air cooled and smelled fresher.

There stood the Meduse. I could not tell how many of them, for they were transparent and when they stood together, all I could see were a tangle of translucent tentacles and undulating domes. I clutched the edan to my chest as I pressed myself on the other side of the room, against the window.

It happened fast like the desert wolves who attack travelers at night back home. One of the Meduse shot toward me. I watched it come. I saw my parents, sisters, brothers, aunts, and uncles, all gathered at a remembrance for me—full of pain and loss. I saw my spirit break from my body and return to my planet, to the desert, where I would tell stories to the sand people.

Time must have slowed down because the Meduse was motionless, yet suddenly it was hovering over me, its tentacles hanging an inch from my head. I gasped, bracing myself for pain and then death. Its pink withered tentacle brushed my arm firmly enough to rub off some of the otjize there. Soft, I thought. Smooth.

There it was. So close now. White like the ice I'd only seen in pictures and entertainment streams, its stinger was longer than my leg. I stared at it, jutting from its bundle of tentacles. It crackled and dried, wisps of white mist wafting from it. Inches from my chest. Now it went from white to a dull light-gray. I looked down at my cramped hands, the edan between them. The current flowing from it washed over the Meduse and extended beyond it. Then I looked up at the Meduse and grinned. "I hope it hurts," I whispered.

The Meduse's tentacles shuddered and it began to back away. I could see its pink deformed tentacle, part of it smeared red with my otjize.

"You are the foundation of evil," it said. It was the one called Okwu. I nearly laughed. Why did this one hate me so strongly?

"She still holds the shame," I heard one say from near the door.

Okwu began to recover as it moved away from me. Quickly, it left with the others.

* * *

Ten hours passed.

I had no food left. No water. I packed and repacked my things. Keeping busy staved off the dehydration and hunger a bit, though my constant need to urinate kept reminding me of my predicament. And movement was tricky because the edan's current still wouldn't release my hands' muscles, but I managed. I tried not to indulge in my fear of the Meduse finding a way to get the ship to stop producing and circulating air and maintaining its internal pressure, or just coming back and killing me.

When I wasn't packing and repacking, I was staring at my edan, studying it; the patterns on it now glowed with the current. I needed to know how it was allowing me to communicate. I tried different soft equations on it and received no response. After a while, when not even hard equations affected it, I lay back on my bed and let myself tree. This was my state of mind when the Meduse came in.

"What is that?"

I screamed. I'd been gazing out the window, so I heard the Meduse before I saw it.

"What?" I shrieked, breathless. "I . . . what is what?"

Okwu, the one who'd tried to kill me. Contrary to how it had looked when it left, it was very much alive, though I could not see its stinger.

"What is the substance on your skin?" it asked firmly. "None of the other humans have it."

"Of course they don't," I snapped. "It is otjize, only my people wear it and I am the only one of my people on the ship. I'm not Khoush."

"What is it?" it asked, remaining in the doorway.

"Why?"

It moved into my room and I held up the edan and quickly said, "Mostly . . . mostly clay and oil from my homeland. Our land is desert, but we live in the region where there is sacred red clay."

"Why do you spread it on your skins?"

"Because my people are sons and daughters of the soil," I said. "And . . . and it's beautiful."

It paused for a long moment and I just stared at it. Really looking at the thing. It moved as if it had a front and a back. And though it seemed to be fully transparent, I could not see its solid white stinger within the drapes of hanging tentacles. Whether it was thinking about what I'd said or considering how best to kill me, I didn't know. But moments later, it turned and left. And it was only after several minutes, when my heart rate slowed, that I realized something odd. Its withered tentacle didn't look as withered. Where it had been curled up tightly into itself, now it was merely bent.

*　　*　　*

It came back fifteen minutes later. And immediately, I looked to make sure I'd seen what I knew I'd seen. And there it was, pink and not so curled up. That tentacle had been different when Okwu had accidently touched me and rubbed off my otjize.

"Give me some of it," it said, gliding into my room.

"I don't have any more!" I said, panicking. I only had one large jar of otjize, the most I'd ever made in one batch. It was enough to last me until I could find red clay on Oomza Uni and make more. And even then, I wasn't sure if I'd find the right kind of clay. It was another planet. Maybe it wouldn't have clay at all.

In all my preparation, the one thing I didn't take enough time to do was research the Oomza Uni planet itself, so focused I was on just getting there. All I knew was that though it was much smaller than earth, it had a similar atmosphere and I wouldn't have to wear a special suit or adaptive lungs or anything like that. But its surface could easily be made of something my skin couldn't tolerate. I couldn't give all my otjize to this Meduse; this was my culture.

"The chief knows of your people, you have much with you."

"If your chief knows my people, then he will have told you that taking it from me is like taking my soul," I said, my voice cracking. My jar was under my bed. I held up my edan.

But Okwu didn't leave or approach. Its curled pink tentacle twitched.

I decided to take a chance, "It helped you, didn't it? Your tentacle."

It blew out a great puff of its gas, sucked it in and left.

It returned five minutes later with five others.

"What is that object made of?" Okwu asked, the others standing silently behind it.

I was still on my bed and I pushed my legs under the covers. "I don't know. But a desert woman once said it was made from something called 'god stone.' My father said there is no such . . ."

"It is shame," it insisted.

None of them moved to enter my room. Three of them made loud puffing sounds as they let out the reeking gasses they inhaled in order to breathe.

"There is nothing shameful about an object that keeps me alive," I said.

"It poisons Meduse," one of the others said.

"Only if you get too close to me," I said, looking straight at it. "Only if you try and kill me."

Pause.

"How are you communicating with us?"

"I don't know, Okwu." I spoke its name as if I owned it.

"What are you called?"

I sat up straight, ignoring the fatigue trying to pull my bones to the bed. "I am Binti Ekeopara Zuzu Dambu Kaipka of Namib." I considered speaking its single name to reflect its cultural simplicity compared to mine, but my strength and bravado were already waning.

Okwu moved forward and I held up the edan. "Stay back! You know what it'll do!" I said. However, it did not try to attack me again, though it didn't start to shrivel up as it approached, either. It stopped feet away, beside the metal table jutting from the wall carrying my open suitcase and one of the containers of water.

"What do you need?" it flatly asked.

I stared, weighing my options. I didn't have any. "Water, food," I said.

Before I could say more, it left. I leaned against the window and tried not to look outside into the blackness. Feet away from me, the door was crushed to the side, the path of my fate was no longer mine. I lay back and fell into the deepest sleep I'd had since the ship left Earth.

*   *   *

The faint smell of smoke woke me up. There was a plate on my bed, right before my nose. On it was a small slab of smoked fish. Beside it was a bowl of water.

I sat up, still tightly grasping the edan. I leaned forward, and sucked up as much water from the bowl as I could. Then, still holding the edan, I pressed my forearms together and worked the food onto them. I brought the fish up, bent forward and took a bite of it. Smoky salty goodness burst across my taste buds. The chefs on the ship fed these fish well and allowed them to grow strong and mate copiously. Then they lulled the fish into a sleep that the fish never woke from and slow cooked their flesh long enough for flavor and short enough to maintain texture. I'd asked the chefs about their process as any good Himba would before eating it. The chefs were all Khoush, and Khoush did not normally perform what they called "superstitious ritual." But these chefs were Oomza Uni students and they said they did, even lulling the fish to sleep in a similar way. Again, I'd been assured that I was heading in the right direction.

The fish was delicious, but it was full of bones. And it was as I was using my tongue to work a long, flexible, but tough bone from my teeth that I looked up and noticed the Meduse hovering in the doorway. I didn't have to see the withered tentacle to know it was Okwu. Inhaling with surprise, I nearly choked on the bone. I dropped what was left, spat out the bone and opened my mouth to speak. Then I closed it.

I was still alive.

Okwu didn't move or speak, though the blue current still connected us.

Moments passed, Okwu hovering and emitting the foul-smelling gasp as it breathed and me sucking bits of fish from my mouth wondering if this was my last meal. After a while, I grasped the remaining hunk of fish with my forearms and continued eating.

"You know," I finally said, to fill the silence. "There are a people in my village who have lived for generations at the edge of the lake." I looked at the Meduse. Nothing. "They know all the fish in it," I continued. "There is a fish that grows plenty in that lake and they catch and smoke them like this. The only difference is that my people can prepare it in such a way where there are no bones. They remove them all." I pulled a bone from between my teeth. "They have studied this fish. They have worked it out mathematically. They know where every bone will be, no matter the age, size, sex of the fish. They go in and remove every bone without disturbing the body. It is delicious!" I put down the remaining bones. "This was delicious, too." I hesitated and then said, "Thank you."

Okwu didn't move, continuing to hover and puff out gas. I got up and walked to the counter where a tray had been set. I leaned down and sucked up the water from this bowl as well. Already, I felt much stronger and more alert. I jumped when it spoke.

"I wish I could just kill you."

I paused. "Like my mother always says, 'we all wish for many things,'" I said, touching a last bit of fish in my back tooth.

"You don't look like a human Oomza Uni student," it said. "Your color is darker and you . . ." It blasted out a large plume of gas and I fought not to wrinkle my nose. "You have okuoko."

I frowned at the unfamiliar word. "What is okuoko?"

And that's when it moved for the first time since I'd awakened. Its long tentacles jiggled playfully and a laugh escaped my mouth before I could stop it. It plumed out more gas in rapid succession and made a deep thrumming sound. This made me laugh even harder. "You mean my hair?" I asked shaking my thick plaits.

"Okuoko, yes," it said.

"Okuoko," I said. I had to admit, I liked the sound of it. "How come the word is different?"

"I don't know," it said. "I hear you in my language as well. When you said okuoko it is okuoko." It paused. "The Khoush are the color of the flesh of the fish you ate and they have no okuoko. You are red brown like the fish's outer skin and you have okuoko like Meduse, though small."

"There are different kinds of humans," I said. "My people don't normally leave my planet." Several Meduse came to the door and crowded in. Okwu moved closer, pluming out more gas and inhaling it. This time I did cough at the stench of it.

"Why have you?" it asked. "You are probably the most evil of your people."

I frowned at it. Realizing something. It spoke like one of my brothers, Bena. I was born only three years after him yet we'd never been very close. He was angry and always speaking out about the way my people were maltreated by the Khoush majority despite the fact that they needed us and our astrolabes to survive. He was always calling them evil, though he'd never traveled to a Khoush country or known a Khoush. His anger was rightful, but all that he said was from what he didn't truly know.

Even I could tell that Okwu was not an elder among these Meduse; it was too hotheaded and . . . there was something about it that reminded me of me. Maybe its curiosity; I think I'd have been one of the first to come see, if I were it, too. My father said that my curiosity was the last obstacle I had to overcome to be a true master harmonizer. If there was one thing my father and I disagreed on, it was that; I believed I could only be great if I were curious enough to seek greatness. Okwu was young, like me. And maybe that's why it was so eager to die and prove itself to the others and that's why the others were fine with it.

"You know nothing of me," I said. I felt myself grow hot. "This is not a military ship, this is a ship full of professors! Students! All dead!! You killed everyone!"

It seemed to chuckle. "Not your pilot. We did not sting that one."

And just like that, I understood. They would get through the university's security if the security people thought the ship was still full of living breathing unmurdered professors and students. Then the Meduse would be able to invade Oomza Uni.

"We don't need you. But that one is useful."

"That's why we are still on course," I said.

"No. We can fly this creature ship," it said. "But your pilot can speak to the people on Oomza Uni in the way they expect." It paused, then moved closer. "See? We never needed you."

I felt the force of its threat physically. The sharp tingle came in white bursts in my toes and traveled up my body to the top of my head. I opened my mouth, suddenly short of breath. This was what fearing death truly felt like, not my initial submission to it. I leaned away, holding up my edan. I was sitting on my bed, its red covers making me think of blood. There was nowhere to go.

"That shame is the only reason you are alive," it said.

"Your okuoko is better," I whispered, pointing at the tentacle. "Won't you spare me for curing that?" I could barely breathe. When it didn't respond, I asked, "Why? Or maybe there is no reason."

"You think we are like you humans?" it asked, angrily. "We don't kill for sport or even for gain. Only for purpose."

I frowned. They sounded like the same thing to me, gain and purpose.

"In your university, in one of its museums, placed on display like a piece of rare meat is the stinger of our chief," it said. I wrinkled my face, but said nothing. "Our chief is . . ." It paused. "We know of the attack and mutilation of our chief, but we do not know how it got there. We do not care. We will land on Oomza Uni and take it back. So you see? We have purpose."

It billowed out gas and left the room. I lay back in my bed, exhausted.

*   *   *

But they brought me more food and water. Okwu brought it. And it sat with me while I ate and drank. More fish and some dried-up dates and a flask of water. This time, I barely tasted it as I ate.

"It's suicide," I said.

"What is . . . suicide," it asked.

"What you are doing!" I said. "On Oomza Uni, there's a city where all the students and professors do is study, test, create weapons. Weapons for taking every form of life. Your own weapons were probably made there!"

"Our weapons are made within our bodies," it said.

"What of the current-killer you used against the Khoush in the Meduse-Khoush War?" I asked.

It said nothing.

"Suicide is death on purpose!"

"Meduse aren't afraid of death," it said. "And this would be honorable. We will show them never to dishonor Meduse again. Our people will remember our sacrifice and celebrate . . ."

"I . . . I have an idea!" I shouted. My voice cracked. I pushed forward. "Let me talk to your chief!" I shrieked. I don't know if it was the delicious fish I'd eaten, shock, hopelessness, or exhaustion. I stood up and stepped to it, my legs shaky and my eyes wild. "Let me . . . I'm a master harmonizer. That's why I'm going to Oomza Uni. I am the best of the best, Okwu. I can create harmony anywhere." I was so out of breath that I was wheezing. I inhaled deeply, seeing stars explode before my eyes. "Let me be . . . let me speak for the Meduse. The people in Oomza Uni are academics, so they'll understand honor and history and symbolism and matters of the body." I didn't know any of this for sure. These were only my dreams . . . and my experience of those on the ship.

"Now you speak of 'suicide' for the both of us," it said.

"Please," I said. "I can make your chief listen."

"Our chief hates humans," Okwu said. "Humans took his stinger. Do you know what . . ."

"I'll give you my jar of otjize," I blurted. "You can put it all over your . . . on every okuoko, your dome, who knows, it might make you glow like a star or give you super-powers or sting harder and faster or . . ."

"We don't like stinging."

"Please," I begged. "Imagine what you will be. Imagine if my plan works. You'll get the stinger back and none of you will have died. You'll be a hero." And I get to live, I thought.

"We don't care about being heroes." But its pink tentacle twitched when it said this.

*   *   *

The Meduse ship was docked beside the Third Fish. I'd walked across the large chitinous corridor linking them, ignoring the fact that the chances of my returning were very low.

Their ship stank. I was sure of it, even if I couldn't smell it through my breather. Everything about the Meduse stank. I could barely concentrate on the spongy blue surface beneath my bare feet. Or the cool gasses Okwu promised would not harm my flesh even though I could not breathe it. Or the Meduse, some green, some blue, some pink, moving on every surface, floor, high ceiling, wall, or stopping and probably staring at me with whatever they stared with. Or the current-connected edan I still grasped in my hands. I was doing equations in my head. I needed everything I had to do what I was about to do.

The room was so enormous that it almost felt as if we were outside. Almost. I'm a child of the desert; nothing indoors can feel like the outdoors to me. But this room was huge. The chief was no bigger than the others, no more colorful. It had no more tentacles than the others. It was surrounded by other Meduse. It looked so much like those around it that Okwu had to stand beside it to let me know who it was.

The current from the edan was going crazy—branching out in every direction bringing me their words. I should have been terrified. Okwu had told me that requesting a meeting like this with the chief was risking not only my life, but Okwu's life as well. For the chief hated human beings and Okwu had just begged to bring one into their "great ship."

Spongy. As if it were full of the firm jelly beads in the milky pudding my mother liked to make. I could sense current all around me. These people had deep active technology built into the walls and many of them had it running within their very bodies. Some of them were walking astrolabes, it was part of their biology.

I adjusted my facemask. The air that it pumped in smelled like desert flowers. The makers of the mask had to have been Khoush women. They liked everything to smell like flowers, even their privates. But at the moment, I could have kissed those women, for as I gazed at the chief, the smell of flowers burst into my nose and mouth and suddenly I was imagining the chief hovering in the desert surrounded by the dry sweet-smelling flowers that only bloomed at night. I felt calm. I didn't feel at home, because in the part of the desert that I knew, only tiny scentless flowers grew. But I sensed Earth.

I slowly stopped treeing, my mind clean and clear, but much stupider. I needed to speak, not act. So I had no choice. I held my chin up and then did as Okwu instructed me. I sunk to the spongy floor. Then right there, within the ship that brought the death of my friends, the boy I was coming to love, my fellow Oomza Uni human citizens from Earth, before the one who had instructed its people to perform moojh-ha ki-bira, also called the "great wave" of death, on my people—still grasping the edan, I prostrated. I pressed my face to the floor. Then I waited.

"This is Binti Ekeopara Zuzu Dambu Kaipka of Namib, the one . . . the one who survives," Okwu said.

"You may just call me Binti," I whispered, keeping my head down. My first name was singular and two syllabled like Okwu's name and I thought maybe it would please the chief.

"Tell the girl to sit up," the chief said. "If there is the slightest damage to the ship's flesh because of this one, I will have you executed first, Okwu. Then this creature."

"Binti," Okwu said, his voice was hard, flat. "Get up."

I shut my eyes. I could feel the edan's current working through me, touching everything. Including the floor beneath me. And I could hear it. The floor. It was singing. But not words. Just humming. Happy and aloof. It wasn't paying attention. I pushed myself up, and leaned back on my knees. Then I looked at where my chest had been. Still a deep blue. I looked up at the chief.

"My people are the creators and builders of astrolabes," I said. "We use math to create the currents within them. The best of us have the gift to bring harmony so delicious that we can make atoms caress each other like lovers. That's what my sister said." I blinked as it came to me. "I think that's why this edan works for me! I found it. In the desert. A wild woman there once told me that it is a piece of old old technology; she called it a 'god stone.' I didn't believe her then, but I do now. I've had it for eight years, but it only worked for me now." I pounded my chest. "For me! On that ship full of you after you'd all done . . . done that. Let me speak for you, let me speak to them. So no more have to die."

I lowered my head, pressing my edan to my belly. Just as Okwu told me. I could hear others behind me. They could have stung me a thousand times.

"You know what they have taken from me," the chief asked.

"Yes," I said, keeping my head down.

"My stinger is my people's power," it said. "They took it from us. That's an act of war."

"My way will get your stinger back," I quickly said. Then I braced myself for the rough stab in the back. I felt the sharpness press against the nape of my neck. I bit my lower lip to keep from screaming.

"Tell your plan," Okwu said.

I spoke fast. "The pilot gets us cleared to land, then I leave the ship with one of you to negotiate with Oomza Uni to get the stinger back . . . peacefully."

"That will take our element of surprise," the chief said. "You know nothing about strategy."

"If you attack, you will kill many, but then they will kill you. All of you,"

I said. "Ahh," I hissed as the stinger pointed at my neck was pressed harder against my flesh. "Please, I'm just . . ."

"Chief, Binti doesn't know how to speak," Okwu said. "Binti is uncivilized. Forgive it. It is young, a girl."

"How can we trust it?" the Meduse beside the chief asked Okwu.

"What would I do?" I asked, my face squeezed with pain. "Run?" I wiped tears from my face. I wiped and wiped, but they kept coming. The nightmare kept happening.

"You people are good at hiding," another Meduse sneered. "especially the females like you." Several of the Meduse, including the chief, shook their tentacles and vibrated their domes in a clear display of laughter.

"Let Binti put down the edan," Okwu said.

I stared at Okwu, astonished. "What?"

"Put it down," it said. "You will be completely vulnerable. How can you be our ambassador, if you need that to stay safe from us."

"It's what allows me to hear you!" I shrieked. And it was all I had.

The chief whipped up one of its tentacles and every single Meduse in that enormous room stopped moving. They stopped as if the very currents of time stopped. Everything stopped as it does when things get so cold that they become ice. I looked around and when none of them moved, slowly, carefully I dragged myself inches forward and turned to see the Meduse behind me. Its stinger was up, at the height of where my neck had been. I looked at Okwu, who said nothing. Then at the chief. I lowered my eyes. Then I ventured another look, keeping my head low.

"Choose," the chief said.

My shield. My translator. I tried to flex the muscles in my hands. I was greeted with sharp intense pain. It had been over three days. We were five hours from Oomza Uni. I tried again. I screamed. The edan pulsed a bright blue deep within its black and gray crevices, lighting up its loops and swirls. Like one of the bioluminescent snails that invaded the edges of my home's lake.

When my left index finger pulled away from the edan, I couldn't hold the tears back. The edan's blue-white glow blurred before my eyes. My joints popped and the muscles spasmed. Then my middle finger and pinky pulled away. I bit my lip so hard that I tasted blood. I took several quick breaths and then flexed every single one of my fingers at the same time. All of my joints went CRACK! I heard a thousand wasps in my head. My body went numb. The edan fell from my hands. Right before my eyes, I saw it and I wanted to laugh. The blue current I'd conjured danced before me, the definition of harmony made from chaos.

There was a soft pap as the edan hit the floor, rolled twice, then stopped. I had just killed myself. My head grew heavy . . . and all went black.

*   *   *

The Meduse were right. I could not have represented them if I was holding the edan. This was Oomza Uni. Someone there would know everything there was to know about the edan and thus its toxicity to the Meduse. No one at Oomza Uni would have really believed I was their ambassador unless I let go.

Death. When I left my home, I died. I had not prayed to the Seven before I left. I didn't think it was time. I had not gone on my pilgrimage like a proper woman. I was sure I'd return to my village as a full woman to do that. I had left my family. I thought I could return to them when I'd done what I needed to do.

Now I could never go back. The Meduse. The Meduse are not what we humans think. They are truth. They are clarity. They are decisive. They are sharp lines and edges. They understand honor and dishonor. I had to earn their honor and the only way to do that was by dying a second time.

I felt the stinger plunge into my spine just before I blacked out and just after I'd conjured up the wild line of current that I guided to the edan. It was a terrible pain. Then I left. I left them, I left that ship. I could hear the ship singing its half-word song and I knew it was singing to me. My last thought was to my family, and I hoped it reached them.

*   *   *

Home. I smelled the earth at the border of the desert just before it rained, during Fertile Season. The place right behind the Root, where I dug up the clay I used for my otjize and chased the geckos who were too fragile to survive a mile away in the desert. I opened my eyes; I was on my bed in my room, naked except for my wrapped skirt. The rest of my body was smooth with a thick layer of otjize. I flared my nostrils and inhaled the smell of me. Home . . .

I sat up and something rolled off my chest. It landed in my crotch and I grabbed it. The edan. It was cool in my hand and all dull blue as it had been for years before. I reached behind and felt my back. The spot where the stinger had stabbed me was sore and I could feel something rough and scabby there. It too was covered with otjize. My astrolabe sat on the curve of the window and I checked my map and stared outside for a very long time. I grunted, slowly standing up. My foot hit something on the floor. My jar. I put the edan down and picked it up, grasping it with both hands. The jar was more than half-empty. I laughed, dressed and stared out the window again. We were landing on Oomza Uni in an hour and the view was spectacular.

* * *

They did not come. Not to tell me what to do or when to do it. So I strapped myself in the black landing chair beside the window and stared at the incredible sight expanding before my eyes. There were two suns, one that was very small and one that was large but comfortably far away. Hours of sunshine on all parts of the planet were far more than hours of dark, but there were few deserts on Oomza Uni.

I used my astrolabe in binocular vision to see things up close. Oomza Uni, such a small planet compared to Earth. Only one third water, its lands were every shade of the rainbow—some parts blue, green, white, purple, red, white, black, orange. And some areas were smooth, others jagged with peaks that touched the clouds. And the area we were hurtling toward was orange, but interrupted by patches of the dense green of large forests of trees, small lakes, and the hard gray-blue forests of tall skyscrapers.

My ears popped as we entered the atmosphere. The sky started to turn a light pinkish color, then red orange. I was looking out from within a fireball. We were inside the air that was being ripped apart as we entered the atmosphere. There wasn't much shaking or vibrating, but I could see the heat generated by the ship. The ship would shed its skin the day after we arrived as it readjusted to gravity.

We descended from the sky and zoomed between monstrously beautiful structures that made the skyscrapers of Earth look miniscule. I laughed wildly as we descended lower and lower. Down down, we fell. No military ships came to shoot us out of the sky. We landed and, moments after smiling with excitement, I wondered if they would kill the pilot now that he was useless? I had not negotiated that with the Meduse. I ripped off my safety belt and jumped up and then fell to the floor. My legs felt like weights.

"What is . . ."

I heard a horrible noise, a low rumble that boiled to an angry-sounding growl. I looked around, sure there was a monster about to enter my room. But then I realized two things. Okwu was standing in my doorway and I understood what it was saying.

I did as it said and pushed myself into a sitting position, bringing my legs to my chest. I grasped the side of my bed and dragged myself up to sit on it.

"Take your time," Okwu said. "Your kind do not adjust quickly to jadevia."

"You mean gravity?" I asked.

"Yes."

I slowly stood up. I took a step and looked at Okwu, then past it at the empty doorway. "Where are the others?"

"Waiting in the dining room."

"The pilot?" I asked.

"In the dining room as well."

"Alive?"

"Yes."

I sighed, relieved, and then paused. The sound of its speech vibrating against my skin. This was its true voice. I could not only hear at its frequency, but I saw its tentacles quiver as it spoke. And I could understand it. Before, it had just looked like their tentacles were quivering for no reason.

"Was it the sting?" I asked.

"No," it said. "That is something else. You understand, because you truly are what you say you are—a harmonizer."

I didn't care to understand. Not at the moment.

"Your tentacle," I said. "Your okuoko." It hung straight, still pink but now translucent like the others.

"The rest was used to help several of our sick," it said. "Your people will be remembered by my people."

The more it spoke, the less monstrous its voice sounded. I took another step.

"Are you ready?" Okwu asked.

I was. I left the edan behind with my other things.

*   *   *

I was still weak from the landing, but this had to happen fast. I don't know how they broke the news of their presence to Oomza Uni authorities, but they must have. Otherwise, how would we be able to leave the ship during the brightest part of the day?

I understood the plan as soon as Okwu and the chief came to my room. I followed them down the hallway. We did not pass through the dining room where so many had been brutally killed, and I was glad. But as we passed the entrance, I saw all the Meduse in there. The bodies were all gone. The chairs and tables were all stacked on one side of the large room as if a windstorm had swept through it. Between the transparent folds and tentacles, I thought I glimpsed someone in the red flowing uniform of the pilot, but I wasn't sure.

"You know what you will say," the chief said. Not a question, but a statement. And within the statement, a threat.

I wore my best red shirt and wrapper, made from the threads of well-fed silkworms. I'd bought it for my first day of class at Oomza Uni, but this was a more important occasion. And I'd used fresh otjize on my skin and to thicken my plaited hair even more. As I'd palm rolled my plaits smooth like the bodies of snakes, I noticed that my hair had grown about an inch since I'd left home. This was odd. I looked at the thick wiry new growth, admiring its dark brown color before pressing the otjize onto it, making it red. There was a tingling sensation on my scalp as I worked the otjize in and my head ached. I was exhausted. I held my otjize-covered hands to my nose and inhaled the scent of home.

Years ago, I had snuck out to the lake one night with some other girls and we'd all washed and scrubbed off all our otjize using the lake's salty water. It took us half the night. Then we'd stared at each other horrified by what we'd done. If any man saw us, we'd be ruined for life. If our parents saw us, we'd all be beaten and that would only be a fraction of the punishment. Our families and people we knew would think us mentally unstable when they heard, and that too would ruin our chances of marriage.

But above all this, outside of the horror of what we'd done, we all felt an awesome glorious . . . shock. Our hair hung in thick clumps, black in the moonlight. Our skin glistened, dark brown. Glistened. And there had been a breeze that night and it felt amazing on our exposed skin. I thought of this as I applied the otjize to my new growth, covering up the dark brown color of my hair. What if I washed it all off now? I was the first of my people to come to Oomza Uni, would the people here even know the difference? But Okwu and the chief came minutes later and there was no time. Plus, really, this was Oomza Uni, someone would have researched and known of my people. And that person would know I was naked if I washed all my otjize off . . . and crazy.

I didn't want to do it anyway, I thought as I walked behind Okwu and the chief. There were soldiers waiting at the doorway; both were human and I wondered what point they were trying to make by doing that. Just like the photos in the books I read, they wore all-blue kaftans and no shoes.

"You first," the chief growled, moving behind me. I felt one of its tentacles, heavy and smooth, shove me softly in the back right where I'd been stung. The soreness there caused me to stand up taller. And then more softly in a voice that only tickled my ear with its strange vibration. "Look strong, girl."

Following the soldiers and followed by two Meduse, I stepped onto the surface of another planet for the first time in my life. My scalp was still tingling, and this added to the magical sensation of being so far from home. The first thing I noticed was the smell and weight of the air when I walked off the ship. It smelled jungly, green, heavy with leaves. The air was full of water. It was just like the air in the ship's plant-filled breathing chambers!

I parted my lips and inhaled it as I followed the soldiers down the open black walkway. Behind me, I heard the Meduse, pluming out and sucking in gas. Softly, though, unlike on the ship. We were walking toward a great building, the ship port.

"We will take you to the Oomza Uni Presidential Building," one of the soldiers said in to me in perfect Khoush. He looked up at the Meduse and I saw a crease of worry wrinkle his brow. "I don't know . . . their language. Can you . . ."

I nodded.

He looked about twenty-five and was dark brown skinned like me, but unlike the men of my people, his skin was naked, his hair shaven low, and he was quite short, standing a head shorter than me. "Do you mind swift transport?"

I turned and translated for Okwu and the chief.

"These people are primitive," the chief responded. But it and Okwu agreed to board the shuttle.

*   *   *

The room's wall and floor were a light blue, the large open windows letting in sunshine and a warm breeze. There were ten professors, one from each of the ten university departments. They sat, stood, hovered, and crouched behind a long table of glass. Against every wall were soldiers wearing blue uniforms of cloth, color, and light. There were so many different types of people in the room that I found it hard to concentrate. But I had to or there would be more death.

The one who spoke for all the professors looked like one of the sand people's gods and I almost laughed. It was like a spider made of wind, gray and undulating, here and not quite there. When it spoke, it was in a whisper that I could clearly hear despite the fact that I was several feet away. And it spoke in the language of the Meduse.

It introduced itself as something that sounded like "Haras" and said, "Tell me what you need to tell me."

And then all attention was suddenly on me.

*   *   *

"None of you have ever seen anyone like me," I said. "I come from a people who live near a small salty lake on the edge of a desert. On my people's land, fresh water, water humans can drink, is so little that we do not use it to bathe as so many others do. We wash with otjize, a mix of red clay from our land and oils from our local flowers."

Several of the human professors looked at each other and chuckled. One of the large insectile people clicked its mandibles. I frowned, flaring my nostrils. It was the first time I'd received treatment similar to the way my people were treated on Earth by the Khoush. In a way, this set me at ease. People were people, everywhere. These professors were just like anyone else.

"This was my first time leaving the home of my parents. I had never even left my own city, let alone my planet Earth. Days later, in the blackness of space, everyone on my ship but the pilot was killed, many right before my eyes, by a people at war with those who view my own people as near slaves." I waited for this to sink in, then continued. "You've never seen the Meduse, either. Only studied them . . . from afar. I know. I have read about them too." I stepped forward. "Or maybe some of you or your students have studied the stinger you have in the weapons museum up close."

I saw several of them look at each other. Some murmured to one another. Others, I did not know well enough to tell what they were doing. As I spoke, I fell into a rhythm, a meditative state very much like my math-induced ones.

Except I was fully present, and before long tears were falling from my eyes. I told them in detail about watching Heru's chest burst open, desperately grabbing food, staying in that room waiting to die, the edan saving me and not knowing how or why or what.

I spoke of Okwu and how my otjize had really been what saved me. I spoke of the Meduse's cold exactness, focus, violence, sense of honor, and willingness to listen. I said things that I didn't know I'd thought about or comprehended. I found words I didn't even know I knew. And eventually, I told them how they could satisfy the Meduse and prevent a bloodbath in which everyone would lose.

I was sure they would agree. These professors were educated beyond anything I could imagine. Thoughtful. Insightful. United. Individual. The Meduse chief came forward and spoke its piece, as well. It was angry, but thorough, eloquent with a sterile logic. "If you do not give it to us willingly, we have the right to take back what was brutally stolen from us without provocation," the chief said.

After the chief spoke, the professors discussed among themselves for over an hour. They did not retreat to a separate room to do this. They did it right before the chief, Okwu, and me. They moved from the glass table and stood in a group.

Okwu, the chief, and I just stood there. Back in my home, the elders were always stoic and quiet and they always discussed everything in private. It must have been the same for the Meduse, because Okwu's tentacles shuddered and it said, "What kind of people are these?"

"Let them do the right thing," the chief said.

Feet away from us, beyond the glass table, these professors were shouting with anger, sometimes guffawing with glee, flicking antennae in each other's faces, making ear-popping clicks to get the attention of colleagues. One professor, about the size of my head, flew from one part of the group to the other, producing webs of gray light that slowly descended on the group. This chaotic method of madness would decide whether I would live or die.

I caught bits and pieces of the discussion about Meduse history and methods, the mechanics of the Third Fish, the scholars who'd brought the stinger. Okwu and the chief didn't seem to mind hovering there waiting. However, my legs soon grew tired and I sat down right there on the blue floor.

* * *

Finally, the professors quieted and took their places at the glass table again. I stood up, my heart seeming to pound in my mouth, my palms sweaty. I glanced at the chief and felt even more nervous; its okuoko were vibrating and its blue color was deeper, almost glowing. When I looked at Okwu, where its okuoko hung, I caught a glimpse of the white of its stinger, ready to strike.

The spiderlike Haras raised two front legs and spoke in the language of the Meduse and said, "On behalf of all the people of Oomza Uni and on behalf of Oomza University, I apologize for the actions of a group of our own in taking the stinger from you, Chief Meduse. The scholars who did this will be found, expelled, and exiled. Museum specimen of such prestige are highly prized at our university, however such things must only be acquired with permission from the people to whom they belong. Oomza protocol is based on honor, respect, wisdom, and knowledge. We will return it to you immediately."

My legs grew weak and before I knew it, I was sitting back on the floor. My head felt heavy and tingly, my thoughts scattered. "I'm sorry," I said, in the language I'd spoken all my life. I felt something press my back, steadying me. Okwu.

"I am all right," I said, pushing my hands to the floor and standing back up. But Okwu kept a tentacle to my back.

The one named Haras continued. "Binti, you have made your people proud and I'd personally like to welcome you to Oomza Uni." It motioned one of its limbs toward the human woman beside it. She looked Khoush and wore tight-fitting green garments that clasped every part of her body, from neck to toe. "This is Okpala. She is in our mathematics department. When you are settled, aside from taking classes with her, you will study your edan with her. According to Okpala, what you did is impossible."

I opened my mouth to speak, but Okpala put up a hand and I shut my mouth.

"We have one request," Haras said. "We of Oomza Uni wish Okwu to stay behind as the first Meduse student to attend the university and as a showing of allegiance between Oomza Uni governments and the Meduse and a renewal of the pact between human and Meduse."

I heard Okwu rumble behind me, then the chief was speaking up. "For the first time in my own lifetime, I am learning something completely outside of core beliefs," the chief said. "Who'd have thought that a place harboring human beings could carry such honor and foresight." It paused and then said, "I will confer with my advisors before I make my decision."

The chief was pleased. I could hear it in its voice. I looked around me. No one from my tribe. At once, I felt both part of something historic and very alone. Would my family even comprehend it all when I explained it to them? Or would they just fixate on the fact that I'd almost died, was now too far to return home and had left them in order to make the "biggest mistake of my life"?

I swayed on my feet, a smile on my face.

"Binti," the one named Okpala said. "What will you do now?"

"What do you mean?" I asked. "I want to study mathematics and currents. Maybe create a new type of astrolabe. The edan, I want to study that and . . ."

"Yes," she said. "That is true, but what about your home? Will you ever return?"

"Of course," I said. "Eventually, I will visit and . . ."

"I have studied your people," she said. "They don't like outsiders."

"I'm not an outsider," I said, with a twinge of irritation. "I am . . ." And that's when it caught my eye. My hair was rested against my back, weighed down by the otjize, but as I'd gotten up, one lock had come to rest on my shoulder. I felt it rub against the front of my shoulder and I saw it now.

I frowned, not wanting to move. Before the realization hit me, I knew to drop into meditation, treeing out of desperation. I held myself in there for a moment, equations flying through my mind, like wind and sand. Around me, I heard movement and, still treeing, I saw that the soldiers were leaving the room. The professors were getting up, talking among themselves in their various ways. All except Okpala. She was looking right at me.

I slowly lifted up one of my locks and brought it forward I rubbed off the ojtize. It glowed a strong deep blue like the sky back on earth on a clear day, like Okwu and so many of the other Meduse, like the uniforms of the Oomza Uni soldiers. And it was translucent. Soft, but tough. I touched the top of my head and pressed. They felt the same and . . . I felt my hand touching them. The tingling sensation was gone. My hair was no longer hair. There was a ringing in my ear as I began to breathe heavily, still in meditation. I wanted to tear off my clothes and inspect every part of my body. To see what else that sting had changed. It had not been a sting. A sting would have torn out my insides, as it did for Heru.

"Only those," Okwu said. "Nothing else."

"This is why I understand you?" I flatly asked. Talking while in meditation was like softly whispering from a hole deep in the ground. I was looking up from a cool dark place.

"Yes."

"Why?"

"Because you had to understand us and it was the only way," Okwu said.

"And you needed to prove to them that you were truly our ambassador, not prisoner," the chief said. It paused. "I will return to the ship; we will make our decision about Okwu." It turned to leave and then turned back. "Binti, you will forever hold the highest honor among the Meduse. My destiny is stronger for leading me to you." Then it left.

I stood there, in my strange body. If I hadn't been deep in meditation I would have screamed and screamed. I was so far from home.

*   *   *

I'm told that news of what had happened spread across all Oomza Uni within minutes. It was said that a human tribal female from a distant blue planet saved the university from Meduse terrorists by sacrificing her blood and using her unique gift of mathematical harmony and ancestral magic. "Tribal": that's what they called humans from ethnic groups too remote and "uncivilized" to regularly send students to attend Oomza Uni.

Over the next two days, I learned that people viewed my reddened dark skin and strange hair with wonder. And when they saw me with Okwu, they grew tense and quiet, moving away. Where they saw me as a fascinating exotic human, they saw Okwu as a dangerous threat. Okwu was of a warlike people who, up until now, had only been viewed with fear among people from all over. Okwu enjoyed its infamy, whereas I just wanted to find a quiet desert to walk into so I could study in peace.

"All people fear decisive proud honor," Okwu proclaimed.

We were in one of the Weapons City libraries, staring at the empty chamber where the chief's stinger had been kept. A three-hour transport from Math City, Weapons City was packed with activity on every street and crowded with sprawling flat gray buildings made of stone. Beneath each of these structures were inverted buildings that extended at least a half-mile underground where only those students, researchers, and professors involved knew what was being invented, tested, or destroyed. After the meeting, this was where they'd taken me, the chief, and Okwu for the retrieval of the stinger.

We'd been escorted by a person who looked like a small green child with roots for a head, who I later learned was the head professor of Weapons City. He was the one who went into the five-by-five-foot case made of thick clear crystal and opened it. The stinger was placed atop a slab of crystal and looked like a sharp tusk of ice.

The chief slowly approached the case, extended an okuoko, and then let out a large bluish plume of gas the moment its okuoko touched the stinger. I'll never forget the way the chief's body went from blue to clear the moment the stinger became a part of it again. Only a blue line remained at the point of demarcation where it had reattached—a scar that would always remind it of what human beings of Oomza Uni had done to it for the sake of research and academics.

Afterward, just before the chief and the others boarded the Third Fish that would take them back to their own ship just outside the atmosphere, upon Okwu's request, I knelt before the chief and placed its stinger on my lap. It was heavy and it felt like a slab of solid water and the edge at its tip looked like it could slice into another universe. I smeared a dollop of my otjize on the blue scar where it had reattached. After a minute, I wiped some of it away. The blue scar was gone. Their chief was returned to its full royal translucence, they had the half jar of otjize Okwu had taken from me, which healed their flesh like magic, and they were leaving one of their own as the first Meduse to study at the great Oomza University. The Meduse left Oomza Uni happier and better off than when they'd arrived.

*   *   *

My otjize. Yes, there is a story there. Weeks later, after I'd started classes and people had finally started to leave me be, opting to simply stare and gossip in silence instead, I ran out of otjize. For days, I'd known it would happen. I'd found a sweet-smelling oil of the same chemical makeup in the market. A black flower that grew in a series of nearby caverns produced the oil. But a similar clay was much harder to find. There was a forest not far from my dorm, across the busy streets, just beyond one of the classroom buildings. I'd never seen anyone go into it, but there was a path opening.

That evening, before dark, I walked in there. I walked fast, ignoring all the stares and grateful when the presence of people tapered off the closer I got to the path entrance. I carried my satchel with my astrolabe, a bag of nuts, my edan in my hands, cool and small. I squeezed my edan as I left the road and stepped onto the path. The forest seemed to swallow me within a few steps and I could no longer see the purpling sky. My skin felt near naked, the layer of otjize I wore was so thin.

I frowned, hesitating for a moment. We didn't have such places where I came from and the denseness of the trees, all the leaves, the small buzzing creatures, made me feel like the forest was choking me. But then I looked at the ground. I looked right there, at my sandaled feet and found precisely what I needed.

I made the otjize that night. I mixed it and then let it sit in the strong sunshine for the next day. I didn't go to class, nor did I eat that day. In the evening, I went to the dorm and showered and did that which my people rarely do: I washed with water. As I let the water run through my hair and down my face, I wept. This was all I had left of my homeland and it was being washed into the runnels that would feed the trees outside my dorm.

When I finished, I stood there, away from the running stream of water that flowed from the ceiling. Slowly, I reached up. I touched my "hair." The okuoko were soft but firm and slippery with wetness. They touched my back, soft and slick. I shook them, feeling them otjize-free for the first time.

I shut my eyes and prayed to the Seven; I hadn't done this since arriving on the planet. I prayed to my living parents and ancestors. I opened my eyes. It was time to call home. Soon.

I peeked out of the washing space. I shared the space with five other human students. One of them just happened to be leaving as I peeked out. As soon as he was gone, I grabbed my wrapper and came out. I wrapped it around my waist and I looked at myself in the large mirror. I looked for a very very long time. Not at my dark brown skin, but where my hair had been. The okuoko were a soft transparent blue with darker blue dots at their tips. They grew out of my head as if they'd been doing that all my life, so natural looking that I couldn't say they were ugly. They were just a little longer than my hair had been, hanging just past my backside, and they were thick as sizable snakes.

There were ten of them and I could no longer braid them into my family's code pattern as I had done with my own hair. I pinched one and felt the pressure. Would they grow like hair? Were they hair? I could ask Okwu, but I wasn't ready to ask it anything. Not yet. I quickly ran to my room and sat in the sun and let them dry.

Ten hours later, when dark finally fell, it was time. I'd bought the container at the market; it was made from the shed exoskeleton of students who sold them for spending money. It was clear like one of Okwu's tentacles and dyed red. I'd packed it with the fresh otjize, which now looked thick and ready.

I pressed my right index and middle finger together and was about to dig out the first dollop when I hesitated, suddenly incredibly unsure. What if my fingers passed right through it like liquid soap? What if what I'd harvested from the forest wasn't clay at all? What if it was hard like stone?

I pulled my hand away and took a deep breath. If I couldn't make otjize here, then I'd have to . . . change. I touched one of my tentacle-like locks and felt a painful pressure in my chest as my mind tried to take me to a place I wasn't ready to go to. I plunged my two fingers into my new concoction . . . and scooped it up. I spread it on my flesh. Then I wept.

I went to see Okwu in its dorm. I was still unsure what to call those who lived in this large gas-filled spherical complex. When you entered, it was just one great space where plants grew on the walls and hung from the ceiling. There were no individual rooms, and people who looked like Okwu in some ways but different in others walked across the expansive floor, up the walls, on the ceiling. Somehow, when I came to the front entrance, Okwu would always come within the next few minutes. It would always emit a large plume of gas as it readjusted to the air outside.

"You look well," it said, as we walked down the walkway. We both loved the walkway because of the winds the warm clear seawater created as it rushed by below.

I smiled. "I feel well."

"When did you make it?"

"Over the last two suns," I said.

"I'm glad," it said. "You were beginning to fade."

It held up an okuoko. "I was working with a yellow current to use in one of my classmate's body tech," it said.

"Oh," I said, looking at its burned flesh.

We paused, looking down at the rushing waters. The relief I'd felt at the naturalness, the trueness of the otjize immediately started waning. This was the real test. I rubbed some otjize from my arm and then took Okwu's okuoko in my hand. I applied the otjize and then let the okuoko drop as I held my breath. We walked back to my dorm. My otjize from Earth had healed Okwu and then the chief. It would heal many others. The otjize created by my people, mixed with my homeland. This was the foundation of the Meduse's respect for me. Now all of it was gone. I was someone else. Not even fully Himba anymore. What would Okwu think of me now?

When we got to my dorm, we stopped.

"I know what you are thinking," Okwu said.

"I know you Meduse," I said. "You're people of honor, but you're firm and rigid. And traditional." I felt sorrow wash over and I sobbed, covering my face with my hand. Feeling my otjize smear beneath it. "But you've become my friend," I said. When I brought my hand away, my palm was red with otjize. "You are all I have here. I don't know how it happened, but you are . . ."

"You will call your family and have them," Okwu said.

I frowned and stepped away from Okwu. "So callous," I whispered.

"Binti," Okwu said. It plumed out gas, in what I knew was a laugh. "Whether you carry the substance that can heal and bring life back to my people or not, I am your friend. I am honored to know you." It shook its okuoko, making one of them vibrate. I yelped when I felt the vibration in one of mine.

"What is that?" I shouted, holding up my hands.

"It means we are family through battle," it said. "You are the first to join our family in this way in a long time. We do not like humans."

I smiled.

He held up an okuoko. "Show it to me tomorrow," I said, doubtfully.

"Tomorrow will be the same," it said.

When I rubbed off the otjize the burn was gone.

*   *   *

I sat in the silence of my room looking at my edan as I sent out a signal to my family with my astrolabe. Outside was dark and I looked into the sky, at the stars, knowing the pink one was home. The first to answer was my mother.

EXCERPT FROM *RAISING CAINE*

CHARLES E. GANNON

Dr. Charles E. Gannon's award-winning Caine Riordan/Terran Republic hard sf novels have been multiply best-selling and Nebula finalists He also collaborates with Eric Flint in the NYT and WSJ best-selling Ring of Fire alternate history series. His other novels and short fiction straddle the divide between hard SF and technothrillers and have appeared through various imprints and in various magazines. He also worked extensively in game design and writing, as well as being a scriptwriter and producer in New York City, where his clients included the United Nations, the World Health Organization, and PBS.

A Distinguished Professor of English and Fulbright Senior Specialist, his book Rumors of War and Infernal Machines *won the 2006 American Library Association Choice Award for Outstanding Book. He is a recipient of five Fulbright Fellowships and Travel Grants and has been a subject matter expert both for national media venues such as NPR and the Discovery Channel, as well as for various intelligence and defense agencies, including DHS, Pentagon, every service branch, NATO, DARPA, ONR, NRO, NASA, and several other organizations with which he signed NDAs.*

FROM THE AUTHOR

Writing Raising Caine *started with me poring over almost 40,000 words of notes, and then listening to something like four hours of audio notes.*

Here's why: the Caine Riordan/Terran Republic series (of which it is the third volume) is, in part, a chronicle of humanity's transition from thinking itself alone in the universe to realizing that it is not. It's not, however, a polarized, "us-them," first contact saga, because there are several different races (four, or five, depending upon how you count them). But the confusions and conflicts that arise are not merely (or even primarily) caused by contemporary differences, but are revealed to emerge from a local history of which humanity has not yet been apprised. In short, much of the deeper narrative action is how the layers of hidden knowledge are peeled away like the layers of an onion, and how that process results in both new perceptions and misperceptions. Consequently, understanding any (let alone all) of the exosapients occurs not all at once, or even in one book, but over time, particularly as the humans come to understand what was happening in this stellar cluster before they emerged into it.

To put it lightly, a story (well, a mosaic) like this has a lot of moving parts. Not just in terms of characters and current events, but the constantly changing state of knowledge of the various entities (human and otherwise) who are involved in these uncertain and often half-veiled exchanges. This means resolving threads set out in prior books, evolving others which will only be resolved later, and starting new ones. Raising Caine had a lot of this traffic, even though it did not dominate the "text" of the narrative. Rather, it was the subtext which, like bedrock, shapes the topography of the surface: of the unfolding and immediate events of the story. So, although I am partially a "pantser" when it comes to individual scenes, my "plotter" hat was jammed firmly on my head as I wove this tale of misdirection, survival, and betrayal during a diplomatic effort to forge a relationship with another species.

Chapter Twenty-Two

BIOBAND'S VALLAND
GJ 1248 ONE ("ADUMBRATUS")

As Caine worked his way to the head of the legation, Yiithrii'ah'aash continued on into a grove of immense, hypertrophied bushes which were simultaneously reminiscent of pointy mushrooms and very squat Christmas trees. "These are one of our most effective organisms for inducing xenobiots to become receptive to our own flora. And ultimately, to our settlers and other fauna."

Trent Howarth looked around, puzzled. "Isn't this planet already inhabited by Slaasriithi?" He glanced meaningfully at the ambassador's shorter, thicker assistants.

"What you see, Mr. Howarth, are pioneer inducers of change, not colonists. Their life work is to shape the environment by fostering symbiotic or cooperative relationships between the indigenous biota and our own. Where that is not possible, we will establish preserves of our own biota by crowding out the native ones. These plants excel at that task." Yiithrii'ah'aash gestured toward what Riordan was already thinking of as a cone tree. "By using their canopy to capture all the light and water that would normally find its way down to the ground, and by selectively sharing the resulting resources with our own—or receptive indigenous—biota, the trees claim the area beneath them for our exploitation. We introduce our own biota into it, and then work at inducing further mutations to maximize the harmony between the two families of bioforms."

Phil Friel's soft voice rose from the rear of the group. "You keep using the word 'induce' when you speak about changing an organism. Since you seem to have a wide command of our language, I'm wondering if that repetition is not merely intentional, but important." Tina Melah glanced at the quiet Irishman with unveiled admiration. Of course, Tina didn't seem to bother with veils of any type.

Yiithrii'ah'aash purred. "Indeed, we use the word 'induce' quite purposefully. It describes how we prefer to transform biota: to provide the correct environmental circumstances and monitoring to encourage natural change in a desired direction. Creating change by using sudden force, whether by traumatic stimuli or mechanistic alteration, rarely produces stable environmental blending."

They left the grove of cone trees along a path that straddled an irregular border between day-glo green lichens struggling out from beneath the Slaasriithi plants on one side and a diffuse violet moss pierced by intermittent black spikes on the other side. Caine tried to recall an analog for the latter flora, but the only image that came to mind was of sea urchins trying to push up through a carpet of violet cotton candy. The ground between the two masses of plants was a tangle of runners from both, many of which were brown and lank: die-off where the two families of vegetation met, fought, and died.

Oleg Danysh squinted along their probable path, which remained in the shade of the brightside wall: the high terminal moraine that sheltered both the indigenous and exogenous biota from the steady red-gold light of GJ 1248. "It seems, Ambassador, that you mean to follow the contact margin between your own imported species, and those native to this planet."

"Very astute, Dr. Danysh. In addition to keeping us in the shade of the ridgeline, it allows us to visit where we are making our greatest progress to transform the native life. And so, it offers you the best opportunities to learn about us."

"Well, about your work as planet-changers, at least," Tina Melah drawled.

Yiithrii'ah'aash's head turned back in her direction; he did not slow his forward progress. "You may find, Ms. Melah, that the latter reveals the former more profoundly than any other behavior of ours. What we do here is no different from what we do everywhere."

"Even on your homeworld?" she wondered.

"Especially on our homeworld," Yiithrii'ah'aash emphasized. "We seek to reconcile and blend different species, taxae, individuals. It is the great challenge and conundrum of life, wherever it exists, that stability is only achieved by acknowledging the inevitability of change, and is only preserved by working with the forces of entropy to create a dynamic equilibrium in the natural order."

Gaspard aimed his chin toward the rose-tinted cream sky. "And if those endeavors reveal the nature of the Slaasriithi best, which behaviors would you say reveal humanity's nature most clearly to you?"

"We have not known you for that long." Yiithrii'ah'aash might have sounded evasive.

"True, but you have had reports on us from the Custodians while we were a protected species, and you have had access to a full compendium of our history and media for almost a year now. Surely you have some sense of which endeavors reveal the most about us."

"I do," Yiithrii'ah'aash admitted slowly. "Human nature, we find, is best revealed in endeavors characterized by uncertainty, innovation and crisis. So, we find depictions of your exploration, and of rescue operations, particularly informing."

Caine waited for the third category of activity and, when he did not hear it, asked outright. "And war?"

Yiithrii'ah'aash slowed slightly, swiveled his head back at Riordan. "Yes. Most especially, war."

They continued up the rough trail in silence.

* * *

The legation descended into a flat expanse where the native "forest"—stacks of vine-bound cream-teal tumbleweeds—were embroiled in a war of econiche flanking maneuvers against the cone trees and giant ferns of Slaasriithi origin. Arrayed just in front of that latter mass of Kelly- and lime-green vegetation, Slaasriithi were patiently watching some of their own fauna roll what looked like unripe grapefruits toward a waiting clutch of indigenous animals. The Slaasriithi creatures, which resembled a nutria–flying squirrel hybrid with far too many eyes, deposited the fruits in the midground between the two groups, then backed off a few steps and waited.

Their local counterparts—smooth, leather-backed creatures with six squat legs, four small eyes, and a head that resembled an armor-plated badger crossbred with a catfish—waited, watched, and began side-winding forward. Several emitted a crackling hiss as they approached. In response to those which hissed, the surprisingly swift Slaasriithi nutria-squirrels scuttled forward and grabbed their fruits back to safety. In the case of the local creatures that approached more placidly, the flap-legged nutrias edged forward slightly. In most cases, the local creatures retreated. In several cases, they tolerated the modest advance of the alien animals until they could grab the fruit and scramble away. When the more truculent catfish-badgers then tried to muscle in and get some of the water-rich fruits retrieved by their fellows, the Slaasriithi summoned an almost invisible drone, which made a quick pass between the contending local creatures. The drone was noiseless and did not visibly discharge any payload, but it must have released a marker spore which repulsed the less cooperative local creature: in each case, the would-be fruit hijacker scuttled away empty-handed.

Another group of Slaasriithi, a taxon subtly different in physiology, unobtrusively followed the more cooperative local creatures. When they began tearing into their fruit, the Slaasriithi released insects which quickly caught the familiar scent. They hovered over the backs of the greedily feeding indigenous creatures until they abandoned the stripped rind. Then the insects descended to scavenge the remains.

"Let me guess," Ben Hwang muttered, his arms folded. "By hovering over the local animals, these insects inadvertently 'marked' them. That allows you to follow the individuals which grabbed the fruit and to encourage their propagation."

Yiithrii'ah'aash seemed pleased. "You are an exceptionally quick study, Doctor Hwang. Your surmise is correct. The rest is, I trust, obvious."

Hirano Mizuki nodded. "The indigenous creatures which have tolerated greater proximity with your own species, being better fed and hydrated, now have better survival and breeding odds. In that way, you are increasing the prevalence of whatever combination of predisposition and learned behaviors made them more tolerant. Conversely, by ensuring that the aggressive ones cannot hijack the fruit, you reduce their breeding odds and, consequently, their ability to impart the unwanted traits to subsequent generations. Over time, you will provide the changed species with additional training opportunities and consequent survival and breeding advantages. And the final step will be to increase their toleration for your own fauna until they are comfortable mingling, and even sharing the fruit."

Dora Veriden was watching the flapped nutria-squirrels. "Must be handy to have those trained muskrats ready to work for you. How long does it take to bribe them into submission?"

Yiithrii'ah'aash turned, as did several of the legation, at the facetiousness of Dora's tone. "The species you refer to, Ms. Veriden, has several of our own traits, which we find not only useful but crucial. Specifically, Slaasriithi intelligence arose not so much from tool use, but from our reflex to establish relationships with other species, and thereby increase our social sophistication, specialization, and survival strategies."

The ambassador gestured back toward the nutria-squirrels. "We did not *train* these creatures to apply a crude version of operant conditioning upon these indigenous species. It is a reflex, coded into their genetic matrix. This is how they, and we, survive and ultimately thrive in new environments."

NEBULA AWARD NOMINEE
BEST NOVEL

EXCERPT FROM *THE FIFTH SEASON*

N. K. JEMISIN

N. K. Jemisin is a Brooklyn author who won the Hugo Award for Best Novel for The Fifth Season, *which was also a New York Times Notable Book of 2015. She previously won the Locus Award for her first novel,* The Hundred Thousand Kingdoms, *and her short fiction and novels have been nominated multiple times for Hugo, World Fantasy, and Nebula awards, and shortlisted for the Crawford and the James Tiptree, Jr. awards. She is a science fiction and fantasy reviewer for the* New York Times, *and you can find her online at nkjemisin.com.*

FROM THE AUTHOR

I actually talked about this on my blog back when I first started it, in the blog post "Carving a New World" (nkjemisin.com/2011/12/ carving-a-new-world/). Basically, I wrote a simple synopsis, then wrote some test chapters to get a better feel for the voice I needed; this is something I do for every new novel. Then I wrote something that I call a "proof of concept" short story—not necessarily the same characters, but giving the worldbuilding a road test. The proof of concept story for The Fifth Season *was actually published in Clarkesworld as "Stone Hunger" (clarkesworldmagazine.com/jemisin_07_14/). I did spend a while doing research into seismology, because I'm nothing but an armchair enthusiast. This involved a lovely, exhausting four-day trip to Hawai'i, in which I visited a volcano per day. Then I settled into writing. The whole thing took me about a year and a half.*

prologue
you are here

Let's start with the end of the world, why don't we? Get it over with and move on to more interesting things.

First, a personal ending. There is a thing she will think over and over in the days to come, as she imagines how her son died and tries to make sense of something so innately senseless. She will cover Uche's broken little body with a blanket—except his face, because he is afraid of the dark—and she will sit beside it numb, and she will pay no attention to the world that is ending outside. The world has already ended within her, and neither ending is for the first time. She's old hat at this by now.

What she thinks then, and thereafter, is: *But he was free.*

And it is her bitter, weary self that answers this almost-question every time her bewildered, shocked self manages to produce it:

He wasn't. Not really. But now he will be.

*   *   *

But you need context. Let's try the ending again, writ continentally.

Here is a land.

It is ordinary, as lands go. Mountains and plateaus and canyons and river deltas, the usual. Ordinary, except for its size, and its dynamism. It moves a lot, this land. Like an old man lying restlessly abed it heaves and sighs, puckers and farts, yawns and swallows. Naturally this land's people have named it *the Stillness.* It is a land of quiet and bitter irony.

The Stillness has had other names. It was once several other lands. It's one vast, unbroken continent at present, but at some point in the future it will be more than one again.

Very soon now, actually.

The end begins in a city: the oldest, largest, and most magnificent living city in the world. The city is called Yumenes, and once it was the heart of an empire. It is still the heart of many things, though the empire has wilted somewhat in the years since its first bloom, as empires do.

Yumenes is not unique because of its size. There are many large cities in this part of the world, chain-linked along the equator like a continental girdle.

Elsewhere in the world villages rarely grow into towns, and towns rarely become cities, because all such polities are hard to keep alive when the earth keeps trying to eat them . . . but Yumenes has been stable for most of its twenty-seven centuries.

Yumenes is unique because here alone have human beings dared to build not for safety, not for comfort, not even for beauty, but for bravery. The city's walls are a masterwork of delicate mosaics and embossing detailing its people's long and brutal history. The clumping masses of its buildings are punctuated by great high towers like fingers of stone, hand-wrought lanterns powered by the marvel of hydroelectricity, delicately-arching bridges woven of glass and audacity, and architectural structures called *balconies* that are so simple, yet so breathtakingly foolish, that no one has ever built them before in written history. (But much of history is unwritten. Remember this.) The streets are paved not with easy-to-replace cobbles, but with a smooth, unbroken, and miraculous substance the locals have dubbed *asphalt*. Even the shanties of Yumenes are daring, because they're just thin-walled shacks that would blow over in a bad windstorm, let alone a shake. Yet they stand, as they have stood, for generations.

At the core of the city are many tall buildings, so it is perhaps unsurprising that one of them is larger and more daring than all the rest combined: a massive structure whose base is a star pyramid of precision-carved obsidian brick. Pyramids are the most stable architectural form, and this one is pyramids times five because why not? And because this is Yumenes, a vast geodesic sphere whose faceted walls resemble translucent amber sits at the pyramid's apex, seeming to balance there lightly—though in truth, every part of the structure is channeled toward the sole purpose of supporting it. It *looks* precarious; that is all that matters.

The Black Star is where the leaders of the empire meet to do their leaderish things. The amber sphere is where they keep their emperor, carefully preserved and perfect. He wanders its golden halls in genteel despair, doing what he is told and dreading the day his masters decide that his daughter makes a better ornament.

None of these places or people matter, by the way. I simply point them out for context.

But here is a man who will matter a great deal.

You can imagine how he looks, for now. You may also imagine what he's thinking. This might be wrong, mere conjecture, but a certain amount of likelihood applies nevertheless. Based on his subsequent actions, there are only a few thoughts that could be in his mind in this moment.

He stands on a hill not far from the Black Star's obsidian walls. From here he can see most of the city, smell its smoke, get lost in its gabble. There's a group of young women walking along one of the asphalt paths below; the hill is in a park much beloved by the city's residents. (*Keep green land within the walls*, advises stonelore, but in most communities the land is fallow-planted with legumes and other soil-enriching plants. Only in Yumenes is greenland sculpted into prettiness.) The women laugh at something one of them has said, and the sound wafts up to the man on a passing breeze. He closes his eyes and savors the faint tremolo of their voices, the fainter reverberation of their footsteps like the wingbeats of butterflies against his sessapinae. He can't sess all seven million residents of the city, mind you; he's good, but not that good. Most of them, though, yes, they are there. *Here.* He breathes deeply and becomes a fixture of the earth. They tread upon the filaments of his nerves; their voices stir the fine hairs of his skin; their breaths ripple the air he draws into his lungs. They are on him. They are in him.

But he knows that he is not, and will never be, one of them.

"Did you know," he says, conversationally, "that the first stonelore was actually *written* in stone? So that it couldn't be changed to suit fashion or politics. So it wouldn't wear away."

"I know," says his companion.

"Hnh. Yes, you were probably there when it was first set down, I forget." He sighs, watching the women walk out of sight. "It's safe to love you. You won't fail me. You won't die. And I know the price up front."

His companion does not reply. He wasn't really expecting a response, though a part of him hoped. He has been so lonely.

But hope is irrelevant, as are so many other feelings that he knows will bring him only despair if he considers them again. He has considered this enough. The time for dithering is past.

"A commandment," the man says, spreading his arms, "is set in stone."

Imagine that his face aches from smiling. He's been smiling for hours: teeth clenched, lips drawn back, eyes crinkled so the crow's feet show. There is an art to smiling in a way that others will believe. It is always important to include the eyes; otherwise, people will know you hate them.

"Chiseled words are absolute."

He speaks to no one in particular, but beside the man stands a woman—of sorts. Her emulation of human gender is only superficial, a courtesy. Likewise the loose drapelike dress that she wears is not cloth. She has simply shaped a portion of her stiff substance to suit the preferences of the fragile, mortal creatures among whom she currently moves. From a distance the illusion would work to pass her off as a woman standing still, at least for a while. Up close, however, any hypothetical observer would notice that her skin is white porcelain; that is not a metaphor. As a sculpture, she would be beautiful, if too relentlessly realistic for local tastes. Most Yumenescenes prefer polite abstraction over vulgar actuality.

When she turns to the man—slowly; stone eaters are slow aboveground, except when they aren't—this movement pushes her beyond artful beauty into something altogether different. The man has grown used to it, but even so, he does not look at her. He does not want revulsion to spoil the moment.

"What will you do?" he asks her. "When it's done. Will your kind rise up through the rubble and take the world in our stead?"

"No," she says.

"Why not?"

"Few of us are interested in that. Anyway, you'll still be here."

The man understands that she means you in the plural. *Your kind. Humanity.* She often treats him as though he represents his whole species. He does the same to her. "You sound very certain."

She says nothing to this. Stone-eaters rarely bother stating the obvious. He's glad, because her speech annoys him in any case; it does not shiver the air the way a human voice would. He doesn't know how that works. He doesn't *care* how it works, but he wants her silent now.

He wants *everything* silent.

"End," he says. "Please."

EXCERPT FROM *ANCILLARY MERCY*

ANN LECKIE

Ann Leckie is the author of the Hugo, Nebula, and Arthur C. Clarke Award winning novel Ancillary Justice. *She has also published short stories in* Subterranean Magazine, Strange Horizons, *and* Realms of Fantasy. *Her story "Hesperia and Glory" was reprinted in* Science Fiction: The Best of the Year, 2007, *edited by Rich Horton.*

Ann has worked as a waitress, a receptionist, a rodman on a land-surveying crew, and a recording engineer. She lives in St. Louis, Missouri.

FROM THE AUTHOR

I have yet to outline. Maybe I will someday. I knew how I wanted this story to end, but not exactly how it would end up there, so it was kind of nerve-wracking, especially when I could see people online saying things like "I can't wait to find out what happens in this book!" and I would think, "Neither can I!"

. . . The hatch clicked, and thunked, and swung open. Governor Giarod stiffened, trying, I supposed, to stand straighter than she already was. The person who came stooping through the open hatchway looked entirely human. Though of course that didn't mean she necessarily was. She was quite tall—there must have barely been room for her to stretch out in her tiny ship. To look at her, she might have been an ordinary Radchaai. Dark hair, long, tied simply behind her head. Brown skin, dark eyes, all quite unremarkable. She wore the white of the Translators Office—white coat and gloves, white trousers, white boots. Spotless. Crisp and unwrinkled, though in such a small space there could barely have been room for a change of clothes, let alone to dress so carefully. But not a single pin, or any other kind of jewelry, to break that shining white.

She blinked twice, as though adjusting to the light, and looked at me and at Governor Giarod, and frowned just slightly. Governor Giarod bowed, and said, "Translator. Welcome to Athoek Station. I'm System Governor Giarod, and this"—she gestured toward me—"is Fleet Captain Breq."

The translator's barely perceptible frown cleared, and she bowed. "Governor. Fleet Captain. Honored and pleased to make your acquaintance. I am Presger Translator Dlique."

The governor was very good at looking as though she were quite calm. She drew breath to speak, but said nothing. Thinking, no doubt, of Translator Dlique herself, whose corpse was even now in suspension in Medical. Whose death we were going to have to explain.

That explanation was apparently going to be even more difficult than we had thought. But perhaps I could make at least that part of it a bit easier. When I had first met Translator Dlique, and asked her who she was, she had said, I said just now I was Dlique but I might not be, I might be Zeiat.

"Begging your very great pardon, Translator," I said, before Governor Giarod could make a second attempt at speech, "but I believe that you're actually Presger Translator Zeiat."

The translator frowned, in earnest this time. "No. No, I don't think so. They told me I was Dlique. And they don't make mistakes, you know. When you think they have, it's just you looking at it wrong. That's what they say, anyway." She sighed. "They say all sorts of things. But you say I'm Zeiat, not Dlique. You wouldn't say that unless you had a reason to." She seemed just slightly doubtful of this.

"I'm quite certain of it," I replied.

"Well," she said, her frown intensifying for just a moment, and then clearing. "Well, if you're certain. Are you certain?"

"Quite certain, Translator."

"Let's start again, then." She shrugged her shoulders, as though adjusting the set of her spotless, perfect coat, and then bowed again. "Governor, Fleet Captain. Honored to make your acquaintance. I am Presger Translator Zeiat.

And this is very awkward, but now I really do need to ask you what's happened to Translator Dlique."

I looked at Governor Giarod. She had frozen, for a moment not even breathing. Then she squared her broad shoulders and said, smoothly, as though she had not been on the edge of panic just the moment before, "Translator, we're so very sorry. We do owe you an explanation, and a very profound apology."

"She went and got herself killed, didn't she," said Translator Zeiat. "Let me guess, she got bored and went somewhere you'd told her not to go."

"More or less, Translator," I acknowledged.

Translator Zeiat gave an exasperated sigh. "That would be just like her. I am so glad I'm not Dlique. Did you know she dismembered her sister once? She was bored, she said, and wanted to know what would happen. Well, what did she expect? And her sister's never been the same."

"Oh," said Governor Giarod. Likely all she could manage.

"Translator Dlique mentioned it," I said.

Translator Zeiat scoffed. "She would." And then, after a brief pause, "Are you certain it was Dlique? Perhaps there's been some sort of mistake. Perhaps it was someone else who died."

"Your very great pardon, Translator," replied Governor Giarod, "but when she arrived, she introduced herself as Translator Dlique."

"Well, that's just the thing," Translator Zeiat replied. "Dlique is the sort of person who'll say anything that comes into her mind. Particularly if she thinks it will be interesting or amusing. You really can't trust her to tell the truth."

I waited for Governor Giarod to reply, but she seemed paralyzed again. Perhaps from trying to follow Translator Zeiat's statement to its obvious conclusion.

"Translator," I said, "are you suggesting that since Translator Dlique isn't entirely trustworthy, she might have lied to us about being Translator Dlique?"

"Nothing more likely," replied Zeiat. "You can see why I'd much rather be Zeiat than Dlique. I don't much like her sense of humor, and I certainly don't want to encourage her. But I'd much rather be Zeiat than Dlique just now, so I suppose we can just let her have her little bit of fun this time. Is there anything, you know . . ." She gestured doubt. "Anything left? Of the body, I mean."

"We put the body in a suspension pod as quickly as we could, Translator," said Governor Giarod, trying very hard not to look or sound aghast. "And . . . we didn't know what . . . what customs would be appropriate. We held a funeral . . ."

Translator Zeiat tilted her head and looked very intently at the governor. "That was very obliging of you, Governor."

She said it as though she wasn't entirely sure it was obliging.

The governor reached into her coat, pulled out a silver-and-opal pin. Held it out to Translator Zeiat. "We had memorials made, of course."

Translator Zeiat took the pin, examined it. Looked back up at Governor Giarod, at me. "I've never had one of these before! And look, it matches yours." We were both wearing the pins from Translator Dlique's funeral. "You're not related to Dlique, are you?"

"We stood in for the translator's family, at the funeral," Governor Giarod explained. "For propriety's sake."

"Oh, propriety." As though that explained everything. "Of course. Well, it's more than I would have done, I'll tell you. So. That's all cleared up, then."

"Translator," I said, "may one properly inquire as to the purpose of your visit?"

Governor Giarod added, hastily, "We are of course pleased you've chosen to honor us." With a very small glance my way that was as much objection as she could currently make to the directness of my question.

"The purpose of my visit?" asked Zeiat, seeming puzzled for a moment. "Well, now, that's hard to say. They told me I was Dlique, you recall, and the thing about Dlique is—aside from the fact that you can't trust a word she says—she's easily bored and really far too curious. About the most inappropriate things, too. I'm quite sure she came here because she was bored and wanted to see what would happen. But since you tell me I'm Zeiat, I suspect I'm here because that ship is really terribly cramped and I've been inside it far too long. I'd really like to be able to walk around and stretch a bit, and perhaps eat some decent food." A moment of doubt. "You do eat food, don't you?"

It was the sort of question I could imagine Translator Dlique asking. And perhaps she had asked it, when she'd first arrived, because Governor Giarod replied, calmly, "Yes, Translator." On, it seemed, firmer ground for the moment. "Would you like to eat something now?"

"Yes, please, Governor!"

EXCERPT FROM *THE GRACE OF KINGS*

KEN LIU

Ken Liu (http://kenliu.name) is an author and translator of speculative fiction, as well as a lawyer and programmer. A winner of the Nebula, Hugo, and World Fantasy awards, he has been published in the Magazine of Fantasy & Science Fiction, Asimov's, Analog, Clarkesworld, Lightspeed, and Strange Horizons, among other places. His debut novel, The Grace of Kings (2015), is the first volume in a silkpunk epic fantasy series, The Dandelion Dynasty. It won the Locus Best First Novel Award and was a Nebula finalist. He has a collection of short fiction, The Paper Menagerie and Other Stories (2016). He lives with his family near Boston, Massachusetts.

In addition to his original fiction, Ken is also the translator of numerous literary and genre works from Chinese to English. His translation of The Three-Body Problem, by Liu Cixin, won the Hugo Award for Best Novel in 2015, the first translated novel ever to receive that honor.

FROM THE AUTHOR

The Grace of Kings *began as a suggestion from my wife to try to re-imagine one of the foundational narratives of Chinese culture, the founding of the Han Dynasty, as a modern epic fantasy. Ultimately, I decided to reject many of the popular techniques of contemporary epic fantasy and draw inspiration instead from both Western epics* and Chinese historical romances. *That decision led to some challenges as I had to think through what made modern narratives "modern" and what it meant to consciously evoke much older narrative traditions. Working through the voice and characterization techniques that I wanted to employ—many of which are no longer popular in contemporary fiction—taught me a lot about the arbitrary nature of many of our judgments about what a "good story" was. And I was glad that I chose to write an extremely challenging book for my first novel.*

Outside Zudi: the ninth month in the third year of the Reign of Righteous Force.

The night before, Kuni Garu still had under his charge fifty prisoners—a few from Zudi, but most from far away, men who had committed some kind of crime and received sentences of hard labor in the corvée gangs.

The prisoners had been walking slowly because one of the men had a lame leg. Since they couldn't make it to the next town in time, Kuni had decided to make camp in the mountains.

In the morning, only fifteen prisoners were left.

"What are they thinking?" Kuni fumed. "There is nowhere to hide anywhere in the Islands. They'll be caught and their families will be executed or conscripted for hard labor to make up for their desertion. I treated them well and didn't have them chained at night, and this is how they repay me? I'm dead meat!"

Kuni had been promoted to head of the Corvée Department two years ago. Ordinarily, escorting a team of prisoners was something one of his underlings would do. But he had taken this particular assignment himself because he knew that the gang would probably not get to their destination on time because of the man with the bad leg—Kuni was sure he could convince the commander at Pan to let it go. Besides, he had never been to Pan, and he had always wanted to see the Immaculate City.

"I just *had* to do the most *interesting* thing," he berated himself. "Am I having *fun* now?" At that moment, he wished more than anything to be home with Jia, drinking a cup of herbal tea made from some recipe she was experimenting with, safe and bored.

"You didn't know?" one of the soldiers, a man by the name of Hupé, asked, incredulous. "The prisoners had been whispering and plotting all of yesterday. I thought you knew and were letting them go on purpose because you believed in the prophecy. They want to join the rebels who declared war on the emperor and pledged to free all prisoners and conscripted laborers."

Kuni did remember the prisoners whispering an unusual amount yesterday. And he, like everyone else in Zudi, had heard rumors about the rebellion. But he had been too distracted by the beauty of the mountains they were hiking through, and didn't connect the dots.

Abashed, he asked Hupé to tell him more about what he knew of the rebels.

"A scroll in a fish!" Kuni exclaimed. "A fish that they just happened to have bought. That con stopped working on me when I turned five. And people believe this?"

"Don't speak ill of the gods," Hupé, who was very religious, said stiffly.

"Well, this is a bit of a pickle," Kuni muttered. To calm himself, he took a plug of chewing herbs out of his waist pouch and put it into his mouth, letting it sit under his tongue. Jia knew how to make herbal mixes that made him feel like he was flying and caused him to see rainbow-haloed crubens and dyrans everywhere—he and Jia had fun with those—but she also knew how to make mixes that did the opposite: slowed things down and helped him see choices more clearly when he was stressed, and he definitely needed some clarity.

What was the point of bringing fifteen prisoners to Pan when the quota was fifty? He'd have an appointment with the executioner no matter how he tried to talk his way out of it. And most likely Jia, too. His life as a servant of the emperor was over; there was no longer any path back to safety. All the options he had were dangerous.

But some choices are more interesting than others, and I did make a promise to myself.

Could this rebellion finally be the opportunity that he had been seeking all his life?

"Emperor, king, general, duke," he whispered to himself. "These are just labels. Climb up the family tree of any of them high enough and you'll find a commoner who dared to take a chance."

He got up on a rock and faced the soldiers and the remaining prisoners, all of whom were terrified: "I'm grateful that you stayed with me. But there's no point in going any farther. Under the laws of Xana, we're all going to be punished severely. Feel free to go wherever you want or to join the rebels."

"Aren't you going to join the rebels?" Hupé asked in a fervent voice. "The prophecy!"

"I can't think about any prophecies right now. I'm going to hide in the mountains first and figure out a way to save my family."

"You're thinking of becoming a bandit then?"

"The way I look at it is this: If you try to obey the law, and the judges call you a criminal anyway, then you might as well live up to the name."

To his satisfaction but not surprise, everyone volunteered to stay with him.

The best followers are those who think it was their own idea to follow you.

EXCERPT FROM
BARSK: THE ELEPHANTS' GRAVEYARD

LAWRENCE M. SCHOEN

Lawrence M. Schoen holds a PhD in cognitive psychology, has been nominated for the Campbell, Hugo, and Nebula awards, is a world authority on the Klingon language, operates the small press Paper Golem, and is a practicing hypnotherapist specializing in authors' issues.

His previous science fiction includes many light and humorous adventures of a space-faring stage hypnotist and his alien animal companion. His most recent book, Barsk, takes a very different tone, exploring issues of prophecy, intolerance, friendship, conspiracy, and loyalty, and redefines the continua between life and death. He lives near Philadelphia, Pennsylvania, with his wife and their dog. In 2015, Barsk won the Cóyotl Award for Best Novel.

FROM THE AUTHOR

I started writing Barsk in 1988, during my second year as a college professor. The first two chapters were published in a fan magazine in 1990, and I went on to write the entire novel, all fifty chapters of it! I was very proud of the book, as it was the first novel I had written from beginning to end. I tried to find a publisher, and fortunately I failed, primarily because it was a horrible book! It wasn't that the story was bad, just that I didn't know how to write without endless exposition and overdone tropes. I hadn't learned enough or acquired the necessary tools to tell it well. Eventually this fact bypassed my ego and percolated through to my awareness and I put the damn manuscript in a drawer. I went back to writing, to studying, to improving. I joined a regular writing group. I attended James Gunn's two-week workshop at the University of Kansas. I climbed the mountain and took part in Walter Jon Williams's master class in Taos, New Mexico. And I practiced, practiced, practiced. Twenty plus years later, I had what I needed to do it right, and here we are.

Jorl filled the resulting darkness with images from his own memory, imagining a familiar room in a house on the island of Keslo. The dimensions and materials, the colors and textures and scents formed around him. That easily, he sat in a small alcove that lay just off of the kitchen of the home maintained by his friend's widow. The walls were beech, yellow, bright in their own right and polished to a high sheen. A hand-braided rug covered the floor from the kitchen's threshold to the hidden door in the back wall that provided a less obvious entrance to the house. A tapestry woven of wild flowers hung on that wall, filling the air with light, sweet fragrance. Two comfortably curved benches faced one another, set far back against opposite sides such that their occupants would be unseen by anyone passing the opening. Jorl saw it all in his mind, just as he had seen it before taking the koph and settling into that very spot after dinner.

While his best friend's widow busied herself with after-dinner tasks, he muttered a name aloud, "Arlo," and began summoning particles, luring them with memories: sitting in a classroom in his grandmother's hall learning to cipher . . . sampling their first efforts at distillation . . . introducing him to Tolta, the daughter of a friend of his mother . . . laughing in the rain as they took a raft to Gerd for the first time . . . embracing him, trunks wrapped around one another's ears, the day he left Barsk . . .

When he had a sufficient number, he willed the particles to coalesce into his friend's form, occupying the bench opposite him, visible to anyone who possessed the Speaker's gift.

"Your wife made the most amazing dinner tonight," said Jorl, the mental construct of himself smacking his lips with satisfaction while in the real world his head pressed back against the wall, his trunk draping languidly down his chest, a trickle of drool starting at the corner of his flaccid mouth.

Arlo smiled. It started at his eyes and spread with exaggerated slowness across his face, until his ears gave a little flap of merriment. "Did she? You say that like you're surprised. Tolta's always been a great cook. You know that."

"Of regional dishes, sure. The safe and same traditional meals that everyone's aunt knows how to make. I'm talking about recipes from other worlds, places where no Fant has been in centuries."

"Now you're just being foolish. No one is going to bother venturing into space just for dinner. Not even you."

"I didn't say we left Barsk, only that the recipes, the spices, were from off world. Pay attention."

"Or what? You'll banish me? Spread the glowing bits of me far and wide?"

"I'd never—don't even joke about that!"

"I'm dead, Jorl. You can't tell me what to do. More importantly, you shouldn't be trying to tell me anything. This is what, the thirtieth time you've summoned me? It's not healthy."

"I'm a Speaker. It's a rare gift, even on Barsk. Why shouldn't I use it?"

"Just because a thing can be done doesn't mean it should be done. I'm not telling you not to use your gift. You're a historian, and I imagine it must be a powerful tool in your work, talking directly to the people who made history. That's incredible. Do more of that. But you shouldn't keep talking to me. Let me go. Even a historian can't keep living in the past."

"I don't want to have this argument with you."

Arlo spread his hands, his trunk lifting in an ironic gesture. "Stop summoning me and you won't."

"I needed to talk to you. Something's going on and I don't understand it. I thought discussing it with you might help."

The smile fell away from Arlo's face. "Something more than Tolta's cooking?"

"I've been studying the prophecies of the Matriarch since our school days." He grew still, head bowed, hands clasping the nubs of his trunk and one another in his lap. Even his ears had stopped moving. "I think one of the dire ones is coming to pass."

"I've long since forgotten the details of her warnings. Of all the areas of history to study, I never understood why you made her life your focus. Most of her writings bored me, and the prophecies were so weird they made little sense, at least at the time we covered them in class. Which one are you going on about here?"

"The Silence."

Arlo scrunched up his trunk and spat. "I hate that one. You remember how my mam told us stories about it when we were small, years before we got to that section in school? Scared the leaves out of us."

"I remember. I had nightmares. Sometimes I think I grew up to study them as a reaction. You know, so that I could really understand what scared me."

"Yeah? Well, be sure and thank her for your livelihood next time you see her."

Jorl looked down, finding a sudden interest in the cuticles of one hand.

"What?" said Arlo.

"Your mom is part of the problem. I wasn't going to bother you with the knowledge, but she sailed off a season ago. I'm sorry."

"Oh."

"Kembü had a full life, Ar. It didn't have anything to do with your own passing. It was just her time."

"What do you mean, she's 'part of the problem'?"

"Do you remember when we were eight and crazy for insects? We spent the summer collecting every bug we could find? I got to thinking about it, and I found myself wanting the specimen jar you used. Just a sentimental reminder. And you know how your mother never threw anything away. . . . So I tried to ask her if she knew where it was."

"What do you mean, you *tried*?"

"I couldn't summon her."

"How long ago?"

"Weeks. More than enough time for her to finish her last voyage and be summonable. Something set me off, thinking about that long ago summer. I snatched up a pellet of koph and reached out to pull your mother's nefshons together, only . . . I couldn't."

NEBULA AWARD NOMINEE
BEST NOVEL

UPDRAFT

FRAN WILDE

Fran Wilde's work includes the novels Updraft *(Tor, 2015) and* Cloud-bound *(Tor, 2016). Her short stories appear in* Asimov's, Tor.com, *and* Nature. *Her novella "The Jewel and Her Lapidary," came out from* Tor.com *in May 2016. She writes for publications including the* Washington Post, SF Signal, *and* Clarkesworld.

Editor's Note: Updraft *was also nominated for the Andre Norton Award and won in that category. Please go to page 251 to read an extended excerpt of this novel.*

EXCERPT FROM *UPROOTED*

NAOMI NOVIK

Naomi Novik is the acclaimed author of the Temeraire series, begun with His Majesty's Dragon. *Her latest novel,* Uprooted, *is a new fantasy influenced by the Polish fairy tales of her childhood. She is a founder of the Organization for Transformative Works and the Archive of Our Own.*

FROM THE AUTHOR

I started writing Uprooted *from an impulse to tell a story about a completely different kind of dragon than the ones in my Temeraire series—that's where the first line came from. The narrator's voice came to me very clearly after that and from there I wrote the first 11–12 thousand words very quickly, in a few weeks, and by the end of that I had discovered it took place in a kind of fairytale version of Poland, shaped by the stories I grew up with.*

Our Dragon doesn't eat the girls he takes, no matter what stories they tell outside our valley. We hear them sometimes, from travelers passing through. They talk as though we were doing human sacrifice, and he were a real dragon. Of course that's not true: he may be a wizard and immortal, but he's still a man, and our fathers would band together and kill him if he wanted to eat one of us every ten years. He protects us against the Wood, and we're grateful, but not that grateful.

He doesn't devour them really; it only feels that way. He takes a girl to his tower, and ten years later he lets her go, but by then she's someone different. Her clothes are too fine and she talks like a courtier and she's been living alone with a man for ten years, so of course she's ruined, even though the girls all say he never puts a hand on them. What else could they say? And that's not the worst of it—after all, the Dragon gives them a purse full of silver for their dowry when he lets them go, so anyone would be happy to marry them, ruined or not.

But they don't want to marry anyone. They don't want to stay at all.

"They forget how to live here," my father said to me once, unexpectedly. I was riding next to him on the seat of the big empty wagon, on our way home after delivering the week's firewood. We lived in Dvernik, which wasn't the biggest village in the valley or the smallest, or the one nearest the Wood: we were seven miles away. The road took us up over a big hill, though, and at the top on a clear day you could see along the river all the way to the pale grey strip of burned earth at the leading edge, and the solid dark wall of trees beyond. The Dragon's tower was a long way in the other direction, a piece of white chalk stuck in the base of the western mountains.

I was still very small—not more than five, I think. But I already knew that we didn't talk about the Dragon, or the girls he took, so it stuck in my head when my father broke the rule.

"They remember to be afraid," my father said. That was all. Then he clucked to the horses and they pulled on, down the hill and back into the trees.

It didn't make much sense to me. We were all afraid of the Wood. But our valley was home. How could you leave your home? And yet the girls never came back to stay. The Dragon let them out of the tower, and they came back to their families for a little while—for a week, or sometimes a month, never much more. Then they took their dowry-silver and left. Mostly they would go to Kralia and go to the University. Often as not they married some city man, and otherwise they became scholars or shopkeepers, although some people did whisper about Jadwiga Bach, who'd been taken sixty years ago, that she became a courtesan and the mistress of a baron and a duke. But by the time I was born, she was just a rich old woman who sent splendid presents to all her grandnieces and nephews, and never came for a visit.

So that's hardly like handing your daughter over to be eaten, but it's not a happy thing, either. There aren't so many villages in the valley that the chances are very low—he takes only a girl of seventeen, born between one October and the next. There were eleven girls to choose from in my year, and that's worse odds than dice. Everyone says you love a Dragon-born girl differently as she gets older; you can't help it, knowing you so easily might lose her. But it wasn't like that for me, for my parents. By the time I was old enough to understand that I might be taken, we all knew he would take Kasia.

Only travelers passing through, who didn't know, ever complimented Kasia's parents or told them how beautiful their daughter was, or how clever, or how nice. The Dragon didn't always take the prettiest girl, but he always took the most special one, somehow: if there was one girl who was far and away the prettiest, or the most bright, or the best dancer, or especially kind, somehow he always picked her out, even though he scarcely exchanged a word with the girls before he made his choice.

And Kasia was all those things. She had thick wheat-golden hair that she kept in a braid to her waist, and her eyes were warm brown, and her laugh was like a song that made you want to sing it. She thought of all the best games, and could make up stories and new dances out of her head; she could cook fit for a feast, and when she spun the wool from her father's sheep, the thread came off the wheel smooth and even without a single knot or snarl.

I know I'm making her sound like something out of a story. But it was the other way around. When my mother told me stories about the spinning princess or the brave goose-girl or the river-maiden, in my head I imagined them all a little like Kasia; that was how I thought of her. And I wasn't old enough to be wise, so I loved her more, not less, because I knew she would be taken from me soon.

She didn't mind it, she said. She was fearless, too: her mother Wensa saw to that. "She'll have to be brave," I remember hearing her say to my mother once, while she prodded Kasia to climb a tree she'd hung back from, and my mother hugging her, with tears.

We lived only three houses from one another, and I didn't have a sister of my own, only three brothers much older than me. Kasia was my dearest. We played together from our cradles, first in our mothers' kitchens keeping out from underfoot and then in the streets before our houses, until we were old enough to go running wild in the woods. I never wanted to be anywhere inside when we could be running hand-in-hand beneath the branches. I imagined the trees bending their arms down to shelter us. I didn't know how I would bear it, when the Dragon took her.

My parents wouldn't have feared for me, very much, even if there hadn't been Kasia. At seventeen I was still a too-skinny colt of a girl with big feet and tangled dirt-brown hair, and my only gift, if you could call it that, was I would tear or stain or lose anything put on me between the hours of one day. My mother despaired of me by the time I was twelve and let me run around in castoffs from my older brothers, except for feast days, when I was obliged to change only twenty minutes before we left the house, and then sit on the bench before our door until we walked to church. It was still even odds whether I'd make it to the village green without catching on some branch, or spattering myself with mud.

"You'll have to marry a tailor, my little Agnieszka," my father would say, laughing, when he came home from the forest at night and I went running to meet him, grubby-faced, with at least one hole about me, and no kerchief. He swung me up anyway and kissed me; my mother only sighed a little: what parent could really be sorry, to have a few faults in a Dragon-born girl?

Our last summer before the taking was long and warm and full of tears. Kasia didn't weep, but I did. We'd linger out late in the woods, stretching each golden day as long as it would go, and then I would come home hungry and tired and go straight to lie down in the dark. My mother would come in and stroke my head, singing softly while I cried myself to sleep, and leave a plate of food by my bed for when I woke up in the middle of the night with hunger. She didn't try to comfort me otherwise: how could she? We both knew that no matter how much she loved Kasia, and Kasia's mother Wensa, she couldn't help but have a small glad knot in her belly—not *my* daughter, not *my* only one. And of course, I wouldn't really have wanted her to feel any other way.

It was just me and Kasia together, nearly all that summer. It had been that way for a long time. We'd run with the crowd of village children when we were young, but as we got older, and Kasia more beautiful, her mother had said to her, "It's best if you don't see much of the boys, for you and them." But I clung to her, and my mother did love Kasia and Wensa enough not to try and pry me loose, even though she knew that it would hurt me more in the end.

On the last day, I found us a clearing in the woods where the trees still had their leaves, golden and flame-red rustling all above us, with ripe chestnuts all over the ground. We made a little fire out of twigs and dry leaves to roast a handful. Tomorrow was the first of October, and the great feast would be held to show honor to our patron and lord. Tomorrow, the Dragon would come.

"It would be nice to be a troubadour," Kasia said, lying on her back with her eyes closed. She hummed a little: a traveling singer had come for the festival, and he'd been practicing his songs on the green that morning. The tribute wagons had been arriving all week. "To go all over Polnya, and sing for the king."

She said it thoughtfully, not like a child spinning clouds; she said it like someone really thinking about leaving the valley, going away forever. I put my hand out and gripped hers. "And you'd come home every Midwinter," I said, "and sing us all the songs you'd learned." We held on tight, and I didn't let myself remember that the girls the Dragon took never wanted to come back.

Of course at that moment I only hated him ferociously. But he wasn't a bad lord. On the other side of the northern mountains, the Baron of the Yellow Marshes kept an army of five thousand men to take to Polnya's wars, and a castle with four towers, and a wife who wore jewels the color of blood and a white fox-fur cloak, all on a domain no richer than our valley. The men had to give one day a week of work to the baron's fields, which were the best land, and he'd take likely sons for his army, and with all the soldiers wandering around, girls had to stay indoors and in company once they got to be women. And even he wasn't a *bad* lord.

The Dragon only had his one tower, and not a single man-at-arms, or even a servant, besides the one girl he took. He didn't have to keep an army: the service he owed the king was his own labor, his magic. He had to go to court sometimes, to renew his oath of loyalty, and I suppose the king could have called him to war, but for the most part his duty was to stay here and watch the Wood, and protect the kingdom from its malice.

His only extravagance was books. We were well read by the standards of villagers, because he would pay gold for a single great tome, and so the book-peddlers came all this way, even though our valley was at the very edge of Polnya. And as long as they were coming, they filled up the saddlebags of their mules with whatever worn-out or cheaper stock of books they had and sold them to us for our pennies. It was a poor house in the valley that didn't have at least two or three books proudly displayed upon the walls.

These might all seem like small and petty things, little enough cause to give up a daughter, to anyone who didn't live near enough the Wood to understand. But I had lived through the Green Summer, when a hot wind carried pollen from the Wood west a long way into the valley, into our fields and gardens. The crops grew furiously lush, but also strange and misshapen. Anyone who ate of them grew sick with anger, struck at their families, and in the end ran into the Wood and vanished, if they weren't tied down.

I was six years old at the time. My parents tried to shelter me as much as they could, but even so I remembered vividly the cold clammy sense of dread everywhere, everyone afraid, and the never-ending bite of hunger in my belly. We had eaten through all our last year's stores by then, counting on the spring. One of our neighbors ate a few green beans, driven foolish by hunger. I remember the screams from his house that night, and peering out the window to see my father running to help, taking the pitchfork from where it leaned against our barn.

One day that summer, too young to understand the danger properly, I escaped my tired, thin mother's watch and ran into the forest. I found a half-dead bramble, in a nook sheltered from the wind. I pushed through the hard dead branches to the protected heart and dug out a miraculous handful of black-berries, not misshapen at all, whole and juicy and perfect. Every one was a burst of joy in my mouth. I ate two handfuls and filled my skirt; I hurried home with them soaking purple stains through my dress and my mother wept with horror when she saw my smeared face. I didn't sicken: the bramble had somehow escaped the Wood's curse, and the blackberries were good. But her tears frightened me badly; I shied from blackberries for years after.

The Dragon had been called to court that year. He came back early and rode straight to the fields and called down magic fire to burn all that tainted harvest, every poisoned crop. That much was his duty, but afterwards he went to every house where anyone had sickened, and he gave them a taste of a magic cordial that cleared their minds. He gave orders that the villages farther west, which had escaped the blight, should share their harvest with us, and he even gave up his own tribute that year entirely so none of us would starve. The next spring, just before the planting season, he went through the fields again to burn out the few corrupted remnants before they could take fresh root.

But for all he'd saved us, we didn't love him. He never came out of his tower to stand a drink for the men at harvest-time the way the Baron of the Yellow Marshes would, or to buy some small trinket at the fair as the baron's lady and her daughters so often did. There were plays sometimes put on by traveling shows, or singers would come through over the mountain pass from Rosya. He didn't come to hear them. When the carters brought him his tribute, the doors of the tower opened by themselves, and they left all the goods in the cellar without even seeing him. He never exchanged more than a handful of words with the headwoman of our village, or even the mayor of Olshanka, the largest town of the valley, very near his tower. He didn't try to win our love at all; none of us knew him.

And of course he was also a master of dark sorcery. Lightning would flash around his tower on a clear night, even in the winter. Pale wisps that he set loose from his windows drifted along the roads and down the river at night, going to the Wood to keep watch for him. And sometimes when the Wood caught someone—a shepherd girl who had drifted too close to its edge, following her flock; a hunter who had drunk from the wrong spring; an unlucky traveler who came over the mountain pass humming a snatch of music that sank claws into your head—well, the Dragon would come down from his tower for them, too; and the ones he took away never came back at all.

He wasn't evil, but he was distant and terrible. And he was going to take Kasia away, so I hated him, and had hated him for years and years.

My feelings didn't change on that last night. Kasia and I ate our chestnuts. The sun went down and our fire went out, but we lingered in the clearing as long as the embers lasted. We didn't have a long way to go in the morning. The harvest feast was usually held in Olshanka, but in a choosing year, it was always held in a village where at least one of the girls lived, to make the travel a little easier for their families. And our village had Kasia.

I hated the Dragon even more the next day, putting on my new green over-dress. My mother's hands were shaking as she braided up my hair. We knew it would be Kasia, but that didn't mean we weren't still afraid. But I held my skirts up high off the ground and climbed into the wagon as carefully as I could, looking twice for splinters and letting my father help me. I was determined to make a special effort. I knew it was no use, but I wanted Kasia to know that I loved her enough to give her a fair chance. I wasn't going to make myself look a mess or squint-eyed or slouching, the way girls sometimes did.

We gathered on the village green, all eleven of us girls in a line. The feasting-tables were set out in a square, loaded too heavily because they weren't really big enough to hold the tribute of the entire valley. Everyone had gathered behind them. Sacks of wheat and oats were piled up on the grass at the corners in pyramids. We were the only ones standing on the grass, with our families and our headwoman Danka, who paced nervously back and forth in front of us, her mouth moving silently while she practiced her greeting.

I didn't know the other girls much. They weren't from Dvernik. All of us were silent and stiff in our nice clothes and braided hair, watching the road. There was no sign of the Dragon yet. Wild fantasies ran in my head. I imagined flinging myself in front of Kasia when the Dragon came, and telling him to take me instead, or declaring to him that Kasia didn't want to go with him. But I knew I wasn't brave enough to do any of that.

And then he came, horribly. He didn't come from the road at all, he just stepped straight out of the air. I was looking that way when he came out: fingers in midair and then an arm and a leg and then half a man, so impossible and wrong that I couldn't look away even though my stomach was folding itself over in half. The others were luckier. They didn't even notice him until he took his first step towards us, and everyone around me tried not to flinch in surprise.

The Dragon wasn't like any man of our village. He should have been old and stooped and grey; he had been living in his tower a hundred years, but he was tall, straight, beardless, his skin taut. At a quick glance in the street I might have thought him a young man, only a little older than me: someone I might have smiled at across the feast-tables, and who might have asked me to dance. But there was something unnatural in his face: a crow's-nest of lines by his eyes, as though years couldn't touch him, but use did. It wasn't an ugly face, even so, but coldness made it unpleasant: everything about him said, *I am not one of you, and don't want to be, either.*

His clothes were rich, of course; the brocade of his zupan would have fed a family for a year, even without the golden buttons. But he was as lean as a man whose harvest had gone wrong three years out of four. He held himself stiff, with all the nervous energy of a hunting dog, as though he wanted nothing more than to be off quickly. It was the worst day of all our lives, but he had no patience for us; when our headwoman Danka bowed and said to him, "My lord, let me present to you these—" he interrupted her and said, "Yes, let's get on with it."

My father's hand was warm on my shoulder as he stood beside me and bowed; my mother's hand was clenched tight on mine on the other side. They reluctantly stepped back with the other parents. Instinctively the eleven of us all edged closer to one another. Kasia and I stood near the end of the line. I didn't dare take her hand, but I stood close enough that our arms brushed, and I watched the Dragon and hated him and hated him as he stepped down the line and tipped up each girl's face, under the chin, to look at her.

He didn't speak to all of us. He didn't say a word to the girl next to me, the one from Olshanka, even though her father, Borys, was the best horse-breeder in the valley, and she wore a wool dress dyed brilliant red, her black hair in two long beautiful plaits woven with red ribbons. When it was my turn, he glanced at me with a frown—cold black eyes, pale mouth pursed—and said, "Your name, girl?"

"Agnieszka," I said, or tried to say; I discovered my mouth was dry. I swallowed. "Agnieszka," I said again, whispering. "My lord." My face was hot. I dropped my eyes. I saw that for all the care I'd taken, my skirt had three big mud stains creeping up from the hem.

The Dragon moved on. And then he paused, looking at Kasia, the way he hadn't paused for any of the rest of us. He stayed there with his hand under her chin, a thin pleased smile curving his thin hard mouth, and Kasia looked at him bravely and didn't flinch. She didn't try to make her voice rough or squeaky or anything but steady and musical as she answered, "Kasia, my lord."

He smiled at her again, not pleasantly, but with a satisfied-cat look. He went on to the end of the line only perfunctorily, barely glancing at the two girls after her. I heard Wensa drag in a breath that was nearly a sob, behind us, as he turned and came back to look at Kasia, still with that pleased look on his face. And then he frowned again, and turned his head, and looked straight at me.

I'd forgotten myself and taken Kasia's hand after all. I was squeezing the life out of it, and she was squeezing back. She quickly let go and I tucked my hands together in front of me instead, hot color in my cheeks, afraid. He only narrowed his eyes at me some more. And then he raised his hand, and in his fingers a tiny ball of blue-white flame took shape.

"She didn't mean anything," Kasia said, brave brave brave, the way I hadn't been for her. Her voice was trembling but audible, while I shook rabbit-terrified, staring at the ball. "Please, my lord—"

"Silence, girl," the Dragon said, and held his hand out towards me. "Take it."

"I—what?" I said, more bewildered than if he'd flung it into my face.

"Don't stand there like a cretin," he said. *"Take it."*

My hand was shaking so when I raised it that I couldn't help but brush against his fingers as I tried to pluck the ball from them, though I hated to; his skin felt feverish-hot. But the ball of flame was cool as a marble, and it didn't hurt me at all to touch. Startled with relief, I held it between my fingers, staring at it. He looked at me with an expression of annoyance.

"Well," he said ungraciously, "you then, I suppose." He took the ball out of my hand and closed his fist on it a moment; it vanished as quickly as it had come. He turned and said to Danka, "Send the tribute up when you can."

I still hadn't understood. I don't think anyone had, even my parents; it was all too quick, and I was shocked by having drawn his attention at all. I didn't even have a chance to turn around and say a last good-bye before he turned back and took my arm by the wrist. Only Kasia moved; I looked back at her and saw her about to reach for me in protest, and then the Dragon jerked me impatiently and ungently stumbling after him, and dragged me with him back into thin air.

I had my other hand pressed to my mouth, retching, when we stepped back out of the air. When he let go my arm, I sank to my knees and vomited without even seeing where I was. He made a muttered exclamation of disgust— I had spattered the long elegant toe of his leather boot—and said, "Useless. Stop heaving, girl, and clean that filth up." He walked away from me, his heels echoing upon the flagstones, and was gone.

I stayed there shakily until I was sure nothing more would come up, and then I wiped my mouth with the back of my hand and lifted my head to stare. I was on a floor of stone, and not just any stone, but a pure white marble laced through with veins of brilliant green. It was a small round room with narrow slitted windows, too high to look out of, but above my head the ceiling bent inward sharply. I was at the very top of the tower.

There was no furniture in the room at all, and nothing I could use to wipe up the floor. Finally I used the skirt of my dress: that was already dirty anyway. Then after a little time sitting there being terrified and more terrified, while nothing at all happened, I got up and crept timidly down the hallway. I'd have taken any way out of the room but the one he had used, if there had been any other way. There wasn't.

He'd already gone on, though. The short hallway was empty. It had the same cold hard marble underfoot, illuminated with an unfriendly pale white light from hanging lamps. They weren't real lamps, just big chunks of clear polished stone that glowed from inside. There was only one door, and then an archway at the end that led to stairs.

I pushed the door open and looked in, nervously, because that was better than going past it without knowing what was inside. But it only opened into a small bare room, with a narrow bed and a small table and a wash-basin. There was a large window across from me, and I could see the sky. I ran to it and leaned out over the sill.

The Dragon's tower stood in the foothills on the western border of his lands. All our long valley lay spread out to the east, with its villages and farms, and standing in the window I could trace the whole line of the Spindle, running silver-blue down the middle with the road dusty brown next to it. The road and the river ran together all the way to the other end of the Dragon's lands, dipping into stands of forest and coming out again at villages, until the road tapered out to nothing just before the huge black tangle of the Wood. The river went on alone into its depths and vanished, never to come out again.

There was Olshanka, the town nearest the tower, where the Grand Market was held on Sundays: my father had taken me there, twice. Beyond that Poniets, and Radomsko curled around the shores of its small lake, and there was my own Dvernik with its wide green square. I could even see the big white tables laid out for the feasting the Dragon hadn't wanted to stay for, and I slid to my knees and rested my forehead on the sill and cried like a child.

But my mother didn't come to rest her hand on my head; my father didn't pull me up and laugh me out of my tears. I just sobbed myself out until I had too much of a headache to go on crying, and after that I was cold and stiff from being on that painfully hard floor, and I had a running nose and nothing to wipe it with.

I used another part of my skirt for that and sat down on the bed, trying to think what to do. The room was empty, but aired-out and neat, as if it had just been left. It probably had. Some other girl had lived here for ten years, all alone, looking down at the valley. Now she had gone home to say good-bye to her family, and the room was mine.

A single painting in a great gilt frame hung on the wall across from the bed. It made no sense, too grand for the little room and not really a picture at all, just a broad swath of pale green, grey-brown at the edges, with one shining blue-silver line that wove across the middle in gentle curves and narrower silver lines drawn in from the edges to meet it. I stared at it and wondered if it was magic, too. I'd never seen such a thing.

But there were circles painted at places along the silver line, at familiar distances, and after a moment I realized the painting was the valley, too, only flattened down the way a bird might have looked down upon it from far over-head. That silver line was the Spindle, running from the mountains into the

Wood, and the circles were villages. The colors were brilliant, the paint glossy and raised in tiny peaks. I could almost see waves on the river, the glitter of sunlight on the water. It pulled the eye and made me want to look at it and look at it. But I didn't like it, at the same time. The painting was a box drawn around the living valley, closing it up, and looking at it made me feel closed up myself.

I looked away. It didn't seem that I could stay in the room. I hadn't eaten a bite at breakfast, or at dinner the night before; it had all been ash in my mouth. I should have had less appetite now, when something worse than anything I'd imagined had happened to me, but instead I was painfully hungry, and there were no servants in the tower, so no one was going to get my dinner. Then the worse thought occurred to me: what if the Dragon expected me to get his?

And then the even worse thought than that: what about *after* dinner? Kasia had always said she believed the women who came back, that the Dragon didn't put a hand on them. "He's taken girls for a hundred years now," she always said firmly. "*One* of them would have admitted it, and word would have got out."

But a few weeks ago, she'd asked my mother, privately, to tell her how it happened when a girl was married—to tell her what her own mother would have, the night before she was wed. I'd overheard them through the window, while I was coming back from the woods, and I'd stood there next to the window and listened in with hot tears running down my face, angry, so angry for Kasia's sake.

Now that was going to be *me*. And I wasn't brave—I didn't think that I could take deep breaths, and keep from clenching up tight, like my mother had told Kasia to do so it wouldn't hurt. I found myself imagining for one terrible moment the Dragon's face so close to mine, even closer than when he'd inspected me at the choosing—his black eyes cold and glittering like stone, those iron-hard fingers, so strangely warm, drawing my dress away from my skin, while he smiled that sleek satisfied smile down at me. What if all of him was fever-hot like that, so I'd feel him almost glowing like an ember, all over my body, while he lay upon me and—

I shuddered away from my thoughts and stood up. I looked down at the bed, and around at that small close room with nowhere to hide, and then I hurried out and went back down the hall again. There was a staircase at the end, going down in a close spiral, so I couldn't see what was around the next turn. It sounds stupid to be afraid of going down a staircase, but I was terrified. I nearly went back to my room after all. At last I kept one hand on the smooth stone wall and went down slowly, putting both my feet on one step and stopping to listen before I went down a little more.

After I'd crept down one whole turn like that, and nothing had jumped out at me, I began to feel like an idiot and started to walk more quickly. But then I went around another turn, and still hadn't come to a landing; and another, and I started to be afraid again, this time that the stairs were magic and would just keep going forever, and—well. I started to go quicker and quicker, and then I skidded three steps down onto the next landing and ran headlong into the Dragon.

I was skinny, but my father was the tallest man in the village and I came up to his shoulder, and the Dragon wasn't a big man. We nearly tumbled down the stairs together. He caught the railing with one hand, quick, and my arm with the other, and somehow managed to keep us from landing on the floor. I found myself leaning heavily on him, clutching at his coat and staring directly into his startled face. For one moment he was too surprised to be thinking, and he looked like an ordinary man startled by something jumping out at him, a little bit silly and a little bit soft, his mouth parted and his eyes wide.

I was so surprised myself that I didn't move, just stayed there gawking at him helplessly, and he recovered quick; outrage swept over his face and he heaved me off him onto my feet. Then I realized what I'd just done and blurted in a panic, before he could speak, "I'm looking for the kitchen!"

"*Are* you," he said silkily. His face didn't look at all soft anymore, hard and furious, and he hadn't let go of my arm. His grip was clenching, painful; I could feel the heat of it through the sleeve of my shift. He jerked me towards him and bent towards me—I think he would have liked to loom over me, and because he couldn't was even more angry. If I'd had a moment to think about it, I would have bent back and made myself smaller, but I was too tired and scared. So instead his face was just before mine, so close his breath was on my lips and I felt as much as heard his cold, vicious whisper: "Perhaps I'd better show you there."

"I can—I can—" I tried to say, trembling, trying to lean back from him. He spun away from me and dragged me after him down the stairs, around and around and around again, five turns this time before we came to the next landing, and then another three turns down, the light growing dimmer, before at last he dragged me out into the lowest floor of the tower, just a single large bare-walled dungeon chamber of carven stone, with a huge fireplace shaped like a downturned mouth, full of flames leaping hellishly.

He dragged me towards it, and in a moment of blind terror I realized he meant to throw me in. He was so strong, much stronger than he ought to have been for his size, and he'd pulled me easily stumbling down the stairs after him. But I wasn't going to let him put me in the fire. I wasn't a lady-like quiet girl; all my life I'd spent running in the woods, climbing trees and tearing through brambles, and panic gave me real strength. I screamed as he pulled me close to it, and then I went into a fit of struggling and clawing and squirming, so this time I really did trip him to the floor.

I went down with him. We banged our heads on the flagstones together, and dazed lay still for a moment with our limbs entwined. The fire was leaping and crackling beside us, and as my panic faded, abruptly I noticed that in the wall beside it were small iron oven doors, and before it a spit for roasting, and above it a huge wide shelf with cooking-pots on it. It was only the kitchen.

After a moment, he said, in almost marveling tones, "Are you deranged?"

"I thought you were going to throw me in the oven," I said, still dazed, and then I started to laugh.

It wasn't real laughter—I was half-hysterical by then, wrung out six ways and hungry, my ankles and knees bruised from being dragged down the stairs and my head aching as though I'd cracked my skull, and I just couldn't stop.

But *he* didn't know that. All he knew was the stupid village girl he'd picked was laughing at him, the Dragon, the greatest wizard of the kingdom and her lord and master. I don't think anyone had laughed at him in a hundred years, by then. He pushed himself up, kicking his legs free from mine, and getting to his feet stared down at me, outraged as a cat. I only laughed harder, and then he turned abruptly and left me there laughing on the floor, as though he couldn't think what else to do with me.

After he left, my giggles tapered off, and I felt somehow a little less hollow and afraid. He hadn't thrown me into the oven, after all, or even slapped me. I got myself up and looked around the room: it was hard to see, because the fireplace was so bright and there were no other lights lit, but when I kept my back to the flames I could start to make out the huge room: divided after all, into alcoves and with low walls, with racks full of shining glass bottles—wine, I realized. My uncle had brought a bottle once to my grandmother's house, for Midwinter.

There were stores all over: barrels of apples packed in straw, potatoes and carrots and parsnips in sacks, long ropes of onions braided. On a table in the middle of the room I found a book standing with an unlit candle and an ink-stand and a quill, and when I opened it I found a ledger with records of all the stores, written in a strong hand. At the bottom of the first page there was a note written very small; when I lit the candle and bent down to squint I could just make it out:

Breakfast at eight, dinner at one, supper at seven. Leave the meal laid in the library, five minutes before, and you need not see him—no need to say who—*all the day. Courage!*

Priceless advice, and that *Courage!* was like the touch of a friend's hand. I hugged the book against me, feeling less alone than I had all day. It seemed near midday, and the Dragon hadn't eaten at our village, so I set about dinner. I was no great cook, but my mother had kept me at it until I could put together a meal, and I did do all the gathering for my family, so I knew how to tell the fresh from the rotten, and when a piece of fruit would be sweet. I'd never had so many stores to work with: there were even drawers of spices that smelled like Midwinter cake, and a whole barrel full of fresh soft grey salt.

At the end of the room there was a strangely cold place, where I found meat hanging up: a whole venison and two great hares; there was a box of straw full of eggs. There was a fresh loaf of bread already baked wrapped in a woven cloth on the hearth, and next to it I discovered a whole pot of rabbit and buckwheat and small peas all together. I tasted it: like something for a feast day, so salty and a little sweet, and meltingly tender; another gift from the anonymous hand in the book.

I didn't know how to make food like that at all, and I quailed thinking that the Dragon would expect it. But I was desperately grateful to have the pot ready nonetheless. I put it back on the shelf above the fire to warm—I splashed my dress a little as I did—and I put two eggs in a dish in the oven to bake, and found a tray and a bowl and a plate and a spoon. When the rabbit was ready, I set it out on the tray and cut the bread—I had to cut it, because I had torn off the end of the loaf and eaten it myself while I waited for the rabbit to heat up—and put out butter. I even baked an apple, with the spices: my mother had taught me to do that for our Sunday supper in winter, and there were so many ovens I could do that at the same time as everything else cooked. I even felt a little proud of myself, when everything was assembled on the tray together: it looked like a holiday, though a strange one, with just enough for one man.

I took it up the stairs carefully, but too late I realized I didn't know where the library was. If I'd thought about it a little, I might have reasoned out that it wouldn't be on the lowest floor, and indeed it wasn't, but I didn't find that out until I'd wandered around carrying the tray through an enormous circular hall, the windows draped with curtains and a heavy throne-like chair at the end. There was another door at the far end, but when I opened that I found only the entry hall and the huge doors of the tower, three times the height of my head and barred with a thick slab of wood in iron brackets.

I turned and went back through the hall to the stairs, and up another landing, and here found the marble floor covered in soft furry cloth. I'd never seen a carpet before. That was why I hadn't heard the Dragon's footsteps. I crept anxiously down the hall, and peered through the first door. I backed out hastily: the room was full of long tables, strange bottles and bubbling potions and unnatural sparks in colors that came from no fireplace; I didn't want to spend another moment inside there. But I managed to catch my dress in the door and tear it, even so.

Finally the next door, across the hall, opened on a room full of books: wooden shelves up and up from floor to ceiling crammed with them. It smelled of dust, and there were only a few narrow windows throwing light in. I was so glad to find the library that I didn't notice at first that the Dragon was there: sitting in a heavy chair with a book laid out on a small table across his thighs, so large each page was the length of my forearm, and a great golden lock hanging from the open cover.

I froze staring at him, feeling betrayed by the advice in the book. I'd somehow assumed that the Dragon would conveniently keep out of the way until I'd had a chance to put down his meal. He hadn't raised his head to look at me, but instead of just going quietly with the tray to the table in the center of the room, laying it out, and scurrying away, I hung in the doorway and said, "I've—I've brought dinner," not wanting to go in unless he told me to.

"Really?" he said, cuttingly. "Without falling into a pit along the way? I'm astonished." He only then looked up at me and frowned. "Or *did* you fall into a pit?"

I looked down at myself. My skirt had one enormous ugly stain, from the vomit—I'd wiped it off best as I could in the kitchen, but it hadn't really come out—and another from where I'd blown my nose. There were three or four dripping stains from the stew, and some more spatters from the dish-pan where I'd wiped the pots. The hem was still muddy from this morning, and I'd torn a few other holes in it without even noticing. My mother had braided and coiled my hair that morning and pinned it up, but the coils had slid mostly down off my head and were now a big snarled knot of hair hanging half off my neck.

I hadn't noticed; it wasn't anything out of the usual for me, except that I was wearing a nice dress underneath the mess. "I was—I cooked, and I cleaned—" I tried to explain.

"The dirtiest thing in this tower is *you*," he said—true, but unkind anyway. I flushed and with my head low went to the table. I laid everything out and looked it over, and then I realized sinkingly that with all the time I'd taken wandering around, everything had gone cold, except the butter, which was a softened runny mess in its dish. Even my lovely baked apple was all congealed.

I stared down at it in dismay, trying to decide what to do; should I take it all back down? Or maybe he wouldn't mind? I turned to look and nearly yelped: he was standing directly behind me peering over my shoulder at the food. "I see why you were afraid I might roast you," he said, leaning over to lift up a spoonful of the stew, breaking the layer of cooling fat on its top and dumping it back in. "You would make a better meal than this."

"I'm not a splendid cook, but—" I started, meaning to explain that I wasn't quite so terrible at it, I'd only not known my way, but he snorted, interrupting me.

"Is there anything you *can* do?" he asked, mockingly.

If only I'd been better trained to serve, if only I'd ever really thought I might be chosen and had been more ready for all of it; if only I'd been a little less miserable and tired, and if only I hadn't felt a little proud of myself in the kitchen; if only he hadn't just twitted me for being a rag, the way everyone who loved me did, but with malice instead of affection—if any of those things, and if only I hadn't run into him on the stairs, and discovered that he *wasn't* going to fling me into a fire, I would probably have just gone red, and run away.

Instead I flung the tray down on the table in a passion and cried, "Why did you take me, then? Why didn't you take Kasia?"

I shut my mouth as soon as I'd said it, ashamed of myself and horrified. I was about to open my mouth and take it back in a rush, to tell him I was sorry, I didn't mean it, I didn't mean he should go take Kasia instead; I would go and make him another tray—

He said impatiently, "Who?"

I gaped at him. "Kasia!" I said. He only looked at me as though I was giving him more evidence of my idiocy, and I forgot my noble intentions in confusion. "You were going to take her! She's—she's clever, and brave, and a splendid cook, and—"

He was looking every moment more annoyed. "Yes," he bit out, interrupting me, "I do recall the girl: neither horse-faced nor a slovenly mess, and I imagine would not be yammering at me this very minute: enough. You village girls are all tedious at the beginning, more or less, but you're proving a truly remarkable paragon of incompetence."

"Then you needn't keep me!" I flared, angry and wounded—*horse-faced* stung.

"Much to my regret," he said, "that's where you're wrong."

He seized my hand by the wrist and whipped me around: he stood close behind me and stretched my arm out over the food on the table. "*Lirintalem*," he said, a strange word that ran liquidly off his tongue and rang sharply in my ears. "Say it with me."

"What?" I said; I'd never heard the word before. But he pressed closer against my back, put his mouth against my ear, and whispered, terrible, "*Say it!*"

I trembled, and wanting only for him to let me go said it with him, "*Lirintalem*," while he held my hand out over the meal.

The air rippled over the food, horrible to see, like the whole world was a pond that he could throw pebbles in. When it smoothed again, the food was all changed. Where the baked eggs had been, a roast chicken; instead of the bowl of rabbit stew, a heap of tiny new spring beans, though it was seven months past their season; instead of the baked apple, a tartlet full of apples sliced paper-thin, studded with fat raisins and glazed over with honey.

He let go of me. I staggered with the loss of his support, clutching at the edge of the table, my lungs emptied as if someone had sat on my chest; I felt like I'd been squeezed for juice like a lemon. Stars prickled at the edge of my sight, and I leaned over half-fainting. I only distantly saw him looking down at the tray, an odd scowl on his face as though he was at once surprised and annoyed.

"What did you do to me?" I whispered, when I could breathe again.

"Stop whining," he said dismissively. "It's nothing more than a cantrip." Whatever surprise he might have felt had vanished; he flicked his hand at the door as he seated himself at the table before his dinner. "All right, get out. I can see you'll be wasting inordinate amounts of my time, but I've had enough for the day."

I was glad to obey that, at least. I didn't try to pick up the tray, only crept slowly out of the library, cradling my hand against my body. I was still stumbling-weak. It took me nearly half an hour to drag myself back up all the stairs to the top floor, and then I went into the little room and shut the door, dragged the dresser before it, and fell onto the bed. If the Dragon came to the door while I slept, I didn't hear a thing.

F. J. Bergmann edits poetry for Star*Line, the journal of the Science Fiction Poetry Association (sfpoetry.com) and Mobius: The Journal of Social Change (mobiusmagazine.com), and imagines tragedies on or near exoplanets. An alumna of Viable Paradise, she previously won the Rhysling Award for the Short Poem in 2008.

100 REASONS TO HAVE SEX WITH AN ALIEN

F. J. BERGMANN

after *237 More Reasons to Have Sex*, by Denise Duhamel and Sandy McIntosh

1. More than one tentacle.
2. With suckers.
3. I mistook the blaster in his pocket for happiness.
4. He asked me what a being like me was doing on a planet like this.
5. His ventral cluster was magnified in the curved side of my rocket.
6. His ventral cluster was like a bouquet of blue flowers.
7. I said, "For me?"
8. He felt like a cross between astrakhan and curly endive.
9. I thought I was shaking his hand.
10. He thought he was stroking my prehensile appendage.
11. We both thought it was a diplomatic formality.
12. We thought we were responsible for the fates of our respective worlds.
13. I felt lonely because the universe was expanding.
14. I felt small because the universe was so vast.

15. I felt reassured because his presence meant we were not alone, after all.
16. The gravity field caused genital engorgement.
17. The anti-grav generator caused dizziness.
18. The solar wavelength triggered hormone production.
19. The Coriolis effect made my senses swirl.
20. Lit only by Cherenkov radiation, I still cast a spell.
21. Such unusual sex toys!
22. Which he referred to as "probes."
23. When he unfurled his wings to stretch, I thought it was a mating display.
24. I mistook his yawning for sexual arousal.
25. I mistook his indifference for sexual arousal.
26. I mistook his urgent need to micturate for sexual arousal.
27. He mistook my sneezing for sexual arousal.
28. He mistook my laughter for sexual arousal.
29. He mistook my sulking for sexual arousal.
30. He mistook my tattoos for a mating display.
31. My piercings were highly magnetic.
32. He thought my breasts were egg-sacs.
33. He said he didn't have DNA, so I didn't have to worry about pregnancy.
34. Parthenogenesis, on the other hand.
35. I had had it with humanity.
36. Not much else to do on an asteroid.
37. We were both too far from home.
38. The starlight was so ancient.
39. He said he'd let me fly his spaceship.
40. He said he'd let me play with his matter transmitter.
41. He said he'd let me play with his matter transmuter.
42. He said he'd let me play with his time machine.
43. He told me he was a divine messenger, and I believed him.
44. His silicon-based wings fanned my lust.
45. His pheromonal signature was intriguing.
46. His subvocal rumblings made me squirm rapturously.
47. His buzzing vocalizations gave me a migraine, so I closed my eyes.
48. Next thing I knew . . .
49. He didn't have a name to remember.

50. He looked nothing like my father.
51. He looked nothing like my ex.
52. He looked nothing like anything I'd ever seen before.
53. I was ripe for mischief.
54. The bubbles in his creamy center turned me on.
55. His outer integument was my favorite color, periwinkle.
56. His outer integument had a fishnet-stocking pattern, and those things really turn me on.
57. Including the seam up the back.
58. And 9-inch stiletto heels.
59. His emanations smelled like roast pork and cinnamon.
60. I was hungry.
61. I just wanted irregular sex.
62. I'd never done it in free fall.
63. He read my mind and knew exactly what I wanted.
64. A myriad of moonlets intensified my longing.
65. We were trying to establish each other's respective genders.
66. I told myself it was my duty as a Terran citizen.
67. I told myself it was my duty as a xenoanthropologist.
68. I told myself it was my duty as a xenolinguist.
69. I told myself it was the best available treatment for xenophobia.
70. We slowly climbed out of each other's Uncanny Valley.
71. He said he wanted to serve me.
72. He said he wanted to eat me.
73. He said he liked my "Cthulhu for President" t-shirt.
74. I was hoping someone would pay big money for the videos of our encounter.
75. Someone on *his* home world.
76. He said he'd take me on a trip aboard his magic swirling ship.
77. Which had a really cool hood ornament.
78. He said he'd take me 2,000 light years from home.
79. He said he'd set the controls for the heart of the sun.
80. He said his mother was a Space Lord.
81. He said he was a Time Lord.
82. He was way hotter than I expected.
83. I had a fetish for long striped scarves.

84. I had a fetish for the writhing of his ventral cluster.
85. And the plumes on his dorsal ridge.
86. His violet eyes turned me on. All fifteen of them.
87. He said he was a famous rock star on his planet.
88. He offered to let me make a plaster cast of his ventral cluster.
89. He said he was a famous artist on his planet.
90. He offered to show me his Rigelian-sandworm-excreta sculptures.
91. He said he was a famous poet on his planet.
92. I didn't believe him, but I didn't want to hurt his feelings.
93. He said he'd come all the way from Rigel just to hear *me* read *my* poetry.
94. He wanted me so much he put his space ship on autopilot.
95. He wanted me so much he didn't notice when we overshot our destination.
96. The stimulating vibration as our vessel entered the atmosphere.
97. I thought the ship would blow up any minute and this would be my last chance.
98. It was my last chance.
99. Our vessel was about to crash.

> The smoke of our burning intertwined and rose up
> toward the stars.

ABOUT THE RAY BRADBURY AWARD FOR OUTSTANDING DRAMATIC PRESENTATION

The Ray Bradbury Award for Outstanding Dramatic Presentation is not a Nebula Award, but it follows Nebula nomination, voting, and award rules and guidelines, and it is given each year at the annual awards banquet. Founded in 2009, it replaces the earlier Nebula Award for Best Script. It was named in honor of science fiction and fantasy author Ray Bradbury, whose work appeared frequently in movies and on television.

The winner in 2016 was *Mad Max: Fury Road*, written by George Miller, Brendan McCarthy, and Nick Lathouris.

A REMARKABLE WIN

MARK ASKWITH

Mark Askwith is a Canadian television producer and writer. From 1982–87 he was the manager of Toronto's Silver Snail comic book store. He left to work with director Ron Mann on a documentary called Comic Book Confidential, *and to collaborate with Dean Motter on* The Prisoner: Shattered Visage, *a graphic novel based on the groundbreaking television series. In 1989 he co-created the award-winning TV show* Prisoners of Gravity, *a show that featured interviews with writers and artists who worked in the field of speculative fiction. When PoG ended its five-year run, Askwith became the producer of* Imprint, *Canada's flagship literary TV show. In 1997 he became a founding producer of a national Canadian television channel—SPACE—where he is the producer of special projects.*

The Ray Bradbury Award for Outstanding Dramatic Presentation was awarded to *Mad Max: Fury Road*, written by George Miller, Brendan McCarthy, Nick Lathouris. The category was very competitive this year, and the other nominees showcased the finest writing in animation (*Inside Out*), television (*Jessica Jones*), and feature films (*Ex Machina*, *The Martian*, and *Star Wars: The Force Awakens*).

Mad Max: Fury Road is the fourth film in the Mad Max franchise, and it continues the story of a former policeman who now inhabits a bleak post-apocalyptic world. The film begins when Max is captured by an army of War Boys led by a despot called Immortan Joe. When one of Immortan Joe's lieutenants, Imperator Furiosa, goes rogue, she drives away with his five wives, and thus begins a roughly two-hour chase through a windswept desert.

George Miller's initial idea for the script was a simple one: could he write a film that was a continuous chase scene? Miller enlisted artist Brendan McCarthy to collaborate on the design and storyboards, and they broke down each sequence as if they were working on an animated movie. McCarthy called the document "a surreal fusion of graphic novel and Hollywood screenplay"—and this manuscript, with 3,500 panels of artwork, became the "Mad Max Bible." Rumors began to circulate that there was no script, but Charlize Theron (Furiosa) stated "there was a script; it just wasn't a conventional script, in the sense that we kind of know scripts with scene numbers. Initially it was just a storyboard, and we worked off that storyboard for almost three years. And then eventually, there was a kind of written version of the storyboard, which just felt like a written version of the storyboard, again not like a script."

Mad Max: Fury Road's win is remarkable given how troubled the production of the film was. The film was to begin shooting in Australia in 2001, but after the events of September 11 the American dollar collapsed. In 2003 the film was set to film in the Australian desert, but the locations were ruined by rainfall. In 2009 the project had morphed into an R-rated animated film, to be released in 2012. After years of delays, principal photography began in the Namibian desert in 2012.

Mad Max: Fury Road was a critical success and was chosen by many publications as one of the top ten films of 2015. In fact, it ranks first on Metacritic and Rotten Tomatoes as the highest reviewed film of 2015. It was the second most nominated film with ten Academy Award nominations, including Best Director, and Best Picture, and it took home six awards.

The movie is an energetic whirlwind of action. The plot and dialogue are stripped to the bare minimum, but the visuals are so rich and evocative that the story becomes mythic. Fittingly, the film ends with a quote from Albert Camus: "Where must we go, we who wander this wasteland, in search of our better selves."

ABOUT THE ANDRE NORTON AWARD FOR YOUNG ADULT SCIENCE FICTION AND FANTASY

The Andre Norton Award for Young Adult Science Fiction and Fantasy is an annual award presented by SFWA to the author of the best young-adult or middle-grade science fiction or fantasy book published in the United States in the preceding year.

The Andre Norton Award is not a Nebula Award, but it follows Nebula nomination, voting, and award rules and guidelines. It was founded in 2005 to honor popular science fiction and fantasy author and Grand Master Andre Norton.

EXCERPT FROM *UPDRAFT*

FRAN WILDE

Fran Wilde's work includes the novels Updraft *(Tor, 2015) and* Cloud-bound *(Tor, 2016). Her short stories appear in* Asimov's, Tor.com *and* Nature. *Her novella "The Jewel and Her Lapidary" came out from* Tor.com *in May 2016. She writes for publications including the* Washington Post, SF Signal, *and* Clarkesworld.

FROM THE AUTHOR

I'd just finished work on an SF novel when I wrote a short story (the second or third) set in the world of Updraft. *The original story set in that world was written as a response to a workshop challenge. This short story was about a winged knife fight in a wind tunnel . . . and I discovered (with help from my critique pals) that I had a lot more to say than would fit in a short story.*

The first draft of Updraft *took six weeks to write. The next draft, about six months.*

Ch. 1. Densira

My mother selected her wings as early morning light reached through our balcony shutters. She moved between the shadows, calm and deliberate, while downtower neighbors slept behind their barricades. She pushed her arms into the woven harness. Turned her back to me so that I could cinch the straps tight against her shoulders.

When two bone horns sounded low and loud from Mondarath, the tower nearest ours, she stiffened. I paused as well, trying to see through the shutters' holes. She urged me on while she trained her eyes on the sky.

"No time to hesitate, Kirit," she said. She meant *no time to be afraid.*

On a morning like this, fear was a blue sky emptied of birds. It was the smell of cooking trapped in closed towers, of smoke looking for ways out. It was an ache in the back of the eyes from searching the distance, and a weight in the stomach as old as our city.

Today Ezarit Densira would fly into that empty sky—first to the east, then southwest.

I grabbed the buckle on her left shoulder, then put the full weight of my body into securing the strap. She grunted softly in approval.

"Turn a little, so I can see the buckles better," I said. She took two steps sideways. I could see through the shutters while I worked.

Across a gap of sky, Mondarath's guards braved the morning. Their wings edged with glass and locked for fighting, they leapt from the tower. One shouted and pointed.

A predator moved there, nearly invisible—a shimmer among exploding gardens. Nets momentarily wrapped two thick, sky-colored tentacles. The sky-mouth shook free and disappeared. Wails built in its wake. Mondarath was under attack.

The guards dove to meet it, the sun dazzling their wings. The air roiled and sheared. Pieces of brown rope netting and red banners fell to the clouds far below. The guards drew their bows and gave chase, trying to kill what they could not see.

"Oh, Mondarath," Ezarit whispered. "They never mind the signs."

The besieged tower rose almost as tall as ours, sun-bleached white against the blue morning. Since Lith fell, Mondarath marked the city's northern edge. Beyond its tiers, sky stretched uninterrupted to the horizon.

A squall broke hard against the tower, threatening a loose shutter. Then the balcony's planters toppled and the circling guards scattered. One guard, the slowest, jerked to a halt in the air and flew, impossibly, backwards. His leg yanked high, flipping his body as it went, until he hung upside down in the air. He flailed for his quiver, spilling arrows, as the sky opened below him, red and wet and filled with glass teeth. The air blurred as slick, invisible limbs tore away his brown silk wings, then lowered what the monster wanted into its mouth.

By the time his scream reached us, the guard had disappeared from the sky.

My own mouth went dry as dust.

How to help them? My first duty was to my tower, Densira. To the Laws. But what if we were under attack? My mother in peril? What if no one would help then? My heart hammered questions. What would it be like to open our shutters, leap into the sky, and join this fight? To go against Laws?

"Kirit! Turn away." Ezarit yanked my hand from the shutters. She stood beside me and sang the Law, Fortify:

Tower by tower, secure yourselves,
Except in city's dire need.

She had added the second half of the Law to remind me why she flew today. Dire need.

She'd fought for the right to help the city beyond her own tower, her own quadrant. Someday, I would do the same.

Until then, there was need here too. I could not turn away.

The guards circled Mondarath, less one man. The air cleared.

The horns stopped for now, but the three nearest towers—Wirra, Densira, and Viit—kept their occupied tiers sealed.

Ezarit's hand gripped the latch for our own shutters. "Come on," she whispered. I hurried to tighten the straps at her right shoulder, though I knew she didn't mean me. Her escort was delayed.

She would still fly today.

Six towers in the southeast stricken with a coughing illness needed medicines from the north and west. Ezarit had to trade for the last ingredients and make the delivery before Allmoons, or many more would die.

The buckling done, she reached for her panniers and handed them to me.

Elna, my mother's friend from downtower, bustled in the kitchen, making tea. After the first migration warnings, Ezarit had asked her to come uptower, for safety's sake—both Elna's and mine, though I no longer needed minding.

Elna's son, Nat, had surprised us by helping her climb the fiber ladders that stretched from the top of the tower to the last occupied tier. Elna was pale and huffing as she finally cleared the balcony. When she came inside, I saw why Nat had come. Elna's left eye had a cloud in it—a skyblindness.

"We have better shutters," Ezarit had said. "And are farther from the clouds. Staying higher will be safer for them."

A mouth *could* appear anywhere, but she was right. Higher was safer, and on Densira, we were now highest of all.

At the far side of our quarters, Nat kept an eye on the open sky. He'd pulled his sleeping mat from behind a screen and knelt, peering between shutters, using my scope. When I finished helping my mother, I would take over that duty.

I began to strap Ezarit's panniers around her hips. The baskets on their gimbaled supports would roll with her, no matter how the wind shifted.

"You don't have to go," I said as I knelt at her side. I knew what her reply would be. I said my part anyway. We had a ritual. Skymouths and klaxons or not.

"I will be well escorted." Her voice was steady. "The west doesn't care for the north's troubles, or the south's. They want their tea and their silks for Allmoons and will trade their honey to the highest bidder. I can't stand by while the south suffers, not when I've worked so hard to negotiate the cure."

It was more than that, I knew.

She tested the weight of a pannier. The silk rustled, and the smell of dried tea filled the room. She'd stripped the bags of their decorative beads. Her cloak and her dark braids hung unadorned. She lacked the sparkle that trader Ezarit Densira was known for.

Another horn sounded, past Wirra, to the west.

"See?" She turned to me. Took my hand, which was nearly the same size as hers. "The skymouths take the east. I fly west. I will return before Allmoons, in time for your wingtest."

Elna, her face pale as a moon, crossed the room. She carried a bowl of steaming tea to my mother. "For your strength today, Risen," she said, bowing carefully in the traditional greeting of lowtower to high.

My mother accepted the tea and the greeting with a smile. She'd raised her family to the top of Densira through her daring trades. She had earned the greeting. It wasn't always so, when she and Elna were young downtower mothers. But now Ezarit was famous for her skills, both bartering and flying. She'd even petitioned the Spire successfully once. In return, we had the luxury of quarters to ourselves, but that only lasted as long as she kept the trade flowing.

As long as she could avoid the skymouths today.

Once I passed my wingtest, I could become her apprentice. I would fly by her side, and we'd fight the dangers of the city together. I would learn to negotiate as she did. I'd fly in times of dire need while others hid behind their shutters.

"The escort is coming," Nat announced. He stood; he was much taller than me now. His black hair curled wildly around his head, and his brown eyes squinted through the scope once more.

Ezarit walked across the room, her silk-wrapped feet swishing over the solid bone floor. She put her hand on Nat's shoulder and looked out. Over her shoulders, between the point of her furled wings and through the shutters, I saw a flight of guards circle Mondarath, searching out more predators. They yelled and blew handheld horns, trying to scare skymouths away with noise and their arrows. That rarely worked, but they had to try.

Closer to us, a green-winged guard soared between the towers, an arrow nocked, eyes searching the sky. The guards atop Densira called out a greeting to him as he landed on our balcony.

I retightened one of Ezarit's straps, jostling her tea. She looked at me, eyebrows raised.

"Elna doesn't need to watch me," I finally said. "I'm fine by myself. I'll check in with the aunts. Keep the balcony shuttered."

She reached into her pannier and handed me a stone fruit. Her gold eyes softened with worry. "Soon." The fruit felt cold in my hand. "I need to know you are all safe. I can't fly without knowing. You'll be free to choose your path soon enough."

After the wingtest. Until then, I was a dependent, bound by her rules, not just tower strictures and city Laws.

"Let me come out to watch you go, then. I'll use the scope. I won't fly." She frowned, but we were bartering now. Her favorite type of conversation.

"Not outside. You can use the scope inside. When I return, we'll fly some of my route around the city, as practice." She saw my frustration. "Promise me you'll keep inside? No visiting? No sending whipperlings? We cannot lose another bird."

"For how long?" A mistake. My question broke at the end with the kind of whine that hadn't slipped out in years. My advantage dissipated like smoke.

Nat, on Ezarit's other side, pretended he wasn't listening. He knew me too well. That made it worse.

"They will go when they go." She winced as sounds of Mondarath's mourning wafted through the shutters. Peering out again, she searched for the rest of her escort. "Listen for the horns. If Mondarath sounds again, or if Viit goes, stay away from the balconies."

She looked over her shoulder at me until I nodded, and Nat too.

She smiled at him, then turned and wrapped her arms around me. "That's my girl."

I would have closed my eyes and rested my head against the warmth of her chest if I'd thought there was time. Ezarit was like a small bird, always rushing. I took a breath, and she pulled away, back to the sky. Another guard joined the first on the balcony, wearing faded yellow wings.

I checked Ezarit's wings once more. The fine seams. The sturdy battens. They'd worn in well: no fraying, despite the hours she'd flown in them. She'd traded five bolts of raw silk from Naza tower to the Viit wingmaker for these, and another three for mine. Expensive but worth it. The wingmaker was the best in the north. Even Singers said so.

Furled, her wings were a tea-colored brown, but a stylized kestrel hid within the folds. The wingmaker had used tea and vegetable dyes—whatever he could get—to make the rippling sepia pattern.

My own new wings leaned against the central wall by our sleeping area, still wrapped. Waiting for the skies to clear. My fingers itched to pull the straps over my shoulders and unfurl the whorls of yellow and green.

Ezarit cloaked herself in tea-colored quilted silks to protect against the chill winds. They tied over her shoulders, around her trim waist and at her thighs and ankles. She spat on her lenses, her dearest treasure, and rubbed them clean. Then she let them hang around her neck. Her tawny cheeks were flushed, her eyes bright, and she looked, now that she was determined to go, younger and lighter than yesterday. She was beautiful when she was ready to fly.

"It won't be long," she said. "Last migration through the northwest quadrant lasted one day."

Our quadrant had been spared for my seventeen years. Many in the city would say our luck had held far too long while others suffered. Still, my father had left to make a trade during a migration and did not return. Ezarit took his trade routes as soon as I was old enough to leave with Elna.

"How can you be sure?" I asked.

Elna patted my shoulder, and I jumped. "All will be well, Kirit. Your mother helps the city."

"And," Ezarit said, "if I am successful, we will have more good fortune to celebrate."

I saw the gleam in her eye. She thought of the towers in the west, the wealthier quadrants. Densira had scorned us as unlucky after my father disappeared, family and neighbors both. The aunts scorned her no longer, as they enjoyed the benefits of her success. Even last night, neighbors had badgered Ezarit to carry trade parcels for them to the west. She'd agreed, showing respect for family and tower. Now she smiled. "Perhaps we won't be Ezarit and Kirit Densira for long."

A third guard clattered to a landing on the balcony, and Ezarit signaled she was ready. The tower marks on the guards' wings were from Naza. Out of the migration path; known for good hunters with sharp eyes. No wonder Nat stared at them as if he would trade places in a heartbeat.

As Ezarit's words sank in, he frowned. "What's wrong with Densira?"

"Nothing's wrong with Densira," Elna said, reaching around Ezarit to ruffle Nat's hair. She turned her eyes to the balcony, squinting. "Especially since Ezarit has made this blessed tower two tiers higher."

Nat sniffed, loudly. "This tier's pretty nice, even if it reeks of brand-new."

My face grew warm. The tier did smell of newly grown bone. The central core was still damp to the touch.

Still, I held my chin high and moved to my mother's side. Not that long ago, Nat and I had been inseparable. Practically wing-siblings. Elna was my second mother. My mother, Nat's hero. We'd taken first flights together. Practiced rolls and glides. Sung together, memorizing the towers, all the Laws. Since our move, I'd seen him practicing with other flightmates. Dojha with her superb dives. Sidra, who had the perfect voice for Laws and already wore glorious, brand-new wings. Whose father, the tower councilman, had called my mother a liar more than once after we moved uptower, above their tier.

I swallowed hard. Nat, Elna, and I would be together in my still-new home until Ezarit returned. Like old times, almost.

In the air beyond the balcony, a fourth figure appeared. He glided a waiting circle. Wings shimmered dove gray. Bands of blue at the tips. A Singer.

A moment of the old childhood fear struck me, and I saw Nat pale as well. Singers sometimes took young tower children to the Spire. It was a great honor. But the children who went didn't return until they were grown. And when they came back, it was as gray-robed strangers, scarred and tattooed and sworn to protect the city.

The guards seemed to relax. The green-winged guard nudged his nearest companion, "Heard tell no Singer's ever been attacked by a skymouth." The other guards murmured agreement. One cracked his knuckles. Our Magister for flight and Laws had said the same thing. No one ever said whether those who flew with Singers had the same luck, but the guards seemed to think so.

I hoped it was true.

Ezarit signaled to the guards, who assembled in the air near the Singer. She smiled at Elna and hugged her. "Glad you are here."

"Be careful, Ezarit," Elna whispered back. "Speed to your wings."

Ezarit winked at Nat, then looked out at the sky. She nodded to the Singer. Ready. She gave me a fierce hug and a kiss. "Stay safe, Kirit."

Then she pushed the shutters wide, unfurled her wings, and leapt from the balcony into the circle of guards waiting for her with bows drawn.

The Singer broke from their formation first, dipping low behind Wirra. I watched from the threshold between our quarters and the balcony until the rest were motes against the otherwise empty sky. Their flight turned west and disappeared around Densira's broad curve.

For the moment, even Mondarath was still.

*　　*　　*

Nat moved to pull the shutters closed, but I blocked the way. I wanted to keep watching the sky.

"Kirit, it's Laws," he said, yanking my sleeve. I jerked my arm from his fingers and stepped farther onto the balcony.

"You go inside," I said to the sky. I heard the shutter slam behind me. I'd broken my promise and was going against Laws, but I felt certain that if I took my eyes off the sky, something would happen to Ezarit and her guards.

We'd seen signs of the skymouth migration two days ago. House birds had molted. Silk spiders hid their young. Densira prepared. Watchmen sent black-feathered kaviks to all the tiers. They cackled and shat on the balconies while families read the bone chips they carried.

Attempting to postpone her flight, Ezarit had sent a whipperling to her trading partners in the south and west. They'd replied quickly, "We are not in the migration path." "We can sell our honey elsewhere." There would be none left to mix with Mondarath's herbs for the southeast's medicines.

She made ready. Would not listen to arguments. Sent for Elna early, then helped me strip the balcony.

Mondarath, unlike its neighbors, paid little mind to preparations. The skymouth migration hadn't passed our way for years, they'd said. They didn't take their fruit in. They left their clotheslines and the red banners for Allmoons flapping.

Around me now, our garden was reduced to branches and leaves. Over the low bone outcrop that marked Aunt Bisset's balcony, I saw a glimmer. A bored cousin with a scope, probably. The wind took my hair and tugged the loose tendrils. I leaned out to catch one more glimpse of Ezarit as she passed beyond the tower's curve.

The noise from Mondarath had eased, and the balconies were empty on the towers all around us. I felt both entirely alone and as if the eyes of the city were on me.

I lifted my chin and smiled, letting everyone behind their shutters know I wasn't afraid, when they were. I panned with our scope, searching the sky. A watchman. A guardian.

And I saw it. It tore at my aunt's gnarled trees, then shook loose the ladder down to Nat's. It came straight at me fast and sure: a red rip in the sky, sharp beak edges toothed with ridge upon ridge of glass teeth. Limbs flowed forward like thick tongues.

I dropped the scope.

The mouth opened wider, full of stench and blood.

I felt the rush of air and heard the beat of surging wings, and I screamed. It was a child's scream, not a woman's. I knew I would die in that moment, with tears staining my tunic and that scream soiling my mouth. I heard the bone horns of our tower's watch sound the alarm: We were unlucky once more.

My scream expanded, tore at my throat, my teeth.

The skymouth stopped in its tracks. It hovered there, red and gaping. I saw the glittering teeth and, for a moment, its eyes, large and side-set to let its mouth open even wider. Its breath huffed thick and foul across my face, but it didn't cross the last distance between us. My heart had stopped with fear, but the scream kept on. It spilled from me, softening. As the scream died, the skymouth seemed to move again.

So I hauled in a deep breath through my nose, like we were taught to sing for Allmoons, and I kept screaming.

The skymouth backed up. It closed its jaws. It disappeared into the sky, and soon I saw a distant ripple, headed away from the city.

I tried to laugh, but the sound stuck in my chest and strangled me. Then my eyes betrayed me. Darkness overtook the edges of my vision, and white, wavy lines cut across everything I saw. The hard slats of the shutters counted the bones of my spine as I slid down and came to rest on the balcony floor.

My breathing was too loud in my ears. It roared.

Clouds. I'd shouted down a skymouth and would still die blue-lipped outside my own home? I did not want to die.

Behind me, Nat battered at the shutters. He couldn't open them, I realized groggily, because my body blocked the door.

Cold crept up on me. My fingers prickled, then numbed. I fought my eyelids, but they won, falling closed against the blur that my vision had become.

I thought for a moment I was flying with my mother, far beyond the city. Everything was so blue.

Hands slid under my back and legs. Someone lifted me. The shutters squealed open.

Dishes swept from our table hit the floor and rolled. Lips pressed warm against mine, catching my frozen breath. The rhythm of in and out came back. I heard my name.

When I opened my eyes, I saw the Singer's gray robes first, then the silver lines of his tattoos. His green eyes. The dark hairs in his hawk nose. Behind him, Elna wept and whispered, "On your wings, Singer. Mercy on your wings."

He straightened and turned from me. I heard his voice for the first time, stern and deep, telling Elna, "This is a Singer concern. You will not interfere."

Ch. 2. Sent Down

The Singer came and went from my side. He checked my breathing. His fingers tapped my wrist.

Elna and Nat swirled around the table like clouds. I heard Elna whisper angrily.

When I found I could hold my eyes open without growing dizzy, Nat had disappeared. The Singer sat at my mother's worktable. His draped robes puddled on the floor and obscured her stool. As the sun passed below the clouds, he sat there fingering a skein tied with blank message chips.

In the dark, his knife scraped against one bone chip, then another.

The room felt tight-strung, an instrument waiting to be played.

With the sunrise, Densira neighbors began clattering onto our balcony. They brought a basket of fruit, a string of beads.

"The tower is talking," Elna said. "About the miracle. That it's a skyblessing."

The Singer waved away our visitors. He positioned a tower guard on the balcony.

Occasionally, the guard peered through the shutters and shook his head, like kaviks did when they were molting. "Lawsbreaker," he muttered. He told any who would listen how stupid I'd been.

I caught pieces of his words on the wind.

"It came right for her. The fledge stood out on the balcony with the lens of that scope glinting in the sun. Should have gobbled her up. Would have shot her myself, attracting a mouth to the tower like that." He waved our neighbors away. "Don't waste your goods on her. She's not skyblessed. She's bad luck. Should tie enough Laws on her that she'll rattle when she moves."

The people of Densira did not listen. Elna scrambled to find places for everything they brought.

She took the guard a cup of tea. "Luck was with her, Risen. The tower has luck now, because of Kirit. The skymouth fled."

The Singer cleared his throat loudly. Elna jostled the cup. Nearly spilled the tea. The Singer looked as if he wanted to have Elna swept from the tower and silenced.

I tried to say something helpful, but my voice rasped in my throat.

"Don't try to speak, Kirit." Elna returned to my side. The Singer glared again, then rose, muttering about needing a new sack of rainwater. He must have decided to keep me alive a little longer.

She propped me up. Around me, the bone lanterns' glow cast halos and small stars against the pale walls. The rugs and cushions of the place I'd shared with my mother since the tower rose were swathed in shadow.

Elna wrapped me in a quilt, tucking the down-filled silk beneath me. Instead of warming, I shook harder. The Singer returned and held my wrist between his thumb and forefinger. He reached into his robe. Took out a small bag that smelled rich and dark. Metal glittered in the light.

A moment later, he handed me a tiny cup filled with sharp-smelling liquid.

It burned my throat as it went down, then warmed my chest and belly. It took me a moment to realize I wasn't drinking rainwater from my usual bone cup. He'd given me a brass cup so old the etching was nearly worn away. It warmed in my hands as the glow crept up my arms. Calm followed warmth until I was able to focus on the room, the smell of chicory brewing, the sound of voices.

Elna disappeared when the Singer glared at her a third time. He gave me a stern look. Waited for me to speak. I wished Ezarit sat beside me.

"They think you are skyblessed," he said when I did not speak on his cue.

I blinked at the words and closed my eyes again. Skyblessed. Like the people in the songs, who escaped the clouds, or those who survived Lith.

The Singer's tone made it clear that he thought me nothing of the sort.

"Your example will tempt people to risk themselves. We have Laws for a reason, Kirit. To keep the city safe."

I found that hard to argue. I sat up straighter. My head pounded. I looked around the empty tier, at the lashed shutters, anywhere but at the Singer standing before me, his hands folded into his robe.

"You are old enough to understand duty to your tower. You know our history. Why we can never go back to disorder."

I nodded. This was why we sang. To remember.

"Yet you are still part of a household. Your mother is still responsible for you. Even while she's on a trading run."

He was right. She wouldn't learn what I'd done until she flew close enough to the north quadrant for the gossip to catch up with her. I imagined her sipping tea at a stopover tower. Varu, perhaps. And hearing. What her face would look like as she tallied the damage to her reputation. To mine. Bile rose in my throat, despite the calming effect of whatever was in that cup.

The Singer leaned close. "You know what you did."

I'd broken Laws. I knew that. I'd attracted a skymouth with my actions. A punishable offense. Worse, I drew a Singer's attention, which could affect Densira. Councilman Vant, Sidra's father, would sanction me, and my mother too, for my deeds.

But that fell below the Singers' jurisdiction. They only dealt with the big Laws. I sipped at the cup to conceal my confusion. Cut my losses. "I broke tower Laws."

He lowered his voice. "Not only that, you lived to tell about it. How did you do that, Kirit Densira?" His eyes bored into mine, his breath rich with spices. He looked like a hawk, looming over me.

Elna was nowhere to be seen. I looked at my fingers, the soft pattern on the sleeve of my robe that Ezarit brought back from her last trip. Stall, my brain said. Someone would come.

I met the Singer's gaze. Hard as stone, those eyes.

"I am waiting." He spoke each word slowly, as if I wouldn't understand otherwise.

"I don't know."

"Don't know what?"

"Why I am still alive."

"You've never been in skymouth migration before?"

I shook my head. Never. Wasn't that hard to believe. Everyone knew the northwest quadrant had been lucky.

"What about the Spire? Never to a market there, nor for Allsuns?"

Shaking my head repeatedly made the room spin. A low throb gripped the base of my skull. My voice rasped. "She said we'd go when we were both traders."

He frowned. Perhaps he thought I lied. "Don't all citizens love to visit the Spire's hanging markets at Allsuns, pick over the fine bone carvings, and watch the quadrant wingfights?"

I shook my head. Not once. Ezarit never wanted to go, nor Elna. They avoided the Singers more than most. How could I convince him I told the truth?

"Do you know what you've done?"

I shook my head a third time, while pressure pounded my temples. I did not know, and I felt nauseated. I could see no way for me to get away from this Singer. Even seated, he loomed over me, tall and thin and sour-faced. Despite this, his hands were smooth, no deep lines marked his face beneath the tattoos; he might not have been much older than me.

"I don't know what you want me to say. I went on the balcony. A skymouth came. I screamed, and it—"

I stopped speaking. I'd screamed. The skymouth had halted. Why? People who were close enough to a skymouth to scream died.

The Singer's gaze bored into mine. His frown deepened. He turned away from me and looked at the balcony. Then back to me.

"There are those who can hear the city all the time. Not only when it roars. They learn to speak its language. You know that, right?"

I bowed my head. "They become Singers. They make sure we continue to rise, instead of falling like Lith." Our Magister, Florian, had taught us this long ago. If tower children became Singers, their families were rewarded with higher tiers; their towers with bridges. But the Singers themselves were family no longer. Tower no longer. They severed themselves from city life; enforced Laws even on those they once loved. Nat's father, for instance. Though I'd been too young to see it, I'd heard stories. I imagined now a Laws-weighted figure thrown to the clouds. Arms and legs churning in place of missing wings. Failing. Falling. Tears pricked my eyes.

This Singer took my arm and squeezed hard. I locked my teeth together to avoid crying out. His fingers pressed into my skin, dimpling pale rings around the pressure points. "Kirit Densira, daughter of Ezarit Densira, I place you under Spire fiat. If you reveal anything that I say now to anyone, you will be thrown down. If you fail to tell the truth, you will be thrown down. Do you understand?"

My head throbbed worse than ever, and I leaned hard against his grip. "Yes." Anything to get free of this man.

"Some among the Singers can speak to monsters."

"What do you mean?"

"There are five people in the city who can stop a skymouth with a shout. All Singers. Except one."

He stared at me. He meant me. I was the fifth.

"Kirit." He paused. "You are not skyblessed."

I bowed my head. I hadn't thought so.

He released a breath. Scent of garlic. "But you could be something more. Someone who helps to keep the city safe in its direst need."

As my mother did. I raised my eyebrows. "How?"

"You must come into the Spire with me."

The way he said it, I knew he didn't mean for a visit. I jerked backwards. Neck and shoulder muscles tensed into a rejection of him. And yet he held me. Tried to shake me out of it. *No.*

I would not leave the towers. I would not go into the Spire. Not for anything.

Traders flew the quadrants freely, making elegant deals. They connected the city, helped weave it together. Better still, traders were not always tied to a single tower and its fate; they saw the whole city, especially if they were very good, like Ezarit. That was what I wanted. What I would choose when I was able.

I stalled. "I have already put my name in for the next wingtest."

His turn to shake his head. "That hardly matters. Come with me. Your mother will be well honored for your sacrifice. Your tower too."

Sacrifice? No. Not me. I would ply the winds and negotiate deals that let the towers help one another. I would be brave and smart and weave beads in my hair. I would not get locked in an obelisk of bone and secrets. I wouldn't make small children cry, nor etch my face with silver tattoos.

I yanked my arm away. Scrambled off the table, my knees wobbly, toes tingling. Two steps, and I hit the floor. I tried to crawl to the balcony, to get to Aunt Bisset's, to get back to Elna.

The Singer grabbed me up by the neck of my robe. His words were soft, his grip fierce. "You have broken the Laws of your tower. Endangered everyone here. Some think you're skyblessed, but that will wear off. Others think you are a danger, unlucky."

"I am no danger!"

"I will encourage these thoughts. What then? Soon the tower will grow past you. Your bad luck will sour your trades and your family's status. You will be left behind. Or worse. You will be Densira's pariah for every bad thing."

I saw my future as he drew it. The tower turned against me, against my mother. Ezarit, living within a cage of shame.

"As a Singer, you will be respected and feared. Your mother and Elna and Nat will be forgiven your Lawsbreaks."

The household. He would punish Elna and Nat too. And Ezarit. For my decisions. I needed to bargain with this man. How did I do that? How would Ezarit have done it? I groped for memories of her trading stories, for how she would have turned him away. She would have tried to trade, to haggle. If she'd nothing to trade, she'd bluff.

"I am too old to take." I'd never heard of someone nearly at wingtest being taken by the Singers.

"You are still a dependent in the eyes of your tower."

"In that case," I said, resisting the urge to argue his point, "my mother would never permit this." I was certain of that.

"Your mother is not here. Won't be back until nearly Allmoons."

"You can't take me without her permission," I said. "It says so in Laws."

And once I have my wingmark, Singer, I will be an apprentice. Able to decide my own path. Singers do not take apprentices from the city, except for egregious Lawsbreaks. I coughed to conceal my shudder at that possibility. Then I straightened. "Ezarit would bring down a storm on the Spire so great, you'd be begging the clouds to pull you back up." I yanked my arm from his grip.

The Singer smiled, all but his eyes. My skin crawled. "Singers are more powerful than traders, Kirit. Even Ezarit. No matter what your mother thinks."

I drew a deep breath. "I will not go with you."

The Singer straightened. "Very well. You would be unteachable at this age if you did not desire to become a Singer anyway."

I'd changed his mind. I couldn't believe it. It felt too easy.

"You will stay in Densira until the wingtest. Then we will talk again." He rose and reached back to release his wings. He was leaving. Then he paused. Frowned. The tattoos on his cheeks and chin creased and buckled.

"Of course," he said, "you did break tower Law." He drew a cord from his sleeve, tied with four bone chips. "The tower councilman has sent you, Elna, Nat, and your mother a message. Vant is of the opinion, which I have reinforced, that you are in no way skyblessed, no way lucky. That the guard must have driven away the skymouth with noise and arrows. That you must be censured severely to avoid future danger to the tower."

I took the chips. Freshly carved. Approved by Councilman Vant. Two were thin, light: Nat's and mine. We were assigned hard labor, cleaning four tiers downtower.

I gasped. That could take well past the wingtest to finish.

Heavier still were Elna's and Ezarit's chips. They felt thick. Not the thickest, I knew, but still true Laws chips. Permanent, unless Ezarit could bargain with Vant so that he let her untie them.

As promised, they were punished for my deeds. For both the Lawsbreak and for refusing the Singer. Nat and I could miss the wingtest. We would certainly miss the last flight classes, when the Magister did his most intensive review. I could lose my chance at becoming an apprentice this year. Perhaps forever.

My head ached, and I tried hard to swallow. I knew I could have been thrown down for endangering the tower. But censure was bad too. Everything was wrong now.

And not just for me. I held Elna's, Nat's, and my mother's fates in my hand.

The Singer raised his eyebrows. Would I change my mind? Would I give in and go with him?

I stared back at him. Swallowed. Shook my head. Densira seemed to fall silent as we stared each other down.

"My name is Wik. Remember it," he said. "I will find you at Allmoons, Kirit Densira. By then, you will want to come with me."

Trapped behind walls. Gray wings and robes, silver tattoos. Lawsbreakers thrown down, arms flailing. No family. No tower but the Spire.

I would find a way to avoid that. I had to.

* * *

The sound of Elna and Nat returning startled the Singer. He swept from our quarters, unfurling his wings as he crossed to the balcony. Nat dodged left to avoid being struck.

I walked unsteadily to greet them, waving my hand to dissuade Elna from bowing in custom.

Shading my eyes against the sunset, I watched the Singer's silhouette shrink as the breeze carried him away. He soared towards the city's center, towards the Spire.

My shoulders dropped. I sank down to rest on my mother's stool. Nat came to stand by me. "I'm sorry," he murmured. "For locking you out."

I looked up at him. Wished I had words. But anything I said could reveal me, break the Singer's fiat, and endanger Nat and Elna even more. They had enough trouble coming because of me.

I held out the markers, with their sentences on them.

Elna read hers and sucked in her breath. Then she read Nat's and mine, saw they were blessedly temporary. Her eyes watered. "Serves you right," she said. But she heaved the words at us with such relief, I knew she'd been afraid.

I did not want to think of Naton, Nat's father, now. But I was sure Elna thought of the bone markers she'd held the day Naton was thrown down. A skein of Treason Laws, making him first chosen for Conclave, the ritual to appease the city.

Those chips were the heaviest the Singers dispensed.

Ours were much lighter. Tower Laws. Warnings. We would not have to wear them forever.

After he read his chip, Nat's face was a puzzle. "Why do I get punished for what Kirit did?"

Because I would not sacrifice myself for you, Nat. Because I would not go with the Singer, you are punished. I opened my mouth to tell him. To say I was sorry.

But Elna turned on him. "Oh, you're not innocent. You stood by and watched." Her look stopped him cold. He glanced at me from under his lids instead. She huffed and began piling foods from the offerings into a basket. "Might as well get packed up, then. The council will be up."

"Packed?" I couldn't fathom why.

"They'll want you two as low as they can send you," Elna said. "Closer to your duties, but also much more shameful, isn't it? So they'll move you down, to my tier."

ABOUT THE
KATE WILHELM SOLSTICE AWARD

Among the changes SFWA made in 2016 was to rename the Solstice Award to the Kate Wilhelm Solstice Award. It was felt that doing so acknowledged the important role that Ms. Wilhelm has played not just in SFWA's history, but overall in the field of speculative fiction.

This decision also brought the award's name more in line with the naming of other SFWA awards, such as the Ray Bradbury Award for Outstanding Dramatic Presentation, the Andre Norton Award for Outstanding Young Adult Science Fiction, and the Kevin O'Donnell Jr. Service to SFWA Award.

Created in 2008 and given at the discretion of the SFWA President and Board, the award is for individuals who have had a significant impact on the science fiction or fantasy landscape, and is particularly intended for those who have consistently made a major positive difference within the speculative fiction field, much like its namesake.

Sir Terry Pratchett (28 April 1948–12 March 2015) has been named the recipient of the Kate Wilhelm Solstice Award. "In his long career, Sir Terry used humor and satire to entertain and educate, becoming one of the best-selling British authors of the twentieth century. His work has inspired numerous authors and readers. Pratchett has donated his time and money to orangutan conservation efforts and Alzheimer's research. Pratchett was knighted by Queen Elizabeth for his service to Literature in 2009." Kathryn Baker for SFWA.

SFWA President Cat Rambo wrote, "I deeply regret Sir Terry's untimely passing, and my inability to give him the award in person. He's shaped the genre in ways that will resonate for centuries."

I HAVE READ THEM ALL, NOW

MICHELLE SAGARA

Michelle's author bio was written with care, thought, and incredible attention to detail. Unfortunately, while reading a fantasy novel, she folded it in half and stuck it in the book as a bookmark, and she hasn't been able to find it. Her house is also full of books, and sadly, completely lacking in shelf-space, which gives the entire place the untidy look of an accident waiting to happen.

Michelle writes as Michelle West, Michelle Sagara, and has been published as Michelle Sagara West. She is married to the world's best husband, and they live with their two sons.

You can find her online at http://michellesagara.com, when she is not hiding from distraction and trying to meet deadlines.

I write this as a reader.

I didn't know Terry Pratchett in any other way. I can go to Wikipedia and look up the relevant dates—birth, death—and locations, but . . . I would be going to Wikipedia to look them up solely for this introduction. To me as a reader, the dates are like many dry historical facts. They tell me nothing about why Terry Pratchett was so important to me.

I did meet him in real life, twice when he came to the bookstore I work at for signings. The first time was early enough that he hadn't gained reading traction in Canada yet. In the pauses between readers, he took out a tiny PDA and wrote. He was working on a scene with Death in it; I recognized the all caps style of conversation when I glanced at it. I'd offered to run out to buy coffee, food, or anything legal he wanted; he said, "I'm fine. I've done more of these than you've had hot meals. In your life."

I said, "I think you're underestimating my age."

He said, "Probably not."

The second time, he had a much larger Canadian following, and there were no gaps in the line. One reader had brought, oh, everything he'd ever written. His final signature was: "Bugger off and go bother Douglas Adams," which the reader was so tickled at, he showed it to me. Well, to everyone actually. But years and years later, on a different continent, at a different signing, Pratchett signed his latest book with "I guess it's too late to bother Douglas now." He'd *remembered*. He'd remembered this man who had brought an unsigned copy of everything he'd written practically ever.

I saw him on panels, thereafter. At conventions at a distance. I liked to listen to him speak.

But that's ancillary. I wasn't his friend. I wasn't his family. He was incredibly important to me, regardless.

*　　*　　*

I remember when I first heard about the early onset Alzheimer's. I remember where I was. I remember standing in place for one long beat, because the ground that I'd been walking across had suddenly become hugely unstable, as if a chunk of it had been excised, as if solidity was in question.

I will not lie: I cried.

People often find this kind of reaction confusing. Or overly sentimental. Or even self-aggrandizing. Because I didn't know him. At best, I knew of him. I had no *right* to feel bereavement. And this is actually true. His family—wife, children—and his real life friends, did. But I felt bereaved, regardless, because I'm a reader, and he was one of my authors.

Let me explain. A new Terry Pratchett novel filled the house with joy. Or glee. When I got an ARC (Advanced Review Copy) and brought it home, there would be war at the dinner table about who got to read it first. Cutlery and personal stress were weapons in these battles.

There was no frame of mind in which I could not read a Terry Pratchett novel. On the very worst days, when the sun seemed to have permanently sunk, never to rise again, a Pratchett novel could still draw me in, when everything else had moved far, far out of reach. Pratchett could make me laugh. Pratchett could make me cry. I took to saving one unread novel. I stopped being the person who read every word as it was published. I *bought* everything as it was published—but I kept one book in its inviolate "in case of emergencies" position. It was my retreat. It was my place of safety. No matter what Pratchett wrote about, I would laugh, I would cry, it would be a reminder that I was still capable of both of those things.

I was so grateful for that. I was grateful that Terry Pratchett was prolific. I was grateful that he continued to write his Discworld novels (although I did read *Nation*, and pretty much everything else). Is this all about me? Yes. Of course it is.

Because the only real way we intersected was through the act of reading. I don't read in a crowd. I don't act out what I'm reading. I don't discuss it until after the fact. (Well, okay, I discuss it if I've woken people up because I'm laughing too hard, and they want to know why and I owe them that, but.) No two readers perceive or experience the same book the same way.

Tens of millions of people read Pratchett novels; tens of millions of people loved the books, each in their own way. I work in a bookstore, so I've met and discussed Pratchett with hundreds of them. As we inevitably do, we talk about the novels and questions arise. So: as one reader to another, my favorite Pratchett was *Night Watch*. My first Pratchett was *Reaper Man*, followed swiftly by *Men At Arms*.

I have read them all.

ABOUT THE DAMON KNIGHT MEMORIAL GRAND MASTER AWARD

In addition to giving the Nebula Awards each year, SFWA also may present the Damon Knight Grand Master Award to a living author for a lifetime of achievement in science fiction and/or fantasy. In accordance with SFWA's bylaws, the president shall have the power, at his or her discretion, to call for the presentation of the Grand Master Award. Nominations for the Damon Knight Memorial Award are solicited from the officers, with the advice of participating past presidents, who vote with the officers to determine the recipient. This award was first presented in 1975.

DAMON KNIGHT GRAND MASTER: C. J. CHERRYH

BETSY WOLLHEIM

Betsy Wollheim, the daughter of veteran paperback editor, Donald A. Wollheim, is a second generation science fiction editor with over four decades of book publishing experience. She is the president and co-publisher of DAW Books, and not only edits but also art directs all the books she acquires. She has edited numerous award-winning and bestselling authors, including C. J. Cherryh, Tad Williams (with co-publisher Sheila Gilbert), Patrick Rothfuss, Nnedi Okorafor, Mercedes Lackey, Marion Zimmer Bradley, Kristen Britain, Tanith Lee, C. S. Friedman, and Saladin Ahmed. In 2012, Betsy was awarded the Hugo for Best Editor Long Form.

I was twenty-three years old when I returned to New York from six years away attending college, grad school, and working for printing houses. It was 1975, and my dad, Don Wollheim, handed me a well-worn paper manuscript. It was from a new author, someone he was clearly very excited about. The author had two books on submission to DAW, and he had bought both but had decided to publish *Gate of Ivrel*, the one he handed me, first. He said he intended to suggest to the author, Carolyn Janice Cherry, that she use her initials and add a silent "h" to the end of her name, because her legal name was more appropriate for a romance writer, and she was anything but that. C. J. Cherryh had an almost exotic look to it. It seemed right, somehow.

I read *Gate of Ivrel* in my childhood bedroom, in my parents' house in Queens. My father was right—Carolyn Cherry was definitely not a romance writer. *Gate of Ivrel* was different from anything I had ever read. The heroine, Morgaine, was an ancient interstellar operative whose mission was to close the dangerous space-time Gates on planets, setting them to self-destruct as she moved through them to her next location. The novel was clearly hard science fiction, because the greatest danger was the possibility of catastrophically mutating the past by manipulation of the space-time continuum in the Gates. But all the trappings were more typical of a heroic fantasy. Because the story is told from the viewpoint of her vassal-and-partner, Vanye, a warrior from a primitive culture, Morgaine herself is veiled in mystery. She has a high-tech implement that resembles a sword, and this "sword" even has a name: Changeling. It was a perfect illustration of how advanced technology would seem like magic to a tribal culture. It was also the first book where Carolyn pairs an alpha female with a subservient or beta male. This would be one of many ongoing themes in C.J.'s writing. Quite a switch from the sexism that had been traditional in our field for decades.

After reading *Gate of Ivrel*, in October 1975, I started work at DAW Books, moved into my first apartment in Manhattan, and soon thereafter met C.J. Cherryh.

Carolyn was a high school classics teacher from Oklahoma City, and despite her Masters from Johns Hopkins, and extensive world travel, she seemed almost pathologically shy. She developed a very close relationship with my parents and would stay in their home in Queens whenever she was in NYC. Because Carolyn and I didn't speak much in those early years (she was shy, as I've said) I didn't really get to know her until the late 70s. But even in the earliest years, I observed that she was a very determined individual who was not only extremely prolific but also incredibly brave. She entered fandom with a vengeance—traveling to multiple conventions a month, and when her foot was bitten by a brown recluse spider, she was undeterred. For four months she traveled to conventions in a wheelchair with her foot elevated above her heart. Nothing could stop her. She joined the filksingers, she relaxed, we became friends.

And I began to learn about Carolyn. I learned that she first started writing when her favorite childhood television show, *Flash Gordon*, was cancelled. She decided to write her own episodes. Carolyn's parents told her that she couldn't use the typewriter if her younger brother David was sleeping, so on weekend mornings, she would routinely wake David by tossing a wet washcloth in his face and then escape his fury by locking herself in her bedroom to write. She was determined, even at ten.

I read all her manuscripts. But the first manuscript I edited (along with my dad) was *Downbelow Station*. It was a long book for the early 80s, and it needed two rewrites at a time when there were no computers. Carolyn added physical description at Don's suggestion, then chapter headings for clarity, at mine. The book was complex, and the reader needed to know the where, who, and when at the beginning of each chapter; Carolyn had to figure out time relative to space. It was a massive amount of work. The manuscript came back to us cut up in pieces—new parts attached to old with scotch tape. It was an enormous relief when it went to the printer and nothing had fallen out. I have been editing Carolyn's DAW books ever since.

People told Carolyn that a DAW original paperback could never win the Hugo. Despite all odds: mass market original publication, and the pulp-image DAW had at that time, *Downbelow Station* prevailed and won Carolyn her first Best Novel Hugo. I don't remember how many times a C.J. Cherryh title has been nominated for a Hugo, but I vividly remember that *The Pride of Chanur* ran on a slot with the "big three": Heinlein, Asimov, and Clarke. [Ed. note: an excerpt follows.] It was an honor to be on that ballot, and though Asimov won (he got everyone's second place votes) *Pride* got more first place votes than any of the competing books. Carolyn was happy, even though she lost the award.

Downbelow Station was a formative book not only for Carolyn but also for me and for all her readers. It was in this book that Carolyn first laid out her plan for humanity to go to the stars. She charted a route, via Tau Ceti, that would define all of her subsequent science fiction and even some of her already published work. The Alliance-Union Universe is a massive exploration of how humans can reach the stars, and what could happen. It is realistic and believable. It came from the heart and mind of a woman who wanted to go to space— *really wanted it*. So she figured out how to do it, and what might happen if we went. Every star system in CJ's science fiction novels really exists, only the names have changed.

All of Carolyn's science fiction novels, even the offshoots that primarily feature aliens, fit under the huge umbrella of the Alliance-Union universe. In the Chanur series, Tully is the lone human survivor of a captured Alliance exploration ship. The Foreigner series is about a colony ship from Alliance-Union that becomes lost in space. But perhaps Carolyn's greatest literary achievement is the study of how humanity itself can change when the planet of our birth is no longer accessible. The books that comprise the heart of the Alliance-Union novels develop a space-centric culture where the human genome must be protected.

She describes her writing voice as "intense internal," and indeed, her books are very intimate and personal, often about fear and uncertainty in the face of unfamiliar circumstance and extreme danger. Yet her heroes and heroines are as brave as their author and always find a way to survive.

It's a considerable achievement not only to envision a future interstellar human civilization but also to respect the many bona fide parameters of science. It's an even greater achievement to also respect the social and biological complexities of the evolution of a human society without a home world. But it's amazing that she's managed to do it while making her stories so personal.

I'm very proud to have worked with and to continue to work with C.J. Cherryh. Now, after forty years, Carolyn and I are closer than ever—we're family. I'm always learning new things from her. I learned last year that she is the many-times-great grandniece of Daniel Boone. But however much I learn from Carolyn, I learn even more from her work. From the Foreigner series she showed me how a lone human diplomat, within a mere two decades, can lead a steam-age alien civilization to interstellar travel and more. [Ed. note: an excerpt follows.] The acceleration of this technological development makes for an incredibly exciting read. Now in its sixteenth volume, this massive series has expanded its horizons and become more important with each successive book. I look forward to each new novel with all the enthusiasm of an avid fan.

It's an enormous pleasure for me to see Carolyn made a Grand Master by SFWA. No editor understands more than I do how much she deserves it.

EXCERPT FROM *PRIDE OF CHANUR*

C. J. CHERRYH

Chapter 1

There had been something loose about the station dock all morning, skulking in amongst the gantries and the lines and the canisters which were waiting to be moved, lurking wherever shadows fell among the rampway accesses of the many ships at dock at Meetpoint. It was pale, naked, starved-looking in what fleeting glimpse anyone on *The Pride of Chanur* had had of it. Evidently no one had reported it to station authorities, nor did *The Pride.* Involving oneself in others' concerns at Meetpoint Station, where several species came to trade and provision, was ill-advised—at least until one was personally bothered. Whatever it was, it was bipedal, brachiate, and quick at making itself unseen. It had surely gotten away from someone, and likeliest were the kif, who had a thieving finger in everything, and who were not above kidnapping. Or it might be some large, bizarre animal: the mahendo'sat were inclined to the keeping and trade of strange pets, and Station had been displeased with them in that respect on more than one occasion. So far it had done nothing. Stolen nothing. No one wanted to get involved in question and answer between original owners and station authorities; and so far no official statement had come down from those station authorities and no notice of its loss had been posted by any ship, which itself argued that a wise person should not ask questions. The crew reported it only to the captain and chased it, twice, from *The Pride*'s loading area. Then the crew got to work on necessary duties, having settled the annoyance to their satisfaction.

It was the last matter on the mind of the noble, the distinguished captain Pyanfar Chanur, who was setting out down her own rampway for the docks. She was hani, this captain, splendidly maned and bearded in red-gold, which reached in silken curls to the middle of her bare, sleek-pelted chest, and she was dressed as befitted a hani of captain's rank, blousing scarlet breeches tucked up at her waist with a broad gold belt, with silk cords of every shade of red and orange wrapping that about, each knotted cord with a pendant jewel on its dangling end. Gold finished the breeches at her knees. Gold filigree was her armlet. And a row of fine gold rings and a large pendant pearl decorated the tufted sweep of her left ear. She strode down her own rampway in the security of ownership, still high-blooded from a quarrel with her niece—and yelled and bared claws as the intruder came bearing down on her.

She landed one raking, startled blow which would have held a hani in the encounter, but the hairless skin tore and it hurtled past her, taller than she was. It skidded round the bending of the curved ramp tube and bounded right into the ship, trailing blood all the way and leaving a bloody handprint on the rampway's white plastic wall.

Pyanfar gaped in outrage and pelted after, claws scrabbling for traction on the flooring plates. "*Hilfy!*" she shouted ahead; her niece had been in the lower corridor. Pyanfar made it into the airlock, hit the bar of the com panel there and punched all-ship. "Alert! *Hilfy!* Call the crew in! Something's gotten aboard. Seal yourself into the nearest compartment and call the crew." She flung open the locker next to the com unit, grabbed a pistol and scrambled in pursuit of the intruder. No trouble at all tracking it, with the dotted red trail on the white decking. The track led left at the first cross-corridor, which was deserted—the intruder must have gone left again, starting to box the square round the lift shafts. Pyanfar ran, heard a shout from that intersecting corridor and scrambled for it: *Hilfy!* She rounded the corner at a slide and came up short on a tableau, the intruder's hairless, red-running back and young Hilfy Chanur holding the corridor beyond with nothing but bared claws and adolescent bluster.

"Idiot!" Pyanfar spat at Hilfy, and the intruder turned on *her* of a sudden, much closer. It brought up short in a staggered crouch, seeing the gun aimed two-handed at itself. It might have sense not to rush a weapon; might . . . but that would turn it right back at Hilfy, who stood unarmed behind. Pyanfar braced to fire on the least movement.

It stood rigidly still in its crouch, panting from its running and its wound. "Get out of there," Pyanfar said to Hilfy. "Get back." The intruder knew about hani claws now; and guns; but it might do anything, and Hilfy, an indistinction in her vision which was tunnelled wholly on the intruder, stayed stubbornly still. "*Move!*" Pyanfar shouted.

The intruder shouted too, a snarl which almost got it shot; and drew itself upright and gestured to the center of its chest, twice, defiant. *Go on and shoot,* it seemed to invite her.

That intrigued Pyanfar. The intruder was not attractive. It had a bedraggled gold mane and beard, and its chest fur, almost invisible, narrowed in a line down its heaving belly to vanish into what was, legitimately, clothing, a rag almost nonexistent in its tatters and obscured by the dirt which matched the rest of its hairless hide. Its smell was rank. But a straight carriage and a wild-eyed invitation to its enemies . . . that deserved a second thought. It knew guns; it wore at least a token of clothing; it drew its line and meant to hold its territory. Male, maybe. It had that over-the-brink look in its eyes.

"Who are you?" Pyanfar asked slowly, in several languages one after the other, including kif. The intruder gave no sign of understanding any of them. "Who?" she repeated.

It crouched slowly, with a sullen scowl, all the way to the deck, and extended a blunt-nailed finger and wrote in its own blood which was liberally puddled about its bare feet. It made a precise row of symbols, ten of them, and a second row which began with the first symbol prefaced by the second, second with second, second with third . . . patiently, with increasing concentration despite the growing tremors of its hand, dipping its finger and writing, mad fixation on its task.

"What's it doing?" asked Hilfy, who could not see from her side.

"A writing system, probably numerical notation. It's no animal, niece."

The intruder looked up at the exchange—stood up, an abrupt move which proved injudicious after its loss of blood. A glassy, desperate look came into its eyes, and it sprawled in the puddle and the writing, slipping in its own blood in trying to get up again.

"Call the crew," Pyanfar said levelly, and this time Hilfy scurried off in great haste. Pyanfar stood where she was, pistol in hand, until Hilfy was out of sight down another corridor, then, assured that there was no one to see her lapse of dignity, she squatted down with the gun in both hands and loosely between her knees. The intruder still struggled, propped itself up with its bloody back against the wall, elbow pressed against that deeper starting-point of the scratches on its side, which was the source of most of the blood. Its pale blue eyes, for all their glassiness, seemed to have sense in them. It looked back at her warily, with seeming mad cynicism.

"You speak kif?" Pyanfar asked again. A flicker of those eyes, which might mean anything. Not a word from it. It started shivering, which was shock setting in. Sweat had broken out on its naked skin. It never ceased to look at her.

Running broke into the corridors. Pyanfar stood up quickly, not to be caught thus engaged with the creature. Hilfy came hurrying back from her direction, the crew arriving from the other, and Pyanfar stepped aside as they arrived and the intruder tried to scramble off in retreat. The crew laid hands on it and jerked it skidding along the bloody puddle. It cried out and tried to grapple with them, but they had it on its belly in the first rush and a blow dazed it. "*Gently!*" Pyanfar yelled at them, but they had it then, got its arms lashed at its back with one of their belts, tied its ankles together and got off it, their fur as bloody as the intruder, who continued a feeble movement.

"Do it no more damage," Pyanfar said. "I'll have it clean, thank you, watered, fed, and healthy, but keep it restrained. Prepare me explanations how it got face to face with me in the rampway, and if one of you bleats a word of this outside the ship I'll sell you to the kif."

"Captain," they murmured, down-eared in deference. They were second and third cousins of hers, two sets of sisters, one set large and one small, and equally chagrined.

"*Out*," she said. They snatched the intruder up by the binding of its arms and prepared to drag it. "Careful!" Pyanfar hissed, reminding them, and they were gentler in pulling it along.

"You," Pyanfar said then to Hilfy, her brother's daughter, who lowered her ears and turned her face aside—short-maned, with an adolescent's beginning beard, Hilfy Chanur presently wore a air of martyrdom. "I'll send you back shaved if you disobey another order. Understand me?"

Hilfy made a bow facing her, duly contrite. "Aunt," she said, and straightened, contriving to make it all thoughtfully graceful; looked her straight in the eyes with offended worship.

"Huh," Pyanfar said. Hilfy bowed a second time and padded past as softly as possible. In common blue breeches like the crew, was Hilfy, but the swagger was all Chanur, and not quite ludicrous on so young a woman. Pyanfar snorted, fingered the silk of her beard into order, looked down in sober thought at the wallowed smear where the Outsider had fallen, obliterating all the writing from the eyes of the crew.

So, so, so.

Pyanfar postponed her trip to station offices, walked back to the lower-deck operations center, sat down at the com board amid all the telltales of cargo status and lines and grapples and the routine operations *The Pride* carried on automatically. She keyed in the current messages, sorted through those and found nothing, then delved into *The Pride's* recording of all messages received since docking, and all which had flowed through station communications aimed at others. She searched first for anything kif-sent, a rapid flicker of lines on the screen in front of her, all operational chatter in transcription—a very great deal of it. Then she queried for notice of anything lost, and after that, for anything escaped.

Mahendo'sat? she queried then, staying constantly to her own ship's records of incoming messages, of the sort which flowed constantly in a busy station, and in no wise sending any inquiry into the station's comp system. She recycled the whole record last of all, ran it past at eye-blurring speed, looking for any key word about escapes or warnings of alien presence at Meetpoint.

So indeed. No one was going to say a word on the topic. The owners still did not want to acknowledge publicly that they had lost this item. The Chanur were not lack-witted, to announce publicly that they had found it. Or to trust that the kif or whoever had lost it were not at this moment turning the station inside out with a surreptitious search.

Pyanfar turned off the machine, flicked her ears so that the rings on the left one jangled soothingly. She got up and paced the center, thrust her hands into her belt and thought about alternatives, and possible gains. It would be a dark day indeed when a Chanur went to the kif to hand back an acquisition. She could justifiably make a claim on it regarding legal liabilities and the invasion of a hani ship. Public hazard, it was called. But there were no outside witnesses to the intrusion, and the kif, almost certainly to blame, would not yield without a wrangle; which meant court, and prolonged proximity to kif, whose gray, wrinkle-hided persons she loathed; whose naturally dolorous faces she loathed; whose jeremiad of miseries and wrongs done them was constant and unendurable. A Chanur, in station court with a howling mob of kif . . . and it would go to that extreme if kif came claiming this intruder. The whole business was unpalatable, in all its ramifications.

Whatever it was and wherever it came from, the creature was educated. That hinted in turn at other things, at cogent reasons why the kif might indeed be upset at the loss of this item and why they wished so little publicity in the search.

She punched in intraship. "Hilfy."

"*Aunt?*" Hilfy responded after a moment.

"Find out the intruder's condition."

"*I'm watching them treat it now. Aunt, I think it's he, if there's any analogy of form and—*"

"Never mind zoology. How badly is it hurt?"

"*It's in shock, but it seems stronger than it was a moment ago. It—he—got quiet when we managed to get an anesthetic on the scratches. I think he figured then we were trying to help, and he quit fighting. We thought the drug had got him. But he's breathing better now.*"

"It's probably just waiting its chance. When you get it safely locked up, you take your turn at dockwork, since you were so eager to have a look outside. The others will show you what to do. Tell Haral to get herself to lowerdeck op. Now."

"*Yes, aunt.*" Hilfy had no sulking in her tone. The last reprimand must not have worn off. Pyanfar shut down the contact and listened to station chatter in the interim, wishing in vain for something to clarify the matter.

Haral showed up on the run, soaking wet, blood-spattered and breathless. She bowed shortly in the doorway, straightened. She was oldest of the crew, was Haral, tall, with a dark scar across her broad nose and another across the belly, but those were from her rash youth.

"Clean up," Pyanfar said. "Take cash and go marketing, cousin. Shop the second-hand markets as if you were on your own. The item I want may be difficult to locate, but not impossible, I think, in such a place as Meetpoint. Some books, if you will: a mahendo'sat lexicon; a mahendo'sat version of their holy writings. The philosopher Kohboranua or another of that ilk, I'm completely indifferent. And a mahendo'sat symbol translator, its modules and manuals, from elementary up, as many levels as you can find . . . above all that item. The rest is all cover. If questioned—a client's taken a religious interest."

Haral's, eyes flickered, but she bowed in acceptance of the order and asked nothing. Pyanfar put her hand deep into her pocket and came up with a motley assortment of large-denomination coinage, a whole stack of it.

"And four gold rings," Pyanfar added.

"Captain?"

"To remind you all that *The Pride* minds its own business. Say so when you give them. It'll salve your feelings, I hope, if we have to miss taking a liberty here, as well we may. But talk and rouse suspicion about those items, Haral Araun, and you won't have an ear to wear it on."

Haral grinned and bowed a third time.

"Go," said Pyanfar, and Haral darted out in zealous application.

So. It was a risk, but a minor one. Pyanfar considered matters for a moment, finally walked outside the op room and down the corridor, took the lift up to central level, where her own quarters were, out of the stench and the reek of disinfectant which filled the lower deck.

She closed the door behind her with a sigh, went to the bath and washed her hands, seeing that there remained no shred of flesh in the undercurve of her claws— checked over her fine silk breeches to be sure no spatter of blood had gotten on them. She applied a dash of cologne to clear the memory from her nostrils.

Stupidity. She was getting dull as the stsho, to have missed a grip on the intruder in the first place: *old* was not a word she preferred to think about. Slow of mind, woolgathering, that she struck like a youngster on her first forage. Lazy. That was more like it. She patted her flat belly and decided that the year-old complacent outletting of her belt had to be taken in again. She was losing her edge. Her brother Kohan was still fit enough, planet-bound as he was and not gifted with the time-stretch of jump: he managed. Inter-male bickering and a couple of sons to throw out of the domicile kept his blood circulating, and there was usually a trio of mates in the house at any one time, with offspring to chastise. About time, she thought, that she put *The Pride* into home dock at Anuurn for a thorough refitting, and spend a layover with her own mate Khym, high in the Kahin hills, in the Mahn estates. Get the smell of the homeworld wind in her nostrils for a few months. Do a little hunting, run off that extra notch on the belt. Check on her daughter Tahy and see whether that son of hers was still roving about or whether someone had finally broken his neck for him. Surely the lad would have had the common courtesy to send a message through Khym or Kohan if he had settled somewhere; and above all to her daughter, who was, gods knew, grown and getting soft hanging about her father's house, among a dozen other daughters, mostly brotherless. Son Kara should settle himself with some unpropertied wife and give his sister some gainful employ-ment making him rich—above all, settle and take himself out of his father's and his uncle's way. Ambitious, that was Kara. Let the young rake try to move in on his uncle Kohan and that would be the last of him. Pyanfar flexed claws at the thought and recalled why all her shoreleaves were short ones.

But this now, this business with this bit of live contraband which had strayed aboard, which might be kif-owned . . . the honorable lord Kohan

Chanur her brother was going to have a word to say about his ship's carelessness in letting such an incident reach their deck. And there was going to be a major rearrangement in the household if Hilfy got hurt—brotherless Hilfy, who had gotten to be too much Chanur to go following after a brother if ever her mother gave her one. Hilfy Chanur *par* Faha, who wanted the stars more than she wanted anything; and who clung to her father as the one who could give them to her. It was Hilfy's lifelong waited chance, this voyage, this apprenticeship on *The Pride.* It had torn Kohan's doting soul to part from his favorite; that was clear in the letter which had come with Hilfy.

Pyanfar shook her head and fretted. Depriving those four rag-eared crew of hers of a shoreleave in the pursuit of this matter was one thing, but taking Hilfy home to Anuurn while she sorted out a major quarrel with the kif was another. It was expensive, curtailing their homeward routing. More, Hilfy's pride would die a death, if she were the cause of that rerouting, if she were made to face her sisters in her sudden return to the household; and Pyanfar confessed herself attached to the imp, who wanted what she had wanted at such an age, who most likely *would* come to command a Chanur ship someday, perhaps even—gods postpone the hour—*The Pride* itself. Pyanfar thought of such a legacy . . . someday, someday that Kohan passed his prime and she did. Others in the house of Chanur were jealous of Hilfy, waiting for some chance to use their jealousy. But Hilfy *was* the best. The brightest and best, like herself and like Kohan, and no one so far could prove otherwise. Whatever young male one day won the Chanur holding from Kohan in his decline had best walk warily and please Hilfy, or Hilfy might take herself a mate who would tear the ears off the interloper. That was the kind Hilfy was, loyal to her father and to the house.

And ruining that spirit or risking her life over that draggled Outsider was not worth it. Maybe, Pyanfar thought, she should swallow the bitter mouthful and go dump the creature on the nearest kif ship. She seriously considered it. Choosing the wrong kif ship might afford some lively amusement: there would be riot among the kif and consternation on the station. But yielding was still, at bottom, distasteful.

Gods! so that was how she proposed teaching young Hilfy to handle difficulties. *That* was the example she set . . . yielding up what she had, because she thought it might be dangerous to hold it.

She *was* getting soft. She patted her belly again, decided against shoreleave at voyage's end, another lying-up and another Mahn offspring to muddle things up. Decided against retreat. She drew in a great breath and put on a grim smile. Age came and the young grew old, but not too old, the gods grant. This voyage, young Hilfy Chanur was going to learn to justify that swagger she cut through the corridors of the ship; so, indeed she was.

There was no leaving the ship with matters aboard still in flux. Pyanfar went to the small central galley, up the starboard curve from her quarters and the bridge, stirred about to take a cup of gfi from the dispenser and sat down at the counter by the oven to enjoy it at leisure, waiting until her crew should have had ample time to have dealt with the Outsider. She gave them a bit more, finally tossed the empty cup in the sterilizer and got up and wandered belowdecks again, where the corridors stank strongly of antiseptic and Tirun was lounging about, leaning against the wall by the lowerdeck washroom door. "Well?" Pyanfar asked.

"We put it in there, captain. Easiest to clean, by your leave. Haral left. Chur and Geran and *ker* Hilfy are out doing the loading. Thought someone ought to stay awhile by the door and listen, to be sure the creature's all right."

Pyanfar laid her hand on the switch, looked back at Tirun—Haral's sister and as broad and solid, with the scars of youth well-weathered, the gold of successful voyages winking from her left ear. The two of them together could handle the Outsider, she reckoned, in any condition. "Does it show any sign of coming out of its shock?"

"It's quiet; shallow breathing, staring somewhere else—but aware what's going on. Scared us a moment; we thought it'd gone into shock with the medicine, but I think it just quieted down when the pain stopped. We tried with the way we handled it, to make it understand we didn't want to hurt it. Maybe it has that figured. We carried it in here and it settled down and lay still . . . moved when made to move, but not surly, more like it's stopped thinking, like it's stopped doing anything it doesn't have to do. Worn out, I'd say."

"Huh." Pyanfar pressed the bar. The dark interior of the washroom smelled of antiseptic too, the strongest they had. The lights were dimmed. The air was stiflingly warm and carried an odd scent under the antiseptic reek. Her eyes missed the creature a moment, searched anxiously and located it in the corner, a heap of blankets between the shower stall and the laundry . . . asleep or awake she could not tell with its head tucked down in its forearms. A large container of water and a plastic dish with a few meat chips and crumbs left rested beside it on the tiles. Well, again. It was then carnivorous and not so delicate after all, to have an appetite left. So much for its collapse. "Is it restrained?"

"It has chain enough to get to the head if it understands what it's for."

Pyanfar stepped back outside and closed the door on it again. "Very likely it understands. Tirun, it *is* sapient or I'm blind. Don't assume it can't manipulate switches. No one is to go in there alone and no one's to carry firearms near it. Pass that order to the others personally, Hilfy too. Especially Hilfy."

"Yes, captain." Tirun's broad face was innocent of opinions. Gods knew what they were going to *do* with the creature if they kept it. Tirun did not ask. Pyanfar strolled off, meditating on the scene behind the washroom door, the heap of deceptive blankets, the food so healthily consumed, the avowed collapse . . . no lackwit, this creature who had twice tried her ship's security and on the third attempt, succeeded in getting through. Why *The Pride?* she wondered. Why her ship, out of all the others at dock? Because they were last in the section, before the bulkhead of the dock seal might force the creature to have left cover somewhat, and it was the last available choice? Or was there some other reason?

She walked the corridor to the airlock and the rampway, and out its curving ribbed length into the chill air of the docks. She looked left as she came out, and there was Hilfy, canister-loading with Chur and Geran, rolling the big cargo containers off the stationside dolly and onto the moving belt which would take the goods into *The Pride*'s holds, paid freight on its way to Urtur and Kura and Touin and Anuurn itself, stsho cargo, commodities and textiles and medicines, ordinary stuff. Hilfy paused at the sight of her, panting with her efforts and already looking close to collapse—stood up straight with her hands at her sides and her ears back, belly heaving. It was hard work, shifting those cans about, especially for the unskilled and unaccustomed. Chur and Geran worked on, small of stature and wiry, knowing the points of balance to an exactitude. Pyanfar affected not to notice her niece and walked on with wide steps and nonchalant, smiling to herself the while. Hilfy had been mightily indignant, barred from rushing out to station market, to roam about unescorted, sightseeing on this her first call at Meetpoint, where species docked which never called at homeworld . . . sights she had missed at Urtur and Kura, likewise pent aboard ship or held close to *The Pride*'s berth. The imp had too much enthusiasm for her own good. So she got the look at Meetpoint's famous docks she had argued to have—now, this very day—but not the sightseeing tour of her young imaginings.

Next station-call, Pyanfar thought, next station-call her niece might have learned enough to let loose unescorted, when the wild-eyed eagerness had worn off, when she had learned from this incident that there were hazards on dockside and that a little caution was in order when prowling the friendliest of ports.

Herself, she took the direct route, not without watching her surroundings.

Chapter 2

A call on Meetpoint Station officials was usually a leisurely and pleasant affair. The stsho, placid and graceful, ran the station offices and bureaus on this side of the station, where oxygen breathers docked. Methodical to a fault, the stsho, tedious and full of endless subtle meanings in their pastel ornament and the tattooings on their pearly hides. They were another hairless species—stalk-thin, tri-sexed and hanilike only by the wildest stretch of the imagination, if eyes, nose, and mouth in biologically convenient order was similarity. Their manners were bizarre among themselves. But stsho had learned to suit their methodical plodding and their ceremoniousness to hani taste, which was to have a soft chair, a ready cup of herbal tea, a plate of exotic edibles and an individual as pleasant as possible about the forms and the statistics, who could make it all like a social chat.

This stsho was unfamiliar. Stsho changed officials more readily than they changed ornament—either a different individual had come into control of Meetpoint Station, Pyanfar reckoned, or a stsho she had once known had entered a New Phase—new doings? Pyanfar wondered, at the nudge of a small and prickly instinct—new doings? Loose Outsiders and stsho power shuffles? All changes were suspect when something was out of pocket. If it was the same as the previous stationmaster, it had changed the pattern of all the elaborate silver filigree and plumes—azure and lime now, not azure and mint; and if it were the case, it was not at all polite to recognize the refurbished person, even if a hani suspected identity.

The stsho proffered delicacies and tea, bowed, folded up *gtst* stalklike limbs—he, she, or even it, hardly applied with stsho—and seated *gtst*-self in *gtst* bowlchair, a cushioned indentation in the office floor. The necessary table rose on a pedestal before it. Pyanfar occupied the facing depression, lounged on an elbow to reach for the smoked fish the stsho's lesser-status servant had placed on a similar table at her left. The servant, ornamentless and no one, sat against the wall, knees tucked higher than *gtst* head, arms about bony ankles, waiting usefulness. The stsho official likewise took a sample of the fish, poured tea, graceful gestures of stsho elegance and hospitality. Plumed and cosmetically augmented brows nodded delicately over moonstone eyes as *gtst* looked up—white brows shading to lilac and azure; azure tracings on the domed brow shaded to lime over the hairless skull. Another stsho, of course, might read the patterns with exactitude, the station in life, the chosen Mood for this Phase of *gtst* existence, the affiliations and modes and thereby, *gtst* approachability. Nonstsho were forgiven their trespasses; and stsho in Retiring mode were not likely filling public offices.

Pyanfar made one attempt on the Outsider topic, delicately: "Things have been quiet hereabouts?"

"Oh, assuredly." The stsho beamed, smiled with narrow mouth and narrow eyes, a carnivore habit, though the stsho were not aggressive. "Assuredly."

"Also on my world," Pyanfar said, and sipped her tea, an aroma of spices which delighted all her sinuses. "Herbal. But what?"

The stsho smiled with still more breadth. "Ah. Imported from my world. We introduce it here, in our offices. Duty free. New cultivation techniques make it available for export. The first time, you understand. The very first shipment offered. Very rare, a taste of my very distant world."

"Cost?"

They discussed it. It was outrageous. But the stsho came down, predictably, particularly when tempted with a case of hani delicacies promised to be carted up from dockside to the offices. Pyanfar left the necessary interview in high spirits. Barter was as good to her as breathing.

She took the lift down to dock level, straight down, without going the several corridors over in lateral which she could have taken. She walked the long way back toward *The Pride*'s berth, strolled casually along the dockside which horizoned upward before and behind, unfurling as she moved, offices and businesses on the one hand and the tall mobile gantries on the other, towers which aimed their tops toward the distant axis of Meetpoint, so that the most distant appeared insanely atilt on the curving horizon. Display boards at periodic intervals gave information of arrivals, departures, and ships in dock, from what port and bearing what sort of cargo, and she scanned them as she walked.

A car shot past her on the dock, from behind: globular and sealed, it wove along avoiding canisters and passers-by and lines with greater speed than an automated vehicle would use. That was a methane-breather, more than likely, some official from beyond the dividing line which separated the incompatible realities of Meetpoint. Tc'a ran that side of the station, sinuous beings and leathery gold, utterly alien in their multipartite brains—they traded with the knnn and the chi, kept generally to themselves and had little to say or to do with hani or even with the stsho, with whom they shared the building and operation of Meetpoint. Tc'a had nothing in common with this side of the line, not even ambitions; and the knnn and the chi were stranger still, even less participant within the worlds and governments and territories of the Compact. Pyanfar watched the vehicle kite along, up the horizon of Meetpoint's docks, and the section seal curtained it from view as it jittered along in zigzag haste which itself argued a tc'a mind at the controls. There was no trouble from *them* . . . no way that they could have dealt with the Outsider: their brains were as unlike as their breathing apparatus. She paused, stared up at the nearby registry boards with a wrinkling of her nose and a stroking of her beard, sorting through the improbable and untranslatable methane-breather names for more familiar registrations—for potential trouble, and for possible allies of use in a crisis. There was scant picking among the latter at this apogee of *The Pride*'s rambling course.

There *was* one other hani ship in dock, *Handur's Voyager.* She knew a few of the Handur family, remotely. They were from Anuurn's other hemisphere, neither rivals nor close allies, since they shared nothing on Anuurn's surface. There were a lot of stsho ships, which was to be expected on this verge of stsho space. A lot of mahendo'sat, through whose territory *The Pride* had lately come.

And on the side of trouble, there were four kif, one of which she knew: *Kut*, captained by one Ikkkukkt, an aging scoundrel whose style was more to allow another ship's canisters to edge up against and among his on dockside; and to bluff down any easily confused owners who might protest. He was only small trouble, alone. Kif in groups could be different, and she did not know about the others.

"Hai," she called, passing a mahendo'sat docking area, at a ship called *Mahijiru*, where some of that tall, dark-furred kind were minding their own business, cursing and scratching their heads over some difficulty with a connection collar, a lock-ring disassembled in order all over the deck among their waiting canisters. "You fare well this trip, *mahe?*"

"Ah, captain." The centermost scrambled up and others did the same as this one stepped toward her, treading carefully among the pieces of the collar. Any well-dressed hani was captain to a mahendo'sat, who had rather err by compliment than otherwise. But this one by his gilt teeth was likely the captain of his own freighter. "You trade?"

"Trade what?"

"What got?"

"Hai, *mahe*, what need?"

The mahendo'sat grinned, a brilliant golden flash, sharp-edged. No one of course began trade by admitting to necessity.

"Need a few less kif onstation." Pyanfar answered her own question, and the mahendo'sat whistled laughter and bobbed agreement.

"True, true," Goldtooth said somewhere between humor and outrage, as if he had a personal tale to tell. "Whining kif we wish you end of dock, good captain, honest captain. *Kut* no good. *Hukan* more no good; and *Lukkur* same. But *Hinukku* make new kind deal no good. Wait at station, wait no get same you course with *Hinukku*, good captain."

"What, *armed*?"

"Like hani, maybe." Goldtooth grinned when he said it, and Pyanfar laughed, pretended it a fine joke.

"When do hani ever have weapons?" she asked.

The *mahe* thought that a fine joke too.

"Trade you two hundredweight silk," Pyanfar offered.

"Station duty take all my profit."

"Ah. Too bad. Hard work, that." She scuffed a foot toward the ailing collar. "I can lend you very good hani tools, fine steel, two very good hani welders, Faha House make."

"I lend you good quality artwork."

"Artwork!"

"Maybe someday great *mahen* artist, captain."

"*Then* come to me; I'll keep my silk."

"Ah, ah, I make you favor with artwork, captain, but no, I ask you take no chance. I have instead small number very fine pearl like you wear."

"Ah."

"Make you security for lend tools and welders. My man he come by you soon borrow tools. Show you pearl same time."

"Five pearls."

"We see tools you see two pearls."

"You bring four."

"Fine. You pick best three."

"All four if they're not of the best, my good, my great *mahe* captain."

"You see," he vowed. "Absolute best. *Three.*"

"Good." She grinned cheerfully, touched hand to hand with the thick-nailed *mahe* and strolled off, grinning still for all passersby to see; but the grin faded when she was past the ring of their canisters and crossing the next berth.

So. Kif trouble had docked. There were kif and kif, and in that hierarchy of thieves, there were a few ship captains who tended to serve as ringleaders for highstakes mischief; and some elect who were very great trouble indeed. Mahendo'sat translation always had its difficulties, but it sounded uncomfortably like one of the latter. Stay in dock, the mahendo'sat had advised; don't chance putting out till it leaves. That was mahendo'sat strategy. It did not always work. She could keep *The Pride* at dock and run up a monstrous bill, and still have no guarantee of a safe course out; or she could pull out early and hope that the kif would *not* suspect what they had aboard—hope that the kif, at minimum, were waiting for something easier to chew than a mouthful of hani.

Hilfy. That worry rode her mind. Ten quiet voyages, ten voyages of aching, bone-weary tranquillity . . . and now this one.

The docks looked all quiet ahead, up where *The Pride* had docked, her people working out by the loading belt as they should be doing, taking aboard the mail and the freight. Haral was back, working among them; she was relieved to see that. That was Tirun outside now, and Hilfy must have gone in: the other two were Geran and Chur, slight figures next to Haral and Tirun. She found no cause to hurry. Hilfy had probably had enough by now, retreated inside to guard duty over the Outsider, gods grant that she stayed outside the door and refrained from meddling.

But the crew caught sight of her as she came, and of a sudden expressions took on desperate relief and ears pricked up, so that her heart clenched with foreknowledge of something direly wrong. "Hilfy," she asked first, as Haral came walking out to meet her: the other three stayed at their loading, all too busy for those looks of anxiety, playing the part of workers thoroughly occupied.

"*Ker* Hilfy's safe inside," Haral said quickly. "Captain, I got the things you ordered, put them in lowerdeck op, all of it; but there were kif everywhere I went, captain, when I was off in the market. They were prowling about the aisles, staring at everyone, buying nothing. I finished my business and walked on back and they were still prowling about. So I ordered *ker* Hilfy to go on in and send Tirun out here. There are kif nosing about *here* of a sudden."

"Doing what?"

"Look beyond my shoulder, captain."

Pyanfar took a quick look, a shift of her eyes. "Nothing," she said. But canisters were piled there at the section seal, twenty, thirty of them, each as tall as a hani and double-stacked, cover enough. She set her hand on Haral's shoulder, walked her companionably back to the others. "Hark, there's going to be a small stsho delivery and a mahendo'sat with a three-pearl deal; both are true . . . watch them both. But no others. There's one other hani ship docked far around the rim, next to the methane docks. I've not spoken with them. It's *Handur's Voyager.*"

"Small ship."

"And vulnerable. We're going to take *The Pride* out, with all decent haste. I think it can only get worse here. Tirun: a small task; get to *Voyager.* I don't want to discuss the situation with them over com. Warn them that there's a ship in dock named *Hinukku* and the word is out among the mahendo'sat that this one is uncommonly bad trouble. And then get yourself back here fast—no, wait. A good tool kit and two good welders—drop them with the crew of the *Mahijiru* and take the pearls in a hurry if you can get them. Seventh berth down. They'll deserve that and more if I've put the kif onto them by asking questions there. Go."

"Yes, captain," Tirun breathed, and scurried off, ears back, up the service ramp beside the cargo belt.

Pyanfar cast a second look at the double-stacked canisters in turning. No kif in sight. *Haste*, she wished Tirun, *hurry it.* It was a quick trip inside to pull the trade items from the automated delivery. Tirun came back with the boxes under one arm and set out directly in the kind of reasonable haste she might use on her captain's order.

"Huh." Pyanfar turned again and looked toward the shadow.

There. By the canisters after all. A kif stood there, tall and black-robed, with a long prominent snout and hunched stature. Pyanfar stared at it directly—*waved* to it with energetic and sarcastic camaraderie as she started toward it.

It stepped at once back into the shelter of the canisters and the shadows. Pyanfar drew a great breath, flexed her claws and kept walking, round the curve of the canister stacks and softly—face to face with the towering kif. The kif looked down on her with its red-rimmed dark eyes and longnosed face and its dusty black robes like the robes of all other kif, of one tone with the gray skin . . . a bit of shadow come to life. "Be off," she told it. "I'll have no canister-mixing. I'm onto your tricks."

"Something of ours has been stolen."

She laughed, helped by sheer surprise. "Something of *yours* stolen, master thief? That's a wonder to tell at home."

"Best it find its way back to us. Best it should, captain."

She laid back her ears and grinned, which was not friendliness.

"Where is your crewwoman going with those boxes?" the kif asked.

She said nothing. Extruded claws.

"It would not be, Captain, that you've somehow found that lost item."

"What, *lost*, now?"

"Lost and found again, I think."

"What ship *are* you, kif?"

"If you were as clever as you imagine you are, captain, you would know."

"I like to know who I'm talking to. Even among kif. I'll reckon you know my name, skulking about out here. What's yours?"

"Akukkakk is mine, Chanur captain. Pyanfar Chanur. Yes, we know you. Know you well, captain. We have become *interested* in you . . . thief."

"Oh. Akukkakk of what ship?" Her vision sharpened on the kif, whose robes were marginally finer than usual, whose bearing had precious little kifish stoop in dealing with shorter species, that hunch of shoulders and thrusting forward of the head. This one looked at her the long way, from all its height. "I'd like to know you as well, kif."

"You will, hani. No. A last chance. We will redeem this prize you've found. I will make you that offer."

Her mustache-hairs drew down, as at some offensive aroma. "Interesting if I had this item. Is it round or flat, this strayed object? Or did one of your own crew rob you, kif captain?"

"You know its shape, since you have it. Give it up, and be paid. Or don't— and be paid, hani, be paid then too."

"Describe this item to me."

"For its safe return—gold, ten bars of gold, fine. Contrive your own descriptions."

"I shall bear it in mind, kif, should I find something unusual and kif-smelling. But so far nothing."

"Dangerous, hani."

"What ship, kif?"

"*Hinukku.*"

"I'll remember your offer. Indeed I will, master thief."

The kif said nothing more. Towered erect and silent. She aimed a dry spitting toward its feet and walked off, slow swagger.

Hinukku, indeed. A whole new kind of trouble, the mahendo'sat had said, and this surly kif or another *might* have seen . . . or talked to those who had seen. *Gold*, they offered. Kif . . . offered ransom; and no common kif, either, not that one. She walked with a prickling between her shoulderblades and a multiplying apprehension for Tirun, who was now a small figure walking off along the upcurving docks. No hope that the station authorities would do anything to prevent a murder . . . not one between kif and hani. The stsho's neutrality consisted in retreat, and their law in arbitrating after the fact.

Stsho ships were the most common victims of marauding kif, and still kif docked unchecked at Meetpoint. Madness. A bristling ran up her back and her ears flicked, jingling the rings. Hani might deal with the kif and teach them a lesson, but there was no profit in it, not until moments like this one. Divert every hani ship from profitable trade to kif-hunting? Madness too . . . until it was *The Pride* in question.

"Pack it up out here," she told her remaining crew when she reached them. "Get those last cans on and shut it down. Get everything ready to break dock. I'm going to call Tirun back here. It's worse than I thought."

"I'll go after her," Haral said.

"Do as I say, cousin—and keep Hilfy out of it."

Haral fell back. Pyanfar started off down the dock—old habit, not to run; a reserve of pride, of caution, of some instinct either good or ill. Still she did not run in front of witnesses. She widened her strides until some bystanders—stsho—did notice, and stared. She gained on Tirun. Almost, almost within convenient shouting distance of Tirun, and still a far, naked distance up the dock's upcurving course to reach *Handur's Voyager*. *Hinukku* sat at dock for Tirun to pass before she should come to the hani ship. But the mahendo'sat vessel *Mahijiru* was docked before that, if only Tirun handled that extraneous errand on the way, the logical thing to do with a heavy load under one arm. Surely it was the logical thing, even considering the urgency of the other message.

Ah. Tirun did stop at the mahendo'sat berth. Pyanfar breathed a gasp of relief, broke her own rule at the last moment and sprinted behind some canisters, strode right into the gathering which had begun to close about Tirun. She clapped a startled mahendo'sat spectator on the arm, pulled it about and thrust her way through to Tirun, grabbed her arm without ceremony. "Trouble. Let's go, cousin."

"Captain," Goldtooth exclaimed from her right. "You come back make new bigger deal?"

"Never mind. The tools are a gift. Come *on*, Tirun."

"Captain," Tirun began, bewildered, being dragged back through the gathering of mahendo'sat. Mahendo'sat gave way before them, their captain still following them with confused chatter about welders and pearls.

Kif. A black-clad half ring of them appeared suddenly on the outskirts of the swirl of dark-furred mahendo'sat. Pyanfar had Tirun's wrist and pulled her forward. "Look out!" Tirun cried suddenly: one of the kif had pulled a gun from beneath its robe. "*Go!*" Pyanfar yelled, and they dived back among cursing and screaming mahendo'sat, out again through a melee of kif who had circled behind the canisters. Fire popped after them. Pyanfar bowled over a kif in their path with a strike that should snap vertebrae and did not break stride to find out. Tirun ran beside her; they sprinted with fire popping smoke curls off the deck plates ahead of them.

Suddenly a shot came from the right hand. Tirun yelped and stumbled, limping wildly. More kif along the dockfront offices, one very tall and familiar. Akukkakk, with friends. "Earless bastard!" Pyanfar shouted, grabbed Tirun afresh and kept going, dragged her behind the canisters of another mahendo'sat ship in a hail of laser pops and the reek of burned plastic. Tirun sagged in shock—a curse and a jerk on the arm got her running again, desperately: the burn ruptured and bled. They darted into an open space, having no choice: shrill harooing rang out behind and on the right, kif on the hunt.

A second shout roared out from before them, another flash from guns, multicolor, at *The Pride*'s berth: *The Pride*'s crew was returning fire, high for their sakes but meaning business. Station alarms started going off, bass-tone whooping. Red lights flashed on the walls and up the curve till the ceiling vanished. Higher up the curve of the dock, station folk scrambled in panic, hunting shelter. If there were kif among them, they would come charging down from that direction too, at the crew's backs.

And Hilfy was out there at that access, fourth in that line of their own guns— laying down a berserk pattern of fire. Pyanfar dragged Tirun through that line of four by the scruff of the neck. Tirun twisted and fell on the plates and Pyanfar helped her up again, not without a wild look back, at a dockside where enemies fired from cover at her crew who had precious little. *"Board!"* she yelled at the others with the last of her wind, and herself skidded on the decking in turning for the rampway. Haral retreated and grabbed Tirun's flailing arm from the other side and Hilfy suddenly took Pyanfar's. Pyanfar looked back again, willing to turn and fight. Geran and Chur were falling back in orderly retreat behind them, still facing the direction of the kif and firing—the kif had been pinned back from advance into better vantage. Hilfy pulled at her arm and Pyanfar shook free as they reached the rampway's first door. "Come *on*," she shouted at Geran and Chur; and the moment they retreated within, still firing, she hit the door seal. The massive steel clanged and thumped shut and the pair stumbled back out of the way; Hilfy darted in from across the door and rammed the lock-lever down.

Pyanfar looked round then at Tirun, who was on her feet, though sagging in Haral's arms, and holding her upper right leg. Her blue breeches were dark with blood from there to the fur of her calf and threading down to her foot in a puddle, and she was muttering a steady stream of curses.

"Move," Pyanfar said. Haral took Tirun up in her arms and outright carried her, no small load. They withdrew up the rampway curve into their own lock, sealed *that* door and felt somewhat safer.

"Captain," Chur said, businesslike. "All lines are loose and cargo ramp is disengaged. In case."

"Well done," Pyanfar said, vastly relieved to hear it. They walked through the airlock and round the bend into the main lower corridor. "Secure the Outsider; sedate it all the way. You—" she looked aside at Tirun, who was trying to walk again with an arm across her sister's shoulders. "Get a wrap on that leg fast. No time for anything more. We're getting loose. I don't imagine *Hinukku* will stand still for this and I don't want kif passing my tail while we're nose-to-station. Everyone rig for maneuvers."

"I can wrap my own leg," Tirun said. "Just drop me in sickbay."

"Hilfy," Pyanfar said, collected her niece as she headed for the lift. "Disobedient," Pyanfar muttered when they were close.

"Forgive," said Hilfy. They entered the lift together; the door shut. Pyanfar fetched the youngster a cuff which rocked her against the lift wall, and pushed the mainlevel button. Hilfy righted herself and disdained even to clap a hand to her ear, but her eyes were watering, her ears flattened and nostrils wide as if she were facing into some powerful wind. "Forgiven," said Pyanfar. The lift let them out, and Hilfy started to run up the corridor toward the bridge, but

Pyanfar stalked along at a more deliberate pace and Hilfy paused and matched her stride, walked with her through the archway into the curved-deck main operations center.

Pyanfar sat down in her cushion in the center of a bank of vid screens and started turning on systems. Station was squalling stsho language protests, objections, outrage. "Get on that," Pyanfar said to her niece without missing a beat in switch-flicking. "Tell station we're cutting loose and they'll have to cope with it."

A delay. Hilfy relayed the message in limping stsho, ignoring the mechanical translator in her haste. "They complain you killed someone."

"Good." The grapples clanged loose and a telltale said they had retracted all the way. "Tell them we rejoice to have eliminated a kif who started firing without provocation, endangering bystanders and property on the dock." She fired the undocking repulse and they were loose, sudden loss of *g* and reacquisition in another direction . . . fired the secondaries which sent *The Pride* out of plane with station, a redirection of up and down. Ship's *g* started up, a slow tug against the thrust aft.

"Station is mightily upset," Hilfy reported. "They demand to talk to you, aunt; they threaten not to let us dock at stsho—"

"Never mind the stsho." Pyanfar flicked from image to image on scan. She spotted another ship loose, in about the right location for *Hinukku*. Abruptly the scan acquired all kinds of flitter on it, chaff more than likely, as *Hinukku* screened itself to do something. "Gods rot them." She reached madly for controls and got *The Pride* reoriented gently enough to save the bones of those aboard who might not yet be secured for maneuvers . . . warning enough for those below to dive for security. "If they fire on us they'll take out half the station. Gods!" She hit general com. "Brace; we're backing hard."

This time things came loose. A notebook sailed across the section and landed somewhere forward, missing controls. Hilfy spat and curses came back from com. *The Pride* was not made for such moves. Nor for the next, which hammered against that backward momentum and, nose dipped, shot them nadir of station (the notebook flew back to its origins) and braked, another career of fluttering pages.

"Motherless bastards," Pyanfar said. She punched controls, linked turret to scan. It would swivel to any sighting, anything massive. "*Now* let them put their nose down here." Her joints were sore. Alarms were ringing and lights were flashing on the maintenance board, cargo having broken loose. She ran her tongue over the points of her teeth and wrinkled her nose for breath, worrying what quadrant of the scan to watch. She put *The Pride* into a slow axis rotation, gambling that the kif would not come underside of station in so obvious a place as the one in line with last-known-position. "Watch scan," she warned Hilfy, diverting herself to monitor the op board half a heartbeat, to see all the telltales what they ought to be. *"Haral, get up here."*

"Aunt!" Hilfy said. Pyanfar swung her head about again. A little dust had appeared on the screen, some of the chaff spinning their way from above. She had the scanlinked fire control set looser than that and the armament did not react. The lift back down the corridor crashed and hummed in operation. Haral had not acknowledged, but she was coming. "We fire on anything that shows solid," Pyanfar said. "Keep watching that chaff cloud, niece. And mind, it could be outright diversion. I don't trust anything."

"Yes," Hilfy said calmly enough. And then: *"Look out!"*

"Chaff," Pyanfar identified the flutter, her heart frozen by the yell. "Be specific to quadrant: number's enough."

Running feet in the corridor. Haral was with them. Hilfy started to yield her place at scan; Haral slid into the third seat, adjusted the restraints.

"Didn't plan to do so much moving," Pyanfar said, never taking the focus of her eyes from scan. "Anyone hurt?"

"No," said Haral. "Everything's secure."

"They're thinking it over up there," Pyanfar said.

"Aunt! 4/2!"

Turret was swiveling. Eye tracked to the number four screen. Energy washed over station's rim: more chaff followed, larger debris.

"Captain, they hit station." Haral's voice was incredulous. "They *fired.*"

"Handur's Voyager." Pyanfar had the origin mapped on the station torus and made the connection. "O gods." She hit repulse and sent them hurtling to station core shadow, tilted their nose with a second burst and cut in main thrust, shooting them nadir of station, nose for infinity. Pyanfar reached and uncapped a red switch, hit it, and *The Pride* rocked with explosion.

"What was *that?*" Hilfy's voice. "Are we hit?"

"I just dumped our holds." Pyanfar sucked air, an expansion of her nostrils. Her claws flexed out and in on the togglegrip. *G* was hauling at them badly. *The Pride of Chanur* was in full rout, having just altered their mass/drive ratio, stripped for running. "Haral, get us a course."

"Working," Haral said. Numbers started coming up on the comp screen at Pyanfar's left.

"Going to have to find us a quiet spot."

"Urtur's just within singlejump range," Haral said, "stripped as we are. Maybe."

"Has to be." Beyond Meetpoint in the other direction was stsho space, with a great scarcity of jump points to help them along, those masses by which *The Pride* or any other jumpship steered; and on other sides were kif regions; and knnn; and unexplored regions, uncharted, without jump coordinates. Jump blind into those and they would never come back again . . . anywhere known.

She livened another board, bringing up jump-graphs. Urtur. That was the way they had come in, two jumps and loaded—a very large system where mahendo'sat did a little mining, a little manufacture, and licensed others. They *might* make that distance in one jump now; kif were not following . . . yet. Did not have to follow. They could figure possible destinations by dumped mass and the logic of the situation. *O my brother*, she thought, wondering how she would face Kohan. He would be affected by this disgrace, this outrage of lost cargo, of flight while a hani ship perished stationbound and helpless. Kohan Chanur might be broken by it; it might tempt young males to challenge him. And if there were enough challenges, and often enough. . . .

No. Not that kind of end for Chanur. There was no going home with that kind of news. Not until kif paid, until *The Pride* got things to rights again.

"Mark fifteen to jump point," Haral said. "Captain, they'll trace us, no question."

"No question," she said. Beyond Haral's scarred face she caught sight of Hilfy's, unmarred and scant-bearded—frightened and trying not to show it. Pyanfar opened allship: "Rig for jump."

The alarm started, a slow wailing through the ship. *The Pride* leapt forward by her generation pulses, borrowed velocity at the interface, several wrenching flickers, whipped into the between. Pyanfar dug her claws in, decades accustomed to this, did that mental wrench which told lies to the inner ears, and kept her balance. *Come on*, she willed the ship, as if intent alone could take it that critical distance farther.

EXCERPT FROM *FOREIGNER*

C.J. CHERRYH

I

The air moved sluggishly through the open garden lattice, heavy with the perfume of the night-blooming vines outside the bedroom. An o'oi-ana went *click-click*, and called again, the harbinger of rain, while Bren lay awake, thinking that if he were wise, he would get up and close the lattice and the doors before he fell asleep. The wind would shift. The sea air would come and cool the room. The vents were enough to let it in. But it was a lethargic, muggy night, and he waited for that nightly reverse of the wind from the east to the west, waited as the first flickers of lightning cast the shadow of the lattice on the stirring gauze of the curtain.

The lattice panels had the shapes of Fortune and Chance, *baji* and *naji*. The shadow of the vines outside moved with the breeze that, finally, finally, flared the curtain with the promise of relief from the heat.

The next flicker lit an atevi shadow, like a statue suddenly transplanted to the terrace outside. Bren's heart skipped a beat as he saw it on that pale billowing of gauze, on a terrace where no one properly belonged. He froze an instant, then slithered over the side of the bed.

The next flash showed him the lattice folding further back, and the intruder entering his room.

He slid a hand beneath the mattress and drew out the pistol he had hidden there—braced his arms across the mattress in the way the aiji had taught him, and pulled the trigger, to a shock that numbed his hands and a flash that blinded him to the night and the intruder. He fired a second time, for sheer terror, into the blind dark and ringing silence.

He couldn't move after that. He couldn't get his breath. He hadn't heard anyone fall. He thought he had missed. The white, flimsy draperies blew in the cooling wind that scoured through his bedroom.

His hands were numb, bracing the gun on the mattress. His ears were deaf to sounds fainter than the thunder, fainter than the rattle of the latch of his bedroom door—the guards using their key, he thought.

But it might not be. He rolled his back to the bedside and braced his straight arms between his knees, barrel trained on the middle of the doorway as the inner door banged open and light and shadow struck him in the face.

The aiji's guards spared not a word for questions. One ran to the lattice doors, and out into the courtyard and the beginning rain. The other, a faceless metal-sparked darkness, loomed over him and pried the gun from his fingers.

Other guards came; while Banichi—it was Banichi's voice from above him—Banichi had taken the gun.

"Search the premises!" Banichi ordered them. "See to the aiji!"

"Is Tabini all right?" Bren asked, overwhelmed, and shaking. "Is he all right, Banichi?"

But Banichi was talking on the pocket-com, giving other orders, deaf to his question. The aiji must be all right, Bren told himself, or Banichi would not be standing here, talking so calmly, so assuredly to the guards outside. He heard Banichi give orders, and heard the answering voice say nothing had gotten to the roof.

He was scared. He knew the gun was contraband. Banichi knew it, and Banichi could arrest him—he feared he might; but when Banichi was through with the radio, Banichi seized him by the bare arms and set him on the side of the bed.

The other guard came back through the garden doors—it was Jago. She always worked with Banichi, "There's blood, I've alerted the gates."

So he'd shot someone. He began to shiver as Jago ducked out again. Banichi turned the lights on and came back, atevi, black, smooth-skinned, his yellow eyes narrowed and his heavy jaw set in a thunderous scowl.

"The aiji gave me the gun," Bren said before Banichi could accuse him. Banichi stood there staring at him and finally said,

"This is *my* gun."

He was confused. He sat there with his skin gone to gooseflesh and finally moved to pull a blanket into his lap. He heard commotion in the garden, Jago yelling at other guards.

"This is *my* gun," Banichi said forcefully. "Can there be any question this is my gun? A noise waked you. I lay in wait for the assassin. *I* fired. What did you see?"

"A shadow. A shadow coming in through the curtains." Another shiver took him. He knew how foolish he had been, firing straight across and through the doors. The bullet might have kept going across the garden, into the kitchens. It could have ricocheted off a wall and hit someone asleep in another apartment. The shock persisted in his hands and in his ears, strong as the smell of gunpowder in the air, that didn't belong with him, in his room. . . .

The rain started with a vengeance. Banichi used his pocket-com to talk to the searchers, and to headquarters, lying to them, saying he'd fired the shot, seeing the intruder headed for the paidhi's room, and, no, the paidhi hadn't been hurt, only frightened, and the aiji shouldn't be wakened, if he hadn't heard the shots. But the guard should be doubled, and the search taken to the south gates, before, Banichi said, the rain wiped out the tracks.

Banichi signed off.

"Why did they come *here?*" Bren asked. Assassins, he understood; but that any ordinary assassin should come into the residential compound, where there were guards throughout, where the aiji slept surrounded by hundreds of willing defenders—nobody in their right mind would do that.

And to assassinate *him*, Bren Cameron, with the aiji at the height of all power and with the nai'aijiin all confirmed in their houses and supportive— where was the sense in it? Where was the gain to anyone at all sane?

"Nadi Bren." Banichi stood over him with his huge arms folded, looking down at him as if he were dealing with some feckless child. "*What* did you see?"

"I told you. Just a shadow, coming through the curtain." The emphasis of the question scared him. He might have been dreaming. He might have roused the whole household and alarmed the guards all for a nightmare. In the way of things at the edge of sleep, he no longer knew for sure what he had seen.

But there had been blood. Jago said so. He *had* shot someone.

"*I* discharged the gun," Banichi said. "Get up and wash your hands, nadi. Wash them twice and three times. And keep the garden doors locked."

"They're only glass," he protested. He had felt safe until now. The aiji had given him the gun two weeks ago. The aiji had taught him to use it, the aiji's doing alone, in the country-house at Taiben, and no one could have known about it, not even Banichi, least of all, surely, the assassin—if he had not dreamed the intrusion through the curtains, if he had not just shot some inno- cent neighbor, out for air on a stifling night.

"Nadi," Banichi said, "go wash your hands."

He couldn't move, couldn't deal with mundane things, or comprehend what had happened—or why, for the gods' sake, *why* the aiji had given him such an unprecedented and disturbing present, except a general foreboding, and the guards taking stricter account of passes and rules . . .

Except Tabini-aiji had said—'Keep it close.' And he had been afraid of his servants finding it in his room.

"Nadi."

Banichi was angry with him. He got up, naked and shaky as he was, and went across the carpet to the bath, with a queasier and queasier stomach.

The last steps were a desperate, calculated rush for the toilet, scarcely in time to lose everything in his stomach, humiliating himself, but there was nothing he could do—it was three painful spasms before he could get a breath and flush the toilet.

He was ashamed, disgusted with himself. He ran water in the sink and washed and scrubbed and washed, until he no longer smelled the gunpowder on his hands, only the pungency of the soap and astringents. He thought Banichi must have left, or maybe called the night-servants to clean the bath.

But as he straightened and reached for the towel, he found Banichi's reflection in the mirror.

"Nadi Bren," Banichi said solemnly. "We failed you tonight."

That stung, it truly stung, coming from Banichi, who would never humiliate himself as he had just done. He dried his face and rubbed his dripping hair, then had to look at Banichi face on, Banichi's black, yellow-eyed visage as impassive and powerful as a graven god's.

"You were brave," Banichi said, again, and Bren Cameron, the descendant of spacefarers, the representative of six generations forcibly earthbound on the world of the atevi, felt it like a slap of Banichi's massive hand.

"I didn't get him. Somebody's loose out there, with a gun or—"

"*We* didn't get him, nadi. It's not your business, to 'get him.' Have you been approached by anyone unusual? Have you seen anything out of order before tonight?"

"No."

"Where did you *get* the gun, nadi-ji?"

Did Banichi think he was lying? "Tabini gave it . . ."

"From what *place* did you get the gun? Was this person moving very slowly?"

He saw what Banichi was asking. He wrapped the towel about his shoulders, cold, with the storm wind blowing into the room. He heard the boom of thunder above the city. "From under the mattress. Tabini said keep it close. And I don't know how fast he was moving, the assassin, I mean. I just saw the shadow and slid off the bed and grabbed the gun."

Banichi's brow lifted ever so slightly. "Too much television," Banichi said with a straight face, and took him by the shoulder. "Go back to bed, nadi."

"Banichi, what's happening? *Why* did Tabini give me a gun? Why did he tell me—?"

The grip tightened. "Go to bed, nadi. No one will disturb you after this. You saw a shadow. You called me. I fired two shots."

"I could have hit the kitchen!"

"Most probably one shot did. Kindly remember bullets travel, nadi-ji. Was it not you who taught *us*? Here."

To his stunned surprise, Banichi drew his own gun from the holster and handed it to him.

"Put that under your mattress," Banichi said, and left him—walked on out of the bedroom and into the hall, pulling the door to behind him.

He heard the lock click as he stood there stark naked, with Banichi's gun in his hand and wet hair trailing about his shoulders and dripping on the floor.

He went and shoved the gun under the mattress where he had hidden the other one, and, hoping Jago would choose another way in, shut the lattice doors and the glass, stopping the cold wind and the spatter of rain onto the curtains and the carpet.

Thunder rumbled. He was chilled through. He made a desultory attempt to straighten the bedclothes, then dragged a heavy robe out of the armoire to wrap about himself before he turned off the room lights and struggled, wrapped in the bulky robe, under the tangled sheets. He drew himself into a ball, spasmed with shivers.

Why me? he asked himself over and over, and asked himself whether he could conceivably have posed so extreme a problem to anyone that that individual would risk his life to be rid of him. He couldn't believe he had put himself in a position like that and never once caught a clue of such a complete professional failure.

Perhaps the assassin had thought him the most defenseless dweller in the garden apartments, and his open door had seemed the most convenient way to some other person, perhaps to the inner hallways and Tabini-aiji himself.

But there were so many guards. That was an insane plan, and assassins were, if hired, not mad and not prone to take such risks.

An assassin might simply have mistaken the room. Someone of importance might be lodged in the guest quarters in the upper terrace of the garden. He hadn't heard that that was the case, but otherwise the garden court held just the guards, and the secretaries and the chief cook and the master of accounts—and himself—none of whom were controversial in the least.

But Banichi had left him his gun in place of the aiji's, which he had fired. He understood, clearer-witted now, why Banichi had taken it with him, and why Banichi had had him wash his hands, in case the chief of general security might not believe the account Banichi would give, and in case the chief of security wanted to question the paidhi and have him through police lab procedures.

He most sincerely hoped to be spared that. And the chief of security had no cause against him that *he* knew of—had no motive to investigate *him*, when he was the victim of the crime, and had no reason that he knew of to challenge Banichi's account, Banichi being in some ways higher than the chief of security himself.

But then . . . who would want to break into his room? His reasoning looped constantly back to that, and to the chilling fact that Banichi had left him another gun. That was dangerous to do. Someone could decide to question him. Someone could search his room and find the gun, which they could surely then trace to Banichi, with all manner of public uproar. Was it prudent for Banichi to have done that? Was Banichi somehow sacrificing himself, in a way he didn't want, and for something he might have caused?

It even occurred to him to question Banichi's integrity—but Banichi and his younger partner Jago were his favorites among Tabini's personal guards, the ones that took special care of him, while they stood every day next to Tabini, capable of any mischief, if they intended any, to Tabini himself—let alone to a far more replaceable human.

Gods, no, suspecting them was stupid. Banichi wouldn't see him harmed. Banichi would directly lie for him. So would Jago, for Tabini's sake—he was the paidhi, the Interpreter, and the aiji needed him, and that was reason enough for either of them. Tabini-aiji would take it very seriously, what had happened, Tabini would immediately start inquiries, make all kinds of disturbance—

And, dammit, he didn't want the whole citadel set on its ear over this. He didn't want notoriety, or to be the center of an atevi feud. Publicity harmed his position among atevi. It completely destroyed his effectiveness the moment politics crept into his personal influence, and politics would creep into the matter—politics would *leap* into it, the minute it hit the television news. Everybody would have an opinion, everybody would have a theory and it could only be destructive to his work.

He huddled under chill covers, trying to get his wits about him, but his empty stomach distracted him and the smell of gunpowder made him queasy. If he called for something to settle his nerves, the night-staff would bring him whatever he asked, or rouse his own servants at his request, but poor Moni and Taigi had probably been roused out of bed to bewildering questions—Did you shoot at the paidhi? Did you leave his door unlatched?

Security was probably going down the list of employees, calling in the whole night-staff and everyone he dealt with—as if anyone in this whole wing could be sleeping now. The shots had probably echoed clear downhill and into the city, the phone lines were probably jammed, the rail station would be under tight restrictions, clear into tomorrow's morning commuter traffic . . . no flattery to him: he'd seen what resulted when someone set off alarms inside Tabini's security.

He wanted hot tea and crackers. But he could only make security's job more difficult by asking for personal errands to be run up and down through halls they were trying to search.

Meanwhile the rain spatted against the glass. And it was less and less likely that they would catch the assassin at all.

Moni and Taigi arrived in the morning with his breakfast cart—and the advisement from staff central that Tabini-aiji wanted him in early audience.

Small surprise, that was. In anticipation of a call, he had showered and shaved and dressed himself unaided before dawn, as far as his accustomed soft trousers and shirt, at least, and braided his hair back himself. He had had the television on before they arrived, listening to the morning news: he feared the case might be notorious by now, but to his perplexity he heard not so much as a passing mention of any incident, only a report on the storm last night, which had generated hail in Shigi township, and damaged roof tiles in Wingin before it had gone roaring over the open plains.

He was strangely disappointed, even insulted, by the silence. One had assassins invading one's room and, on one level, despite his earnest desire for obscurity to the outside world, he did hope to hear confirmed that there had been an intruder in the aiji's estates, the filtered sort of news they might have released—or, better yet, that the intruder was securely in the aiji's hands, undergoing questioning.

Nothing of the sort—at least by the television news; and Moni and Taigi laid out breakfast with not a question nor a comment about what had happened in the garden court last night, or why there were towels all over the bathroom floor. They simply delivered the message they had had from the staff central office, absorbed every disarrangement of the premises without seeming to notice, and offered not a hint of anything wrong, or any taste of rumors that might be running the halls.

The lord second heir of Talidi province had assassinated a remote relative in the water garden last spring in an argument over an antique firearm, and the halls of the complex had buzzed with it for days.

Not this morning. Good morning, nand' paidhi, how are you feeling, nand' paidhi? More berries? Tea?

Then, finally, with a downcast glance, from Moni, who seldom had much to say, "We're very glad you're all right, nand' paidhi."

He swallowed his bite of fruit. Gratified.

Appeased. "Did you hear the commotion last night?"

"The guard waked us," Taigi said. "That was the first we knew of anything wrong."

"You didn't hear anything?"

"No, nand' paidhi."

With the lightning and the thunder and the rain coming down, he supposed that the sharp report of the gunshot could have echoed strangely, with the wind swirling about the hill, and with the gun being set off inside the room, rather than outside. The figure in the doorway last night had completely assumed the character of dream to him, a nightmare occurrence in which details both changed and diminished. His servants' utter silence surrounding the incident had unnerved him, even cast his memory into doubt . . . not to mention his understanding and expectation of atevi closest to him.

He was glad to hear a reasonable explanation. So the echo of it hadn't carried to the lower-floor servants' court, down on the side of the hill and next the ancient walls. Probably the thunder had covered the echoes. Perhaps there'd been a great peal of it as the storm onset and as the assassin made his try—he'd had his own ears full of the gunshot, which to him had sounded like doom, but it didn't mean the rest of the world had been that close.

But Moni and Taigi were at least duly concerned, and, perhaps perplexed by his human behaviors, or their expectation of them, they didn't know quite what else to say, he supposed. It was different, trying to pick up gossip when one was in the center of the trouble. All information, especially in a life-and-death crisis, became significant; appearing to know something meant someone official could come asking, and no one close to him reasonably wanted to let rumors loose—as he, personally, didn't want any speculation going on about him from servants who might be expected to have information.

No more would Moni and Taigi want to hear another knock on their doors, and endure a second round of questions in the night. Classically speaking—treachery and servants were a cliche in atevi dramas. It was too ridiculous—but it didn't mean they wouldn't feel the onus of suspicion, or feel the fear he very well understood, of unspecified accusations they had no witnesses to refute.

"I do hope it's the end of it," he said to them. "I'm very sorry, nadiin. I trust there won't be more police. I *know* you're honest."

"We greatly appreciate your confidence," Moni said, and both of them bowed. "Please be careful."

"Banichi and Jago are on the case."

"That's very good," Taigi said, and set scrambled eggs in front of him.

So he had his breakfast and put on his best summer coat, the one with the leather collar and leather down the front edges to the knee.

"Please don't delay in the halls," Taigi said.

"I assure you," he said.

"Isn't there security?" Moni asked. "Let us call security."

"To walk to the audience hall?" They *were* worried, he decided, now that the verbal dam had broken. He was further gratified. "I assure you there's no need. It was probably some complete lunatic, probably hiding in a storage barrel somewhere. They might go after lord Murida in the water garden at high noon—not me. I assure you. With the aiji's own guards swarming about . . . not highly likely." He took his key and slipped it into his trousers. "Just be careful of the locks. The garden side, especially, for the next few days."

"Nadi," they said, and bowed again—anxious, he decided, as they'd truly been when they'd arrived, just not advertising their state of mind, which atevi didn't. Which reminded him that he shouldn't let his worry reach his face either. He went cheerfully out the door—

Straight into a black uniform and, well above eye-level, a scowling atevi face.

"Nand' paidhi," the guard officer said. "I'm to escort you to the hall."

"Hardly necessary," he said. His heart had skipped a dozen beats. He didn't personally know the man. But the uniform wasn't one an assassin would dare counterfeit, not on his subsequent life, and he walked with the officer, out into the corridors of the complex, past the ordinary residential guard desk and into the main areas of the building—along the crowded colonnade, where wind gusted, fresh with rain and morning chill.

Ancient stonework took sunlight and shadow, the fortress walls of the Bu-javid, the citadel and governmental complex, sprawled over its high hill, aloof and separate from the urban sprawl of Shejidan—and down below those walls the hotels and the hostelries would be full to overflowing. The triennial public audience, beginning this morning, brought hundreds of provincial lords and city and town-ship and district officials into town—by subway, by train—all of them trekking the last mile on foot from the hotels that ringed the ancient Bu-javid, crowds bearing petitions climbing the terraced stone ceremonial road, passing beneath the fortified Gate of the Promise of Justice, and trekking finally up the last broad, flower-bor-dered courses to the renowned Ninefold Doors, a steady stream of tall, broad-shoul-dered atevi, with their night-black skins and glossy black braids, some in rich coats bordered in gilt and satin, some in plain, serviceable cloth, but clearly their courtly best. Professional politicians rubbed shoulder to shoulder with ordinary trade folk, lords of the Associations with anxious, unpracticed petitioners, bringing their color-fully ribboned petitions, rolled and bound, and with them, their small bouquets of flowers to lay on the foyer tables, an old custom of the season.

The hall at the end of the open colonnade smelled of recent rain and flowers, and rang with voices—atevi meeting one another, or falling into line to register with the secretaries, on whose desks, set up in the vast lower foyer, the stacks of documents and petitions were growing.

For the courtiers, a human on his way to court business through this milling chaos was an ordinary sight—a pale, smallish figure head and shoulders shorter than the crowds through which he passed, a presence conservative in his simple, unribboned braid and leather trim—the police escort was uncommon, but no one stared, except the country folk and private petitioners.

"Look!" a child cried, and pointed at him.

A mortified parent batted the offending hand down while the echoes rang, high and clear, in the vaulted ceilings. Atevi looked. And pretended not to have seen either him or his guard.

A lord of the provinces went through the halls attended by his own aides and by his own guards and the aiji's as well, and provoked no rude stares. Bren went with his police escort, in the same pretense of invisibility, a little anxious, since the child's shout, but confident in the visible presence of the aiji's guards at every doorway and every turn, ordinary precaution on audience day.

In that near presence, he bade a courteous farewell to his police escort at the small Whispering Port, which, a small section of one of the great ceremonial doors, led discreetly and without official recognition into the back of the audience hall. He slipped through it and softly closed it again, so as not to disturb the advance meetings in progress.

Late, he feared. Moni and Taigi hadn't advanced the hour of his wake-up at all, simply shown up at their usual time, lacking other orders and perhaps fearing to do anything unusual, with a police guard standing at his door. He hoped Tabini hadn't wanted otherwise, and started over to the reception desk to see where he fitted in the hearings.

Banichi was there. Banichi, in the metal-studded black of the aiji's personal guard, intercepted him with a touch on his arm.

"Nadi Bren. Did you sleep last night?"

"No," he confessed. And hoping: "Did you catch him?"

"No, nadi. There was the storm. We were not so fortunate."

"Does Tabini know what happened?" He cast a glance toward the dais, where Tabini-aiji was talking to governor Brominandi, one of the invitational private hearings. "I think I'm on the agenda. Does he want to talk with me? What shall I tell him?"

"The truth, only in private. It *was* his gun—was it not?"

He threw Banichi a worried look. If Banichi doubted his story, he hadn't left him with that impression last night. "I told you the truth, Banichi."

"I'm sure you did," Banichi said, and when he would have gone on to the reception desk, as he had purposed, to give his name to the secretary, Banichi caught his sleeve and held him back. "Nothing official." Banichi nodded toward the dais, still holding his sleeve, and brought him to the foot of the dais instead.

Brominandi of Entaillan province was finishing his business. Brominandi, whose black hair was shot through with white, whose hands sparkled with rings both ornamental and official, would lull a stone to boredom, and the bystanding guards had as yet found no gracious way to edge the governor off.

Tabini nodded to what Brominandi was saying, nodded a second time, and finally said, "I'll take it before council." It sounded dreadfully like the Alujis river rights business again, two upstream provinces against three downstream which relied on its water for irrigation. For fifty years, that pot had been boiling, with suit and counter-suit. Bren folded his hands in front of him and stood with Banichi, head ducked, making himself as inconspicuous as a human possibly could in the court.

Finally Tabini-aiji accepted the inevitable petition (or was it counter-petition?) from Brominandi, a weighty thing of many seals and ribbons, and passed it to his legislative aides.

At which time Bren slid a glance up to Tabini, and received one back, which was the summons to him and to Banichi, up the several steps to the side of the aiji's chair, in the lull in which the favored early petitioners could mill about and gossip, a dull, echoing murmur in the vaulted, white and gilt hall.

Tabini said, right off, "Do you know who it was, Bren? Do you have any idea?"

"None, aiji-ma, nothing. I shot at him. I missed. Banichi said I should say he fired the shot."

A look went past him, to Banichi. Tabini's yellow eyes were very pale, ghostly in certain lights—frightening, when he was angry. But he didn't seem to be angry, or assigning blame to either of them.

Banichi said, "It removed questions."

"No idea the nature of the intrusion."

"A burglar would be a fool. Assignations . . ."

"No," Bren said, uncomfortable in the suggestion, but Tabini knew him, knew that atevi women had a certain curiosity about him, and it was a joke at his expense.

"Not a feminine admirer."

"No, aiji-ma." He certainly hoped not, recalling the blood Jago had found in the first of the rain, out on the terrace.

Tabini-aiji reached out and touched his arm, apology for the levity. "No one has filed. It's a serious matter. I take it seriously. Be careful with your locks."

"The garden door is only glass," Banichi said. "Alterations would be conspicuous."

"A wire isn't," Tabini said.

Bren was dismayed. The aiji's doors and windows might have such lethal protections. He had extreme reservations about the matter.

"I'll see to it," Banichi said.

"I might walk into it," Bren said.

"You won't," Tabini said. And to Banichi: "See to it. This morning. One on either door. His key to disarm. Change the locks."

"Aiji," Bren began to say.

"I have a long list today," Tabini said, meaning shut up and sit down, and when Tabini-aiji took that tone about a matter, there was no quarrel with it. They left the top of the dais. Bren stopped at the fourth step, which was his ordinary post.

"You *stay* here," Banichi said. "I'll bring you the new key."

"Banichi, is anybody after me?"

"It would seem so, wouldn't it? I do doubt it was a lover."

"Do you know anything I don't?"

"Many things. Which interests you?"

"My *life*."

"Watch the wire. The garden side will activate with a key, too. I'm moving your bed from in front of the door."

"It's summer. It's hot."

"We all have our inconveniences."

"I wish someone would tell me what's going on!"

"You shouldn't turn down the ladies. Some take it badly."

"You're not serious."

No, Banichi wasn't. Banichi was evading the question again. Banichi damned well knew something. He stood in frustration as Banichi went cheerfully to turn his room into a death-trap, mats in front of doors, lethal wires to complete the circuit if a foolish, sleepy human forgot and hurried to shut his own garden door in a sudden rainstorm.

He had been scared of the events last night. Now he was mad, furiously angry at the disruption of his life, his quarters, his freedom to come and go in the city—he foresaw guards, restrictions, threats . . . without a damned reason, except some lunatic who possibly, for whatever reason, didn't like humans. That was the only conclusion he could come to.

He sat down on the step where the paidhi-aiji was entitled to sit, and listened through the last pre-audience audience with the notion that he might hear something to give him a clue, at least, whether there was some wider, more political reason to worry, but the way Banichi seemed to be holding information from him, and Tabini's silence, when Tabini himself probably knew something he wasn't saying, all began to add up to him to an atevi with a grudge.

No licensed assassin was going to file on a human who was an essential, treatied presence in the aiji's household—a presence without the right to carry arms, but all the same, a court official and a personal intimate of the aiji of the Western Association. No professional in his right mind would take *that* on.

Which left some random fool attacking him as a symbol, perhaps, or someone mad at technology or at some equally remote grievance, who could know? Who could track such a thing?

The only comforting thought was that, if it wasn't a licensed assassin, it was the lunatic himself or an amateur who couldn't get a license—the sort that might mow down bystanders by mistake, true, dangerous in that regard.

But Banichi, unlike the majority of the aiji's guards, had a license. You didn't take him on. You didn't take on Jago, either. The rain last night had been a piece of luck for the intruder—who had either counted on the rain wiping out his tracks on the gravel and cement of the garden walkways, or he'd been stupid, and lucky.

Now the assassin wasn't lucky. Banichi was looking for him. And if he'd left a footprint in a flower bed or a fingerprint anywhere, that man—assuming it was a man—was in trouble.

He daren't go to a licensed doctor, for one thing. There had been blood on the terrace. Bren personally hoped he'd made life uncomfortable for the assassin, who clearly hadn't expected the reception he'd met. Most of all he hoped, considering Banichi's taking on the case, that life would become uncomfortable for the assassin's employer, if any, enough for the employer to withdraw the contract.

The doors opened. The guards and marshals let the crowd in, and the secretary accepted from the Day Marshal the towering stack of ribboned, sealed petitions and affidavits and filings.

There were some odd interfaces in the dealings of atevi and humans. One *couldn't* blame the atevi for clinging to traditional procedures, clumsy as the stacks were, and there *was* a computer record. The secretaries in the foyer created it.

But ask the atevi to use citizen numbers or case numbers? Convince them first that their computer-assigned personal numbers were auspicious in concert with their other numerologies. Convince them that changing those numbers caused chaos and lost records—because if things started going wrong, an ateva faulted his number and wanted it changed, immediately.

Create codes for the provinces, simply to facilitate computer sorting? Were *those* numbers auspicious, or was it some malevolent attempt of the aiji's court in Shejidan to diminish their importance and their power?

Then, of course, there was the dire rumor that typing the names in *still* produced numbers in the computers, numbers of devious and doubtless malevolent intent on the part of the aiji, conspiring, of course, with the humans who had brought the insidious device to earth.

Not all that humans brought to earth was anathema, of course. Television was an addiction. Flight was an increasingly essential convenience, practiced as see-and-avoid by frighteningly determined provincials, although the aiji had laid down the law within his domains, requiring flight plans, after the famous Weinathi Bridge crash.

Thank the atevi gods Tabini-aiji was a completely irreligious man.

The matters before the aiji had one turn of the glass apiece—a summation, by the petitioner. Most were rural matters, some involved trade, a few regarded public works projects—highways and dams and bridges, harbors and hunting and fishing rights which involved the rights of the Associations united under the aiji's influence. Originating projects and specific details of allocation and budget involved the two houses of the legislature, the hasdrawad and the tashrid—such bills were not the aiji's to initiate, only to approve or disapprove. But so much, so incredibly much, still needed the aiji's personal seal and personal hearing.

For chief example, there were the feuds to register, two in number, one a wife against an ex-husband, over illegal conversion of her property.

"It's better to go to court," Tabini said plainly. "You could get the money back, in installments, from his income."

"I'd rather kill him," the wife said, and Tabini said, "Record it," waved his hand and went on to the next case.

That was *why* humans preferred their enclave on Mospheira. Mospheira was an island, it was under human administration, computers had undisputed numbers, and laws didn't have bloodfeud as an alternative.

It did, however, mean that for all the sixty so-called provinces and conservatively three hundred million people under the aiji's hand, there was a single jail, which generally held less than fifty individuals awaiting trial or hearing, who could not be released on their own recognizance. There were a number of mental hospitals for those who needed them. There were four labor-prisons, for the incorrigibly antisocial—the sort, for instance, who took the assassins' function into their own hands, after refusal by a guild who did truly refuse unwarranted solicitation.

Sane, law-abiding atevi simply avoided argumentative people. One tried to have polite divorces. One tried not to antagonize or embarrass one's natural opponents. Thank God atevi generally did prefer negotiation or, as a last reasonable resort before filing feud, a physical, unarmed confrontation—equally to be avoided. Tall, strong humans still stood more than a head shorter and massed a third less than the average atevi, male or female—the other reason humans preferred their own jurisdiction.

He'd clearly annoyed somebody who hadn't followed the rules. His mind kept going back to that. No one had filed a feud. They had to notify him, that was one of the stringent requirements of the filing, but no one had even indicated casual irritation with him—and now Tabini was putting lethal defenses into his quarters.

The shock of the incident last night was still reverberating through his thinking, readjusting everything, until he had suddenly to realize he really wasn't entirely safe walking the halls out there. Professional assassins avoided publicity and preferred their faces not to become famous—but there were instances of the knife appearing out of the faceless crowd, the push on the stairs.

And in no few of the lords' staffs there were licensed assassins he daily rubbed shoulders with and never thought about it—until now.

An elderly gentleman brought the forty-sixth case, which regarded, in sum, a request for the aiji's attendance at a regional conference on urban development. That went onto the stack, for archive.

One day, he'd told the aiji himself, and he knew his predecessors had said it, one day the archives would collapse under the weight of seals, ribbons, and paper, all ten stories of the block-long building going down in a billow of dust. But this had to be the last petition for the session. The secretary called no more names. The reception table looked empty.

But, no, not the last one. Tabini called the secretary, who brought an uncommonly elaborate paper, burdened with the red and black ribbons of high nobility.

"A filing of Intent," Tabini said, rising, and startling the aides and assembled witnesses, and the secretary held up the document and read: "Tabini-aiji against persons unknown, who, without filing Intent, invaded the peace of my house and brought a threat of harm against the person of the paidhi-aiji, Bren Cameron. If harm results henceforth to any guest or person of my household by this agency or by any other agency intending harm to the paidhi-aiji, I personally declare Intent to file feud, because of the offense to the safety of my roof, with Banichi of Dajoshu township of Talidi province as my registered and licensed agent. I publish it and cause it to be published, and place it in public records with its seals and its signatures and sigils."

Bren was thoroughly shocked. He felt altogether conspicuous in the turning heads and the murmur of comment and question that followed as Tabini-aiji left the dais and walked past him, with:

"Be prudent, nadi Bren."

"Aiji-ma," he murmured, and bowed a profound bow, to cover his confusion. The audience was over. Jago was quick to fall in with Tabini, along with a detachment of the household and personal guard, as Tabini cut a swath through the crowd on his way to the side doors and the inner halls.

Bren started away on his own, dreading the course through the halls, wondering if the attempted assassin or his employer was in the room and whether the police escort would still be waiting out there.

But Banichi turned up in his path, and fell in with him, escorting him through the Whispering Port and into the public halls.

"Tabini declared Intent," he said to Banichi, wondering if Banichi had known in advance what Tabini had drafted.

"I'm not surprised," Banichi said.

"I ought to take the next plane to Mospheira."

"Highly foolish."

"We have different laws. And on Mospheira an ateva stands out. Find me the assassin in this crowd."

"You don't even know it was one of us."

"Then it was the broadest damn human I ever saw. —Forgive me." One didn't swear, if one was the paidhi-aiji, not, at least, in the public hall. "It wasn't a human. I know that."

"You know who came to your room. You don't know, however, who might have hired him. There is some smuggling on Mospheira, as the paidhi is aware. Connections we don't know exist are a very dangerous possibility."

The language had common pronouns that didn't specify gender. Him or her, that meant. And politicians and the aiji's staff used that pronoun habitually.

"I know where I'm safer."

"Tabini needs you here."

"For *what*?" That the aiji was undertaking anything but routine business was news to him. He hadn't heard. Banichi was telling him something no one else had.

And a handful of weeks ago Tabini had found unprecedented whimsy in arming him and giving him two hours of personal instruction at his personal retreat. They had joked, and shot melons on poles, and had supper together, and Tabini had had all the time he could possibly want to warn him if something was coming up besides the routine councils and committee meetings that involved the paidhi.

They turned the corner. Banichi, he did not fail to note, hadn't noticed his question. They walked out onto the colonnade, with the walls of the ancient Bu-javid pale and regular beyond them, the traffic flow on the steps reversed, now, downward bound. Atevi who had filed for hearing had their numbers, and the aiji would receive them in their established order.

But when they walked into the untrafficked hall that led toward the garden apartments, Banichi gave him two keys. "These are the only valid ones," Banichi said. "Kindly don't mix them up with your old ones. The old ones work. They just don't turn off the wires."

He gave Banichi a disturbed stare—which, also, Banichi didn't seem to notice. "Can't you just shock the bastard? Scare him? He's not a professional. There's been no notice . . ."

"I'm within my license," Banichi said. "The Intent is filed. Didn't you say so? The intruder would be very foolish to try again."

A queasy feeling was in his stomach. "Banichi, damn it . . ."

"I've advised the servants. Honest and wise servants, capable of serving in this house, will request admission henceforth. Your apartment is no different than mine, now. Or Jago's. I change my own sheets."

As well as he knew Jago and Banichi, he had had no idea of such hazards in their quarters. It made sense in their case or in Tabini's. It didn't, in his.

"I trust," Banichi said, "you've no duplicate keys circulating. No ladies. No—hem—other connections. You've not been gambling, have you?"

"No!" Banichi knew him, too, knew he had female connections on

Mospheira, one and two not averse to what Banichi would call a one-candle night. The paidhi-aiji hadn't time for a social life, otherwise. Or for long romantic maneuverings or hurt feelings, lingering hellos or good-byes—most of all, not for the peddling of influence or attempts to push this or that point on him. His friends didn't ask questions. Or want more than a bouquet of flowers, a phone call, and a night at the theater.

"Just mind, if you've given any keys away."

"I'm not such a fool."

"Fools of that kind abound in the Bu-javid. I've spoken severely to the aiji."

Give atevi a piece of tech and sometimes they put it together in ways humans hadn't, in their own history—inventors, out of their own social framework, connected ideas in ways you didn't expect, and never intended, either in social consequence, or in technical ramifications. The wire was one. Figure that atevi had a propensity for inventions regarding personal protection, figure that atevi law didn't forbid lethal devices, and ask how far they'd taken other items and to what uses they didn't advertise.

The paidhi tried to keep ahead of it. The paidhi tried to keep abreast of every technology and every piece of vocabulary in the known universe, but bits and tags perpetually got away and it was accelerating—the escape of knowledge, the recombination of items into things utterly out of human control.

Most of all, atevi weren't incapable of making technological discoveries completely on their own . . . and had no trouble keeping them prudently under wraps. They were not a communicative people.

They reached the door. He used the key Banichi had given him. The door opened. Neither the mat nor the wire was in evidence.

"Ankle high and black," Banichi said. "But it's down and disarmed. You did use the right key."

"*Your* key." He didn't favor Banichi's jokes. "I don't see the mat."

"Under the carpet. *Don't* walk on it barefoot. You'd bleed. The wire is an easy step in. You can walk on it while it's off. Just don't do that barefoot, either."

He could scarcely see it. He walked across the mat. Banichi stayed the other side of it.

"It cuts its own way through insulation," Banichi said. "And through boot leather, paidhi-ji, if it's live. Don't touch it, even when it's dead. Lock the door and don't wander the halls."

"I have an energy council meeting this afternoon."

"You'll want to change coats, nadi. Wait here for Jago. She'll escort you."

"What is this? I'm to have an escort everywhere I go? I'm to be leapt upon by the minister of Works? Assaulted by the head of Water Management?"

"Prudence, prudence, nadi Bren. Jago's witty company. She's fascinated by your brown hair."

He was outraged. "You're enjoying this. It's not funny, Banichi."

"Forgive me." Banichi was unfailingly solemn. "But humor her. Escort is so damned boring."

PAST NEBULA AWARD WINNERS

1965

Novel: *Dune* by Frank Herbert
Novella: "He Who Shapes" by Roger Zelazny and "The Saliva Tree" by Brian Aldiss (tie)
Novelette: "The Doors of His Face, the Lamps of His Mouth" by Roger Zelazny
Short Story: "'Repent, Harlequin!' Said the Ticktockman" by Harlan Ellison

1966

Novel: *Babel-17* by Samuel R. Delany and *Flowers for Algernon* by Daniel Keyes (tie)
Novella: "The Last Castle" by Jack Vance
Novelette: "Call Him Lord" by Gordon R. Dickson
Short Story: "The Secret Place" by Richard McKenna

1967

Novel: *The Einstein Intersection* by Samuel R. Delany
Novella: "Behold the Man" by Michael Moorcock
Novelette: "Gonna Roll the Bones" by Fritz Leiber
Short Story: "Aye, and Gomorrah" by Samuel R. Delany

1968

Novel: *Rite of Passage* by Alexei Panshin
Novella: "Dragonrider" by Anne McCaffrey
Novelette: "Mother to the World" by Richard Wilson
Short Story: "The Planners" by Kate Wilhelm

1969

Novel: *The Left Hand of Darkness* by Ursula K. Le Guin
Novella: "A Boy and His Dog" by Harlan Ellison
Novelette: "Time Considered as a Helix of Semi-Precious Stones" by Samuel R. Delany
Short Story: "Passengers" by Robert Silverberg

1970

Novel: *Ringworld* by Larry Niven
Novella: "Ill Met in Lankhmar" by Fritz Leiber
Novelette: "Slow Sculpture" by Theodore Sturgeon
Short Story: No Award

1971

Novel: *A Time of Changes* by Robert Silverberg
Novella: "The Missing Man" by Katherine MacLean
Novelette: "The Queen of Air and Darkness" by Poul Anderson
Short Story: "Good News from the Vatican" by Robert Silverberg

1972

Novel: *The Gods Themselves* by Isaac Asimov
Novella: "A Meeting with Medusa" by Arthur C. Clarke
Novelette: "Goat Song" by Poul Anderson
Short Story: "When It Changed" by Joanna Russ

1973

Novel: *Rendezvous with Rama* by Arthur C. Clarke
Novella: "The Death of Doctor Island" by Gene Wolfe
Novelette: "Of Mist, and Grass, and Sand" by Vonda N. McIntyre
Short Story: "Love Is the Plan, the Plan Is Death" by James Tiptree Jr.
Dramatic Presentation: *Soylent Green*

1974

Novel: *The Dispossessed* by Ursula K. Le Guin
Novella: "Born with the Dead" by Robert Silverberg
Novelette: "If the Stars Are Gods" by Gordon Eklund and Gregory Benford
Short Story: "The Day before the Revolution" by Ursula K. Le Guin
Dramatic Presentation: *Sleeper* by Woody Allen
Grand Master: Robert Heinlein

1975

Novel: *The Forever War* by Joe Haldeman
Novella: "Home Is the Hangman" by Roger Zelazny
Novelette: "San Diego Lightfoot Sue" by Tom Reamy
Short Story: "Catch That Zeppelin" by Fritz Leiber
Dramatic Presentation: *Young Frankenstein* by Mel Brooks and Gene Wilder
Grand Master: Jack Williamson

1976

Novel: *Man Plus* by Frederik Pohl
Novella: "Houston, Houston, Do You Read?" by James Tiptree Jr.
Novelette: "The Bicentennial Man" by Isaac Asimov
Short Story: "A Crowd of Shadows" by C. L. Grant
Grand Master: Clifford D. Simak

1977

Novel: *Gateway* by Frederik Pohl
Novella: "Stardance" by Spider and Jeanne Robinson
Novelette: "The Screwfly Solution" by Racoona Sheldon
Short Story: "Jeffty Is Five" by Harlan Ellison

1978

Novel: *Dreamsnake* by Vonda N. McIntyre
Novella: "The Persistence of Vision" by John Varley
Novelette: "A Glow of Candles, A Unicorn's Eye" by C. L. Grant
Short Story: "Stone" by Edward Bryant
Grand Master: L. Sprague de Camp

1979

Novel: *The Fountains of Paradise* by Arthur C. Clarke
Novella: "Enemy Mine" by Barry B. Longyear
Novelette: "Sandkings" by George R. R. Martin
Short Story: "GiANTS" by Edward Bryant

1980

Novel: *Timescape* by Gregory Benford
Novella: "Unicorn Tapestry" by Suzy McKee Charnas
Novelette: "The Ugly Chickens" by Howard Waldrop
Short Story: "Grotto of the Dancing Deer" by Clifford D. Simak
Grand Master: Fritz Leiber

1981

Novel: *The Claw of the Conciliator* by Gene Wolfe
Novella: "The Saturn Game" by Poul Anderson
Novelette: "The Quickening" by Michael Bishop
Short Story: "The Bone Flute" by Lisa Tuttle [declined by author]

1982

Novel: *No Enemy but Time* by Michael Bishop
Novella: "Another Orphan" by John Kessel
Novelette: "Fire Watch" by Connie Willis
Short Story: "A Letter from the Clearys" by Connie Willis

1983

Novel: *Startide Rising* by David Brin
Novella: "Hardfought" by Greg Bear
Novelette: "Blood Music" by Greg Bear
Short Story: "The Peacemaker" by Gardner Dozois
Grand Master: Andre Norton

1984

Novel: *Neuromancer* by William Gibson
Novella: "Press Enter []" by John Varley
Novelette: "Blood Child" by Octavia Butler
Short Story: "Morning Child" by Gardner Dozois

1985

Novel: *Ender's Game* by Orson Scott Card
Novella: "Sailing to Byzantium" by Robert Silverberg
Novelette: "Portraits of His Children" by George R. R. Martin
Short Story: "Out of All Them Bright Stars" by Nancy Kress
Grand Master: Arthur C. Clarke

1986

Novel: *Speaker for the Dead* by Orson Scott Card
Novella: "R&R" by Lucius Shepard
Novelette: "The Girl Who Fell into the Sky" by Kate Wilhelm
Short Story: "Tangents" by Greg Bear
Grand Master: Isaac Asimov

1987

Novel: *The Falling Woman* by Pat Murphy
Novella: "The Blind Geometer" by Kim Stanley Robinson
Novelette: "Rachel in Love" by Pat Murphy
Short Story: "Forever Yours, Anna" by Kate Wilhelm
Grand Master: Alfred Bester

1988

Novel: *Falling Free* by Lois McMaster Bujold
Novella: "The Last of the Winnebagos" by Connie Willis
Novelette: "Schrödinger's Kitten" by George Alec Effinger
Short Story: "Bible Stories for Adults, No. 17: The Deluge" by James Morrow
Grand Master: Ray Bradbury

1989

Novel: *The Healer's War* by Elizabeth Ann Scarborough
Novella: "The Mountains of Mourning" by Lois McMaster Bujold
Novelette: "At the Rialto" by Connie Willis
Short Story: "Ripples in the Dirac Sea" by Geoffrey A. Landis

1990

Novel: *Tehanu: The Last Book of Earthsea* by Ursula K. Le Guin
Novella: "The Hemingway Hoax" by Joe Haldeman
Novelette: "Tower of Babylon" by Ted Chiang
Short Story: "Bears Discover Fire" by Terry Bisson
Grand Master: Lester del Rey

1991

Novel: *Stations of the Tide* by Michael Swanwick
Novella: "Beggars in Spain" by Nancy Kress
Novelette: "Guide Dog" by Mike Conner
Short Story: "Ma Qui" by Alan Brennert

1992

Novel: *Doomsday Book* by Connie Willis
Novella: "City Of Truth" by James Morrow
Novelette: "Danny Goes to Mars" by Pamela Sargent
Short Story: "Even the Queen" by Connie Willis
Grand Master: Fred Pohl

1993

Novel: *Red Mars* by Kim Stanley Robinson
Novella: "The Night We Buried Road Dog" by Jack Cady
Novelette: "Georgia on My Mind" by Charles Sheffield
Short Story: "Graves" by Joe Haldeman

1994

The 1994 Nebulas were awarded at a ceremony in New York City in late April 1995.

Novel: *Moving Mars* by Greg Bear
Novella: "Seven Views of Olduvai Gorge" by Mike Resnick
Novelette: "The Martian Child" by David Gerrold
Short Story: "A Defense of the Social Contracts" by Martha Soukup
Grand Master: Damon Knight
Author Emeritus: Emil Petaja

1995

Novel: *The Terminal Experiment* by Robert J. Sawyer
Novella: "Last Summer at Mars Hill" by Elizabeth Hand
Novelette: "Solitude" by Ursula K. Le Guin
Short Story: "Death and the Librarian" by Esther M. Friesner
Grand Master: A. E. van Vogt
Author Emeritus: Wilson "Bob" Tucker

1996

Novel: *Slow River* by Nicola Griffith
Novella: "Da Vinci Rising" by Jack Dann
Novelette: "Lifeboat on a Burning Sea" by Bruce Holland Rogers
Short Story: "A Birthday" by Esther M. Friesner
Grand Master: Jack Vance
Author Emeritus: Judith Merril

1997

Novel: *The Moon and the Sun* by Vonda N. McIntyre
Novella: "Abandon in Place" by Jerry Oltion
Novelette: "Flowers of Aulit Prison" by Nancy Kress
Short Story: "Sister Emily's Lightship" by Jane Yolen
Grand Master: Poul Anderson
Author Emeritus: Nelson Slade Bond

1998

Novel: *Forever Peace* by Joe Haldeman
Novella: "Reading the Bones" by Sheila Finch
Novelette: "Lost Girls" by Jane Yolen
Short Story: "Thirteen Ways to Water" by Bruce Holland Rogers
Grand Master: Hal Clement (Harry Stubbs)
Author Emeritus: William Tenn (Philip Klass)

1999

Novel: *Parable of the Talents* by Octavia E. Butler
Novella: "Story of Your Life" by Ted Chiang
Novelette: "Mars Is No Place for Children" by Mary A. Turzillo
Short Story: "The Cost of Doing Business" by Leslie What
Script: *The Sixth Sense* by M. Night Shyamalan
Grand Master: Brian W. Aldiss
Author Emeritus: Daniel Keyes

2000

Novel: *Darwin's Radio* by Greg Bear
Novella: "Goddesses" by Linda Nagata
Novelette: "Daddy's World" by Walter Jon Williams
Short Story: "macs" by Terry Bisson
Script: *Galaxy Quest* by Robert Gordon and David Howard
Ray Bradbury Award: Yuri Rasovsky and Harlan Ellison
Grand Master: Philip José Farmer
Author Emeritus: Robert Sheckley

2001

Novel: *The Quantum Rose* by Catherine Asaro
Novella: "The Ultimate Earth" by Jack Williamson
Novelette: "Louise's Ghost" by Kelly Link
Short Story: "The Cure for Everything" by Severna Park
Script: *Crouching Tiger, Hidden Dragon* by James Schamus, Kuo Jung Tsai, and
    Hui-Ling Wang
President's Award: Betty Ballantine

2002

Novel: *American Gods* by Neil Gaiman
Novella: "Bronte's Egg" by Richard Chwedyk
Novelette: "Hell Is the Absence of God" by Ted Chiang
Short Story: "Creature" by Carol Emshwiller
Script: *Lord of the Rings: The Fellowship of the Ring* by Frances Walsh, Phillipa Boyens, and Peter Jackson
Grand Master: Ursula K. Le Guin
Author Emeritus: Katherine MacLean

2003

Novel: *Speed of Dark* by Elizabeth Moon
Novella: "Coraline" by Neil Gaiman
Novelette: "The Empire of Ice Cream" by Jeffrey Ford
Short Story: "What I Didn't See" by Karen Joy Fowler
Script: *Lord of the Rings: The Two Towers* by Frances Walsh, Phillipa Boyens, Stephen Sinclair, and Peter Jackson
Grand Master: Robert Silverberg
Author Emeritus: Charles L. Harness

2004

Novel: *Paladin of Souls* by Lois McMaster Bujold
Novella: "The Green Leopard Plague" by Walter Jon Williams
Novelette: "Basement Magic" by Ellen Klages
Short Story: "Coming to Terms" by Eileen Gunn
Script: *Lord of the Rings: Return of the King* by Frances Walsh, Phillipa Boyens, and Peter Jackson
Grand Master: Anne McCaffrey

2005

Novel: *Camouflage* by Joe Haldeman
Novella: "Magic for Beginners" by Kelly Link
Novelette: "The Faery Handbag" by Kelly Link
Short Story: "I Live with You" by Carol Emshwiller
Script: *Serenity* by Joss Whedon
Grand Master: Harlan Ellison
Author Emeritus: William F. Nolan

2006

Novel: *Seeker* by Jack McDevitt
Novella: "Burn" by James Patrick Kelly
Novelette: "Two Hearts" by Peter S. Beagle
Short Story: "Echo" by Elizabeth Hand
Script: *Howl's Moving Castle* by Hayao Miyazaki, Cindy Davis Hewitt, and Donald H. Hewitt
Andre Norton Award: *Magic or Madness* by Justine Larbalestier
Grand Master: James Gunn
Author Emeritus: D. G. Compton

2007

Novel: *The Yiddish Policemen's Union* by Michael Chabon
Novella: "Fountain of Age" by Nancy Kress
Novelette: "The Merchant and the Alchemist's Gate" by Ted Chiang
Short Story: "Always" by Karen Joy Fowler
Script: *Pan's Labyrinth* by Guillermo del Toro
Andre Norton Award: *Harry Potter and the Deathly Hallows* by J. K. Rowling
Grand Master: Michael Moorcock
Author Emeritus: Ardath Mayhar
SFWA Service Awards: Melisa Michaels and Graham P. Collins

2008

Novel: *Powers* by Ursula K. Le Guin
Novella: "The Spacetime Pool" by Catherine Asaro
Novelette: "Pride and Prometheus" by John Kessel
Short Story: "Trophy Wives" by Nina Kiriki Hoffman
Script: *WALL-E* by Andrew Stanton and Jim Reardon. Original story by
  Andrew Stanton and Pete Docter
Andre Norton Award: *Flora's Dare: How a Girl of Spirit Gambles All to Expand
  Her Vocabulary, Confront a Bouncing Boy Terror, and Try to Save Califa from a
  Shaky Doom (Despite Being Confined to Her Room)* by Ysabeau S. Wilce
Grand Master: Harry Harrison
Author Emeritus: M. J. Engh
Solstice Award: Kate Wilhelm, Martin H. Greenberg, and the late Algis Budrys
SFWA Service Award: Victoria Strauss

2009

Novel: *The Windup Girl* by Paolo Bacigalupi
Novella: "The Women of Nell Gwynne's" by Kage Baker
Novelette: "Sinner, Baker, Fabulist, Priest; Red Mask, Black Mask, Gentleman,
  Beast" by Eugie Foster
Short Story: "Spar" by Kij Johnson
Ray Bradbury Award: *District 9* by Neill Blomkamp and Terri Tatchell
Andre Norton Award: *The Girl Who Circumnavigated Fairyland in a Ship of Her
  Own Making* by Catherynne M. Valente
Grand Master: Joe Haldeman
Author Emeritus: Neal Barrett Jr.
Solstice Award: Tom Doherty, Terri Windling, and the late Donald A. Wollheim
SFWA Service Awards: Vonda N. McIntyre and Keith Stokes

2010

Novel: *Blackout/All Clear* by Connie Willis

Novella: "The Lady Who Plucked Red Flowers beneath the Queen's Window" by Rachel Swirsky

Novelette: "That Leviathan Whom Thou Hast Made" by Eric James Stone

Short Story: "Ponies" by Kij Johnson and "How Interesting: A Tiny Man" by Harlan Ellison (tie)

Ray Bradbury Award: *Inception* by Christopher Nolan

Andre Norton Award: *I Shall Wear Midnight* by Terry Pratchett

2011

Novel: *Among Others* by Jo Walton

Novella: "The Man Who Bridged the Mist" by Kij Johnson

Novelette: "What We Found" by Geoff Ryman

Short Story: "The Paper Menagerie" by Ken Liu

Ray Bradbury Award: *Doctor Who*: "The Doctor's Wife" by Neil Gaiman (writer), Richard Clark (director)

Andre Norton Award: *The Freedom Maze* by Delia Sherman

Damon Knight Grand Master Award: Connie Willis

Solstice Award: Octavia Butler (posthumous) and John Clute

SFWA Service Award: Bud Webster

2012

Novel: *2312* by Kim Stanley Robinson

Novella: *After the Fall, Before the Fall, During the Fall* by Nancy Kress

Novelette: "Close Encounters" by Andy Duncan

Short Story: "Immersion" by Aliette de Bodard

Ray Bradbury Award: *Beasts of the Southern Wild* by Benh Zeitlin & Lucy Abilar (writers), Benh Zeitlin (director)

Andre Norton Award: *Fair Coin* by E. C. Myers

2013

Novel: *Ancillary Justice* by Ann Leckie
Novella: "The Weight of the Sunrise" by Vylar Kaftan
Novelette: "The Waiting Stars" by Aliette de Bodard
Short Story: "If You Were a Dinosaur, My Love" by Rachel Swirsky
Ray Bradbury Award: *Gravity* by Alfonso Cuarón, Jonás Cuarón, (writers), Alfonso
    Cuarón (director)
Andre Norton Award: *Sister Mine* by Nalo Hopkinson
Damon Knight Grand Master Award: Samuel R. Delany
2013 Distinguished Guest: Frank M. Robinson
Kevin O'Donnell Jr. Service to SFWA Award: Michael Armstrong

2014

Novel: *Annihilation* by Jeff VanderMeer
Novella: *Yesterday's Kin* by Nancy Kress
Novelette: "A Guide to the Fruits of Hawai'i" by Alaya Dawn Johnson
Short Story: "Jackalope Wives" by Ursula Vernon
Ray Bradbury Award: *Guardians of the Galaxy* by James Gunn and Nicole
    Perlman (writers)
Andre Norton Award: *Love Is the Drug* by Alaya Dawn Johnson
Damon Knight Grand Master Award: Larry Niven
Solstice Award: Joanna Russ (posthumous), Stanley Schmidt
Kevin O'Donnell Jr. Service to SFWA Award: Jeffry Dwight

2015

Novel: *Uprooted* by Naomi Novik

Novella: *Binti* by Nnedi Okorafor

Novelette: "Our Lady of the Open Road" by Sarah Pinsker

Short Story: "Hungry Daughters of Starving Mothers" by Alyssa Wong

Ray Bradbury Award: *Mad Max: Fury Road* by George Miller, Brendan McCarthy, and Nick Lathouris

Andre Norton Award: *Updraft* by Fran Wilde

Damon Knight Grand Master Award: C.J. Cherryh

Kate Wolhelm Solstice Award: Sir Terry Pratchett (posthumous)

Kevin O'Donnell Jr. Service to SFWA Award: Dr. Lawrence M. Schoen

ABOUT THE EDITOR

Since 1997, Canadian author / former biologist **Julie E. Czerneda** has shared her curiosity about living things through her science fiction and fantasy, published by DAW Books. Julie's edited/co-edited fifteen anthologies of SF/F, including the Aurora Award–winning: *Space Inc.* and *Under Cover of Darkness*. She's presented internationally on writing, scientific literacy, and SF in the classroom; produced the award-winning Tales from the Wonder Zone and Realms of Wonder themed anthologies; and was Toast-

Photo by Roger Czerneda Photography

master for Anticipation, the Montreal Worldcon. Julie is presently completing her SF series, the Clan Chronicles, with the final book, *To Guard Against the Stars*, to be released October 2017. She is honored to have been invited to edit this volume and work with such stellar authors. Please visit www.czerneda.com for more.

ABOUT THE COVER ARTIST

Maurizio Manzieri is a science fiction and fantasy illustrator dreaming his Universes in a small oasis in the heart of Turin, Italy. His artwork has been showcased in exhibits all around the world and included in many annuals, such as *Spectrum*, *The Best in Contemporary Fantastic Art*, and *Infected by Art*. He has won the Cesley Award, the Europe Award, the Italia Award, and the Asimov's Readers' Award. More information is available online at http://www.manzieri.com/.